Monsoon Mists

Monsoon Mists

Christina Courtenay

Published 2014 by Choc Lit Limited
Penrose House, Crawley Drive, Camberley, Surrey GU15 2AB, UK
www.choc-lit.com

A CIP catalogue record for this book is available
from the British Library

ISBN 978-1-78189-167-4

MIX
Paper from
responsible sources
FSC® C020471

Printed and bound by CPI Group (UK) Ltd, Croydon, CR0 4YY

To Fu-Tsi, Fudge and Shendu
– I'm so lucky to have you!

Acknowledgements

From the moment I wrote *Highland Storms*, telling the story of Brice Kinross and his supposedly treacherous brother, I knew Jamie had to be given the opportunity to give his version of events. I might not have persevered in writing this though if it hadn't been for one person – Liv Thomas – who kept telling me she wanted to read about him. So many thanks, Liv, for encouraging me to put fingers to keyboard and I hope you like Jamie now he's finally here!

A big thank you, as always, to the rest of the ChocLiteers – stars one and all – and the amazing Choc Lit team and their Tasting Panel, without whom none of this would be possible. It's an honour to work with you all!

Massive thanks to Sue Moorcroft for keeping me sane through my first year as Chair of the RNA, for being my brilliant "roomie" at various conventions and for teaching me so much about professionalism and perseverance in the face of adversity – respect! To Gill Stewart for always being there and for being a wonderful critique partner. To Henriette Gyland for making our Swedish adventures such fun and for being an equally wonderful critique partner, and to all my other writing friends who make it such a joy to be an author.

And last, but not least, huge thanks to my hero-at-home, Richard, who makes it possible for me to write and to go places, to my lovely daughters, Josceline and Jessamy, and to Fu-Tsi, Fudge and Shendu, my constant companions to whom this book is dedicated and who are the inspiration for all my canine characters. Thank you all!

Author's Note

This book could not have been written without the superb diary of one man – Christopher Hinric Braad (b. 1728–d. 1781). A Swede who travelled with the Swedish East India Company on some of their journeys to the Far East, he kept the most meticulous journals you could possibly imagine, which were invaluable to me in trying to describe the city of Surat in the late 1750s.

Braad travelled on board the ship Götha Leijon when it sailed to Canton in China in 1750–52, stopping at Surat and several other destinations. His journal (called *Beskrifning på skeppet Götha Leijons resa till Surat och åtskillige andre indianske orter*, which can be found at Gothenburg University Library in the Swedish East India Company collection) contains not only copious notes and descriptions, but also superb drawings of all manner of things – fish, plants, buildings and places. These too helped me immensely in picturing the sights the hero of my story would have seen during his travels.

Braad seems to have gone on the journey with the Götha Leijon purely as a scientific spectator and writer, rather than a trader. He went out of his way to seek out the most obscure facts about each of the places they visited along the route, recording it all carefully, even going so far as to measure out the size of a town's square in number of footsteps! He gives measurements, longitudes and latitudes for everything, but the most interesting parts of his accounts (for me anyway) are those where he describes the people and sights he encounters. Quite often you can almost hear the amazement in Braad's writing voice as he witnesses things most of his countrymen would never see and marvels at how different they are to what he is used to.

Writing his diary in old-fashioned Swedish, Braad's account was a bit difficult to decipher at times, not to mention somewhat long-winded (although I thoroughly enjoyed his erratic spelling!). I hope I have understood him correctly – any mistakes are obviously my own. I am truly indebted to Braad and others like him, who had the courage to sail to what they must have thought of as the ends of the earth, and then felt it their duty to tell others what they had seen.

Prologue

It was well after midnight and the farmhouse was eerily silent, apart from the slight creaking of the floorboards as Jamie Kinross paced back and forth in the parlour. He was too restless to sleep, but he wished now he'd brought his eiderdown bolster downstairs with him. This room was so cold he was sure he'd freeze to death if he sat down on any of the stiff-backed furniture. The only way to stay warm enough was to keep moving.

Damn Elisabet!

Could you damn someone who was already dead? And who might, at this very moment, be standing by the gates of hell being judged and condemned for her sins? Jamie didn't care and muttered another curse about conniving women in general and his deceased wife in particular, even though he knew he was probably being unfair. She'd had her reasons. If only she'd played her little games with someone other than him …

He stopped briefly to glance out the window, rimed with ice both inside and out. The yard was ringed with drifts of snow so deep you sank in up to your thighs if you tried walking through them. The moonlight bathed the scene in a surreal glow, making the surfaces glitter like a thousand diamond fragments. Jamie loved this sight, loved the snow, but tonight he felt as though the deep cold outside penetrated right to his core. He shivered and turned away.

He couldn't stay here. He had to leave. Needed to leave.

But he had responsibilities.

Granhult farm and everything in it was his now and had been since Elisabet's father died the previous month, leaving her sole heiress and Jamie, as her husband, owner by default. The problem was he didn't want it. Had never wanted it.

Or her.

He sighed and continued his pacing. It was all so complicated and he'd been trying for months to come to terms with the fact that he couldn't change his fate. He had to accept it and live with it. Live with *her*. And truly, he'd intended to make the best of it as soon as the baby was born. Only, now it was too late.

And the baby, currently sleeping upstairs – he couldn't leave her here. *Think, man, think!*

Just before dawn he made up his mind and went to speak to the farm steward, Jonas Nilsson, who lived in a cottage just the other side of the yard. 'I need you to take over the day-to-day running for now, please,' Jamie told the man. 'I may be away some time, but I trust you to look after everything.'

Nilsson nodded, sympathy and understanding showing clearly in his sleep-hazy eyes. 'Aye, I'll take care of it, don't you worry, sir.' And Jamie knew he would. Nilsson was a good sort, honest to a fault and entirely dependable.

Unlike some people.

Jamie shook off his dark thoughts and went back to the main house. He woke the wet nurse, Lina, and told her to get herself and the baby dressed and packed. 'Put as many layers of clothing on her as possible, please. I'll find sheepskin rugs and Elisabet's fur-lined cloak to wrap around her.'

Jamie waited for Lina to protest at his orders and try

to reason with him. He'd have welcomed an argument; anything to let out his suppressed feelings of anger, resentment, grief and guilt. But she took one look at his face and did as she was told.

Half an hour later, the horses were stamping their hooves on the icy surface outside the front door. They shook their heads, jingling the bells on the harnesses while whinnying softly, as eager to be off as their master. Jamie exhaled a misty breath of impatience while he watched the wet nurse settle under the covers with her precious burden. Thank the Lord the baby wasn't crying at least. That would have set his teeth on edge for sure.

'Mr Kinross, you can't mean to take a day-old baby out in this cold, surely? It's madness!'

Jamie turned to see that Karin, his dead wife's personal maid and confidante, had followed him out of the house and now stood wringing her hands on the porch.

'She's well wrapped up and we're not going far,' he told her, his curt tone indicating that he didn't intend to take any notice of her views on the matter. Never had, never would. He could barely stand the sight of the woman and if he'd been a more vindictive man he would have told her to go to hell. With a huge effort of will, he held his tongue and settled himself on the driver's seat in the sleigh.

'But it's going to snow! Look at the clouds.' Karin seemed to be on the verge of tears, but Jamie hardly noticed and cared even less. Karin's tears were usually of the fake variety and although they may be genuine now, it made no difference.

'It will hold off for half an hour or so, which is all I need. Lina has hot bricks under the covers and if you'd just let us be on our way, all will be well. Stand aside.'

The snow had been shovelled into piles around the

edges of the yard, but the leaden skies threatened to undo this good work in the very near future. Jamie knew time was of the essence and perhaps he was mad to go travelling with a newborn infant today, but he simply couldn't stay here another minute. And he was only going as far as the next estate – to Askeberga, his parents' manor house.

When he gave the horses the command to walk on, the sleigh glided easily on the smooth surface.

'But, Mr Kinross …!'

Jamie heard Karin calling one last protest, but he ignored her and concentrated on the narrow road. He'd never been much for praying, but he did so now. 'Please, dear God, keep the snow from falling, just for a short while, so we don't get stuck in a snow drift somewhere. *And get me the hell out of here!*' He realised belatedly that this probably wasn't an appropriate way of addressing the Lord, even in your thoughts, but perhaps He would understand the feeling was heartfelt and make allowances?

Jamie's eyes stung from the cold and he buried his nose inside the scarf wrapped around the lower half of his face. Turning to the wet nurse on the seat behind him inside the sleigh, he saw that she was submerged under the sheepskin rugs and wolf pelts with her charge. 'Are you warm enough?' he asked, raising his voice a little to be heard over the swishing sound of the runners.

'Yes, at the moment.'

The woman's eyes, which were all Jamie could see, were wary. He couldn't blame her. She probably thought him crazed with grief and was humouring him. That almost made him smile, it was so far from the truth. Out of his mind he may be, but not because he was sorrowing for Elisabet.

Or at least not in the way Lina thought. He didn't mourn the loss of his wife, but he did feel sad about someone dying so young. It seemed a terrible waste and he couldn't help but wonder if it was partly his fault. He should have made peace with her before the birth, extended an olive branch perhaps ... Would it have made a difference? Put her in a more positive frame of mind?

He shook his head. Childbirth was a risky business and it was in the hands of God.

Somehow, miraculously, the roads were passable. The landscape flew by, a glimmering blur in shades of white and silver, and after half an hour or so they entered the avenue of ash trees that led to Askeberga and which gave the estate its name. A medium-sized manor house, painted a cheerful yellow with white windows, it was mostly buried under layers of snow like everything else around it. The smoking chimney indicated the welcome warmth within though and the fact that at least some of the servants were up already. Hopefully his mother would be too as she was an early riser. Jamie flicked the reins for a last burst of speed towards the entrance steps.

The moment the sleigh swooshed to a stop, he was out of it and rushing up to hammer on the door with the side of his gloved fist. Then, taking the steps two at a time, he went down again, helping Lina out and up towards the door, which had now been opened.

'Master James! What ...?'

'Please, fetch my mother. Now!' He pushed the wet nurse past the surprised maid and slammed the door shut behind him. 'And find someone to take care of the horses immediately.'

'Yes, sir.'

'Jamie, is that you? Is something wrong? Oh!' Jamie's

mother, Jessamijn, had come into the hall and stopped at the sight of the woman holding a telltale bundle. 'The baby, it's arrived!' She rushed over and bent to free the child from the outermost sheepskin and some of its layers so that she could gaze at the tiny face. Jamie averted his eyes. He knew what the baby looked like and didn't want to see her again. Black hair, dark eyes, magnolia skin ... Nothing like him. He took a deep breath.

'It's a girl and she's to be christened Margot. Her mother is ... dead. Please, Mama, will you look after her for me for a while? I have to leave. I can't stay here, not now.'

Jessamijn stopped her intense scrutiny of the baby and came to put her hands on her son's shoulders instead, looking him straight in the eye. 'Jamie, listen to me. Whatever happened, you have a responsibility now. The farm, this baby, you have to take care of them and—'

'No, Mama. I've left the farm in the hands of Nilsson. You know he's trustworthy, a good man. And Karin will see to the funeral arrangements, I'm sure.'

'But you have to attend! Elisabet was your wife.' His mother looked shocked.

'In name only. I'm sure the entire county is aware of the circumstances of our nuptials by now.' Jamie gritted his teeth. 'I can't play the grieving husband while everyone laughs behind my back. I'm not that good an actor.' When Jessamijn opened her mouth to protest further, he added, 'Tell them I've run mad, whatever you want, it doesn't matter. I don't care what they think.' He pulled a sheaf of papers out of an inside pocket. 'Here are the deeds to the farm and a signed and witnessed document giving it all to Margot. I want nothing that belonged to Elisabet, nothing, do you hear me? I trust you to look after the child. When … if I can, I will return, but right now, I need to go as far away from here as possible. I'm sorry, but I can't bear to stay. Please say you understand?'

He blinked and stared at his mother, so small and yet so strong. They had always shared a special bond, for he was her youngest son, her favourite, although she'd never said so out loud. And she'd been the only one who empathised with him, who didn't try and curb his high spirits or wild ways. She didn't now either.

Stretching up a hand to caress his cheek, she nodded. 'Then go if you must, my love, but you *will* come back, understand? This is temporary, to give you a chance to regain your equilibrium, but it's not forever. I expect better of you.'

He nodded, although he doubted he could follow her order.

She opened her arms and he embraced her, crushing her slight frame to him so hard he wondered afterwards if he'd hurt her. She hugged him back, then stood on tiptoe to kiss his cheek. 'Godspeed, Jamie. Take care of yourself, for me.'

She was wise enough not to mention the baby and as he stepped back out into the cold, Jamie hoped he could forget the little scrap altogether.

He couldn't bear to even think about her.

Chapter One

'I say, it's rather warm in here, isn't it?'

'Do you think so?' Zarmina Miller swallowed a sigh and tried to resist rolling her eyes. *Here we go again.* Honestly, couldn't he think of anything more original?

To be fair, the young man next to her – George Carmichael – was newly arrived from England to take up his post as writer, or junior tally clerk, to the English East India Company's factors in Surat. It would probably take months before he became acclimatised to the Indian heat and, unlike her, he seemed to be in genuine discomfort. The months of April and May were the hottest of the year, with temperatures soaring daily and the humidity nigh unbearable. Zar could see perspiration pouring down the sides of Mr Carmichael's face, from his temples all the way into the folds of his neckcloth, and his cheeks were mottled red with prickly heat rash. She guessed the itchy areas covered other parts of him as well and felt a pang of sympathy.

Still, it was the same excuse they all used to get her on her own. She swept a gaze round the large dining hall of the so called Factory, where this gathering was taking place, while she waited for the inevitable next sentence. It wasn't long in coming.

'Would you care to take a turn with me in the roof garden? I'm sure it will be much cooler up there.'

Zar could have given him a hundred reasons why she didn't want to go anywhere with him, but thought it best to get this over with. 'Yes, thank you, why not?' she said in a falsely cheerful voice. In order to avoid taking his arm, however, she swept off in the direction of the stairs before he had time to register her acquiescence.

The roof garden wasn't really a garden as such. It was just a large space, enclosed by a balustrade, with a few plants in pots and some benches placed at discreet intervals. A slight breeze whispered round the greenery, which usually made it a pleasant spot for a leisurely stroll in the evening, but at this time of year it was still stiflingly hot. At least to foreigners. There were times when Zar blessed the fact that she was a half-caste. The blood of Indian ancestors coursing through her veins gave her a distinct advantage when it came to coping with the weather conditions.

Zar glanced behind her and saw Mr Carmichael draw in a deep breath, as if he was relieved to escape the stuffiness of the room below. He wiped his brow with a large handkerchief and surreptitiously loosened his neckcloth a little, pulling it away from where it stuck to his skin. Then he hurried after her as she began to walk towards the nearest bench.

'Shall we …' he began, but Zar had already stopped.

'Sit down? Yes, of course.' She gathered her skirts and seated herself, spreading them out around her, which left him only a small space at the end of the bench. Normally she preferred Indian clothing, as it was much more suited to the climate here, but she had to acknowledge that English fashions came in useful for keeping suitors at a distance. The small hoop with its wide petticoat and overdress was a very effective barrier. If Mr Carmichael noticed her deliberate ploy, he was too much of a gentleman to comment, but he swivelled towards her as much as her gown would allow.

He cleared his throat. 'I, er ... understand you are a widow, Mrs Miller.'

'Yes, that's right. My husband died last year.' Zar was sure he already knew this and much more besides, but she humoured him for the sake of politeness. No one ever mentioned her wealth; that would be plain vulgar.

'Then you must be very lonely. It's difficult for a woman on her own, I dare say.'

'Not at all, I enjoy solitude.'

He looked baffled for a moment, then forced a laugh. 'Oh, I see, you jest.' Another guffaw. 'Very funny, to be sure.'

Zar kept quiet. She'd learned that the less she said, the sooner the ordeal would be over and done with.

'The thing is ...' Mr Carmichael cleared his throat again. 'The thing is, Mrs Miller, I was wondering ... that is to say, as you do not seem to have formed an attachment to anyone presently stationed here at the Factory, I thought ... what I mean is ...'

Zar wanted to scream. *For heaven's sake, spit it out, man!*

'Would you do me the honour of becoming my wife?' Mr Carmichael finally forced the words out in such a rush that, had Zar not been expecting them, she might have missed what he said.

She looked out over the balustrade to the more or less sleeping city around them and shook her head. 'I thank you for your kind offer, but I'm afraid the answer is no, Mr Carmichael. I'm very sorry.'

'I know it's a bit sudden and we haven't known each other very long. I own, perhaps, I should have waited a bit, but I thought that with you in such a precarious situation and—'

'Mr Carmichael.' Zar turned to him and pinned him to his seat with her most earnest gaze. 'Please believe me when I say that *nothing* would induce me to marry at this time. I'm perfectly happy without a husband and should I need any male assistance, I have a stepson who can take care of anything I ask him to.' No need to tell Mr Carmichael that William was the last man on earth she'd go to for help.

'But …'

Zar stifled another sigh. Some men were incredibly obtuse. 'I consider this matter closed, Mr Carmichael, and would thank you not to refer to it again. At any time,' she added, just to make it perfectly clear.

'I see.' Mr Carmichael's expression turned sulky, in the manner of a small boy, which did nothing to make Zar change her mind. He wasn't bad-looking and she had no doubt he was a decent enough man, but she didn't feel anything for him and couldn't imagine marrying him, so she kept her eyes fixed on his. He finally seemed to understand and backed down. 'Well, then, I suppose I should take my leave,' he muttered.

Feeling sorry for his wounded pride, Zar took pity on him. 'I thought you wished to take the air as it's a bit cooler up here.' She stood up and waited. 'Shall we at least walk around the perimeter? There is a lovely view of the river in the moonlight.'

He hesitated for a moment, then offered her his arm, which she accepted, although she was careful only to place a few fingers on his sleeve with the lightest of touches. 'By all means, Mrs Miller, by all means.'

Zar breathed a sigh of relief. Thank goodness for that. Now perhaps she'd be left alone until the next new arrivals.

Chapter Two

The so called 'Black Town' of Madras was an area to the north of the English Fort St George, laid out in a neat grid pattern of streets. As Jamie entered it late one afternoon, a fresh sea breeze made the air temperature bearable and went some way towards diminishing the usual city odours. He glimpsed the waters of the Bay of Bengal in the distance to his right, glittering invitingly. Although he didn't notice the heat as much as he once had, having been in this part of the world for so many years now, the thought of a swim was still tempting. The fact that he was wearing native clothing kept him relatively cool though. He'd adopted the Mohammedan style – loose fitting trousers, a shirt with long narrow sleeves and a long coat, all made of fine white cotton. A turban protected his head from the sun's rays, and the simple Hindu shoes that looked like slippers on his bare feet helped too.

He headed for the northern half of the town where Indian merchants and craftsmen had their newly built houses. Earlier in the year, during January and February, the French had besieged Madras. Their artillery fire had gutted most of the houses, especially in the Black Town, but buildings were springing up everywhere now the French were routed. It was with some satisfaction that Jamie recalled what he'd heard recently – the English troops were on the offensive, winning victories everywhere.

'And good riddance, *messieurs*,' he muttered. Not that he had anything against the French personally, but their infernal warmongering here hindered his trading activities. He'd be glad if they were evicted from the sub-continent for good or a peace of some sort could be agreed.

Passing whitewashed houses, some in a better state than others, he reached the one he was looking for. Its walls hadn't been affected much by the recent fighting, although he noticed they were freshly painted, but the roof looked new in the fading light. Jamie frowned as he stopped in front of the closed door and listened. He'd expected it to be open, with the usual early evening activity, but no sounds emanated from inside the building. It seemed empty and lifeless.

He rapped on the door, his knuckles making a sound like a pistol shot. 'Hello? Anyone there? Open up.'

Nothing. No footsteps, no voices, not a sound from within.

Jamie took a step back, puzzled, then went over to the house next door. An old man sat on the ground outside, cross-legged. When asked about his neighbour, however, he shook his head and without meeting Jamie's gaze muttered, 'Gone.'

'What do you mean, gone? Where exactly? And why? Has he been arrested? Or do you mean there's illness about?'

'Don't know. Just left. All of them, whole family.' The old man still wouldn't look at Jamie, which made the latter suspicious.

'There must have been some reason.' But he could tell he wouldn't learn what it was from this man.

He went back to stand outside his friend's front door. Akash was a lapidary and gem trader who had, rather reluctantly at first, taken Jamie on as an apprentice four years before. He'd stared at Jamie in disbelief when he arrived unannounced and asked to learn all about gemstones, but Jamie had stood his ground.

'I've been told you speak some English and that you're the best diamond cutter in town. I want to learn. Please, will you teach me? I'll make it worth your while.'

'Why?' The one word and black gaze had told Jamie that Akash thought it the whim of a bored and spoiled rich man, which was partly true. But Jamie had other reasons for wanting to immerse himself in the world of precious stones. He needed to forget his old life, his former self, and fill his mind with new images and knowledge.

To Akash he said only, 'I can't become a successful trader unless I know all about the goods, and I see no better way of learning than by starting at the beginning, when stones are cut and polished. I never do anything by halves and I'm serious about this. I want to become the best foreign gem merchant in India.'

The lapidary seemed to read between the lines and Jamie found out later that Akash had heard the unspoken words too. The desperation of a man at the end of his tether, a man needing the distraction of learning. He was wise enough not to mention this at the time.

From that day on he never questioned Jamie about his reasons again, waiting for the foreigner to be ready to confide his secrets by himself. And he generously taught Jamie everything he knew – splitting, cutting, polishing and valuing – until Jamie was ready to begin to trade. They'd worked together on and off now for a couple of years, their bond growing stronger all the time. Akash wouldn't just up and leave without some sort of message.

So where the hell was he?

Jamie glared at the closed door and gave it an impatient push. It didn't budge. Muttering a curse, he went round to the back of the house where a high wall encircled a courtyard. From nearby homes enticing cooking smells emanated and voices rose and fell as the occupants went about their daily business, but here there were no sounds. The lapidary workshop was silent and the lathe still. And yet …

Jamie cocked his head to one side, listening intently. He was sure he'd heard a slight scuffling noise, as if someone was trying to keep another person quiet or confined. Someone could be holding Akash prisoner. He had to check. Backing up a bit, he took a running jump at the wall and managed to heave himself up to the top, straddling it. He slung the other leg over and dropped to the ground, as lithe as a cat, alert and looking for movement. Just inside the open back door of the main building, he thought he saw a shadow shift ever so slightly.

Right, got you.

He slipped off his footwear and proceeded barefoot across the courtyard, glancing left and right to make sure he wasn't ambushed by some assailant. He slid a long dagger out of the sheath at his belt and held it ready. Then he peeked round the door frame into the house and stopped dead. His friend was sitting on the floor, bent forward with his head in his hands.

'Akash?' He whispered the question, since he didn't yet know what was happening. It was gloomy inside the house and Jamie wasn't sure if they were alone, but at the sound of Jamie's voice, Akash shot upright and blinked.

'Jamie! I thought you were in Burma or Calcutta. By all the gods, am I glad to see you!'

Since Akash wasn't bothering to keep his voice down, Jamie surmised there was no danger and put his dagger away. But something still wasn't right. He looked around the empty room and frowned. 'I came back sooner than expected. What's the matter?'

Akash stood up and came to clasp Jamie in a quick embrace. 'A lot has happened. I would have sent for you if I could, but I didn't know how to reach you.'

'Why? Where is your family? Please tell me what's going on?' Jamie was appalled to find Akash looking drawn and tired. It was unlike the normally even-tempered man who always worked with a smile on his face.

'They've been taken.' Akash seemed to be struggling for composure and a cold shiver of apprehension slithered down Jamie's back.

'Taken? What do you mean?'

Akash swallowed and closed his eyes briefly. 'I will tell you everything, but you must promise not to breathe a word to a soul.'

'Of course. You know you can trust me.' Jamie would never do anything to jeopardise his friend.

'Then come, I want to show you something.' Akash led Jamie outside and into the workshop across the yard, shutting the door behind them.

While staying with Akash, Jamie had lived like a native and without thinking he sank down to sit cross-legged next to his friend on a floor mat. They spoke in Hindi, which Jamie had learned as he worked through his apprenticeship. Unlike most people in the region, Akash and his family didn't speak Tamil at home, because they'd come from the north originally. Jamie was grateful for this, as Hindi had proved more useful when conducting business, although he'd picked up enough Tamil as well to get by since he had an ear for languages.

'So what happened?' he prompted.

Akash fiddled with his belt, then sighed and began his

tale. 'Last night, I went to visit my brother Sanjiv who, as you know, lives only a couple of streets away. I stayed talking to him for a while and by the time I got back here it was fully dark. As I entered the house, a man grabbed me from behind and put a hand over my mouth. He hissed that I had to keep quiet and not struggle – my family's lives depended on it. So, of course, I nodded. What else could I do?'

'Who was this man? And where was your wife and the children?'

Meera, Akash's wife, had treated Jamie like a member of the family while he stayed with them and he'd appreciated her quiet care. As for the two lovely dark-haired and dark-eyed children, Jamie couldn't bear the thought of anyone harming them. He'd come to love them as if they were his own. They had reminded him daily of the baby he'd left behind, but by caring for Akash's offspring he felt he'd atoned somewhat for his shortcomings when it came to Margot.

'I don't know who he was. He said my family had been taken hostage and would be kept somewhere safe until I did what was asked of me. When I became agitated, he assured me they were well and would not be mistreated as long as I cooperated.' Akash passed a hand over his brow, drawing in a deep breath, and Jamie waited for him to continue. 'The man said I had to find a trustworthy person, a courier, to take something to Surat. Something very important, but secret.'

'I see.' Jamie thought he understood and hazarded a guess. 'A valuable gemstone?' Travelling was always a danger, with bandits and other brigands a plague on the roads. A man had to be very careful when transporting something precious.

Akash shook his head. 'Not the way you think.' With jerky movements, he reached underneath his workbench and withdrew a small bundle, which he held out to Jamie. 'Take a look at this.'

Jamie unwrapped the slightly grimy material and drew in a sharp breath. 'Bloody hell,' he muttered in English. On his lap lay a turban ornament of the kind worn by the richest of Indian rulers, the *nawabs,* or the local princes, the *rajahs.* A huge cut red gemstone was set in gold together with a cabochon sapphire, one on top of the other, with feathers sticking out above them to add the final touch. The sapphire was probably very old, judging by its shape, and had been decorated with etched symbols on one side. Jamie had seen this type of thing before and knew he was holding what was in effect a talisman for good luck. An enormously costly one, if not priceless. He studied the jewel more closely and caught his breath at the sheer beauty of it.

'That's never a …?' he began, as the topmost stone flashed with sudden red fire in the faint light.

Akash nodded. 'Yes, a red diamond. Incredibly rare, especially that size.'

'You're sure? It could just be a pale ruby.' But Jamie had never known Akash to be wrong about something like that before. He took a small magnifying glass out of his pocket and looked more closely as he'd been taught, holding it up to the last of the daylight filtering in through the window. Most rubies had small imperfections in them, which helped to distinguish them from diamonds which were essentially clear crystals. This stone was flawless.

Akash just gave him a hard stare, as if questioning his judgement was an insult, which it probably was.

'Hell and damnation! I don't understand what this has to do with you or your family though?'

'I can't be sure, of course, but it's my belief this item has been stolen. If so, it's too distinctive to sell here, where someone might recognise it. Even if I were to take it apart for them to sell the stones individually, it would be too risky. So the thief or thieves want it conveyed to a merchant in Surat, from whence it will probably be transferred to a rich buyer somewhere in another country. Persia perhaps? That would be far enough.'

'But why are they asking you to arrange transport?' Jamie was puzzled as to why any thieves would involve someone like Akash, who was known to be an honest man.

'The man who brought it said he'd heard I had contacts in the gem trade and therefore thought I'd be the best man for the job. No one would think it strange if I sent someone with a valuable consignment to Surat. I've done so before. The man couldn't go himself, because he was needed by his master, or so he claimed. I'm guessing he simply doesn't want to be caught with the stolen jewel. And via him, the trail might lead directly to the original thief. So it has to be someone unknown.' His shoulders slumped and his voice grew hoarse with emotion. 'If I don't comply, Meera and the children will die.'

Jamie considered the talisman one more time. It was very distinctive and anyone caught with it would be branded a thief whether he was connected to the original robber or not. Carrying such a thing all the way across India would be madness.

'Did you get a look at his face? Would you recognise him if you saw him again?'

'No, he kept it covered, apart from his eyes.'

'A shame. Then we can't ask around, try and find out who he is.'

'No, there's no point. Besides, he's coming back tomorrow and if I haven't made satisfactory arrangements by then, he'll ...' Akash swallowed hard, obviously unable to finish the sentence.

Jamie put a hand on his friend's arm and squeezed it in silent sympathy. 'Don't worry. We'll save your family somehow. There must be a way. Perhaps we can fool the thieves and—'

'No! I can't risk anyone hurting my loved ones. I don't know who the real thief or thieves are – I'm sure the man who came here is just a go-between – but I must do exactly as he asks. He's sure to be watching me. If nothing else, to make certain I don't make off with the jewel myself.'

Jamie closed his fist around the valuable item in his hand so hard the gold bit into his palm, hurting him. 'But damn it all, that will make you their accomplice. What if they plan to blame it all on you?'

Akash shrugged, his expression bleak. 'What choice do I have? I just have to hope they don't get caught, then I can't be implicated.'

'They could pin the blame on you even if they escape with the jewel. No, there must be something we can do to even the score a little and make sure that can't happen.' Jamie stared into the growing dusk and tried to come up with a plan. He had to help. Akash had no idea just how much he'd done for Jamie. Simply by accepting him as his unofficial apprentice he'd dragged him out of the deep depression he'd suffered since leaving Sweden. *I owe him so much.*

Jamie's brain turned over the various options. 'If

I deliver the jewel to Surat ...' he mused out loud, but Akash interrupted him.

'You would be ideal, but I can't ask it of you.'

'Of course you can. Who else? I travel all the time and I can go there easily by sea. I know Surat. I've been there before, briefly, when I first arrived in India. Then you can truthfully say you've fulfilled your part of the bargain and if anyone comes looking, you can't be accused of theft.'

'I can't let you take that risk, my friend. What if you're caught in possession of the talisman? You'd be a dead man.'

'And you're not, right now?'

Akash opened his mouth to reply, then closed it again as there was obviously only one answer to that.

Jamie thought some more. 'Listen, do you know who this really belongs to? Which *rajah*?'

'I think so, yes. It's unique and people in the trade talk. The Rajah of Nadhur had something very similar.'

'He'll want it back.'

'Yes, but we can't give it to him. The thieves will take revenge on anyone who thwarts their plans.'

'I know. That's not the point. But the Rajah will have men out looking for his talisman, which is yet another reason not to be caught in possession of it. We wouldn't be able to prove we weren't the original thieves. So we must outwit everyone.' Jamie continued to stare out the window into the dusk, his mind a whirl of possibilities. He held up his hand to stop Akash from talking while he finished his thought processes, then finally he nodded. 'Here's what we have to do – your brother Sanjiv, the one who lives nearby, is a goldsmith, am I right?'

'Yes, but what's he got to do with anything?'

'We'll need his services, in secret of course. We're going

to make a replica of this talisman so that we can confuse the people on its trail.'

'A what? Have you taken leave of your senses?' Akash blinked at Jamie. 'And where are we going to get a red diamond that size?'

Jamie smiled. 'We're not, but I happen to have a pale ruby that's very similar in size, or it will be once we cut it. Just bought it in Burma. With a bit of polishing we can make it almost the same and only an expert would know the difference. Do you have a sapphire that could be used?'

'Well, yes, but—'

'Then all we need is your brother's help to make the gold setting, and some feathers.'

'I don't understand what you're hoping to achieve with this mad scheme,' Akash complained. 'Why would you want to carry two jewels?'

'I won't. The real talisman will be taken to Surat by someone else – your brother perhaps? – while I act as a decoy with the replica and deliberately make the people who are watching follow me. That way, if I'm challenged or anyone steals the jewel from me, it won't mean disaster for either of us, because the real one will still be delivered as promised. And if the thieves are thinking of trying to trick us, I can't be accused of theft because I'll be able to prove that the jewel I'm carrying isn't the real talisman.'

Akash shook his head. 'I'm confused.'

'Good, then maybe everyone else will be too.' Jamie clapped a hand on his friend's shoulder. 'Listen, don't worry about it now, let's just get started. We have to work quickly before anyone realises what we're up to. Can we get your neighbour's son to take a message to your brother? He needs to come over here now.'

* * *

They worked through the night and by the following afternoon they were done.

'The replica would fool most people, wouldn't you say?' Jamie asked with satisfaction. 'But there are still subtle differences to help me prove it's a fake, if necessary.'

Akash and his brother Sanjiv both nodded. The three of them were in the workshop, where Sanjiv had just put the finishing touches to the gold mount and secured the feathers.

'The main thing that could give it away is the diamond,' Akash muttered. 'We managed to copy the inscription on the sapphire perfectly, apart from the one symbol you said to leave out on purpose.'

'Yes, but how many people can tell the difference between a red diamond and a ruby? Besides, we mustn't let anyone get close enough to check. And no one knows, apart from ourselves, that there are now two talismans, so they won't even think to look. Why would they?'

Sanjiv held out his hand for the real one. 'Don't worry, brother, I will deliver it to Jamie in Surat. I can take care of myself and I'll be careful.'

They had decided that Sanjiv would leave a day or two after Jamie, once Meera and the children had been returned safely. He was to go overland, travelling in the guise of a snake charmer. 'I've always loved snakes,' he'd said, 'and I doubt anyone would willingly stick their hand into a snake's basket to check for valuables. It will be the perfect hiding place.'

Jamie was to go by sea, boarding an English ship bound for Surat to sail around the Indian coast. 'Excellent. Akash, you must watch and make sure Sanjiv isn't followed. Now please tell me again how I am to find the contact in Surat in order to hand this over.'

Akash obliged, but his instructions were complicated. 'The man wouldn't give me a name. He said you have to go round to all the gem traders and ask a specific question. Start by saying that the weather has been very unpredictable lately, then the exact phrase "I wonder if the monsoon will bring mists this year?" The man expecting you will reply "Oh, yes, and the mists hide everything". Have you memorised that?'

Jamie nodded. 'Yes, every word.' He turned to Sanjiv. 'I'll see you in Surat. I will hire a house near the English Factory and you can ask for me there. Seek me out at night and we'll confer. We need to be on our guard. They may still hope to trick us somehow – perhaps they'll need scapegoats to throw the Rajah's men off the scent? – so keep your eyes and ears open.'

'Will do.' Sanjiv nodded, a determined set to his mouth, which reassured Jamie. He hadn't really wanted to involve anyone else in this venture, but he couldn't see any other way to make the ruse work.

'I'll try to delay handing over the talisman until you bring me word, Sanjiv, that the thieves have returned Meera and the little ones, safe and sound.'

'Good.'

'Now all we have to do is wait for the man to arrive so we can tell him I'm the courier,' Jamie said.

'What if he's been watching the house and asks about Sanjiv?' Akash wanted to know.

Jamie shrugged. 'Just say you called him over to ask his advice, but that I convinced the two of you to let me be the one to go.'

'I really shouldn't allow either of you to do this.' Akash bit his lip, clearly worried. 'I ought to go myself.'

'You can't. You have a family, people depending on

24

you.' Jamie put a hand on Akash's shoulder. 'Sanjiv and I don't, and anyway we'll be fine.'

'If you say so.'

Jamie nodded, but he wasn't quite as sanguine as he made out. What choice did he have though? This had to work.

Chapter Three

Nadhur, Central India – May 1759

The Rajah of Nadhur paced his opulent quarters, his gold embroidered coat flaring around him with every step and fanning out in an arc each time he turned to retrace his path. He was oblivious to the beauty that surrounded him. Exquisitely painted walls and ceilings, ornately carved pillars and a shining marble floor were all ignored. He should have been a happy man, since he'd recently been given leave to marry Indira, the only daughter of a rich *nawab* from a province in the north-west. A girl so lovely that his rivals would be green with envy, even had she not brought him a small fortune along with the territory as her marriage portion. But he wasn't particularly pleased today and didn't bother with any of the usual pleasantries.

'The sacred talisman is gone, Bijal!' he exclaimed.

The Grand Vizier hid a smile. It wouldn't do to show any joy at his master's misfortune. Not yet anyway. He'd been summoned with an urgency that made him half run along the corridors, but at forty he wasn't as fit as he'd once been and had arrived panting and overheated. He stared at his master, feigning consternation while trying to get his breathing under control. 'Really, Highness? Are you sure?'

'Of course I'm sure! I've looked everywhere and besides, I know exactly where I put it last time I used it. It's not there, I tell you.'

Bijal adopted his most serious expression and tried to look sympathetic at the same time. 'That is indeed unfortunate.'

The Rajah continued to pace. 'I don't understand how it could have just disappeared,' he complained. He stopped his perambulations long enough to gesture angrily at his Grand Vizier. 'No one seems to have seen the thief enter my chambers, and the guards are outside day and night. How? How, I ask you?'

Bijal shrugged, somewhat defensively. 'I will, of course, interrogate everyone, Highness. We should have an answer very soon. Perhaps one of your servants has merely taken it away for cleaning?'

'No one touches it without my permission, you know that,' the Rajah virtually snarled at him.

'Have you asked your half-brother, Highness?'

'Dev? Why would I?'

'He is, er … given to pranks, is he not? Or he may have decided to borrow it. There are only three people who are free to come and go at will into your private quarters – myself, your half-brother and Ravi, your most trusted servant. I sincerely hope you don't suspect either of us …?' He let the sentence hang, making his eyes large and guileless.

The Rajah shook his head. 'Of course not, but … Dev?' His frown deepened. The half-brothers had never been close and of late the rift between them had opened into a veritable chasm. Bijal had fanned the flames on occasion, but for the most part, this wasn't necessary. Dev, being younger, was jealous of his brother's position, power and possessions. Since the announcement of the forthcoming nuptials, things had been worse than usual. Dev must have realised that his chances of ever inheriting his brother's domains would be very slim once the lovely Indira began to produce offspring.

'I heard only yesterday that he has been spending

lavishly,' Bijal said, his voice tinged with fake regret. He shook his head. 'The young live for the moment, don't they? But where are his riches coming from, I wonder?'

Dev was given a generous allowance, but frequently overspent. It was yet another sore point, but it helped to cast suspicion on the half-brother now.

'You're not suggesting …?'

Bijal held up his hands. 'I'm not suggesting anything, Highness, merely stating the facts. Could it be that young Dev has only borrowed the talisman temporarily until he is in funds again? Perhaps it is being held as surety?'

'That would be outrageous! He'd never dare.'

'No, you're right. That is surely a step too far even for a beloved brother.' Which Dev most certainly was not. Bijal kept another smile at bay. 'In that case, the talisman must indeed have been stolen and, if so, I would hazard a guess it's already far away. Any thief would surely sell it as soon as possible and not risk being caught in possession of such a thing.'

The Rajah strode off once more, turning angrily as he reached the farthest wall of the room. 'So what you're saying is that even if we catch the perpetrator, we'll be no nearer to finding the actual jewel? That's just not good enough! How can I marry without it? The talisman brings luck to my family and my people. To go through the wedding ceremony without it is simply in-con-ceivable.' He punctured each syllable of the final word with a furious step. 'It's part of the ritual, you know that.'

Bijal bowed, his gaze lowered so as not to show his triumph. *I know*. Out loud he said, 'I will do my best to find out what has happened to it. Leave it with me.' With another bow, he left the room and heard the Rajah bellowing after him.

'Your best had better be outstanding! I'm not marrying anyone without wearing the talisman of Nadhur. I'd be a laughing stock. It's a symbol of my power, a good luck charm, imbued with magic to bring us fortune and happiness!'

Indeed it was. And, as Bijal well knew, holding a royal wedding without it would mean the most dreadful of bad luck – complete and utter disaster in fact.

Which was just as it should be in his opinion.

Chapter Four

The journey went smoothly and Jamie had been pleased to observe that he was being followed. An Indian sailor joined the ship's crew at the very last moment, and although Jamie pretended not to notice, he'd kept his eyes on the man throughout the trip. The crewman worked hard, but had managed to stay in Jamie's vicinity more often than not. Again, Jamie ignored this, and acted as if he was the type of man who never even saw ordinary sailors but took their presence for granted. He hoped he'd fooled the spy.

At least Jamie knew what he looked like now. The man had an unmistakeable nose that curved like a *tulwar* sword and he knew he'd recognise him anywhere.

He and Akash had made much of Jamie's departure, making sure anyone watching would see him and follow. As agreed, Sanjiv was to set off a few days later, when hopefully no one would notice his departure at all.

'Don't worry, I'll check from a distance,' Akash had promised. 'If anyone so much as looks his way, I'll warn Sanjiv. But I think all eyes will be on you.'

'Let's pray you're right. If not …'

Akash nodded. They both knew what was at stake and what needed to be done. For Meera's and the children's sake, Akash would kill anyone who threatened to disrupt their plans. Hopefully such drastic measures wouldn't prove necessary.

'The man said your family would be returned as soon as I am safely on my way, didn't he?'

'Yes, so I can tell Sanjiv and he'll let you know when you meet up.'

'Good, because I'm not handing over either of the talismans unless I have to without being assured on that point.'

The city of Surat was situated in north-west India, in the province of Gujarat which had a rather marshy coastline full of tidal creeks. Surat itself was slightly inland, however, some six miles up the river Tapi. The entrance to this river was in the Gulf of Cambay where sandbars made navigating difficult. The river wasn't much better – sandbanks were forming in many places and in one particular spot only a narrow and dangerous channel remained for boats to make their way through.

Larger ships anchored at the mouth of the Tapi and passengers continued upstream by barge. Jamie had come this way once before when he first arrived in India on a Swedish trading ship. He watched the landmarks that had been pointed out to him then by a fellow traveller. After some vegetation, in the form of bushes interspersed with tall trees, came a village.

'That's Domus,' the man had said, 'on the southern bank.' And slightly further on, 'There you have the imperial Mughal wharf, followed by another village called Omrah.'

The exotic scents of the Indian countryside carried across to them and Jamie closed his eyes for a moment to really savour them. He was so used to this now, he hardly took the time to register such things any more. And Sweden, with its crisp smells of pine and cool air, seemed a lifetime away. The heat and spices of India were his world now.

They passed another village called Athwa, some private

wharves belonging to the richest of the city's merchants, and finally that of the French *Compagnie des Indes* just before reaching the southern part of the city walls.

Surat lay in a curve of the river on a flat plain and was protected by a double semi-circle of walls – an inner one that surrounded the main town including a castle, and an outer one built around the suburbs. Jamie remembered that the inner wall was called the *sheherpanah*, which meant 'the Safety of the City', while the outer was named the *alampanah*, or 'the Safety of the World', which he found quaint. Both were built of bricks, at least ten foot high, and with numerous gates and fortified points.

The barge passed the castle and its moat, which was just inside the southernmost part of the inner wall, and moored near the *furza*, the customs house, next door. As he disembarked, Jamie saw the Imperial Mint just across the street from the *furza* and on the left was the *daria mahal*, where the harbour master resided. He knew the castle green, in front, was called the *maidan* and it was crammed, as always, with tents, people, animals and goods of every kind. Bullock carts jostled for space with merchants and their customers and the whole scene was one of chaos and noise that assaulted his senses. Chattering, laughter, music, shouting. The scents of humanity, cattle and spices almost overwhelmed him, while heat and dust enveloped him in a suffocating embrace. Even the wind, when it blew, was hot here, leaving him feeling as though he'd been blasted by the draught from an oven.

Jamie looked forward to exploring the city again at a later date, but first he had to pass through customs like everyone else. His trunk was searched and everything inside turned upside down, which annoyed him no end, but he kept his temper in check. When the customs officials searched him, patting his pockets and feeling all along his body, he said nothing. They wouldn't find anything. He'd made sure of that with various secure hiding places. One had to pay customs on anything imported or exported, usually something like two and a half to five and a half per cent. Jamie had no intention of paying such charges unless he had to.

'You bring goods to trade?' the customs official asked.

Jamie shook his head and smiled. 'No, I'm just a traveller, looking at the sights of your lovely country.'

Which was very far from the truth, especially this time.

Released from the customs house at last, Jamie found a couple of *majurs* – common labourers – willing to help carry his belongings. As always, they'd been loitering around the *maidan* in the hope of finding just such work. Jamie travelled fairly light, but had nevertheless brought two chests filled with clothes and all manner of artefacts. He'd learned early on that packing an esoteric collection of Indian and Chinese items, such as figurines, daggers, silk cloth and ornaments of ivory and brass, diverted the customs officials' attention and stopped them from looking too closely at the chests themselves. Had they done so, they would have found several secret compartments filled with gemstones of various kinds. Some of the figurines also contained stones, as did the dagger handles. Jamie had secret hiding places wherever possible, even inside a pair of European shoes whose heels were hollow. Creating these compartments was the first thing he'd done when he began in the gem trade. Now he was doubly pleased he'd taken this precaution, as the fake talisman was hidden inside one of those shoes.

'I'm not taking any chances,' he'd told Akash, and so far, no one had ever found his precious stones.

He headed left, catching a glimpse of the *darbar* – the governor's residence – behind another building beyond the *maidan*. He recalled from his previous visit that most of the population lived inside the inner wall; indeed this part of Surat was so filled with houses you hardly saw any open spaces apart from the squares. He was walking towards Saudagarpura. Here the richest of the city's inhabitants had their mansions, some along the river. It was also where the English Factory was situated and this was Jamie's first port of call.

The Factory was leased from one of the city's richer merchants, and thus the building was in the same style as those around it. A large courtyard, teeming with people, was reached via a gateway. Various buildings surrounded it, among them a chapel without any statues of any kind as no one wanted to offend the Mohammedans – or Moors as the foreigners called them – who objected to such idolatry. Jamie knew from experience that the accommodation offered was good. He didn't want to spend too long there, however, but as a starting point it would serve him well. In the courtyard, he was lucky enough to come across a familiar face.

'Andrew!' he called out. 'Andrew Garwood, by Jove, are you still here?'

The man in question stopped at the sound of his name and turned to stare at Jamie, his startled expression turning into a grin of welcome. 'Kinross! I should have recognised that voice immediately. How are you? What brings you here?'

The two men shook hands. They'd met four years earlier, when the Swedish ship Jamie was travelling on docked at Surat for a time. Andrew was the sort of easy-going man it wasn't difficult to strike up a friendship with and the two had connected immediately.

'Oh, this and that. I'm a gem trader now, have been for a few years. I'm here on business, but thought I'd stay for a while. A couple of weeks, perhaps more. I'll be looking for a house to rent. Do you think there's room for me here until I find somewhere or should I look for an inn?'

'Of course you must stay here, I'll arrange it, but I think you're in luck. I happen to know of a house that's just become vacant which might suit you. First things first, let's get you settled inside. Is that your luggage?'

'Yes.' Jamie directed the *majurs* to follow them.

'Good, good.' Andrew led the way. 'Oh, and you've arrived just in time for a *soiree*. The Chief Factor is having one of his little gatherings tonight. Should be jolly.'

Jamie groaned inwardly. He hadn't really planned on socialising, at least not with the English, but there was nothing for it except to grin and bear it. 'Excellent, I shall look forward to that,' he lied.

Stifling a sigh, he followed Andrew into the building.

Chapter Five

'So I take it you haven't met the "Ice Widow" then?'

'The what?' Jamie raised his eyebrows at Andrew.

'You heard me, and very apt it is too, that nickname. Her frosty glances are enough to freeze off any man's, er ...' Andrew coughed. 'That is to say, she doesn't care much for us gentlemen, as I understand it. Or as husband material, at any rate. Come with me, I'll introduce you.' Andrew's expression betrayed his excitement and expectation and he added sotto voce, 'This should be a treat.'

'Why?'

But Andrew either didn't hear the question or chose to ignore it.

They were part of a gathering in what was normally the dining hall of the English Factory. The large tables that usually filled the space had been removed to allow a sizeable crowd to stand around in groups, chatting, gossiping and laughing. Servants circulated with beverages of various kinds. Despite large fans keeping the air moving, the atmosphere in the room was stifling and Jamie wished he hadn't agreed to come. He hated socialising these days and it was only politeness that had made him give in to Andrew's persuasions.

As they walked across the room, Jamie caught sight of a woman dressed in the English style, and yet somehow different from the few other ladies present. Her gown was made out of shimmering turquoise silk, with a petticoat of a lighter hue in the same material forming an inverted V at the front below the edge of the bodice.

As was the fashion, the sleeves of the gown ended just above the elbow with a flounce. The lace of her chemise peeped out below this and also around the edge of the low-cut décolletage, which emphasised her curves. *And what curves!* His eyes opened slightly at this vision and even wider still when he caught sight of her face. She was breathtakingly lovely in a rather exotic way.

Unfortunately her expression ruined the overall impression. Haughty, with her chin tilted slightly upwards as though she looked down on lesser mortals, she surveyed the room as if she were a *rani*, an Indian queen, at the very least. So this must be the 'Ice Widow'. Jamie's heart sank. By the looks of it she was another spoiled beauty, just like the one he'd been married to. He groaned inwardly. He had no wish to meet her and had to repress an urge to just turn and run out of the room.

She was stunning though, no doubt about it.

Even from a distance he could see that her eyes were luminous and surprisingly light-coloured, a fact that was accentuated by her very dark, long lashes. She turned and stared straight at him as he and Andrew came closer. Jamie couldn't pull his gaze away for a moment as he took in the irises of those eyes – peridot-green in the middle, then turning to iridescent aquamarine. He'd never seen anything like it before. They were a startling contrast to the woman's hair, such a dark brown colour it was almost black and arranged in a simple plait which hung over one shoulder, skimming a high, full breast before falling past her waist. She had flawless skin, a fraction darker than most of the women around her, which made Jamie realise she must be a half-caste – part Asian, part European.

Interesting.

When Andrew stopped in front of her and spoke her

name, 'Mrs Miller,' Jamie could have sworn she hesitated and her mouth tightened for a fraction of a second. It seemed clear she was reluctant to talk to either of them and only good manners forced her to reply.

Haughty, spoiled and rude into the bargain. His jaw tightened even further. Lord, how he hated women like that. What made them feel they were so superior? That they could ride roughshod over every male they encountered? It was unbearable.

'Mr Garwood,' she said politely, but in a cold voice, holding out her hand to Andrew. He bent over it with an old-fashioned flourish, but to Jamie it looked as though she barely curbed a desire to snatch her fingers back. Poor Andrew. Jamie hid a smile as an idea came to him. It would seem the best way to rile her would be to pretend to court her. And for some reason, he suddenly wanted to pay her back for her very obvious disdain by teasing her a little.

'May I introduce Mr Kinross? He's but newly arrived here in the city.' Jamie saw Andrew watch her reaction to the newcomer, as if he expected her to act in a certain way. There was a flash of something – awareness, surprise? – as she took in Jamie's features, but nowhere near the response he normally received from women. Jamie knew he was considered handsome and his good looks often caused a stir, something he'd learned to ignore. On this occasion they had no effect, which for some contrary reason annoyed him. Or perhaps she was just very good at hiding her emotions? Because he felt a definite current between them and couldn't deny that he was physically attracted to her. What warm-blooded man wouldn't be?

She again held out her hand, a small nod acknowledging the introduction. 'Mr Kinross,' she murmured, her voice low and seductive, but Jamie doubted she did that on purpose. Her expression made clear that seducing anyone was definitely not her intention. A shame, but perhaps he could make her change her mind? It would be amusing to try. He bent over her hand, taking her limp fingers in his and grazing her knuckles with the stubble he hadn't shaved off that morning, as well as his lips. The hand was pulled out of his grip quickly and he heard her intake of breath, but he didn't give her the chance to protest.

'It's extremely hot in here, don't you think?' he commented, giving her a half-smile. 'Would you care to take a turn in the roof garden with me, Mrs Miller?'

Since Jamie had been here before, he remembered the haven above them where he and Andrew had spent time chatting during his previous visit. It was the perfect place for courting a woman. Or pretending to.

She glanced around, obviously searching for a way to refuse, but then she straightened her shoulders as though preparing for battle. Very reluctantly she nodded and Jamie saw a mixture of resignation and irritation in her eyes as she placed a few fingers on his outstretched arm. 'Very well. I suppose that would be … nice.'

Andrew grinned and winked at Jamie. He obviously thought Jamie had taken up his unspoken challenge and decided to charm the cool widow. 'Enjoy the sights,' he called after them as they headed slowly for the doors opening onto the stairs.

'I'm sure I shall,' Jamie murmured, looking straight at Mrs Miller, and had the satisfaction of seeing her throw him a disapproving glare. 'Moonlight is so beautiful, don't you think?' he added with a smile. She didn't reply.

Outside in the balmy night air, other people strolled too, but Jamie deliberately headed for an empty corner.

He wasn't going to try and seduce the woman, but he wanted to see what her reaction would be to spending time alone with him, if she was so averse to men. There were lanterns dotted around the balustrade, so the place he steered her to wasn't all that dark, but it still felt a bit too intimate for such a short acquaintance. Jamie wondered if he was doing the right thing, teasing her this way, but then he remembered her expression earlier. As if she was doing them a favour by even talking to them. Jamie resolved to play her at her own game.

'Would you like to …' he began, holding out a hand to indicate the bench, but she interrupted him.

'No, I prefer to stand,' she muttered, turning to stare out across the river which glimmered in the moonlight.

'Very well.' Jamie moved to join her in gazing at the view and she immediately stepped to the side to create a gap between them, even though her skirts kept him well away already. He stayed where he was. For now. 'My friend tells me you are a widow, Mrs Miller,' he said in order to start the conversation.

'Yes, my husband died last year,' she replied, sounding less than enthusiastic at this line of questioning.

He gathered she didn't like to talk about this and thought that perhaps it made her sad. He bowed slightly and commented, 'I'm sorry for your loss. You must feel it keenly, being on your own.'

'Thank you, but I prefer it.'

'You like solitude?' Jamie didn't bother to hide his surprise. It wasn't a sentiment most women shared as far as he'd gathered.

'Yes.'

No explanation seemed to be forthcoming, so he just commented, 'That is … unusual.' He gestured again towards the bench. 'Are you sure you wouldn't like to sit for a while? You can still admire the view, you know.'

She shot him a look which he couldn't interpret, then shrugged. 'We won't be staying up here for very long, but by all means ...' She sank down, spreading her skirts so wide Jamie raised his eyebrows.

'Pardon me, but unless you wish me to sit on your gown, would you mind moving the material slightly? Or are you trying to indicate that you'd prefer me to stand?'

He saw her cheeks take on a tinge of colour, but she moved her skirts enough for him to be able to sit.

'So tell me, why won't we be staying for very long? Have you tired of my company so soon?' he joked.

'No. That is ... we only came up for a quick breath of fresh air.'

'Well, I don't know about you, but I'm not in any hurry to return to the stuffiness below.' She made no response to this, so he guessed she didn't agree, but he'd be damned if he went downstairs quite that quickly. Surely she could give him a few more moments of her time? He continued with the small talk. 'Tell me, do you not find it difficult being on your own here in Surat?'

'No, as I said, I prefer it.'

'You wouldn't rather live in England?'

'Absolutely not.' When he again raised his brows at her, she added, 'I grew up here. England is a foreign country to me.'

'Ah, I see. Then I suppose you'll be looking to marry someone who is planning to stay in India.'

'No, I'm not.'

Jamie was taken aback by this forthright answer, but she pre-empted any reply he would have made by standing up and turning to fix him with a glare.

'Look, I may as well tell you now – I know where this is leading and the answer is no, Mr Kinross,' she said, her voice tight and her expression one of quiet determination. 'And … and now I wish to go downstairs again.'

He stood up as well. 'I beg your pardon? I wasn't aware I'd asked a question.' He tilted his head slightly to one side and gave her his best smile, the one he'd been told could melt a woman's heart at fifty paces. Not this one, apparently. The thought almost made him laugh out loud, but then he wondered what it was about him that she found so offensive. They'd hardly exchanged two sentences.

'I can see that you're the kind of man who usually has all the ladies in a flutter, and no doubt you thought I'd be another easy conquest,' she said, rushing the words out as if she'd recited them many times before.

Perhaps she had, Jamie thought.

'But I'm not looking for a husband so you'd be wasting your breath,' she finished, drawing in a deep gulp of air at last. 'You'll have to make your fortune some other way, as will the gentleman who asked me earlier.'

Anger rushed to the surface, making Jamie forget everything except wanting to punish this woman for her presumption that all men wanted to marry an heiress. *Just like Elisabet.* He deliberately stared at her bosom as it heaved enticingly. This made her blush, so he allowed his gaze to travel up to her face and back down along her body. 'As I said, I wasn't asking,' he drawled. 'And believe me, marriage wasn't the first thing that came to mind when I saw you.'

He had the satisfaction of seeing her eyes widen and her nostrils flare with outrage, but thought to himself that she'd deserved it. Why should he concern himself with her sensibilities when she was so set against every male she encountered without bothering to make their acquaintance properly? The nerve of the woman, to assume he'd want to marry her when they had only just met.

'Well, really! I'm—'

'—not used to men who aren't interested in you? No, I can see that. But rest assured, Mrs Miller, you'd be the last woman on earth I'd want to marry. If you're ever looking for a mere dalliance, however, just let me know. I'd be more than happy to oblige.' He let the words hang in the air for a moment, then gave her a mocking bow. 'And now, since we've established that neither of us is interested in wedded bliss, I'll bid you goodnight. There seems no point in prolonging the conversation or becoming acquainted further. Enjoy your solitary life.'

He turned on his heel and stalked off, more shaken by the encounter than he'd care to admit. Mrs Miller had reminded him of everything he'd been trying to forget and all the reasons why he'd come to India in the first place. Her assumptions about him were as rude as they were unfounded. What was it about spoiled beautiful women that they thought every man within ten miles would want to marry them? They could at least wait to be asked. He gave vent to his anger by downing several glasses of pale punch.

'Bitch,' he muttered, thinking of Mrs Miller but instead startling a matron nearby. He gave her his most charming smile to placate her, but inside he was still seething because in his mind's eye the beautiful Mrs Miller had merged with Elisabet, who'd made the same assumption.

He felt the old resentment well up and threaten to choke him, but he forced it down. He was probably overreacting and, in any case, what did it matter? Mrs Miller wasn't his concern and he need never talk to her again.

To hell with all women.

Zarmina stood frozen to the spot for several long moments, staring at the back of Mr Kinross as he strode off. She brought one trembling hand up to her mouth and tried to calm herself by taking a deep breath. The encounter had been worse than most, despite the fact that Kinross hadn't even tried to touch her. But he'd virtually devoured her with his eyes. She'd felt naked and vulnerable and yet … excited?

'Curse him!'

She didn't know why she was so upset. She ought to be used to this by now, but although she'd received more marriage proposals than she could count, no man had ever made her feel regret. Until now.

Why should she feel anything of the sort? He was no better than the rest. Worse, in fact, because of his rude propositioning.

But, dear Lord, he certainly stood out from the crowd.

Zar had spotted him the moment he entered the room and had studied his progress for a while as his friend introduced him to groups of people. Tall and broad-shouldered, Kinross towered over many of the other men present, but that wasn't what made him conspicuous. Nor was it his exceptional good looks and flashing smile, although these were obviously hard to ignore. Zarmina thought it was more to do with the latent power that radiated from him. She'd noticed he was lean, his tight-fitting clothes hinting at well-trained muscles, and under his polite exterior she sensed he was all primitive male.

Dangerous. At least to susceptible females.

Which was why she'd wanted to nip any possible courtship in the bud immediately.

Only, he wasn't interested so she'd embarrassed herself for nothing.

Zar felt her cheeks heat up at the thought of his rude words. He'd been interested all right, but only in bedding her, something she knew other widows sometimes indulged in. She almost laughed out loud. That would be the last thing she'd ever want to do after … She cut that thought off abruptly. The past was gone. She refused to dwell on it.

Taking another few breaths of sweet night air, she hurriedly made her way back along the roof garden towards the stairs down to the dining room. As always, she held her head high and assumed a mask of indifference. No one could hurt her now. She was her own woman and that's how it was going to stay.

Mr Kinross would soon be forgotten. Wouldn't he?

Yet when she briefly closed her eyes, his mocking smile was the image etched into her memory.

Chapter Six

Jamie woke with a gasp and tried to suck in all the air his dreams had forced out of him. For a moment he felt faint, but somehow he managed to make his lungs do their job. Although he knew the nightmares weren't real, he still had to fight down the panic that had him in its grip. Battling his way out from under the tangled sheets and mosquito curtains, he sat up, running shaking fingers through his shoulder-length hair. His body was covered in a sheen of perspiration, caused by a combination of alarm from the dream and the stultifying heat of the bedroom. Slowly, his heartbeat calmed down and his skin cooled off.

'*Fan i helvetes jävlar!*' He swore viciously in several different languages, switching effortlessly from Swedish to English, then on into his mother's native Dutch, followed by Hindi when he ran out of suitable epithets. The cursing didn't make him feel any better though. What he really wanted was to have his brain cleansed of all memories of Elisabet Grahn. He wished he'd never set eyes on her at all.

She's dead. She's gone, he reminded himself, but the image of her had permeated his dreams and wouldn't leave him.

Awake now, there was no way he'd go back to sleep again, so he pulled on a pair of breeches and went to stand on the narrow balcony outside his room. The air was cooler there, but still hot. This was India, after all, and no matter the time of day, you never froze like you did in his native Scandinavia. How he missed the cold, the crisp air, the cool breeze, the snow. But he couldn't go back.

Not yet.

Perhaps never.

And it was all Elisabet's fault. Or perhaps it was his own?

His tangled thoughts refused to give him respite, so he allowed himself to think back, to remember, hoping this would help put his demons to rest. He'd been such a fool ...

Riding through a deep, dark Swedish forest held no terrors for Jamie. On the contrary, he loved the feeling of solitude, of being at one with nature. The wonderful scent of pine needles and summer greenery enveloped him and he wasn't afraid of the creatures that inhabited the woods. Any wolf or lynx stupid enough to challenge him would regret it. He always carried a lethal dagger and knew how to use it.

It was Midsummer Night's Eve and despite the late hour, it was no darker than at twilight since the sun wouldn't set at all this night. To celebrate, Jamie had spent the evening carousing with friends. He was three sheets to the wind, but it didn't matter. His horse could find the way home without guidance, leaving his master to reminisce about a pretty maidservant who'd promised to meet him in a few days' time.

A piercing scream broke the silence and startled the horse into rearing up. Jamie only just managed to grab the reins and hold on, his fuzzy brain struggling to process what was happening.

'Whoa, Modig, easy boy.' He pulled his dagger out of its sheath, calmed the horse while dismounting and looked around. Another cry came from his right and Jamie plunged in among the trees, towing Modig behind him.

He knew every path for miles around his father's manor house and he remembered there was a river nearby with a very pretty waterfall. The screams had seemed to be coming from that direction so he headed there. Soon after, he burst into a clearing by the water's edge and stopped dead.

'Elisabet? Dear God, what happened to you?'

Feeling suddenly stone cold sober, Jamie took in the dishevelled state of his brother's beloved. Elisabet Grahn was lying on the ground, her clothing torn and dirty, and her bodice covered in what looked like blood. Tears ran down her cheeks and her mouth was swollen. Jamie couldn't help but stare at her half naked upper body, which was covered in scratches.

'J-Jamie, h-help me, please,' she sobbed, stretching out a hand imploringly towards him.

Jamie let go of Modig – he knew the horse wouldn't go far – and rushed forward to help Elisabet off the ground. 'Can you stand? Are you badly hurt?' He searched her face for signs of pain as she stood up with his assistance.

She shook her head, but winced. 'A little, but I ...' She looked downwards and understanding hit him like a punch to the solar plexus. It was clear that she'd been violated. He'd noticed her skirts had been bunched up beneath her, leaving her legs exposed. Even now the material was badly creased.

'Who did this?' he asked, his tone deadly. Elisabet belonged to Brice, Jamie's older brother, everyone knew that. Although no formal betrothal had taken place, it was only a matter of time. The families were just waiting for Brice to come back from a journey to China before making the announcement.

'The ... the blacksmith's apprentice. Luc, the oldest one,' she whispered.

'What, one of the Walloons? Damn it all to hell!'

The local blacksmith was of Belgian extraction, from the Walloon region, and for the last year he'd had some younger relatives apprenticed to him temporarily. They were handsome youths, with black hair, dark eyes, cheeky smiles and tanned skin. At twenty, Jamie was a bit older than them so hadn't been in their company much. But although he'd heard they were prone to picking fights with local boys, he'd never thought any of them would stoop to rape.

Jamie put an arm around Elisabet's shoulders and led her towards the horse. 'Let me take you home, then I'll go after him. He'll not get away with this.'

'No, it's too late,' Elisabet sobbed. 'He said he was leaving. I … I don't know where he's gone. Probably back to … to his country.'

'Don't worry, I'll find him.' Jamie lifted her up onto the horse's back, and mounted behind her. 'Here, take my jacket.' He draped it round her to hide her pale curves. Not because they tempted him, but in case they met someone.

She was a tiny slip of a thing, as fragile as a porcelain doll. Although she was exquisitely beautiful with a perfect face and figure, Jamie had never been as beguiled by her as his brother. It was strange, he thought, but he didn't desire her. Elisabet may be pretty on the outside, but she was spoiled and petulant, a pampered only daughter. Jamie preferred girls who weren't shrews. He'd be damned if he wanted to spend the rest of his life leg-shackled to a tyrant in petticoats.

Poor Brice. Still, to each his own.

At the moment he felt nothing but sympathy for her. And as Brice wasn't here to avenge her honour, the task must be his.

As he turned to check that she was holding on properly, he caught a strange expression on her face but it was gone in an instant. He wondered if he'd imagined it – his brain was still somewhat befuddled with *snaps* after all – and decided he must have done. 'Let's get you home.'

It was only later he realised that he hadn't imagined it, but by then he was well and truly caught.

'There was a message for you, *Sahiba* Zar. That man you insist on employing came while you were out.'

'Priya, not here!'

Zarmina put a finger on her lips to shush the maid, while checking to make sure no one was listening to their conversation. Then she ushered her into a private room, adjoining her bedroom. No one was allowed in there except the two of them.

Priya had been her *ayah*, acting first as nanny and later maid and confidante, but although Zar would trust the woman with her life, Priya didn't always think before acting or speaking. *Still, she's all I've got.* She buried that thought as she'd learned long ago it was no use bemoaning her fate.

'Now then, what did he have to say?'

'Nothing new really.' Priya sniffed. 'Just that your stepson is still meeting with unsavoury characters.'

'Anyone in particular? This is important, I need to know what he's up to. If he's making underhand deals, he could drag me down with him.'

The maid shrugged. 'The usual. And Mansukh the merchant.'

'Mansukh? That's new. Why would he be meeting with him? He's our rival.' Zar frowned and took a turn around the room, trying to order her thoughts. William, her adult stepson, had no head for business whatsoever, which was probably why his father – Zar's former husband – had left half the trading company to her, his widow. She knew William had been first incredulous, then livid, when he found this out, but the will was entirely legal and there was nothing he could do about it. He'd had to accept a partnership with his stepmother, a girl who was younger than himself. Thus, she was a constant thorn in his side.

'Old *sahib* should never have given you this role,' Priya grumbled.

'Maybe not, but I'm glad he did. It's saved me from having to marry again.' Zar shivered at the thought. 'It's given me freedom and you know I'm good at trading. It amused old *sahib* to teach me and I know he was surprised that I learned so quickly, but it's been a blessing. If only I can keep the business from being dragged down by my fool of a partner.' She continued her perambulation. 'What is he up to, I wonder? Why Mansukh?'

The man in question was the most powerful of the local merchants and not one to trifle with. Zar always avoided him, if at all possible, and would never make a deal which she knew went against him in any way. It was much better to stick to goods and deals he wanted no part of.

She sighed. It would seem William didn't have the wits to do the same. Zar came to a quick decision. 'Priya, I'm going out again. I do believe I'll accompany my stepson to the bazaar after all. He said that was where he was going when I met him just now.'

'The bazaar? But you've only just come in and—'

'Now, Priya, hurry please. I need to keep an eye on him and not give him the chance to do something stupid.'

Could she really stop him though?

*　*　*

Sanjiv hadn't yet arrived in Surat, but then Jamie hadn't expected him to. Going by ship was bound to be much faster and he knew he'd have time to kill before the fake snake charmer joined him. He decided he might as well seek out his contact here. Even if he didn't actually hand the fake talisman over immediately, perhaps he could find some useful information by following the man around.

Lord, he was turning into a spy, but he didn't see how else he could learn what he needed to know. Handling stolen goods went against everything he felt was right and he didn't like the fact that his friend had been coerced into accepting this task either. For both reasons, he'd like to unmask the real culprits and if possible perhaps even return the talisman to its rightful owner.

The morning after his encounter with the 'Ice Widow', he'd rented the house Andrew recommended.

'It's not one of the imposing stone mansions along the river, but nonetheless a sizeable property,' Andrew had explained. 'It belongs to a *bania*.'

Jamie knew wealthy Hindu merchants, called *banias*, lived near the English Factory, but in a part of Saudagarpura called Nanavat. Their homes were in less ostentatious buildings made of brick, and in the form of terraced houses, sharing their walls with their neighbours. One of these had been available to rent, and came complete with two servants – a butler cum valet called Kamal and his wife, the cook, Soraya.

'This will suit me fine, thank you.' Jamie had come to an agreement with the owner's representative after a lengthy haggling session, which ended satisfactorily for both parties. It hadn't taken him long to settle in and become bored, which was why he decided to begin his search the following evening, when the worst of the day's heat had subsided.

'I'm going out for a stroll,' Jamie told his temporary manservant. 'Please ask your wife to serve the evening meal in a couple of hours.'

'Very good, *sahib*.'

Leaving the house was like stepping into something tangible, like a moist cloud, the heat so heavy and thick one could almost touch it. Despite the late hour, it enveloped him, weighing down his shoulders, but he was used to it and ignored the discomfort. He thought he'd walk to the nearby bazaar and try to find the street where the gem merchants had their premises. Andrew had told him roughly where it was located and as the town wasn't huge, Jamie was in no hurry to reach his destination. He wandered the crooked lanes, sauntering slowly and taking everything in with interest.

He found it endlessly fascinating to study people going about their daily business and comparing this street scene to those he'd seen in other countries. There were similarities – the merchants trying to attract customers, the housewives or servants buying provisions, the pickpockets and other undesirables sidling around – but the subtle differences in race, clothing and customs made for a unique scene. Here he saw hordes of people dressed mostly in white. The only splashes of colour were provided by the turbans most of the men wore and the sashes tied round their waists.

None of the streets were laid out in an orderly fashion and there were a great many narrow lanes leading off in all directions. Jamie had found during his first visit that it was very easy to get lost as some of the smaller ones sometimes stopped abruptly with no way through. They weren't paved either and a continuous nuisance was the amount of dust swirling around, which was likely to choke you or at the very least make you cough. A stream of conveyances of various kinds didn't help matters.

Along the way, Jamie passed the street where the *sarafs*, or money changers, had their shops. He didn't need their services at present, but he'd made use of them in the past, as everyone did. With the many different types of coin in circulation, it was unavoidable. Beggars held out their hands in pitiful supplication, but Jamie hardened his heart to most of them. He'd be a very poor man now if he had given alms to each and every one. Occasionally he couldn't resist, however, especially if he saw someone maimed in any way.

'Bless you, *sahib,* may the gods send you good fortune.'

Cloth of various kinds was the main product of the province of Gujarat and Jamie lost count of the number of sellers he passed. Mostly they offered their customers cotton – white, coloured, striped or painted – but also some silks and materials embroidered with gold or silver thread. The majority of the shops were situated on the ground floor of the houses and the shopkeepers stood in their doorways calling for customers and crying their wares. If you ignored them, they would sometimes follow you for a while to recommend their goods, presumably in the hope that you'd change your mind.

'Step inside, *sahib*, see best quality cloth in Surat,' they all shouted, trying out various languages and dialects if they knew how.

This made Jamie smile, but he continued on without taking them up on their offers. He would buy a large amount for his mother and sisters if he ever returned to Sweden, but for now, he declined.

At last he reached the bazaar, which was really just a long street, but twice as broad as some of the others. He knew that, with the exception of the hottest part of the day, it was always full of people from early in the morning until late at night, making it difficult to get through the throng. It was a wonderfully colourful scene, the multitude of wares for sale creating a patchwork of bright hues. Also present were a huge number of dogs, barking and yapping, but he'd been told these were highly valued by the *Parsees,* one of the ethnic groups in the city, so no one took much notice.

Various pungent smells assailed him – spicy food, flowers, fruit and incense, as well as less savoury odours. Children with big dark eyes and black hair darted in and out between their elders, making a racket, shrieking and laughing with joy. They were beautiful, with very white teeth in their sunburned faces and ready smiles. Jamie couldn't help but smile back at them, even when they bumped into him by mistake.

About halfway down the street, Jamie suddenly spotted Mrs Miller alighting from a palanquin with a man holding out an impatient hand to help her. While her escort paid off the men carrying it or gave them instructions – Jamie didn't know whether it was a personal conveyance or a hired one – the widow stood beside him with a faraway gaze as if she was deep in thought. Jamie stopped for a moment too, curious despite himself. He'd calmed down considerably since their encounter and admitted to himself that he'd completely over-reacted the other night. Andrew had since confirmed that the poor woman was plagued with suitors, so perhaps it wasn't to be wondered at if she'd assumed he was yet another one.

Still, she could have waited until he actually asked.

Her escort was taking his time, perhaps haggling with their bearers. This gave Jamie the opportunity to admire the view the widow presented. There was no question she was stunning to look at and he reckoned he could safely gawp from a distance as she'd never know. The last thing he wanted was to feed her vanity, but from where he was standing, she wouldn't be able to see him.

But who was the man? An Englishman, or other foreigner of some sort, judging by his fair hair, but with a tanned face as if he'd spent years here. Of normal height, the man wasn't bad looking, but nothing special either. Her lover? Hadn't the widow told Jamie she preferred to be alone? Maybe it had all been lies, designed to discourage him from offering for her. Jamie swallowed down the irritation that rose inside him anew. He shouldn't jump to conclusions without learning the true facts.

In the next instant, he forgot all about their encounter in the roof garden as a flash of white sped past her and Jamie saw her arm jerk as the drawstring bag she'd been holding was snatched out of her hand. Mrs Miller opened her mouth, presumably giving a small shriek, and the man she was with turned and frowned at her. She pointed along the street, where the little thief – for it was a very small one, Jamie saw – was running and dodging between the passers-by with the sinuous dexterity of a snake. The culprit was too fast for Mrs Miller's companion to catch, but he was heading in Jamie's direction.

Without further thought, Jamie looked right and left, then pushed his way across the street, narrowly missing the huge front foot of an elephant lumbering by. Its handler shouted imprecations after him, but Jamie ignored that. He reached the other side just as the thief came charging towards him. Pretending to be walking along like everyone else, Jamie didn't so much as look at the child until he was almost next to him. Then his arm shot out and grabbed the skinniest little wrist he'd ever come across. The thief was pulled to a standstill, his feet practically leaving the ground at such an abrupt halt, and gave an involuntary gasp.

'Aahh!'

Jamie stared into enormous brown eyes, where fear and defiance warred. To his surprise, he realised they were very feminine eyes, with long silky lashes, as was the rest of the dainty face. *So, a girl thief. Why am I not surprised?* Everyone had to survive here; girls as well as boys were sent out to work. But thieving? That was an unusual occupation for a little girl.

He held out his hand and said in English. 'Give me the bag.' Even if, as he was fairly certain, the girl didn't understand his words, there was no mistaking his meaning. She glanced wildly around, as if searching for some kind of escape route and he felt her trembling. They both knew that if she gave it to him, she'd be admitting to theft which probably carried a death sentence here, if not mutilation at the very least. Jamie felt his insides constrict at this possibility. She was so young, she looked no more than six or seven. And she'd probably been ordered to do this by someone else.

Swallowing hard, the girl reluctantly dropped the bag into his outstretched hand, then tried to wriggle out of his hold. Jamie shook his head. 'Not so fast.' Threading his free hand through the strings of Mrs Miller's bag, he dug in his pocket and came up with a silver coin. He held it up in front of the startled girl's face and scowled at her. 'Don't ever do this again, understand?' He nodded at the bag, then shook his head emphatically. Then he flipped her the coin, which she caught with swift dexterity, and let go of her arm. With a final, confused look at his face, as if she couldn't believe what had just happened, she took off and melted into the crowd.

Jamie straightened up and turned to head towards Mrs Miller. He met her, with her companion trailing some way behind her, halfway to where he'd last seen them and held out the bag with a bow. 'Yours I believe?'

'I … yes, thank you, but how …?'

'I was walking along on the other side of the road and saw what happened. I intercepted the thief.' Jamie shrugged. 'Got away though.' He purposely avoided the word 'she'. Mrs Miller didn't need to know she'd been robbed by a girl.

'A shame,' she said, although he noticed she gave him a long, considering look. 'Would have been good to catch him and perhaps guide him into a worthier occupation. Really, they seem to start them on a criminal career from infancy now.'

'I'll try to keep that in mind next time. If there is a next time,' Jamie drawled. 'I doubt it was the child's fault though. It's the people who use little ones for their own nefarious purposes who should be punished, if you ask me.'

'Yes, of course. That's what I meant.'

The man had joined them now and he nodded at Jamie. 'Thank you for your help, Mr, er …?'

'Kinross.' Jamie sketched a small bow.

'Mr Kinross, we're obliged to you.' The man bowed back. 'William Miller, at your service.' Jamie must have looked confused, because Miller added, 'The lady's stepson.' He looked from one to the other. 'I gather you've already met?'

Mrs Miller nodded. 'At the Factory the other evening, when you had another engagement.'

'I see.' He sent his stepmother an impatient glare. 'Well, perhaps this will teach you to hold onto your possessions a bit better in future, Zar.'

'I was! They're just so quick,' she defended herself, but Miller had already turned away. 'Besides, there was nothing of any great value in there.'

'If you say so. Now may we go, please? I have a meeting later so no time to stand around. Good day to you, Mr Kinross.'

Mrs Miller opened her mouth as if she was going to protest, but then obviously thought better of it. She gave Jamie a quick nod, before hurrying off. 'Thank you again, I'm in your debt.'

As he watched her walk away, Jamie almost smiled to himself. That she was.

Perhaps he should demand something in return?

Chapter Seven

'Where have you been, Dev? I thought I asked you to be present yesterday during my meeting with our neighbour, the old Nawab of Bhalagat?'

The Rajah of Nadhur was once again striding around his chamber, while his younger half-brother sprawled on a mountain of cushions in a corner picking his nails with the tip of a dagger. Bijal watched silently from his usual vantage point by the window – present, but not really a part of the scene. The quarrel was between the brothers and he had no need to intervene. It was going very well without any interference from him, in his opinion.

'That old bore. Why should I sit around all day watching him dribble while he eats? He's disgusting,' Dev drawled.

'And you're not? Drinking yourself insensible every night. Bedding every woman in my palace – *my* palace mind – and picking fights with courtiers who dare not oppose you because they fear the consequences. I've had enough of it, I tell you!' Nadhur's fist came down on a small ornamental table and sent a gaming set flying off in all directions. No one came to pick it up as all the servants had been banished for the moment. Nadhur had said he didn't need any witnesses to this confrontation, which was probably wise of him, Bijal thought.

'What else is there to do here? You make all the decisions and there are servants to perform every task. As I see it, it's my duty to be seen to enjoy the privileges of being your brother.'

'Privileges, is it? And what of all the money you're

spending? Don't think I haven't noticed that a few of my possessions have gone missing. Are you giving them to the moneylenders in exchange for coin?'

Dev shrugged. 'So what if I've helped myself to an ugly statue or two. I've only taken the ones my mother told me she brought as part of her dowry.'

'And what of the talisman? She most certainly didn't bring that.'

'Talisman?' Dev looked up at last, genuine confusion in his gaze. 'What do you mean? I wouldn't take that. I may be bored, but I'm not unhinged.'

Nadhur glared at him. 'So you deny "borrowing" it?'

Dev stood up and marched over to stand nose to nose with his older brother. 'I most certainly do. Are you accusing me of something? Because I don't find it amusing to be called a thief.'

They squared off for long moments, then Dev flung away and headed for the door. 'What would be the point of me taking the talisman?' he threw over his shoulder. 'I'd be struck down by the gods, everyone knows that. If you've lost it, you need to look elsewhere for a scapegoat, brother.'

After his departure, Nadhur slumped down onto the pile of cushions so recently vacated by Dev and buried his head in his hands. 'I don't know what to think, Bijal,' he muttered. 'He always looks so innocent … no, guileless, and yet, I know he's trouble personified. I want to believe him, but how can I?'

He lifted his gaze and stared straight at Bijal, who suppressed a sudden urge to squirm. 'I don't know, Highness. Perhaps a search of his quarters will put your mind at ease?' And it would annoy Dev even more, furthering the rift between the brothers.

'You may be right, although if he has taken it, I doubt he'd be stupid enough to conceal it there.'

'I was thinking more along the lines of finding a promissory note, Highness. If he has exchanged it for temporary funds, that is.'

'Ah, yes, of course. Very well, I'll order a search.'

Bijal knew the Rajah's men wouldn't find anything and the whole exercise would leave him even more frustrated, as well as at odds with his brother. But he must remain firm of purpose, he told himself. He had no sympathy for this man. None. He was scum, as was his father before him.

When the time was right, the whole world would find out the truth, but not until all the omens were auspicious.

Zar rushed to catch up with William, but her mind was elsewhere. She was sure she'd seen Mr Kinross flip the little thief a coin before letting him go and she could only reach one conclusion – he'd bribed someone to steal from her so that he could appear in the guise of rescuing hero. But why?

They had already established that neither of them was interested in marriage. So he had no need to impress her, unless he'd been serious about wanting her in his bed? She drew in a hasty breath and almost choked on it as she inhaled a goodly amount of the ever present dust from the streets.

'Are you all right?' William stopped briefly to check on her when he heard her coughing.

'Yes, fine. Dust … everywhere.'

'You should have brought a handkerchief.'

Gallant as always, Zar thought sarcastically. Mr Kinross on the other hand … But Zar didn't utter the words. She knew there was no point arguing with

William. He'd never learned manners and it was probably too late to try to instil any in him now.

Her thoughts returned to her supposed saviour. Except, he was probably no such thing. But he had been even more devastatingly handsome in daylight, his silvery eyes disturbing her equilibrium. She'd noticed he had eyelashes so dark it looked almost as though he'd used kohl to rim his eyes, the way Zar herself sometimes did. But he had no need of such artifice, his features were perfect without. His angular face, with its proud nose and sharp cheekbones, was deeply tanned, which made Zar realise he must have been in India or the Far East for quite some time. And she'd admired the rich colour of his hair – light brown, but glinting with both gold and copper highlights in the sunshine.

She shook her head. What was the matter with her? He was after something and falling under his spell wouldn't help her.

But what did he want?

She was afraid she knew the answer, but what scared her even more was that she wasn't as appalled at the thought as she ought to have been.

William cast a look over his shoulder at his stepmother, who was dawdling with a faraway expression. Stepmother? He almost laughed out loud, except it wasn't funny. It was plain ludicrous. She was several years younger than him and marrying her had made his father a laughing stock. And him.

The whim of a senile old man which had cost William half his inheritance. The hurt this had caused was like an ever present canker inside him, growing daily, as was his frustration.

Damn her.

Of course he could understand that his father had been lonely after his first wife died. He'd not have begrudged him a new one, but why did he have to choose a girl barely out of the schoolroom? One young enough to be his daughter and much too clever for her own good. William's position as favoured only child disappeared almost overnight. Instead, he was constantly compared to the newcomer, whose ability to learn things a woman had no business knowing was uncanny. It was unbearable.

'Why do you persist in teaching her?' he'd asked his father, when the old man crowed over her success while berating his son for his lack of wits.

'Because she has a good head on her shoulders. You'd do well to try and emulate her, instead of falling for every trick the merchants try on you. Use your brain, boy!'

William didn't believe he was that bad at trading, he'd just been a bit unfortunate. Whereas she – the hateful conniving little bitch – had the devil's own luck. Well, no more. Her former husband was gone and William had to put a stop to this.

Zar was a thorn in his side in more ways than one. He'd noticed some of the merchants preferred to trade with her. He wasn't blind. But by using her womanly wiles to make better deals she made William seem like a fool and that wasn't something he could stomach.

His father's will had stipulated that if she married within two years of his death, her new husband would only gain a quarter of the business, even though at present Zar was the owner of half. William didn't know how the legalities of that worked. All he knew was that unless he wanted to lose more of his birthright than necessary, he needed to get her married off soon, whether she wanted to or not.

She'd refused every proposal so far, but William was sure there must be a way of forcing her hand. He just had to find it and then he'd be rid of her.

Jamie visited as many gem dealers as he could find and managed to slip the secret question into the conversation each time.

'I wonder if the monsoon will bring mists this year?'

But no one gave the required reply. They merely looked puzzled. At first he thought perhaps it was his pronunciation that was the problem or the fact that not all the merchants spoke Hindi. He then tried using rudimentary Portuguese, as did most traders along India's coasts, but still had no luck. So he went back, bringing his new servant to use as a translator, but even repeating the words in Gujarati seemed not to have any effect.

During a convivial dinner with Andrew, he mentioned the fact that he'd been to see a lot of local merchants. 'They didn't really have anything of interest to me, though,' he added. 'And I don't think they were in the market to buy the sort of stones I've brought. They're more suited to Europeans, so I'll take them back to Bombay or Madras.'

'What about the foreign merchants here?' Andrew suggested. 'There are a couple of Dutch ones I know of, and Miller, of course. They trade with the Persians and also send goods home to Europe.'

'Miller?' Jamie's ears pricked up at the mention of this name.

'Oh, yes, didn't I say? The widow has a stepson who deals in most things – cloth, indigo, even gems – in partnership with her.' Andrew grinned and took a large sip of wine. 'Now there's a tale …'

'All right, out with it.' Jamie smiled back. 'I can tell you're dying to recount the story of the "Ice Widow", am I right?'

'Absolutely. I'm surprised you didn't ask me more the other night.'

Jamie didn't tell his friend he hadn't been interested at the time, having been so rudely dismissed by her, but now his curiosity was piqued. 'Go on then.'

'Well, as I'm sure you probably noticed, she's of mixed parentage. Her father was an Englishman, Thomas Evans, who married a Parsee woman. A pretty piece, by all accounts, so who can blame him? Evans was employed here at the Factory for a time, but like many others, he was given his marching orders for misusing company funds.'

'Really? Mrs Miller's father was a thief?'

But Andrew waved a hand airily. 'Technically, yes, but it happens all the time. The pay is so bad, you see, a lot of people here "borrow" some money from the company coffers and indulge in a little trading on the side, as it were. Most make a decent profit and pay back the "loan", only Evans wasn't very good at it so he was caught. He actually took the decision to leave before he was officially dismissed, and set up his own private business.'

'I see. And did he prosper then?'

Andrew laughed. 'Not at all. Quite the opposite, in fact, and then, understandably, he got fed up with India and wanted to return home. But there was a small problem – his daughter.'

Jamie frowned. 'Why? And what about the wife?'

'Oh, she'd died long before, which was just as well, I suppose. The daughter had grown into quite the little beauty though, just like her mother, but he couldn't take her back to England for good. Apparently he tried it once and she stuck out like a sore thumb. Stands to reason, I mean, her looks and everything … Can you imagine her in Yorkshire? London maybe, but Evans was from the north.'

As far as Jamie was concerned, Mrs Miller wasn't outrageously different from the wholly European women, but he had to concede she probably would stand out in a group of provincial English girls. 'But surely, with such beauty she could have pulled it off?'

Andrew shook his head. 'I doubt it and the old man was ashamed of her. The Lord knows why – he married her mother, for heaven's sake, but anyway … He hit on another idea.' He paused to take another sip of wine, no doubt hoping to build Jamie's anticipation, then announced with a flourish, 'He sold her.'

'What?' Jamie blinked at him. 'I didn't think there was slavery here.'

'Not as such, no.' Andrew chuckled. 'What I meant was, he practically sold her in marriage to a very old man, Francis Miller. He must have been at least fifty.'

'That's not exactly ancient.' Jamie found himself frowning again, although he wasn't sure why.

'It is if you've spent the larger part of those years in India. Trust me, he looked like a septuagenarian at the very least.' Andrew gave a theatrical shudder. 'Poor girl was barely seventeen.'

'Sounds barbaric.' And it was. Jamie didn't even want to picture the couple in his mind's eye. He could only imagine how she must have felt. 'But it happens, even back home.'

'I know, but still, can't have been a happy day for her. She did well out of it though. The old man died a couple of years later and although he had a grown up son from a previous marriage, William, she inherited half his business. Don't know if you've met young Miller yet?'

Jamie nodded. 'Very briefly.'

'Yes, well, he's not exactly a trading genius, if the gossips are to be believed. Whereas Mrs Miller has a brain as sharp as they come and that's probably why she was entrusted with half the company. Damn millstone round William's neck though, wouldn't you say? Having to work with a woman, I mean. The man was incandescent when he found out.' Andrew smirked.

'I can understand that, but perhaps now he's discovered she's an asset?'

'Not according to him, but I don't know.'

'Well, thanks for telling me.' Jamie lifted his cup of wine in salute. 'I guess I'd better make an appointment to see them. Should make for an interesting meeting.'

Andrew laughed again. 'Good luck, is all I can say.'

'*Sahiba*, you are wanted downstairs. The gentlemen wish to speak to you apparently.' Priya stood just inside the door of Zar's room, frowning. 'Shall I tell them it's too late and you've retired for the evening?'

Zar was tempted to say yes. William had been entertaining some of his English friends from the Factory and she'd heard their laughter echoing round the house. No doubt they'd have had their fair share of imported wine. Who knew how drunk they were by now? But if she didn't go, William might take it into his head to come and fetch her. It had happened before and she hated having to deal with him when he was having one of his tantrums. Much easier to humour him briefly, then make some excuse and leave. He couldn't be rude to her in front of guests.

'No, I'll go down directly. Thank you, Priya.'

As Zar descended the staircase she wondered what she would find. She hoped this wouldn't take long.

'Ah, there you are, Zar. Took your time as usual,' William grumbled when she entered the salon. 'Come, sit over here.'

She'd almost bumped into him in the doorway. Now he put his hand behind her elbow and steered her towards a low settee, where someone was already seated – Mr Richardson, a pompous man she had already refused twice in the last six months. He didn't seem to be able to take no for an answer, but then she'd heard rumours that his trading wasn't going very well and he was becoming desperate for a source of income.

'William, I really don't think this is a good idea,' she hissed at him and tried to shrug out of his grip, but he held on and kept propelling her forward. She continued to try to resist, increasing her efforts when she realised that Richardson was the only guest left. William had no right to order her about. *He's not my keeper.* But he was stronger.

'Don't be a ninny. My friend just wishes a word with you.'

'He's already had several. William, let go, for heaven's sake! Why are you doing this? Do you owe him money or something? We can pay him off,' she whispered.

'Not at all. It's just he told me you were being difficult. Doing him a favour.'

'You're not doing *me* one.'

'Yes, I am. It's time you took another husband.'

'I don't want one.'

But William wasn't listening and she knew he wouldn't care. He'd love to get rid of her, she was sure, but she'd not make it that easy for him. They had reached Richardson, who stood up and bowed. As his eyes raked over Zar, they glittered with what could have been greed, but was probably pure lust. She suppressed a shiver of revulsion and held her breath as she got closer to him. He stank of sweat. Didn't he ever bathe? How could William not notice? But then, he wasn't very fragrant himself.

'Mrs Miller, how charming you look tonight.' Richardson took her hand and placed his dry, chapped lips on her fingers. Zar snatched it out of his grip and inclined her head just a fraction in return, but didn't reply.

'I'll leave you to become better acquainted, shall I?' William said. He strode off without waiting for a reply and Zar's protest died on her lips as the door slammed shut behind him.

How dare he leave me here with this ... this idiot? She resolved to leave immediately.

'I'm sorry, Mr Richardson, but I'm afraid I cannot stay. I must—'

'Not so fast.' His hand shot out and grasped her arm, yanking her back so hard she was flung onto the settee. 'You haven't heard me out yet, Mrs High-and-Mighty.'

Zar tried to straighten her skirts and made sure her bodice wasn't showing more flesh than was seemly, then she scowled at him. 'I have already given you my answer twice, Mr Richardson. I assure you, I haven't changed my mind.'

'Then I'll just have to change it for you, won't I, my beauty.'

He threw himself down onto the settee, effectively trapping her because he sat partly on her skirts and gripped her upper arms with his hands. Zar looked to see if there were any servants around, but in vain. She was quite alone with this horrid man. She shrank away from Richardson and tried to dislodge his hands, pushing on his chest for him to back off. But he held on and almost snarled, 'Now, when I propose marriage to a young lady, especially one like you, I expect to be treated with consideration and not given my *congé* like a naughty schoolboy.'

'What do you mean, "one like me"?' Zar knew very well what he was saying, but his words infuriated her.

'A half-caste. Let's not pretend, because that is what you are, isn't it? So don't think you're too good for me, because I can assure you, you're not.'

'I'm surprised you would even consider marrying so far beneath you then,' she spat, while continuing to struggle against his grip. 'Why don't you look for someone of your own kind? Then you won't have to sully your hands.' She was so angry now, she forgot to be afraid of him.

'Needs must, as they say. Beggars can't be choosers.'

'I thought as much. It's always about the money, isn't it? Well, you can't have it. I'm not marrying you and that's final. In fact, I think you'd be the last man on earth I would wed.'

She twisted and turned and succeeded in dislodging one hand, but he brought it up and put it under her chin, squeezing her windpipe instead. Zar cried out and tried to retreat backwards, but only succeeded in half lying down with Richardson virtually on top of her. With one hand, she tried to fight him off, while the other groped around for something to defend herself with. At first she felt nothing, but then her hand reached a small table which happened to be right next to the settee. On it was a plant in a pot and she tore off a small branch and quickly jabbed it into his eye.

Richardson howled and recoiled, clutching his eye with one hand. Zar didn't wait to see what he'd do next. Instead she struggled into a sitting position, yanked her skirts out from underneath him, and fled towards the door.

'You bitch!' he shouted. 'I *will* have you! Just you wait.'

'Not if I can help it,' she muttered, as she lifted her petticoat and ran up the stairs to her room two at a time. Priya, who must have been waiting for her return, came rushing forward.

'*Sahiba*! Are you all right? What happened?'

'That odious, *odious* man,' Zar hissed through gritted teeth. 'From now on, you are sleeping in here with me, and I want one of the male servants outside my door to guard it. I'll pay him myself and tell him if he lets anyone in, anyone at all, I will have him castrated, understand?'

Priya blinked, obviously startled to see her mistress so vehement, but she nodded. 'I will see to it at once.'

'Thank you.'

Zar threw herself on top of her bed and flung an arm across her eyes. To think she wasn't even safe in her own home – it was the outside of enough and she refused to put up with it.

She intended to make sure this could never happen again. And if William thought he could force her into marriage, he had another thing coming.

Chapter Eight

The Millers lived in a house not unlike the one Jamie himself was renting, only slightly bigger. Like almost all the more affluent ones, it was laid out around a large courtyard, with the rooms on the ground floor a couple of steps up and surrounded by terraces. The courtyard had little paths to divide it, and was planted with flowers, shrubs and small trees, with a pond in the middle. The upper floors – and this particular house had two of them – led off a central walkway, with windows and little holes on both sides to give the rooms a cooling draught. Most houses also had a flat roof with railings around it, where people often slept when the weather was too sultry.

At the front of the building was the main room, the salon or *divan* as they called it here. It was used for conducting business, as now, and for socialising. Jamie was ushered towards it by a grumpy servant.

'This way, *sahib*.'

Once there, Jamie looked around with interest. The room had no fireplace, as heating was never needed here, and it was sparsely furnished. The natives always sat on the floor on beautiful rugs with a latticework frame for guests to lean their backs on, but Jamie noticed that the Millers had stuck to European style furniture. A couple of tables and chairs, a large desk which seemed incongruous in such surroundings, and a low settee against one wall was all the room contained. The floors were made of a hard, shiny material called *puckah*, which looked a little like marble but was usually made out of crushed bricks, some type of glue, chalk and cow hair. This, together with a selection of colourful rugs and wall hangings, added warmth to the decor.

'Come in, Kinross. Have a seat, please.'

Jamie followed his host towards the desk and forgot all about his surroundings as he took in the lovely sight before him. Mrs Miller, standing demurely to one side, was dressed in another shimmering silk gown, this time in pale green. Shafts of sunlight slanting in through the windows made her dark hair gleam and turned her eyes into liquid pools of turquoise and mossy-green, surrounded by those phenomenally long lashes. Jamie had a sudden urge to undo the heavy plait which once again hung over one shoulder. It was so long he felt sure that, unbound, her hair must reach well below her derrière. Hanging loose around her, it would be a silky curtain enveloping her smooth skin like a cape, outlining the contours of her body and ...

He quelled the rest of the thought before his body had time to do more than stir in response. He wasn't here to admire the Ice Widow, he was here on business. And he wasn't interested in her. Definitely not. Taking a deep breath, he resolutely turned to face William Miller. He wouldn't let a woman, even one as beautiful as Mrs Miller, distract him from his purpose – to help Akash.

'Thank you. It was good of you to see me on such short notice.'

Not that the man looked pleased to see him. On the contrary, he wore a sulky expression and twitched, as if impatient to get the meeting over with. Since they barely knew each other, that was intriguing. Jamie settled into his chair and waited.

William was all urbane hospitality as he ushered Mr

Kinross across the *divan* and over to the desk, but Zar knew it was just a façade. He was still angry at what he'd called her 'embarrassing behaviour' towards his friend Richardson, and had been more than usually cross about having to allow Zar to be present at this meeting. He'd also been grumbling earlier about having to do business with Kinross.

'He's probably another amateur trader who thinks he can pull the wool over my eyes and sell me inferior gemstones. A waste of my time.'

Zar refrained from mentioning that *most* merchants sold William mediocre stones unless she intervened, because he simply didn't have an eye for quality. He was fascinated by large gems, no matter their lustre, which made him buy them whether they were good or not. It was infuriating, but she'd given up trying to advise him and now attempted to help out unobtrusively instead, usually by speaking directly to the vendors. Most of them respected her and listened to her views, but a few unscrupulous ones still took advantage of William's gullibility. It was something she'd had to learn to live with.

It was the same with most of the other goods they traded in, but luckily they had a very clever broker to help them make profitable deals. William was too lazy to concern himself much with anything other than gemstones, which was both a blessing and an annoyance.

Zar sat down a little to one side now, while William took the chair behind the large desk that had once been his father's. Mr Kinross made himself comfortable on the opposite side, facing them both. He glanced at Zar, but didn't seem surprised to see her, like some of the other merchants. She surmised he'd been told about her role in the company by someone and it was a relief not to have to explain her presence.

'You had something to discuss with me, er ... us?' William sent a glare in Zar's direction, still visibly irritated at her presence. She ignored him.

'Yes. I've recently been to Golconda and thought you might be interested in some of the stones I purchased there. I'm not returning to Europe myself quite yet, but I understand you have contacts who travel back and forth? I think my finds might be eminently suitable for the European market.'

'You've been to the actual mines?' William stared at Kinross. 'I didn't think foreigners were permitted to travel inland, and certainly not to that destination.'

It was well known that the local *rajahs* had control of the mines and not many people were allowed to go there. Zar had heard tell that they also retained the largest stones for themselves, so it would make sense for them not to want many visitors.

'Yes. It's only a week's travel from Fort St George in Madras. A lapidary friend of mine had contacts there, so we travelled together.'

'I find it hard to believe they'd let you in.' William didn't hide his scepticism.

Kinross smiled, but Zar noticed the smile didn't quite reach his eyes, which were a frosty grey this morning. 'There are ways and means, Mr Miller. I pretended to be a native of northern India where, as I'm sure you know, there are people with blue or grey eyes, like mine.'

William shrugged, as if he wasn't really interested in how Kinross had managed to go to the fabled mines which were supposedly closely guarded at all times. 'Very well, as you're here now, we may as well have a look at what you've brought,' he said, somewhat ungraciously, his polite façade beginning to slip.

From an inner pocket, Kinross pulled out a small white silk bag with a drawstring which he untied. William had a velvet-lined tray on his desk. He pushed it forward and Kinross tipped the contents of the little bag out onto the smooth surface. A large diamond of the so called Peruzzi cut – having fifty-eight facets to enhance its brilliance – tumbled out, together with about ten lesser gems of varying sizes and shapes. Zar saw William's eyes widen at the sight of the big stone and swallowed a sigh. *No!* He was going to fall for it again.

'May I?' At Kinross's nod, William leaned forward and picked up the massive diamond, holding it up to the light. He didn't even look at the rest of the stones, some of which seemed, at least from a distance, to be of excellent quality and lustre. Zar glanced at Kinross and to her surprise, he winked at her. She frowned, wondering what he was up to.

'Do you mind if I look at these?' She indicated the smaller diamonds.

'By all means.'

She picked them all up in turn, while William continued to examine his prize, oblivious to anything else. Zar had been trained by her late husband to check for the 'four C's', namely carat, colour, clarity and cut. These were the criteria by which all stones were evaluated and she knew exactly what to look for. Having studied them, Zar lined them up in order of quality on the tray, then sat back and peeked at Kinross again. She saw him nod as if he was satisfied with her judgement. 'William, may I have a look too?' She held out her hand for the biggest diamond and he reluctantly handed it to her. 'You might want to check the others?' she prompted.

He did so, but she could tell he wasn't focusing. His thoughts were all for the stone in her hand and she'd seen the glitter of greed in his gaze as he looked at it. Stupid man.

Holding it up to the light in her turn, Zar noted that it had quite a few inclusions, as the flaws were called. These were tiny fissures or bits of foreign material that prevented it from being as lustrous as it could have been, although it had been ingeniously polished to mask some of them. 'How much do you want for this?' she asked Kinross, pre-empting William who, she was sure, would pay way over the odds for it. His haggling techniques were abysmal, as she well knew.

Kinross named a staggering price, but Zar saw a glint in his eyes that told her he was just testing her.

'Preposterous,' she said, putting the gemstone back on the tray. 'It's not even worth half that amount.'

'Zar.' William frowned at her. 'I'll handle this.'

'But—'

'If you don't mind?' It wasn't really a request, as she could see from his stormy expression, so Zar backed down.

'Very well.'

He proceeded to haggle half-heartedly and ended up agreeing a price that was much too high, despite the subtle warning she tried to give him. Zar wanted to shake him. Why couldn't he understand that showing such obvious interest right from the start would get him a bad bargain? He was such a fool.

Kinross turned to her. 'Perhaps you'd be interested in some of the smaller gems, Mrs Miller?'

'Yes, why don't you buy a few while I go and fetch the money for this one?' William put in. 'They don't look too bad.' To Kinross he added, 'Excuse me, I'll only be a moment.'

As soon as he'd left the room, Zar rounded on Kinross. 'That was daylight robbery and you know it. You, sir, are no gentleman.'

To her consternation, he smiled and nodded agreement. 'Definitely not, but your stepson deserved that. No one should be in business when they don't have the necessary skills for it. Honestly, I'm surprised he hasn't gone bankrupt long before now.'

'The reason he hasn't is because I usually save his skin.' Zar clenched her teeth together to stop from snarling at the infuriating man. 'But I'm guessing you're not going to listen to reason and lower the price, even though I know you're fleecing us?'

Kinross regarded her for a moment, growing serious. 'Us? Do his deals affect your part of the business then?'

'Unfortunately, yes, although I do some of my own which help.'

He picked up the two most valuable of the smaller stones on the tray and held them out to her, their iridescence sending flashes of fire round the room. 'Then take these, Mrs Miller, as compensation for my alleged "fleecing". They are worth roughly the amount your stepson is overpaying me by, wouldn't you agree?'

Zar blinked. 'You're giving them to me for free?'

'Yes, on condition you don't tell him.' He nodded in the direction of the door William had disappeared out of. 'I wouldn't wish you to suffer on account of his idiocy. I may not be a gentleman, but I make it a rule never to cheat ladies. Here, take them and put them away.'

She had the distinct feeling he might cheat women in other matters, but she was relieved he didn't do so in business. It flustered her, however, and she didn't know what to think of this strange offer. As if he'd divined her thoughts, he dropped the stones into her palm and closed her fingers around them. The touch of his hand on hers made a shiver run up her arm and she looked at him. 'Are you sure?'

He nodded. 'Quite sure. I meant to test Miller and I had my answer. I never thought to involve you.'

Zar tried to calm the fluttering in the pit of her stomach which had been caused by staring into his silvery eyes. They were like the diamonds, clear, sharp and luminous, and quite beautiful … She stopped her thought right there. Mr Kinross had been toying with them and she didn't know what game he was playing. First the supposed robbery and now this. What was he up to? She had no idea, but since William was losing so much on this deal, refusing his offer was out of the question.

'Very well, I thank you, Mr Kinross and you have my word, I won't tell William.'

'Good.' The smile he sent her this time was nothing short of dazzling. Zar was glad she was sitting down as it definitely did something strange to her innards. Then a teasing glint flashed in his eyes.

'So have you thought any more about my proposition?' he asked.

'Which proposition would that be?' Zar frowned, caught off-guard by his question.

'To, er … amuse you if you're in need of a diversion.'

Zar couldn't stop her mouth from falling open, but shut it quickly again as she sent him her most quelling glance. 'Really, Mr Kinross, I don't know to what you are referring.'

'Oh, I think you do.'

He was still smiling and Zar felt unaccountably hot all of a sudden. But she was also outraged. She would make it clear to him she was not that kind of woman.

'I'll have you know I'm a respectable widow. Neither you, nor anyone else, will ever set foot in my bedroom and I'd thank you not to refer to such things again.'

She turned to stare out the window while she tried to force her breathing to return to normal. For some reason she was having trouble inhaling enough air and it was making her chest heave unbecomingly.

'Now that sounds distinctly like a challenge to me. Would you like to bet on it?'

Chapter Nine

'What?' Zar swivelled round and stared at Kinross. The effrontery of the man.

'I'll wager one hundred rupees that I will. Set foot in your bedroom, that is.' He raised his eyebrows at her, as if daring her to accept. 'Say, within the next two weeks?' he added, a teasing note in his voice.

'I don't believe I'm hearing—'

'Very well, two hundred rupees. Deal?'

'Now see here, Mr Kinross—'

'You drive a hard bargain, Mrs Miller. Three hundred it is.'

Zar almost stamped her foot in frustration, but managed to restrain herself at the last minute. 'I'm not making a wager with you!'

'Ah, you're afraid you'll lose. I thought so.'

His smug expression made Zar see red. She clenched her fists by her side and scowled at him. 'I am not.'

'Well, then, you almost certainly stand to gain three hundred rupees. That can't be bad, can it?'

Zar took a deep breath and tried to think, but Kinross's quicksilver gaze held hers and jumbled her thought processes. He was right. It would be the easiest money she'd ever earned. But then why was he even proposing such a thing? There must be a catch … For the life of her, she couldn't think of one though. 'Oh, very well, I accept your wager. But I'm not meeting you anywhere private for you to hand over my winnings, is that clear?'

'Perfectly.' He bowed. 'I will allow you to decide entirely. *If* you win, of course.'

Zar was about to insist that she would, but just then

William came back and she didn't have a chance to say anything else. She winced as she watched him hand over the huge sum of money to Kinross, but she held her tongue as promised. The stones he'd given her would more than make up for the loss, he was right about that too. And William didn't deserve to know.

The transaction completed, Kinross gathered up the stones that were left on the velvet-lined tray, put them back into his white silk bag and stood up. He bowed to them both, then looked out the window at the bright sunlight. 'My servant was telling me the weather has been very unpredictable lately, but you wouldn't think it on a day like today. Still, the rainy season will be upon us before we know it, I expect. I wonder if the monsoon will bring mists this year?'

'Mists?' William stiffened and his gaze suddenly turned sharp. To Zar's surprise, he then replied with a forced laugh, 'Oh, yes, and the mists hide everything.'

Kinross raised his eyebrows at him, then nodded thoughtfully. 'Indeed they do. Good day to you both.'

With another bow he was gone and Zar opened her mouth to ask William what on earth he'd been talking about, but he followed Kinross to the door. 'Must dash. I think I know exactly who to sell this giant diamond to. I'll see you at supper time.'

She was left staring after both of them. Monsoons? Mists? Why had they suddenly started discussing such things? And today of all days? Outside, the weather was as fine as you could possibly wish for in early June and there wasn't even a hint of the coming rains.

Something was going on here. But what?

She determined to find out and went in search of her spy.

* * *

So Miller was the contact – not good.

Jamie had been thinking there may be a way to return the talisman to its rightful owner or at least thwart the thieves somehow. Unless the owner was the person who'd arranged for it to be stolen in the first place? *No, surely not?* Either way, he'd hoped the contact would turn out to be someone he could involve in his plans, but judging by Miller's behaviour that morning, that was out of the question. The man had no business acumen whatsoever and someone was obviously using him.

It seemed clear that Miller had got himself involved in something he probably couldn't handle. Jamie certainly wouldn't trust him for an instant and whoever was behind the theft must be a very clever man. He'd be running rings round Miller. The Englishman would have no idea how valuable the talisman was and Jamie was sure he wouldn't be told either. He wondered why a foreigner had been chosen for the task of sending it out of the country, and such an inept one at that? It seemed bizarre.

He sighed. He'd have to come up with a new plan, but it might be best to wait until Sanjiv arrived. That could be days, even weeks, yet. In the meantime, Jamie would keep his eyes and ears open. It probably wouldn't hurt to have Miller followed. He'd have to see about that.

Jamie was relaxing in the salon of his rented house, lying back on a soft rug and a couple of cushions under a fan which a small boy was operating by pulling on a string from outside on the terrace. It was still hot, but the fan made it slightly more bearable by stirring up the air. He wondered idly whether the beautiful widow was involved in the talisman scheme as well, but dismissed the thought almost immediately.

She had looked thoroughly puzzled when he posed the

question about the monsoon mists. Whereas Miller had caught on straight away.

And she wasn't used to making wagers either. Jamie shook his head at himself. Why on earth had he teased her like that? He'd decided not to have anything more to do with her, hadn't he? But she'd looked so vulnerable, so defeated, when her stepson paid over the odds for the huge diamond. It made Jamie see her in a new light – not as the haughty beauty, but as a woman trying to hold her own in a man's world. And fighting to keep her stepson in check, a seemingly impossible task.

He'd definitely misjudged her during their first encounter. He was sure of it now.

That was still no excuse for flirting, which was what it amounted to. Lord, but he was losing his marbles.

Jamie took a sip of wine and grimaced. It was lukewarm and didn't add much to his comfort. Oh, for a glass of something cold, like Swedish spring water or strong ale ... A knock interrupted his wishful thinking.

'Excuse me, *sahib,* there is, er ... someone to see you. In the hall.' Kamal stood by the door, frowning.

'Who is it?' Jamie wasn't in the mood for visitors of any kind. He wanted to be alone so he could think how best to go forward.

'A very small person, *sahib*. Says she owes you something. Shall I send her away?'

Jamie shot into a sitting position. 'What? A little girl?' The servant nodded, disapproval clearly written on his face, but Jamie was already on his way to the door, swearing under his breath. What did the little thief want with him now? For it couldn't be anyone else.

He was right. She stood very close to the front door, as if it represented an avenue of flight in case Jamie were to change his mind and decide to denounce her to the authorities, he thought. Next to her sat the mangiest little mutt Jamie had ever seen. Small, brown, with a slightly pointy nose and one ear up, the other flopping over. A thin body with a bushy tail curled neatly over its backside. The dog watched Jamie with eyes not dissimilar to those of his young mistress – large, dark and wary.

Jamie stopped in front of them, then hunkered down so he wasn't towering over the child. It must have taken enormous courage to come here. He didn't want to frighten her, so he said hello in Gujarati. He'd already picked up a few phrases, as some of the words were similar to Hindi, but he added a greeting in Hindi for good measure. '*Namaste*. To what do I owe this pleasure?' He was just about to turn to Kamal, who was hovering behind him, to ask him to translate the rest of what he'd said, when a shy smile appeared on the little girl's face.

'You English. I speak you in English. Is good?'

Jamie rocked back on his heels and stared at her. 'Why yes, that is good indeed, but where did you learn?' There weren't that many English people in Surat so he was surprised to find this little thief speaking their language.

'My fader work English family. I listen. I learn.' She nodded, obviously proud of herself. And rightly so, Jamie thought. She must have a very quick mind.

He smiled back at her. 'What is your name?'

'Roshani. And this Kutaro.' She indicated the mutt, whose mouth opened in a wide grin as if he was pleased to see Jamie. The curly tail wagged as well.

'Er, right.' Jamie decided it wouldn't be prudent to stroke the dog, no matter how friendly he looked. He probably came with a whole host of unwanted 'guests' in his fur. 'But why are you here?'

'*Sahib* save Roshani life, now give it you, serve always.'

'What?' Jamie frowned. 'You're ... offering yourself to me as a servant?' Roshani nodded, still smiling. 'But you're only a child! How old are you? You can't be more than, what six?'

'I eight. Want serve *sahib*, all life.' She added something in her own language and Jamie's servant translated sotto voce into Hindi.

'She says because you saved her life, it belongs to you now. She will serve you forever, give her life for you if needed. She knows she is small but she'll grow stronger.'

Jamie shook his head. 'No, this is not necessary. I only wanted you to stop thieving.' He fixed Roshani with his sternest gaze. 'Stealing from people is bad. You should find a job instead if you must earn money. You have no obligation to me whatsoever.'

Her face fell and the big, brown eyes filled with unshed tears. Jamie wasn't sure if she was a phenomenally good actress or if they were genuine, but felt moved all the same.

'You don't owe me your life,' he clarified.

'Don't want steal. Uncle make me. He bad.'

'You live with your uncle?'

'Yes, fader dead. Uncle big thief, outside town. How you say, bandit? Make me little thief. If not ...' She mimed hitting.

'He'll beat you?' Jamie guessed. Roshani nodded. 'And there is nowhere else you can go? No one who can take care of you?'

'No, family all gone.' Her expression turned hopeful. 'Sleep outside *sahib* house? Me and Kutaro. Guard.'

Jamie almost laughed out loud. The idea of him being guarded by a scrawny eight-year-old and a mutt was ludicrous, but he could see that Roshani was in earnest. He stood up and pushed his fingers through his hair, which was hanging in front of his eyes and adding to his irritation. 'Oh, hell,' he muttered, then looked to the servant for support. 'What am I supposed to do with her? I can't have an eight-year-old girl living in my household. It wouldn't be seemly. And I obviously can't send her back to a life of crime.'

'If she stays in the servant quarters, my wife is there,' the servant said, somewhat dubiously.

Jamie weighed his options. He could either have Roshani carry out her threat of sleeping on his doorstep, and probably following him around too with the mangy cur on her heels, or he could compromise by allowing her to stay in the house as a servant. He took a deep breath and decided on the second option.

'Very well, if you're sure Soraya won't mind, Kamal? Perhaps you can find the girl some tasks to perform? Something light, like, I don't know ... chopping vegetables? Running errands? But she's to be thoroughly cleaned first. I'll not have fleas in my house, do you hear? And find her some new clothes, those can be burned.' He glanced at her threadbare tunic, which wasn't fit for anyone. 'I'll pay for new ones.'

'Do you understand, Roshani?' he added, looking at her. 'You can stay here as my servant, but only because I want to help you. You don't owe me your life and you can leave at any time.'

'Yes, *sahib*. Stay here. Kutaro too?'

Jamie eyed the dog, whose grin seemed to widen while the tail thumped on the floor. He nodded. 'Very well, Kutaro too. You can help give him a bath after you've had one yourself.'

Kamal took charge. '*Sahib*, it will be as you command.' He bowed, then fired off a rapid sentence at the girl.

Her face split into a huge grin, the brown eyes shining with happiness. She bounced up and down on the spot, the dog jumping with her. 'Thank you, thank you, *sahib*,' she said.

'Yes, yes, now run along please.' Jamie made a shooing motion and the girl danced off after the servant, the dog running at her heels.

He shook his head and closed his eyes. 'Oh Lord, what have I done?'

But what else *could* he have done? It was the decent thing to do.

'The contact has arrived. The man you asked me to look out for. You should have told me it would be a foreigner. Nearly gave me a heart attack when he said the secret words in front of my stepmother!'

William was sitting with Mansukh, one of the most formidable merchants in Surat. Rotund, with dark intelligent eyes that missed nothing, the man had a reputation as a tough trader who would deal in anything that might turn him a profit, but this was the first time they'd done any business together. William had tried a few times before, but been rebuffed, which was why he'd been very pleased to be approached by the merchant recently. The fact that Mansukh had entrusted him with an important task made it even better.

'If you help me and we succeed, there will be a nice share of the profits for you,' the merchant had promised. And although William suspected the 'goods', whatever it was, would turn out to be something illegal, he didn't care. Why should he? This wasn't his country and he was hoping to leave India soon in any case.

He'd been thinking for some time that he ought to

return to England. His father had talked of the glittering life led by the upper classes there and said that merchants who'd made their fortune in India were accepted into the highest echelons of society, no matter their pedigree.

'They may be sneered at by some of the titled folk, but those with dwindling fortunes and lots of daughters to marry off will turn a blind eye to your lineage. They can't afford to be too choosey.'

William was sure he could find such a girl and marry into that world. It was where he felt he belonged, not here in this godforsaken place where he was a nobody. If he could just force Zar to marry then he could get his hands on half of her inheritance, sell the business and finish this deal with Mansukh. He would then have more than enough capital to satisfy any prospective father-in-law and live comfortably for the rest of his life.

'A foreigner?' Mansukh brought him back to the present. He seemed surprised and not at all pleased. 'Why?'

'How should I know? The man came to my house and spoke the agreed sentence, although in English. I couldn't very well question him in front of an audience.'

'No, I suppose not. We will need to find out more about him. You must arrange a meeting so he can hand over the goods as soon as possible. I need to send it on its way to Persia before the monsoon begins.'

'Are you going to tell me what it is? Or do I have to wait until he hands it to me?'

Mansukh sent him a piercing look, as if he was trying to determine William's trustworthiness and doubting it. 'I'm not sure it would be wise for you to know.'

'Why not? If it's something illegal, I'm certainly not going to inform the authorities. That would be suicide.

And if you don't tell me, how will I know the man is giving me the right thing?'

Mansukh stayed silent for a moment, then nodded. 'Very well, I will tell you. The item he is bringing is a talisman that used to belong to the Rajah of Nadhur. Let's just say, it no longer does. It is highly conspicuous, however, and no one here would buy it.'

'Because it's stolen?'

'I didn't say it was. It changed hands, that's all.'

William didn't believe that for an instant. He wasn't a complete moron. 'Why then?'

'It is imbued with powerful magic which would bring extremely bad luck to a new owner. Any dealer in India worth his salt would know that, which is why it has to be sold abroad as soon as possible. No one must know.'

'I see.' William wasn't convinced. He didn't believe in magic, that was superstitious nonsense, but if that was how Mansukh wanted to explain things, it was fine with him. 'What does it look like? Just so I know I'm not being cheated.'

'It's a beautifully cut red diamond and a cabochon sapphire with some kind of inscription on it, both set in gold and topped with feathers. I'm sure you've seen such things before, turban ornaments, although this one is larger than most. You won't be able to mistake it. I believe it's unique.'

'Very well, I'll set up a meeting with the contact for the handover.' William put his hand into his pocket and pulled out the large diamond he'd bought from Kinross. 'Now I have something else you might be interested in buying ...'

'You are sure my stepson went straight to see Mansukh, the merchant, this morning? He didn't go anywhere else?'

'No, *sahiba,* straight there and then back. Looked very pleased with himself and perhaps even excited, Ali said, at least on the way there.' Priya shrugged.

'I need more information. I want details. Tell Ali from me, please? Whatever it costs, I have to know what's going on. It seems very odd to me, this sudden amicable relationship.'

'Yes, suspicious. But if those two are plotting something, I don't know why you don't give up and just sell your half of the business. It is not seemly, a woman doing such things. And you have no need. You would be rich enough to—'

'Yes, thank you, Priya, I have heard your views on this before and I've told you I'm content for the moment. It gives my life a purpose. I have no husband and no children. What else would I do all day?'

'You could get married again,' Priya muttered, but she knew better than to look at her mistress. That was one subject they'd never agree on.

Zar didn't even reply. What was the point? Priya would never understand. The mere thought of marriage made Zar feel physically sick and she thanked God daily for giving her the means to keep her freedom.

Priya changed tactic. 'I hear you met a very handsome man,' she said with a sudden smile. 'You didn't tell me.'

Zar had to turn away to hide the blush she felt staining her cheeks. There was only one man her servant could be referring to – Kinross. *Damn him!* Every time she thought about their encounter that morning, it made her blood boil. But she was honest enough to admit it wasn't just fury at his presumptuous behaviour that made her hot all over. It was him, the man. He'd had some sort of strange effect on her. Those eyes, so cold one moment and then flashing like gems in sunlight the next. And his smile ... But although he'd made it clear what he wanted, she could never agree. It was no better than marriage; in fact, it was worse.

She wasn't going to let a man touch her that way ever again.

No matter how tempting the man was, she didn't think it would be any different. She would be his plaything. He'd want to put his hands on her, touch her, squeeze her, hurt her ... Zar shuddered as images of Francis's hands on her skin rose in her mind. No, she wouldn't think of it. It was in the past and he was gone. Her former husband couldn't reach her now.

And Kinross wouldn't win that wager. Absolutely not.

Chapter Ten

'What news from Madras?'

Bijal's most trusted servant, Tufan, had entered his quarters via a secret entrance, but they were still talking in hushed whispers to make sure they weren't overheard. The walls most definitely had ears in the palace of Nadhur and one couldn't be too careful.

Situated in a far corner of the large palace complex, Bijal's domain was almost as luxuriously appointed as the Rajah's. Vaulted ceilings, decorated with the most intricate of designs, were supported by innumerable columns similarly adorned. Shining floors were strewn with carpets of high quality and enormous cushions surrounded by low tables where Bijal could enjoy a rest from his endeavours. As Grand Vizier, he could afford to spend lavishly, but he barely noticed his surroundings. To him, these were just temporary quarters until he could put his grand plans into action.

'All is well. The lapidary had a foreign friend who agreed to take the item to Surat. I watched him board an English ship myself and sent someone to keep an eye on him. It will take him a while to find his contact upon arrival, I should think.'

'Excellent. We can't take any chances, however. You must set out for Surat yourself in a few days and make sure all goes as planned. I will follow later this month when the wedding cavalcade leaves. It will pass close to Surat on the way to Ahmedabad and I'll arrange a meeting place for us there.'

The servant's eyebrows rose. 'Will the marriage still go ahead, even without the talisman? I thought ...'

Bijal smiled. 'I have assured him I'm doing my utmost to find it and told him not to worry. He will continue as planned, at least until he gets closer to his destination. Once it becomes clear to him that the jewel won't be found, he will have to turn back, but for now, everything remains the same. It's going to be a huge embarrassment for him.' He felt his smile widen at the thought. 'Don't worry, all will be well.'

Tufan bowed. 'Yes, Master. And the other matter?' The servant glanced around nervously, even though it was the middle of the night and no one was likely to be awake.

'We must proceed as discussed. The Rajah's half-brother is easily led. If I tell him there is a particularly beautiful woman waiting for his attention at the place we agreed, he will go immediately. He is voracious when it comes to females, which is all to our advantage. Along the way, you must make sure he meets with an accident. Elephant, do you think? Better than poison.'

The servant nodded. 'Yes, that would be best. Anyone could fall off one of those, especially if they have imbibed a little too much of that foreign beverage he likes so much. *Shari-* ... no *shori-*, er ...'

'Shiraz wine, yes, I know. Good thinking. I will make sure to send some with him and perhaps share a cup or two before he leaves. And then, the poor elephant would panic and trample him. So sad. Tomorrow night?'

'I'll be waiting.'

The following evening, as she ate her meal alone, Zar's thoughts returned to Priya's words. There was no disputing the fact that she was lonely. William went out almost every night and she was never invited to come along. Not that she wanted to spend time with him or his odious friends, but still …

If only she'd had a child. But she hadn't and now she was by herself yet again.

She'd tried inviting some of the other English women after her husband's death, but it was as if she'd turned into a pariah overnight. Francis's presence at her side had ensured invitations to dine, to receptions and picnics or other outings, but these days the only place she ever went was to the English Factory. And she knew why they continued to invite her.

They were still hoping one of them would win her hand in marriage, and thus, make someone a rich man instantly. Well, they could forget that.

It didn't stop her from going though, however painful she found it having to refuse all the numerous suitors. She was desperate for company and that was her only chance to socialise.

'You could contact your mother's family,' Priya had suggested once, but Zar knew that wouldn't be much better. Her mother, Noor, had been disowned by her Parsee father for marrying a foreigner. Zar doubted a granddaughter would be any more welcome. And she didn't want to meet someone so callous.

The Parsees were the third most numerous ethnic group in Surat and quite distinct from the Hindus and the Moors. They had lighter skin, but the same dark hair as everyone else, and the men all wore beards. Known to be hard workers, most of the town's craftsmen – such as shipbuilders, carpenters and weavers – were Parsees and they also worked the land outside the town. Many of them were servants to the *banias* or Europeans and highly valued as they abhorred laziness.

Zar knew only what her mother and Priya had taught her, but she had learned one thing – the Parsees considered it a dishonour to die childless. So why would her mother's family want her? A woman married for four years without producing any offspring. A failure as a wife. It was a gloomy thought.

With a sigh, she put down her napkin and made her way to the stairs. No point sitting there getting maudlin. She might as well just go to bed.

'You want me to help you, *sahiba*?' Priya made to follow her, but Zar shook her head.

'No, thank you, I'll be all right on my own. You come up when you're ready to retire yourself.' She was wearing native clothing now and didn't need help with unlacing.

Her bedroom was in the corner of the building, overlooking a small alleyway at the back. A servant would come and sit outside on guard soon, as she'd commanded, but as yet it was early and he was probably still having his own evening meal. Deep in thought, she shut the door, leaning her back against it briefly with her eyes closed.

'Good evening, Mrs Miller.'

The deep voice startled her into a gasp and her eyes flew open. She took in the sight of Mr Kinross sitting in a rattan chair in the corner of her room, one leg crossed over the other as if he'd made himself comfortable. Zar put a hand over her heart to still its frantic beating.

'What on earth do you think you're doing?' she hissed at him. She didn't want to call out. If the servants found him here, her reputation would be in shreds in an instant. Although she may have no choice if he … *No!* She swallowed hard.

He stood up, moving unhurriedly, and smiled. 'Winning our wager, I hope? This *is* your bedchamber, is it not?'

He walked over towards her and Zar became aware of just how tall he was. The latent power she'd noticed previously seemed to be emanating from him in invisible waves, making her tremble. She looked up into his eyes, which glittered in the light of the lantern that had been left next to her bed. 'You can't be serious?' she breathed.

'Oh, but I am. I never make bets unless I'm sure I'm going to win them. Perhaps you shouldn't either?' He held out a hand, palm up. 'I believe you owe me three hundred rupees, madam?'

Zar had to restrain herself from boxing his ears. She was furious, but she knew the anger was mostly directed at herself. *Fool! Imbecile!* How could she have been so stupid? She should have known he'd trick her. 'How did you get in? Who did you bribe?' she asked, still keeping her voice down, but making it clear with her icy tone of voice that whoever had helped him would pay for it dearly. Was that why no one was outside her door?

He shook his head. 'No one. I climbed.' He nodded towards the double doors that opened onto a small balcony. 'If you don't want night time visitors, I'd suggest you have your plants pruned more regularly.'

'But there's a nightwatchman who patrols the alleyway. What did you do to him?' Zar didn't want to believe it could be that easy to gain access to her private quarters. If Kinross had managed it, then obviously so could anyone else. Good grief.

'I'm afraid he's asleep and likely to remain so until morning. He was very partial to the drink my servant brought him earlier.'

'Why you ...' Words failed her as she realised the extent of his machinations. 'That means you cheated so I don't owe you anything,' she snapped.

'Oh, I think you do. We didn't agree on any rules for our wager, as I recall? You can't renege now.'

'I don't have three hundred rupees, at least not here. You'll have to wait.' It galled Zar to admit he was right. She should have made sure he couldn't cheat. No, she shouldn't have wagered with him at all.

'Not an option. If you don't have the sum now, you'll have to pay me in kind.'

Zar felt her eyes open wide as a current of fear surged through her, almost paralysing in its intensity. 'What? *No!*'

'Just a kiss?' He glanced at her wrist. 'And perhaps those gold bangles. They must be worth a bit.'

As if in a trance, Zar followed his gaze to the clinking collection of thin gold bracelets encircling her arm. He could have those, sure, but a kiss? No, absolutely not.

'Very well, take these and then the debt is paid. I'm sure you'll find they're worth more than you're asking for.' She pulled them off and held them out to him. They were too big for her anyway and were forever falling down over her hand, restricting her movements. He took them and managed somehow to thread them onto his own wrist. Zar watched in amazement. Didn't he have bones in his hand? It was as if he could squeeze them together, his joints loose.

'Thank you, Mrs Miller. Or may I call you Zarmina?'

'Huh? No, you may not.'

'A shame, because I don't mind if you call me Jamie. My friends do.'

'Well, we're not friends.' Zar took a step back as his gaze seemed to fasten on her lips.

'We could be.' He followed, then lifted his eyes to stare into hers. 'Zarmina.'

He breathed her name and she felt herself shiver. It had never sounded so intimate, so sensual. And no one had ever said it with such reverence, as if she was special. She stood still as his face came nearer, his eyes not leaving hers for a second. Somehow she couldn't move; she could only watch his mouth descend towards hers. A part of her screamed out a warning, urging her legs to run, get away, as fast as she could. But she didn't. She stayed rooted to the spot.

He touched his lips to hers, gently, without any other part of him coming into contact with her. He didn't grab at her upper arms to hold her fast, the way Francis used to, or paw any other part of her anatomy. His mouth was soft, the lips dry, but smooth. He moved it as if he was tasting her, memorising the feel of her, worshipping her. Zar felt her lips tingling and opened them slightly. Kinross – Jamie – seemed to take that as an invitation. His tongue slid slowly through, the tip touching hers. Zar quivered, not sure what to do.

Run! Tell him to stop! But still she didn't.

Instead her treacherous tongue pushed back against his, following his lead to play, spar, taste and explore. She'd never been kissed before, not like this. And never with her consent.

Her consent? Dear Lord …

With a gasp, she broke off the kiss and blinked up at Jamie. Damn it, why couldn't she stop thinking of him by his Christian name now? The corners of his mouth lifted in a lazy smile that made her lungs constrict.

'That wasn't so bad, was it?' he asked, stepping back and giving her the breathing space she sorely needed.

'I …' Zar had lost the power of speech and she had no idea what to say in any case. She couldn't lie. It hadn't been bad, in the sense that she hadn't panicked as she normally would, but it shouldn't have happened in the first place. Even though it was glorious. No, what was she thinking?

'Consider your debt paid.' His smile widened. 'Unless you'd like me to carry on?'

'No! No, please don't.' Zar swallowed, trying to order her thought processes and bring her wayward body under control. She wrapped her arms around her torso for protection, although how that would help she had no idea.

He shrugged. 'Oh well, I'm sure you can easily find out where I live if you change your mind. But now, I must be off. Goodnight, beautiful Zarmina.'

He headed for the balcony and Zar watched as he disappeared over the railing, seemingly without any trouble whatsoever. Feeling dazed, she walked outside and stared down into the alleyway, but all was quiet and Jamie was nowhere to be seen. He'd melted into the night, as if he'd merely been a figment of her imagination.

She put her fingers on her lips. But he wasn't, he was real all right.

And she'd allowed him to kiss her.

What have I done?

And why had he stopped? He could so easily have forced her to carry on. No one would have been any the wiser. But he hadn't so much as laid a finger on her. Just a kiss. That's what he'd said and he'd kept his word. But there was nothing 'just' about it, she realised that now. It had been extraordinary.

Jamie felt like whistling as he made his way home through the dark streets. Well, that didn't go too badly. In fact, it had gone exactly to plan. Except for the part where he'd enjoyed that kiss a little too much.

Damn, but walking away from her was hard.

He'd only meant to give her a small kiss, the merest touch of his lips on hers, but it had turned into something different. It was strange, but she'd been so hesitant he could have sworn she'd never been kissed before. At least not with tongues involved.

He smiled to himself. Well, perhaps she hadn't. He'd come across married women before who had never been wooed properly by their husbands, only used as breeding vessels or for the man's convenience. For a few carefree years before his marriage, Jamie had specialised in 'consoling' these ladies, finding them to be particularly eager for the attentions of someone well versed in the art of lovemaking. And apart from the risk of being found out by an irate husband, bedding such women was always safer than going after the young and unmarried ones. As he'd found to his cost.

Scowling now, Jamie turned his thoughts away from the past and back to the present. Perhaps it was worth pursuing the Ice Widow while he was here? He had plenty of time to amuse himself while he waited for Sanjiv to reach Surat. Mrs Miller – or Zarmina as he'd called her – didn't have a husband any more though, so there could still be consequences. He would have to make sure he didn't take things too far.

A light flirtation, that couldn't hurt, surely? It would help pass the time.

There were many types of coinage in use in the various regions of India, with exotic names like *rupees, pagodas, fanams* and *xeraphims* to name but a few, but Surat had its own currency and at the Mint by the *maidan* anyone could have their silver changed into the local coins. When he'd first arrived there, Jamie had found it very strange that silver was more highly valued than gold. To most Europeans this seemed back to front somehow, but all the coins minted in the city were made of silver and any gold had to be exchanged for the lesser metal unless one wanted an ornament made out of it.

There was a charge for having coins struck, however. Not only that, but unless one paid extra, one could also face an exceedingly long wait because the men who did this work were always busy. Ready-made coins could be bought at a price, but again this would cost more. Only someone in desperate straits would resort to that.

Unfortunately for Jamie, he didn't have time to wait so he'd decided to swallow his resentment against this practice and go see a money changer, or *saraf* as they were called here. He'd been distracted by Zarmina when Miller paid him for the large diamond and it wasn't until afterwards he'd realised the man had given him an odd assortment of coins, none of which could be used here. He must have thought Jamie wouldn't know, since he was a newcomer in Surat. Miller was wrong about that, but now Jamie had to pay for his inattention.

'Bloody thieves,' Andrew had muttered darkly when mentioning the *sarafs*. 'Not only are they in charge of minting, they've got us in their power because they control the exchange rates. It's daylight robbery, I tell you.'

But needs must.

Jamie approached the *maidan*, where the usual hustle and bustle was stirring up the dust. He'd chosen to wear native clothing today, so he used the end of his turban to cover his mouth and nose, thereby avoiding a coughing fit. It helped him to cope with the worst of the stench that hung over the place as well – a pungent mixture of humanity, rubbish, excrement, spices and incense, but he still felt the heat. There was no avoiding that in India, ever, no matter what you wore.

A throng of people mingled with *kafilas*, the rows of bullock carts that brought goods in from the countryside. There were also numerous palanquins and a couple of Arab horses with exquisite saddles. Textiles of every kind were being unloaded from the carts into vendors' tents and official looking individuals went around valuing the goods for customs duties. Nothing could be brought into – or out of – the city for free.

It was complete and utter chaos with so many people you could barely move, and the noise had to be heard to be believed, but Jamie loved it. Not only merchants and *sarafs*, but jugglers and conjurers, contortionists and snake charmers – the *maidan* had them all. For a while he just sauntered around looking at everything going on and storing the scene in his memory. Eventually, however, he made his way over to one of the exchangers who sat under an awning at a small table, literally surrounded by bags of coins.

'Welcome, *sahib*.' He was gestured to sit crosslegged on a rug opposite the man. 'How can I help you?'

A lengthy haggling session followed. The *saraf* had probably thought Jamie would be some poor sap who didn't know how to get a good deal. He was soon proved wrong and the longer it went on, the more the man seemed to be enjoying himself. Jamie, too, derived pleasure from the exchange and although he knew he was probably being fleeced, at least he'd cut this down to a minimum. It could have been worse.

He stuffed the sack of coins into his sash, the way Indians did. They usually didn't have pockets or bags, but used their belts for transporting all manner of things. Jamie had adopted this practice as it seemed sensible. With the money lodged so close to his body, he knew he'd stand more chance of foiling any pickpockets that might be operating in the area.

As he walked away from the *saraf*, he caught the sound of English voices nearby and stopped to listen.

'Take your hands off me, sir. I have already refused your offer and I will *not* be changing my mind. Unhand me this instant!'

Mrs Miller – Zarmina – with a definite tinge of desperation in the tone of her voice. Without hesitation, Jamie plunged through the crowd in her direction.

Chapter Eleven

Zar tried to shake off the hand which was lodged around her wrist like a manacle. Where was Priya? She'd sent the maid to buy some fruit on the other side of the *maidan* but it shouldn't have taken her this long.

'Mrs Miller, really, you are just being coy. We all know you must marry someone, and soon, and it may as well be me. I am the highest-ranking Company employee here at the moment, apart from the Chief Factor himself. You'd be able to lord it over the other ladies. What woman doesn't want that?'

'I have told you, Mr Richardson, I am not interested in marriage. I'm quite happy to remain a widow and "lording it" over other women, as you put it, is not one of my goals, I can assure you.'

'But you must have, er … needs, Mrs Miller. And I can fulfil those. Give you children. You'd like that, wouldn't you?'

He was still holding onto her wrist, despite her struggles to free herself, and Zar felt panic well up inside her. She didn't want him touching her and the thought of him fulfilling any of her 'needs', doing things to her to get her with child, turned her stomach. Bile rose in her throat and she looked around for help, but the money changer she'd been visiting was busy with other customers and had ceased to pay attention to her. The multitude of people around them were also going about their own business and no one seemed to notice the fact that she was being kept here against her will. The crowd jostled her and Mr Richardson repeatedly, but didn't so much as glance at her trapped wrist. She should have thought to bring a weapon. But she hadn't.

'Let. Me. Go!'

She tried to prise off his fingers with her other hand, but his grip was strong. She was pushed against him by someone who bumped into her from behind, and he took the opportunity to put an arm about her waist too, pulling her even closer.

'I think you owe me something for playing that nasty trick on me last time we met.' His face was so near, she could see the veins in his cheeks, reddened by constant exposure to the fierce Indian sun. Although he couldn't be more than ten years older than herself – so in his early thirties – his skin was prematurely wrinkled and his hair thinning at the front. What was left of it was lank and damp with perspiration and Zar didn't think it had been washed in an age.

'Mr Richardson, if you don't let go of my wrist now, I shall be forced to scream and make a scene.'

His mouth curved in a sneer. 'Do you think any of these heathens will care? Their womenfolk do as they're told and they probably think you odd for being out doing business. No, I shan't let you go until I have your agreement this time.'

'I think you would do much better to unhand the lady now, sir.' A new voice entered the conversation and Zar looked up to find Jamie standing in front of her, his arms folded across his chest. She blinked at the sight of him in native clothing. It was a bit strange, but somehow it made him seem even more powerful. Lethal even. The white of his coat and shirt enhanced the deeply tanned colour of his face and made his eyes look like shards of ice.

'What business is it of yours?' Richardson snarled, looking Jamie up and down with a scowl.

Jamie shrugged. 'None, of course, other than the fact that my mother brought me up to be a gentleman. I'm sure yours did the same? And that included not manhandling women who aren't interested in my attentions.'

Zar felt hysterical laughter bubbling up inside her, as that was precisely what he'd done to her the night before. Although 'manhandling' wasn't quite how she'd describe that episode. *And I* was *interested*. She quelled that thought.

'Let her go.' Jamie's voice was low, but colder than a snowy mountain spring, and his gaze bored into the other man's.

Richardson freed her wrist at last, but pushed her away so that she fell backwards and stepped on some unfortunate soul's foot. In the melee that followed, Richardson lunged at Jamie, who had evidently been ready because Zar saw him duck to the left. In the next instant, his right fist shot out and delivered a punch to Richardson's jaw line that was so hard Zar heard it above the din around her. The man's eyes rolled up, showing only the whites, and he went down like an animal felled by a shot.

Angry yelling erupted around them, with people gesticulating and asking what was going on. Jamie shrugged once again, mimed that he believed the man on the ground to be unhinged, then pulled Richardson's inert body to one side next to a tent. The crowd muttered, but soon continued on their way.

Richardson stirred and groaned, but when his eyelids fluttered open, Jamie's face was only inches from his. 'If you so much as lay one finger on Mrs Miller again, I'll hunt you down and put a knife between your shoulder blades. Understand? She's not available.'

Zar saw her former assailant blanch and nod reluctantly. Then Jamie's fingers under her elbow steered her away from the scene and soon after he grabbed her hand and pulled her along, ploughing a way through the mass of humanity without any trouble. She didn't pull her fingers out of his grip. She told herself this was for practical reasons, but the truth was she enjoyed the warm feel of him. Safe. She was safe. And it was thanks to him.

He didn't let go, in fact, until they neared her home. Then he stopped and turned to her, releasing her hand. 'Are you all right?' His gaze searched hers as if he really cared and Zar felt her cheeks heat up.

'Y-yes. Thank you. For ... for rescuing me.' She managed a small smile. 'Your mother would have been proud of you.'

He grinned, his teeth gleaming white against the dark colour of his face. 'I hope so. Strangely enough, she often is, even though I don't deserve it. But that's the way of mothers, I believe.'

Zar nodded. 'Well, thank you again. It seems I'm in your debt once more.'

'Not at all. It gave me great pleasure to hit the man so you've done me a favour. May I give you some advice though?'

'I suppose.'

'If anyone else tries to hold you against your will, pretend that you're going to kick them in the groin. It's a well-used defence tactic, but your assailant would expect that from a woman so instead of following through, try to bash your forehead into his nose as hard and fast as you can. Like this.' He demonstrated slowly, without actually hurting her, and his forehead came to rest on the tip of her nose. Then he looked up. 'See?'

'Yes, but won't it hurt?'

'It might hurt you a little bit, but with luck the man's nose will be much more painful and he'll release his grip on you. Noses are sensitive things.'

'I ... yes, I understand. Thank you. I shall keep that in mind.'

'Excellent. Well, good day to you then, Zarmina.'

He bowed and strode off down the street without so much as a backward glance. Zar stood watching him until he was swallowed up by the crowd. Then she took a deep breath and walked slowly to her home.

Kinross – Jamie – was an enigma, but it would seem he had a chivalrous side to him, despite his roguish tendencies. Zar knew she should have deplored the violence he'd used, but she'd wanted to hit Richardson herself. He got what he deserved and next time, if there was a next time, she'd definitely give him a nose bleed.

As for Jamie, she was appalled to find she'd wanted to kiss him.

'You wanted to see me again, Mr Miller?'

Jamie entered William's *divan* for the second time in as many days, not really surprised to have received a summons. This time, however, they were alone, which he'd also anticipated.

'Indeed. Thank you for coming at such short notice.' They both sat down and William fiddled with some papers on the desk in front of him. 'I'm sure you were expecting to hear from me, following our little exchange the other day?'

Jamie nodded. 'Yes, of course.'

William moistened his lips. 'And do you have it with you? The, er ... object, shall we call it?'

'No. I thought we ought to discuss the handover first, and the payment. Naturally, I need to make sure that all is in order.' Akash had been promised there would be a small sum on delivery of the talisman, although Jamie had a feeling this was just a token as it wasn't nearly enough to compensate his friend for all the trouble he'd been asked to go through. The priority was obviously the return of his family.

'I need to see the object. Otherwise, how do I know you're not cheating us in some way?'

'Us?' Jamie raised his eyebrows at William. It was as he'd suspected, Miller wasn't acting alone.

'I mean myself and the, uhm, person who will transport it during its onward journey to the final destination.' William frowned. 'Besides, I must admit that you being the courier came as something of a surprise. I wasn't expecting an Englishman.'

'Neither was anyone else, hopefully,' Jamie said with a fake smile. 'It made it easier for me to bring the object. And I'm a Swede, actually, or Scotsman if you prefer.' He knew that wasn't important in the scheme of things, but felt he owed it to his parents to clarify the point. His father had fought for the Jacobite cause so his son being taken for a Sassenach would have outraged him.

'Ah, yes, I see,' William said, although he didn't look as if he understood at all. 'Well, when can you bring it?'

'I'm not sure. How do I know you're the right person to give it to?'

'Now see here, Kinross, I gave you the agreed answer to the question you posed. That should be enough.' William's cheeks had taken on a ruddy hue, as if he was keeping his temper in check, but only just.

Jamie regarded the man calmly. 'Perhaps. If you don't

mind though, I'll make a few enquiries first, then we can meet again.'

'But—'

'Let us meet in a week's time in the Dutch cemetery at dusk, near the tomb of Baron van Reede. As I recall, that's impossible to miss.' Jamie had been there during his first visit to Surat and remembered the place, an enormous monument that certainly stood out. 'If I'm reasonably sure that it's the right thing to do, I'll hand over the object then. I'll be in touch.'

Jamie stood up and bowed to William before the man had a chance to protest further. He may have to give him the fake talisman eventually, but he wanted more time first so that Sanjiv could confirm the safe return of Akash's family. No one was getting the talisman until that had happened. Did they think him stupid enough to let go of their only bargaining tool? If so, they could think again. Jamie also wanted to explore other possibilities. And as William was just a puppet, Jamie needed to make sure the man wouldn't have to pay too high a price for his own involvement in this affair.

'Good day to you, Mr Miller.'

William was left grinding his teeth in silent fury. Who did the man think he was? And what was he playing at?

He was just a courier, for heaven's sake.

William stood and jumped up and down, trying to release some of the pent up frustration that had been building during his exchange with Kinross. He couldn't afford to fail in his task. It was too important. And Mansukh wouldn't tolerate it either.

The thought of what the merchant would do to him if he didn't fulfil their agreement made his stomach churn.

112

He simply had to get hold of the talisman and he would, by fair means or foul. If Kinross wouldn't give it to him, as agreed, he'd simply take it. There were men for hire who'd think nothing of burglary. One such could be sent to search Kinross's house without much trouble.

William calmed down. At least he had options and of course he wouldn't fail. He just needed to be patient for a little while longer.

He sat down again, breathing more easily, then another thought suddenly hit him. What if he were to tell Mansukh that Kinross had refused to deliver the 'item' while keeping it for himself? William had contacts in Persia too and had, in fact, traded with some gem dealers there in the past. He could personally take the talisman and sell it. It shouldn't be difficult to buy passage as lots of ships sailed to various parts of that country.

He smiled to himself. Kinross would be blamed and Mansukh would no doubt have him roughed up or worse in order to find out where he'd hidden the 'item'. But no matter what they did to the man, he couldn't tell them where the talisman was because he wouldn't have it. Of course, he'd swear blind that he'd given it to William, but why would Mansukh believe him over someone he'd trusted enough to do business with?

He wouldn't. And by the time the merchant began to suspect he'd been cheated, William would be far away.

If he could have patted himself on the back, he would have done. It was ingenious. All he had to do was to put his affairs in order, sell everything and prepare for departure. He could stop off in Persia on the way to England. Mansukh would never pursue him as far as Europe, surely?

He stopped for a moment and frowned. He still had

one problem – he needed to get Zar married off, and quickly. There was only one thing for it, he'd have to go and see Richardson again.

'He met with Mr Kinross, that new foreigner who's just arrived.'

Priya was once more reporting Ali's words and Zar felt her forehead crease into a frown as she listened.

'Mr Kinross? But why? William already paid him for that big diamond he's been trying to sell without success this week. What possible reason could they have for seeing each other again? I had the distinct impression they didn't get on.'

The strange words Kinross had uttered just before leaving William's office came into her mind. What was it again? Something about the monsoon and misty weather? It hadn't made sense at the time and it still didn't. So had they been speaking in code?

'I don't like it,' she said out loud.

Priya shrugged. 'It's men's business, isn't it?'

'No, it might be mine too. Can you ask Ali to follow Mr Kinross as well, please? Or get one of his friends to do it? I want to know what he's up to.'

'Very well, *sahiba*.' Priya sighed and raised her eyes skywards, as if asking the deities to intervene. Zar ignored her, used to the servant's ways. She knew Priya was loyal to the core so she tolerated her outspokenness and accepted it for what it was – concern for Zar's well-being.

A knock on the bedroom door interrupted their chat and another servant entered and bowed. 'There is a man to see you, mistress. He is waiting in the courtyard.'

'A man?'

'Yes, a *videsi*.'

'A foreigner? Oh, I see. I'll be down in a moment.' Could it be Jamie – *no, Kinross, for heaven's sake, I must remember not to think of him so informally* – come visiting in broad daylight this time? Zar felt a shimmer of anticipation flutter in her stomach, but she put a hand on her abdomen to stop such nonsense. It could be any one of the persistent Englishmen from the Factory too. Not Richardson again? Well, she wouldn't take any chances. 'Priya, accompany me, please.'

'Of course, *sahiba*. I'll sit in a corner where I can see you.'

Priya's presence made Zar feel marginally better, but she still couldn't stop her heart from giving a little leap when she saw that it was indeed Jamie who was sitting on a stone bench in the middle of the courtyard. He stood up as she approached and bowed.

'Mrs Miller. Thank you for taking the time to see me.'

'Please take a seat again, Mr Kinross. To what do I owe this honour? I don't need rescuing today.' Zar couldn't help but infuse a certain amount of sarcasm into her words. After all, he hadn't bothered to ask her permission last time he visited. Nor when he kissed her ... She felt her cheeks heat up at the thought of what he'd done without asking and turned away while she sat down herself. But he had saved her from Richardson.

He didn't answer straight away, but stared at some of the nearby plants first, as if he was weighing his words. Zar felt like the silence was stretching her nerves, so she decided to goad him a little. 'Have you perhaps come to apologise for your intrusion and, er ... taking liberties, the other night?' she said, keeping her voice down so no one else could hear.

He turned to smile at her, amusement glinting in his eyes. In the sunlight, the irises seemed as clear as crystal today and Zar had to drag her own gaze away. 'No, I haven't,' he replied. 'Why, did you expect me to?'

'A gentleman would.'

'Ah. I thought we'd established that I'm no such thing?'

'But you said your mother—'

'Brought me up as one, yes. That doesn't mean I always follow her instructions. Only when there are scoundrels who need thrashing.'

Zar could see he was teasing her now and although it annoyed her, it was also strangely pleasurable. She couldn't remember the last time she'd enjoyed arguing with someone. It made the blood fizz in her veins in the most peculiar way.

'I see,' she said, pretending disdain. 'So what can possibly bring you here today? Nothing good, I'd wager.'

He chuckled. 'And there was I, thinking I'd cured you of making bets with me, Zarmina.'

'It was a figure of speech, as I'm sure you're well aware. And don't call me that,' Zar tried her best to look stern so as to discourage such familiarity, but it only had the effect of widening his smile.

'There's no one near so I think I will anyway, Zarmina.'

She couldn't think of a reply to that, so just waited to hear what he'd come to say. Perhaps he'd changed his mind and intended to propose to her after all? He would receive the same answer as everyone else.

But his next words surprised her. 'I've come to you for advice about a little girl.'

'I beg your pardon?' Zar stared at him. 'What little girl?'

Jamie sighed. 'I have, at present, an eight-year-old girl

living under my roof and I don't quite know what to do with her. She's the little thief who stole your purse the other day and—'

Zar interrupted him. 'Hah, I knew it! You arranged the whole thing in order to make yourself appear in a good light. Just as I thought.'

'What? No!' Jamie looked genuinely horrified, making Zar doubt her conclusion.

'You didn't? But it was all so … so convenient.'

He nodded. 'I can see it might appear that way to you, but I swear on everything I hold dear, I didn't set it up. Roshani really is … *was* a thief. She'd been forced into a life of crime by an evil uncle after her father died and she had no choice. As far as I can make out, her uncle is one of the brigands who roam the countryside, preying on unwary travellers, and he sent her into town each day to pick pockets and steal. But she came to my house the other day and offered me a lifetime of servitude because she said I'd saved hers. I don't know what punishment would have been meted out to her if I'd handed her over to the authorities, but she seemed to think it was bad.'

Zar was still having trouble believing this story and frowned at him. 'Well, of course she would have been punished, although I'm not sure exactly how as she's so young.' She shrugged. 'If you have now employed her, it's up to you to keep an eye on her so she doesn't return to her thieving ways. I don't see why you need advice from me. That should be self-evident, no?'

Jamie, who had stood up again to pace in front of her, sat down abruptly next to Zar. He was so close now their legs touched from upper thigh to knee level, but he didn't seem to notice. She did, however, and had to quell a gasp as the contact sent a wave of warmth through her limbs.

'I trust her not to steal anything ever again,' he said, looking at Zar intently. 'That's not the problem. She's safe for now, under the protection of my servant's wife, and is helping her with cooking and such like. The trouble is that I never stay in one place for very long and I won't be here indefinitely. I've rented the house and the servants are temporary, so what will happen to Roshani when I leave? I doubt they'll keep her on and I can't take her with me. And then there's the dog ...'

'Dog? What dog?'

'Oh, just a mutt Roshani brought with her. I agreed he could stay as well.' He spread his hands in a helpless gesture. 'Well, I couldn't very well separate them. It was obvious they had a close bond.'

Zar continued to stare at him, wondering if he was entirely sane. To take on a former thief as his servant was one thing, but to allow her to bring a dog of indeterminate parentage into his house as well? That was surely taking philanthropy a step too far.

Jamie's mouth quirked and he shook his head. 'I know, I know, it sounds like madness, doesn't it? What can I say? I like dogs. They have this way of looking at you and I fall for it every time.'

'I see.' Zar took a deep breath. For some reason his love of canines and his obviously soft heart when it came to small thieves was making her own heart feel decidedly mushy. She wondered if the whole thing was another set-up. He was an intelligent man. Was he trying to fool her into thinking him different to all the other suitors by deliberately appealing to her tender emotions? But he looked exceedingly earnest, as if the whole subject was really troubling him. There was no guile in his gaze, no apparent deceit. She decided a direct approach would probably be best. The sooner he told her why he'd come, the faster he would leave, which would be heaps better for her equilibrium. 'What, exactly, is it you'd like from me, Mr Kinross?'

Another glint of amusement flashed in his eyes, as if to remind her what it was he really wanted, but then he grew serious. 'I know it's outrageous of me to impose on you, but I was wondering if I could possibly ask you to promise me you'll employ the girl as and when I leave? If not, I think she's stubborn enough to try and follow me, even if I tell her not to. Having rescued her once, I would hate to think of her falling into her uncle's clutches again. The Lord only knows what he'll force her into when she's a bit older …'

He let the sentence hang in the air and Zar caught his meaning loud and clear. A vulnerable young girl could be sold to the highest bidder. She almost snorted. *And don't I know it!*

'Very well, you have my word, but she has to come willingly. I won't force her to work for me so you'll have to persuade her it's her best option.'

Jamie gave her a dazzling smile which made her quite breathless for a moment. He grabbed one of her hands with both of his. 'Thank you, that's a weight off my mind. I owe you a debt of gratitude and I won't forget it.'

She extricated her hand, clasping it with her other one to stop the tingling of the fingers he'd just touched. 'No thanks necessary,' she murmured. 'I'm happy to help a fellow female in need. I just hope I don't regret it. If she steals from me—'

'She won't, I'd swear to it. And if she does, I promise I'll repay you.' He was about to stand up but suddenly stopped. 'Oh, but what about the dog?' His eyes opened wide in consternation and Zar almost laughed out loud. He was seriously concerned about a mongrel? Although truth to tell, as half Parsee, she'd been taught by her mother to hold dogs in high esteem and she had a liking for them herself, only William refused to allow one in the house.

She sighed. 'I suppose he'll have to come too, but he would have to stay in the kitchens. William would kill him else. He's not a lover of animals.'

Jamie nodded. 'Thank you. I'll make sure Roshani knows to keep him out of the way.' He stood at last and bowed deeply to her. 'Would you like to meet them? It might be a good idea for you to become acquainted.'

'Yes, I suppose so.'

'How about if we go on an outing together, a picnic perhaps? I hear people often go on excursions to the gardens in the suburbs. I could rent a conveyance.'

'I ... well ...' Zar wasn't at all sure she wanted to go anywhere with him, even in the company of a small girl and a dog.

'You must bring a maid, of course, and anyone else you'd care to invite. Shall we say tomorrow afternoon or early evening, after the worst of the heat?' When she hesitated, he added with a grin, 'I swear I won't make you any proposals of any kind, if that's what is worrying you. I just want you to get to know Roshani.'

Zar nodded. 'Very well then, tomorrow.'

He took his leave, but she stayed in the courtyard, wondering why his final words had made her feel cross. She ought to be happy he didn't want to marry her, nor proposition her in any other way, so why did his assurance annoy her so? It made no sense. Unless she wanted to marry him. But that was utter nonsense.

She didn't want Jamie or anyone else.

Then why did the words of Shakespeare suddenly pop into her mind? '*The lady doth protest too much, methinks.*'

With an angry swish of her petticoats, she stood up and marched off towards her bedroom. She had better things to do than brood over Mr Kinross. Didn't she?

Chapter Twelve

Jamie had kept an eye out for his shadow from the journey, the man with the *tulwar* nose, and had seen him on several occasions. As he strolled home from Zarmina's house, he noticed the man was following him once again, although as always Jamie didn't let on that he'd spotted him. Tiring of the game, he ducked into a crowded shop and hid behind a particularly large clay pot, waiting for the spy to pass. He wasn't in the mood to humour him today.

'Man still outside. Wait,' a small voice hissed behind him.

Jamie turned to find Roshani and her dog crouching behind another huge pot, while the shopkeeper frowned in their direction. 'What are you doing here?' Jamie said sternly. 'Aren't you supposed to be working in my kitchen?' He didn't mind if she skived off for a while, but he'd rather she didn't get mixed up in the jewel business. What if the man had seen her? Harmed her? The thought made him scowl at her.

'Cook lady no need me today. Said play. Kutaro and me guard.'

'You've been following me?' She nodded and Jamie sighed. 'Look, Roshani, I appreciate your concern, but I can take care of myself. Why do you think I came in here? I was waiting for the man with the big nose to go past.'

'Oh, he gone, but other man over there.' Roshani nodded to the left across the street.

'Other man?' Jamie bent forward slightly to peer around the pot. There was a man loitering near a stall selling fruit, fingering some of them without really looking, while glancing towards the shop Jamie was in. 'What the hell ...?' It annoyed him that he'd been so complacent. He should have been more careful, not assumed that only one spy was following him. He turned back to Roshani. 'I don't suppose you know him?'

It wasn't an unreasonable question. Surat was a teeming city, but if her uncle was a criminal, he might be connected to someone who undertook furtive jobs like spying.

'No, but lady friend do.'

'What?' Jamie felt his eyebrows rise towards his hair line. 'You mean Mrs Miller?'

Roshani nodded. 'She maid talk with man when you leave house.'

Zarmina was having him followed? Why? He'd have to find out and the only way to do that would be to ask.

'Well, thank you for telling me.' Jamie stretched out a hand to the little girl. 'Come on, let's go home. If he wants to follow us, he can, we're not doing anything suspicious.' He grinned at her. 'Although we could play a game with him if you like? Shall we see how long it will take us to lose him in the crowds?'

Roshani's face lit up. 'Yes, fun!'

'Right, let's go.'

'Ali lost him and his daughter.' Priya was combing her mistress's hair in soothing strokes, but her eyes met Zar's in the mirror of her dressing table as she shrugged. 'Maybe you should employ someone else?'

'Mr Kinross doesn't have a daughter as far as I know. That must have been his, er ... ward. But why was she out walking with him? Did he leave her outside my house all by herself while he came in?'

123

'I don't know. Perhaps. So should I fire him, Ali?'

'No! Just make sure he knows I won't pay him for losing sight of the people he's supposed to be following. I need to know what Ja- ... Kinross is up to. There's something strange going on with him and William.'

'Can't be good. Your stepson is a fool.'

'Precisely. So why would Kinross do business with him? And why couldn't he mention it in front of me? It must be an underhand deal of some kind.' A thought struck her. 'You don't think he's a thief? Is anything missing from my jewellery box?' Was that why he was being so lenient with another budding criminal, the little girl? Because he was one himself? It hadn't occurred to Zar to wonder how and where Kinross had obtained those lovely diamonds he'd brought. She had accepted his story of the Golconda mines as truth.

'No, not that I know.'

'Well, check will you, please.'

But nothing was missing. Zar shook her head. 'I still want him watched. Tell Ali to find someone else if he's not capable of doing it himself. He mustn't fail, make that absolutely clear.'

'Yes, *sahiba*.' Priya looked resigned and Zar suspected she would have enjoyed giving the hapless Ali his marching orders. The man hadn't proved very reliable. In the next instant, Priya's expression changed to one of sly amusement. 'Now, what are you going to wear tomorrow? You want to look your best, I assume?'

'Why would you think that? I'm merely going for a picnic.' Zar had been annoyed to note the speculative gleam in Priya's eyes when she told her of the proposed outing.

'Ah, but with a man. A handsome man. You haven't

done that since … well, a very long time.' Priya smiled, as if her mistress was finally seeing sense.

'Don't read anything into it. Mr Kinross is not interested in marrying me, he told me. Besides, you know my feelings on the subject even if he did.'

But Priya didn't seem to be listening and for the rest of the day, she went about her duties with that annoying smile on her face, humming under her breath. It made Zar want to hit her, but she knew she'd never do such a thing.

She'd just have to prove to her the outing meant nothing.

And to herself as well?

There were a lot of beautifully laid out gardens in the suburbs, owned by rich merchants, and Jamie had obtained permission for his party to visit one of them. It was wonderful to escape the cramped conditions and odours of the inner city, especially on such a hot afternoon. In the weeks leading up to the yearly monsoon, the heat always became more intense and well nigh unbearable. The humidity levels rose for each day, relentlessly building to a furnace like crescendo. And with so many people crammed together the stench in towns could become most unpleasant. Rubbish was simply thrown out into the streets and there were no sewers, which meant that the only time the town was cleaned was when the monsoon rains came.

He had hired palanquins to transport them to the picnic site and along the way they passed the huts of ordinary workers who usually lived together in groups according to their occupation. Carpenters, weavers, potters and stonecutters, all passed their skills on to the next generation. And women and children seemed to help with many of the tasks. It was a peaceful, if somewhat uninteresting, view.

When they arrived at their destination, Jamie helped the ladies out of the conveyances by the simple expedient of lifting them. He started with Roshani, followed by the maid, then turned to Zarmina.

'I'm sure I can manage,' she protested, but he took no notice.

'Wouldn't want you to catch your gown or trip,' he said, lifting her without asking permission. He noticed a blush spread over her cheeks, giving them a pleasing glow, and hid a smile. For someone who'd been married for three years or more, she was unaccountably spinsterish. He could only assume her elderly husband hadn't taken much notice of her, at least not in the daytime. And being decrepit, he probably hadn't been able to lift her either. *A shame for him – she's a pleasing armful.* Although fairly tall for a woman, she was soft in all the right places. He felt his body respond to the sensation of holding her like this and set her down as quickly as he could.

This was not the time or the place for desire. He tried to concentrate on other things.

Kamal, who had come with them, helped Jamie to spread out rugs for them to sit on and then Priya assisted him in unpacking the baskets of food. Jamie's cook had provided enough to feed an army and he saw Roshani and the dog stare at the sight of so much sustenance in one place. Presumably they'd both gone hungry on more than one occasion. The thought made his insides clench with anger. Her uncle should have provided for her. But some men cared nothing for their relatives.

Are you any better? A little voice inside his head needled him. *Leaving a defenceless baby in your mother's care without a thought? Your responsibility.* Jamie clenched his jaw. That was different. He'd provided for her. Just because he didn't want to raise her, didn't mean he'd see her want for anything. And he trusted his mother to look after Margot properly.

With an effort, he turned his thoughts back to the present. He wanted to enjoy this day, not think dark thoughts.

The garden was near the river and it was pleasant sitting there on the long rugs, with a warm breeze cooling their cheeks at least a little bit. They had found the perfect spot in which to eat their picnic, in the shade of a large tree. Jamie glanced at the three women seated near him. The first, his main guest Zarmina, was looking around with guarded wariness, as if she was afraid he was going to abduct her. The second, her *ayah*, wore the expression of someone who had just won a major victory, which puzzled Jamie somewhat. And the third, Roshani, was almost bouncing up and down with excitement, as was her canine companion.

Kutaro had scrubbed up well, his fur now several shades lighter and resembling treacle. It was also shiny and clean, which was just as well since Jamie had been unable to resist stroking the little dog whenever he saw him. For a mutt who must often have been badly treated, he was extremely friendly and loved nothing better than to lean into Jamie's hands as he scratched behind the mismatched ears. Jamie knew he was going to find it very difficult to part from the animal when the time came. He'd missed having a dog around. As for Roshani, it would be even harder to leave her behind.

'It's a perfect day for an outing, wouldn't you say, Mrs Miller?' Jamie decided to try and make small talk as politeness dictated. He was on his best behaviour for the sake of propriety and refrained from calling her by her first name.

'Indeed.'

She didn't seem inclined to help him out, he noticed. For every observation he made, she replied in monosyllables. In the end, he turned to Roshani and chatted to her instead. He'd been talking to her as much as possible in order to improve her English and he had been right – she was a fast learner.

Jamie noticed that whenever she did speak, Zarmina made an effort to include Roshani in the conversation and often translated quickly into her own language in order to help her out. The little girl was a bit shy at first but soon opened up and began to chatter away, half in English, half in Gujarati. She seemed pleased when Zarmina made friends with Kutaro as well, and as always, the little dog lapped up all the attention, mouth open in that silly grin of his.

Roshani and the mongrel ate whatever they were offered until both were too full up to manage another mouthful. Taking one of the rugs, they went to lie down near where Kamal was sitting and promptly fell asleep. Priya, although trying valiantly to keep her eyes open, looked as though she'd like to follow their example and have a nap. Jamie took pity on her.

'Mrs Miller, would you care to go for a stroll among the banyan trees? I find it helps to settle the food.' He smiled at Priya. 'Your maid can watch us from here, we won't go far.' To his surprise, the maid winked at him when Zarmina wasn't looking, then made flapping motions with her hands to shoo them off.

'Yes, go, a walk will do you good, *sahiba*.'

Despite throwing her maid an irritated glance, Zarmina nodded agreement and stood up. She unfurled a parasol and placed a couple of fingers on Jamie's sleeve. He steered her towards the shore, wondering why such a small gesture felt so right, as if her fingers belonged there. He shook himself inwardly. He must be going soft in the head, as well as the heart.

She seemed nervous though and he could feel her fingers trembling slightly. He wondered why he would have that effect on her, but before he could ask, she began to talk, presumably to stop him from flirting with her.

'Have you been a gem trader for a long time, Mr Kinross? You seemed very knowledgeable.'

He gave her a small bow. 'Thank you, I'm glad you think so. No, I've only been in the business for four years, but I had a good teacher. One of the best.'

'The man who took you to Golconda?'

'Indeed.' Jamie was surprised that she remembered. She obviously missed nothing.

'And is it only diamonds you trade in?'

'No, any precious stones I can find that are worth having. I've recently been to Burma, in fact, to acquire some rubies.'

'Really? Any pigeon's blood ones? I'd love to get my hands on one of those. Or one with an asterism?'

Jamie raised his eyebrows at her, thoroughly impressed by her knowledge. 'Pigeon's blood' denoted rubies of the most desirable colour, a deep and pure red with a touch of blue. And a ruby with an asterism was one which appeared to have a shimmer in the shape of six rays on the surface whenever you moved the stone. They were very rare.

'I may have,' he replied cryptically. 'But if I did, I'd

want to sell them in Europe. I think I'll get a better price for them there.'

'Yes, of course. I merely wanted to have a look. I've never handled a Burma ruby.'

'I suppose that could be arranged.' He smiled at her and saw her turn away, her long eyelashes fluttering down over her smooth cheeks. He was almost distracted from his main purpose in drawing her away from the others in their party, but now he remembered. It was time to get serious and change the subject.

'So, why are you having me followed?' he asked, making sure they were out of earshot of the others.

'What?' Her eyes flew to his, her mouth open in astonishment.

'The fool I managed to lose in the bazaar the other day. He was in your pay, wasn't he? Or is it your stepson who is spying on me?'

'I … no!' Zarmina's cheeks were flaming now, the colour making its way down her throat towards the top of her bosom, which was enticingly displayed above the neckline of her gown. Jamie tried not to notice and with some difficulty concentrated on her face.

'Which is it? He's not in your pay or he's not in Miller's?' Jamie's gaze bored into hers, even though he continued to walk, giving her no option but to follow.

He saw Zarmina take a deep breath and the colour subsided a little. 'Very well, he's in my pay. Obviously you weren't supposed to see him,' she said through gritted teeth.

Jamie smiled grimly. 'I gathered that. What I'd like to know is why? Are you trying to find out more about me because you've changed your mind about my suitability as a possible husband?'

She gasped. 'No! I mean, I would never … That is to say, of course not. If you must know, Ali reported that you'd met with William and it made me suspicious since I wasn't invited to be present. You'd already concluded your business with each other so there had to be another reason for you to meet up so soon. To be honest, I don't trust William further than I can throw him, and it worried me when I heard of the meeting between you. He's been consorting with some strange people lately and I wanted to know how you fit in.' She stopped and faced him with a determined expression. 'Perhaps you'd care to explain?'

Jamie rubbed his chin, which was smooth for once as he'd made an effort to shave that morning. Should he tell her what was going on or leave her in the dark? She seemed very astute, unlike her stepson, and would most probably make a better ally. He made a snap decision.

'If I tell you, do you swear on your mother's grave not to tell a soul? Especially not Miller?'

She put up a hand to cover her heart – and incidentally drawing his attention to her perfect décolletage again – and nodded. 'I swear, as long as you're not involved in something that's against the law.' She looked very serious, so he believed her.

'I'm not, but other people are. Come, let's walk a bit further.'

As they strolled, he told her why he had come to Surat, leaving out only the reason he was indebted to Akash in the first place. He felt instinctively that he could trust her and if she swore not to tell anyone, she wouldn't, but what was between him and Akash was too private.

When he'd finished his tale, she sighed. 'And you think William is the go-between or the man who's supposed to ferry the stolen goods out of the country?'

'He is. Why else would he know the secret words?'

She shook her head. 'I can't believe he's stupid enough to become embroiled in something like that. But I suppose it explains his recent friendship with Mansukh.'

'Who?'

'A very influential merchant. One you wouldn't want to cross, trust me.' He saw her shudder slightly.

'Does he have contacts with other countries?'

'Undoubtedly. He has a whole fleet of trading ships.'

'Hmm, that must be how they will pass on the talisman to a foreign buyer then. I didn't think Miller was going to do it on his own. But we can't let them, this is all wrong. There must be a way of stopping it. First, I need to know for certain that Akash and his family are safe. Then I want to know who the rightful owner is. I'm hoping Sanjiv will be able to tell me when he arrives as he was supposed to keep his ears open along the way. We can guess, but I need proof.'

'You want to give it back?'

'Possibly. Unless the theft was set up by the owner himself in order to raise funds, in which case I'm not sure how to proceed. That would complicate matters considerably.'

'Assuming he's not behind this, how would you give it back without incriminating yourself? No one would believe you had it if you haven't stolen it.' Worry lurked in Zarmina's eyes and Jamie realised with a jolt that her concern was for him. The thought gave him pause.

'So you wouldn't want me to be caught then?' He couldn't resist teasing her a little. 'I thought you'd be pleased to be rid of me. Another unwanted suitor.'

'You said you were no such thing,' she retorted. 'You only wished to—' She stopped herself just in time as she realised what she'd been about to say. She blushed again and looked away, out across the river.

Jamie chuckled. 'So I did. And I can't do that if I get myself caught.'

She turned back and grabbed his arm, giving it a little shake before letting go. 'Infuriating man, do be serious,' she hissed, casting a glance back towards the picnic rugs as if to check if anyone had seen her gesture. Priya and the others were fast asleep.

'I am.' Seeing her eyes, which were more peridot than turquoise today and flashing angrily, he held up his hands. 'Very well, I'll behave. We need to come up with a plan anyway. Dalliance will have to wait.'

'There won't be any,' she insisted.

'We'll see.' He smiled and ducked out of the way as she threatened to shake him again. 'Now then, how shall we proceed?'

Zarmina pretended to ignore his teasing, but she was still blushing, which pleased Jamie. At least it proved she wasn't entirely immune to his charm, despite her protests. 'I think you must wait until your friend's brother arrives,' she said, 'then try and contact the rightful owner via a third party.'

'I agree. Perhaps the best thing would be to tell the owner when and where the handover to William—' He caught the look of consternation on her face and amended his sentence. 'I mean, to Mansukh or his agents is to take place. Then the owner's men can ambush the merchant and take back what is theirs without involving us.'

Zarmina nodded. 'Good idea. Shall I have Ali follow William some more to see if he can find out anything else?'

'Well, I'd rather he didn't follow me. I have enough trouble shaking off the other man.'

'Fine, I'll tell him, although I doubt the merchant will let William in on anything secret. He must know he's a buffoon who can't be trusted to keep his mouth shut.'

'You may be right.' Jamie stopped for a moment and took her hand, the one that wasn't holding the parasol, and brought it up to his mouth. He brushed her fingers with his lips in a soft kiss. 'Thank you. I promise you can trust me, as I will trust you.'

She lowered her long lashes, but didn't snatch her hand away, like she'd done to poor Andrew the first time Jamie had met her. She looked up at him, her gaze searching his. 'I do,' she whispered.

Chapter Thirteen

'Highness, I'm afraid I bring bad news. Very bad. Your brother …'

Bijal stood in a small alcove next to a pillar and listened as the Rajah's most trusted servant brought his master the bad tidings, his voice breaking with obvious grief.

'Ravi? What's happened?'

'One of your brother's servants just came riding in. Dev *sahib* had an accident, trampled by an elephant. It was all very sudden. I'm so sorry, but … he's dead.'

Ravi kneeled before his master, head bent and shoulders slumped. Dev may not have been universally liked, and Ravi always took his master's side in any arguments of course, but for someone so young to die was still a great tragedy. Bijal regretted that it had been necessary, but there was no other way. Dev had been the only direct heir to the Rajah and now he was gone, the only thing that could save the dynasty was if the marriage to Indira produced offspring.

If there was no wedding, however … Bijal bowed his head to school his features into a sympathetic expression instead of the gloating one he'd prefer. He had to appear to be sincere in his condolences when he made his presence known. On the face of it, this was a tragedy, not just for the Rajah personally, but for the whole country.

'I don't understand. His safety was supposed to be paramount, as I'm sure his guards were aware.' The Rajah's voice shook with a mixture of grief and anger. 'They will account to me for this. Bring them, Ravi.'

'Very well, Highness. But please remember how

headstrong Dev *sahib* is ... was. He often disregarded even those who sought to protect him. And I believe some strong drink had been imbibed by all those present.'

'I know, I know, he could be difficult, but I need to know what happened. Go and find his entourage, please.'

'At once, Highness.'

While the Rajah went to stare out the window, his shoulders slumped in grief, Bijal stepped forward.

'I'm so sorry, Highness. You have my deepest sympathy.'

'Thank you. You may go now. I ... would prefer to be alone for a while.'

'Of course.'

'But wait, what news of the talisman? Have you found it yet?'

Bijal shook his head. 'No, I'm afraid not, but this is a vast country and it takes days to receive messages, so please don't despair.' *Not yet.*

'Well, find it, damn you! I must have it back, you know that.' The Rajah put his face in his hands and bowed his head. 'We need the luck it brings. Just see what losing it has done already – I dread to think what other disasters its absence will cause.'

'I'm doing my best, Highness, I assure you.'

'Very well.' The Rajah's shoulders slumped and he waved his Grand Vizier away. 'Go then, see to it.'

As he left the room, Bijal took a deep breath and smiled. Another bad omen before the wedding. That should make the Rajah think twice, even if the loss of the talisman didn't. He was sure one of his advisors would point that out to him.

Excellent.

* * *

'I'm not going near the blasted woman again, money or no money.'

William stared in surprise at Richardson, whose sulky expression resembled that of a small boy who'd been chastised by a stern parent.

'Why? I thought you said nothing would stop you marrying her? I'm relying on you, Anthony, to take her off my hands. Seriously, I need to be rid of her, and fast.'

'Well, you'll have to find some other sap to enter parson's trap with her. I'm not doing it, I tell you.'

'But what's happened to change your mind?' William felt thoroughly confused. Just a day or two ago the man had been swearing vengeance for Zar's impudence in poking him in the eye or some such. 'Surely you can outwit one measly woman?' He conveniently ignored the fact that Zar wasn't just any woman, but a very canny one, as he knew to his cost.

'Of course I can, but it's not worth a knife blade between the shoulders. That's what her escort threatened and damn me, I believed him.'

'Escort? You mean one of the servants? Of all the ... I'll have him beaten for taking it upon himself to threaten you.'

'No, I don't think it was a servant. Maybe some relative of hers, or something? Seemed very possessive. Big fellow, native, but with lighter coloured eyes. Spoke excellent English. Yes, now I think of it, he must have been a Pathan or maybe Afghan. Very handy with his fists.' William saw Richardson rub his jaw which sported a large bruise.

'I've no idea who that is. She must have hired a personal guard then. A pox on her! Never mind though, I'll get rid of him somehow. Then you can—'

'No!' Richardson shook his head. 'I'm not interested.

I'll make my fortune some other way. Never really wanted a native bitch anyway, they're only good for one thing. Couldn't bring her back to London when I go home. As I said, find someone else, I'm done with her.'

William wanted to slap the man, but could see it probably wouldn't make any difference.

'Very well, if that's your final word? I'm sure I can find plenty of others willing to wed her.'

But as he stormed out of Richardson's room at the Factory, he knew there was no one quite as ruthless and Zar needed a firm hand. A very firm hand.

He gritted his teeth. If the stupid woman wouldn't marry, perhaps he should dispose of her some other way? He may not have a choice.

What on earth made her say 'I do' to him?

Zarmina put her hands up to cheeks that felt overheated as she thought about her response to Jamie that afternoon. It had sounded like a marriage vow, which was the last thing she ever wanted to utter again. Wasn't it?

She may not wish to marry the man, but her treacherous body definitely wanted him in other ways. Zar had no idea why as the mere thought of the act between a man and woman made her skin crawl. But somehow, being lifted and held close by Jamie had made her wonder if perhaps it wouldn't be so bad after all. That not all men hurt you with their pawing and groping. He'd held her as if she was precious porcelain, and despite the opportunity he'd not tried to touch any part of her anatomy other than what was strictly necessary.

What if he was just holding back though? Waiting to pounce the moment she gave her consent?

She shivered. *I can't take the chance.*

Priya had told her men did whatever they wanted when you were their property, their chattel, and women just had to put up with it. Although sympathetic, she'd never understood Zar's deep-rooted fear. But then she hadn't told her *ayah* how vulnerable and exposed she felt, having to stand naked in front of Francis while he gloated over owning her. And then, when his rough fingers started to squeeze and pinch ... She closed her eyes and willed the images away. Francis was dead, he couldn't hurt her any longer.

And as for Jamie, he was probably just trying to lull her into a false sense of security. She wouldn't fall for it.

On his return to the rented house, Jamie found that he had a visitor, but unfortunately it was only Andrew, not Sanjiv. And he brought something Jamie both wanted and feared – a letter from his mother.

'A Swedish ship arrived this morning and they sent a lad round asking if we'd seen you. Lucky I was within earshot or they'd have taken it with them to China or some such. Didn't seem to know where you were at the moment.'

Jamie shrugged. 'They know I move around a lot so they probably instructed the crew to ask wherever they dock. Thank you for bringing it.'

'My pleasure.' Andrew looked around while taking a sip of the drink the ever thoughtful Kamal had provided. 'So how are you settling in? Decided to stay for a bit?'

'Yes, a few more weeks I think. I quite like it here.'

'That wouldn't happen to have anything to do with a certain widow, would it?' Andrew sent him a sly glance, although it was accompanied by a twinkle so Jamie knew there was no malice in the comment.

'Perhaps,' he replied noncommittally, then changed the subject. 'But tell me about yourself, what have you been up to? Found any ladies to entertain you?'

His friend seized on this subject and waxed lyrical about some Indian beauty he'd recently become acquainted with and Jamie let him ramble on until it was time for him to take his leave. Only after Andrew had gone did he open his mother's letter and it made for uncomfortable reading, as he'd known it would.

My dear Jamie,

I hope this finds you well? I was happy to hear that you have found something to do which you enjoy, and your father was most interested in your accounts of the profits to be made in the jewel trade. Perhaps it is something you and he could develop here too when you return?

I don't want to nag, but you are returning soon, are you not? Remember what I said to you when you left – fleeing was only a temporary solution. Little Margot is growing by the day, both in stature and inquisitiveness, and she has started to ask questions. She told me the other day that the other children were being unkind, teasing her about the fact that she looks different. Her hair is so dark – like a midwinter night – and her brown eyes unusual. And you would scarcely credit how her skin tans in the sun! Her heritage is there for anyone to see, I'm afraid, but I told her standing out in a crowd is a good thing and that she will grow to be more beautiful than anyone else, like her mother. She may well do.

The point is though that she needs you, Jamie.

Whatever her true parentage, you are her father in name. I can only do so much to halt the cruel tongues of the gossips and you staying away gives them grist for their evil mills. Please think about this, I urge you. Consider the child's needs before your own. And try to lay your demons to rest. It is all in the past and Margot is not to blame. You know this, as well as I do.

Everyone else is well, including Brice and his wife Marsaili. You know they have two children now? I hope my letter with that piece of news reached you. The little one, a boy, is named after his great-grandfather Kenelm (which would have pleased him). Their daughter Ailsa is thriving and according to her fond papa is growing up to be as wilful and headstrong as her mother. Since Brice is besotted with his wife, I take it that is a compliment. We shall be seeing them in the spring as your father and I are planning a trip to Scotland. He thinks it is safe for him to return now and he's longing to see Rosyth and everyone there again, as am I.

Take care of yourself and stay safe. You are ever in my thoughts.

Much love,

Mama

Jamie leaned back on the cushions and covered his eyes with one hand. He felt his jaw clench as he fought to stem the tide of emotions threatening to swamp him. Damn it all, he didn't want to go home. Didn't want to see that little girl ... But his mother was right, as always. Margot was innocent of blame and couldn't be held to account for her mother's misdeeds. But hell, how was he to cope with seeing her every day? And how could he ever answer her questions? He couldn't possibly tell her the truth of how her mother had tricked him. It wasn't something he ever wanted anyone to know ...

As soon as he had helped Elisabet to mount, they had ridden swiftly through the forest, back the way Jamie had come earlier, towards the large farm, Granhult, where Elisabet lived with her widowed father.

'Can we go in the back way, please?' Elisabet said as they neared the main house. 'Father is away, but my maid should still be awake. Karin said she'd wait up for me.'

'Where were you? How did the Walloon manage to drag you away?' Jamie had been puzzling over this and couldn't stop the questions from tumbling out even though he wasn't sure she was in any state to answer.

'I was with the others in the village, dancing. I had my father's grooms to escort me home, but we were set upon halfway there. He ... Luc had his friends with him at first.' She started to sob again and Jamie regretted having asked.

'I'm sorry,' he said, pulling her back close against him. 'We can talk about it later.'

She turned slightly and leaned her cheek on his chest. 'Thank you, Jamie. I know you want to help, but don't you think it would be better if no one found out about this? I mean, my reputation ...' She left the sentence hanging and Jamie caught her meaning.

'You don't want to report this to the magistrate?' He was incredulous. 'But you were ... attacked.' He didn't want to say 'raped' out loud, in case it started a fresh flood of tears.

'I know.' She put a hand up and braced it against his chest so she could look up at him. 'But I think it's best if we keep it a secret. Only if there are … consequences, then we must tell someone.' She gazed at him with her big, blue eyes, the lashes still sparkling with tears. 'Please, Jamie? Only think what this would do to Brice if he found out.'

Jamie *had* thought of that. Brice was good-natured and slow to anger, but something like this would definitely make him erupt. If Elisabet could handle keeping it a secret, perhaps it was the best thing. Then again, if he were Brice, he'd want to know. His brother would be marrying a girl who was no longer chaste, even if it wasn't her fault. Surely he deserved to be told about that?

'I'll think about it in the morning,' he said. He knew his head wasn't clear at the moment and he wanted his brain free of alcoholic fumes before he came to any decisions.

'Very well.'

Elisabet's maid, Karin, came rushing out of the house, babbling about the two grooms who had returned to the house without their mistress earlier. 'I had to bandage their heads. They were each sporting an egg, having been hit from behind,' she said. 'Oh, but Miss Elisabet, what happened to you?' The woman wrung her hands and ushered her charge into the house. Jamie followed, not quite sure whether he was superfluous now or not.

'Oh, please won't you wait here while I see to her?' Karin said to Jamie, indicating a chair by the kitchen table. 'I may need your help,' she added in a frantic whisper.

Jamie didn't know what assistance he could possibly render when it came to dealing with a newly raped woman, but he sank onto the chair. His head was swimming a bit, so he put his arms on the table and leaned his forehead on them, willing the dizziness to subside.

'*Fan också!*' he muttered. This was a terrible business and he didn't know what to do for the best. Could he really let his brother – his best friend in the world – marry a girl who'd been tainted in this way? What if Brice found out afterwards and blamed Jamie for not telling him? Then there was the revenge – he wanted to tear that foreign youth limb from limb for what he'd done. How dare he? Brice would feel the same.

After what seemed like ages, Karin came back looking grim and tearful at the same time. 'Miss Elisabet would like to see you now,' she said.

'See me? Isn't she asleep?'

'Not yet. She … she wanted to talk to you first, she said.' Karin stared at the floor as if she was embarrassed to look him in the eye. 'Don't worry, I'll be your chaperone.' She bustled over to a cupboard and took down a couple of tankards. 'Let me just fetch some ale. I want to give my charge a sleeping draught.'

Jamie followed Karin upstairs and into Elisabet's bedchamber, trying not to stare at her lying under the covers of a large bed. She was fully dressed now in a nightgown and shawl, her face clean, but he still felt awkward being there. As it was in exceptional circumstances, he tried to suppress his doubts. She probably wanted to make sure he'd keep quiet and he would. For now.

'Jamie, there you are.' Elisabet beckoned him forward. 'I just wanted to thank you again. If you hadn't come when you did …' She blinked, her eyes misty with tears again.

Jamie sat down on the side of her bed, wanting to get

this over and done with. He patted her hand. 'Don't think about it. We'll talk tomorrow. You should sleep now.'

'I agree,' Karin said, coming over with two tankards of ale. 'Here, drink this.' She handed Elisabet one, then gave the other to Jamie. 'And you, young man, could probably do with some ale too, am I right?'

'Well, I've already ...' Jamie started to protest.

'Drink,' Karin said firmly. 'It's only half a mug, it'll do you good.'

Jamie was too tired to argue, so he swallowed the brew as quickly as he could. All he wanted now was to go home. The ale was bitter and he hid a grimace, then watched as Elisabet drank hers down and closed her eyes.

'Thank you again, Jamie,' she whispered. 'It will all work out for the best, you'll see.'

Jamie wasn't sure what she meant by that, but guessed she was too tired to think coherently, so he just smiled and waited. When she looked as though she'd fallen asleep, he stood up to leave, but had to grab hold of the bedpost to steady himself. The room spun and he had the strangest feeling the floor was rising up to meet him.

The next thing he knew, everything went black.

And when he woke up, he was in Elisabet's bed. Naked.

Jamie stood up abruptly, not wanting to think about it any more. It *was* all in the past and he knew he had to do as his mother had said, lay the demons to rest. But he wasn't quite ready yet. Margot would have to wait just a little bit longer, but in the meantime there was another girl he could help. Roshani.

He'd teach her English and how to read and write. Provide her with a dowry perhaps? Then Zarmina could make sure she had a brighter future.

He strode to the door and called for her. The sooner the better. And although an annoying voice inside him insisted he was only salving his conscience, he ignored it.

I will do my duty by Margot, but not yet. It's too soon.

Chapter Fourteen

The Dutch cemetery at dusk should have been eerie, but Jamie found it hauntingly beautiful. There were tombs aplenty, but also lots of what he assumed were mausoleums. They resembled nothing so much as miniature Indian buildings, painted white and with domed roofs. Some were open – pavilions with stone sarcophagi in the centre – others closed like houses for the dead. It felt like a peaceful place to rest for eternity.

The largest by far was that for a Baron Adrian van Reede. As Jamie had seen for himself during his earlier visit, it had a double cupola, with galleries supported by a row of columns. When he reached it, he noticed fading decorations in the form of frescoes and Biblical passages written in Dutch, although he could only read snatches in the fading light. And some of the windows still had lovely carvings.

A man stepped out from behind the monument and Jamie tensed momentarily until he realised that it was the one he'd come to meet – William Miller.

'You're late, Kinross,' was the greeting he received.

'I came as soon as I could.' Jamie wasn't about to justify his actions to Miller. Besides, he'd been tardy on purpose, to test the man's nerves. If he was up to no good, he'd be impatient or nervous. Judging by the look on William's face, he was both.

'You need to hand over what you brought,' William said. 'It's what you were paid to do.'

'No one has paid me anything yet,' Jamie pointed out.

'You will receive what's due to you when you give me the, er … item.'

Jamie pretended to flick some dust off his coat sleeve, then decided to take a gamble. 'You know, Miller, I've been thinking. Perhaps I should just return it to the Rajah. I'd wager he'll pay quite a lot to have it back, eh?'

William froze, his eyes widening. 'You know about him? How?'

'Oh, I have my ways and means.' Jamie suppressed a smile. So Akash was right, the owner was a princeling.

'I doubt Nadhur will do anything other than have you executed as a thief,' William hissed.

Jamie had to swallow hard in order to stop a chuckle from escaping. Nadhur. So Akash was correct about that too. *Miller, you fool, you've just given me his name!* His face as serious as he could make it, he shook his head. 'I don't think so. I'm not stupid enough to show myself.' He sighed and muttered, as if he was debating with himself. 'It would be a tedious business though, as I'll have to travel all the way back again. It would save me time and effort if I just—'

'Yes! Give it to me. As I said, you will receive your due and perhaps I can even add a little extra if you insist.'

Silence stretched between them for a moment, while Jamie pretended to consider this offer. 'I'd like the payment up front,' he said at last. 'Then I might hand it over.'

'What do you mean "might"?' There were beads of perspiration on William's forehead and Jamie guessed they weren't caused by the more than balmy evening air which admittedly was humid and cloying. His own neck was prickling with heat and he wished he'd worn his native clothing instead of the thicker European coat, waistcoat and breeches. 'Now see here, Kinross, if you don't give it to me very soon, you'll be in a lot of trouble. Those who are waiting for it do not have infinite patience, you know. I can't guarantee your safety, should you persist in playing stupid games.'

Jamie wondered who was playing games here. He had a feeling it was William, although perhaps he didn't have the brains for that?

'Someone is waiting for it? I thought you were meant to be taking it abroad yourself.' Jamie was testing William, to see what else he might let slip.

'Well, yes, of course I am, but I have to hire a ship obviously. That's what I meant. I don't own one myself.'

That didn't sound like the whole truth. What exactly was the problem here? According to Zarmina's information, Mansukh was not to be trifled with, if that was indeed the shipowner in question. Then surely William wasn't idiotic enough to try and double-cross someone like that? His stepmother would probably say he was.

Out of the corner of his eye, Jamie saw movement behind another tomb and briefly the shadow of a man's face was outlined against the white background. It wasn't *Tulwar* Man, he would have been unmistakeable. So who was spying on them now? Zar's man? Or someone else?

'Well, I'm in no hurry,' he drawled, deliberately goading William to see just how desperate he was. 'Make me an offer if you'd like the "item" sooner.' He smiled, but knew it was a very fake sort of smile.

William's face darkened and Jamie saw him clench his fists by his side, as if he was contemplating violence. Since Jamie was both taller and fitter, the man obviously thought better of it, but it was clear it cost him a deal of effort to rein in his emotions.

'Very well,' William ground out between gritted teeth.

'Ten per cent extra and not a rupee more. That's my final offer. You will bring me the "item" here, tomorrow evening.'

'No, I won't. I'll be attending a social event at the English Factory. Sorry.' Jamie made sure his tone indicated he wasn't sorry at all. 'I thought you were too? And I'm busy for the following evenings as well.'

'Three days hence.' William was almost growling.

'Sorry, but no. I'm engaged to go out.'

'Fine. I'll give you a week. Seven days from now, just before sundown. Make sure you are here or else.'

William stormed off and Jamie stood still, waiting to see whether anyone would follow him or wait for Jamie. Nothing stirred. *Very well, if you wish to play games with me, I'll oblige.* He sauntered off towards the cemetery gate without hurrying, listening intently for sounds of pursuit. A slight scraping of stone told him he was being followed. But who was it? He had to find out.

He rounded the gatepost, ducked to the side and bent down as if searching for something on the ground. This meant he wasn't visible through the railings, which should hopefully bring whoever it was out through the gate quickly. He was hoping to at least catch a glimpse of him as he passed, but he soon became aware that he wasn't alone. Looking up, he came face to face with Roshani and Kutaro. They were sitting on the ground, leaning against the wall and covered with a tatty old piece of material. In the half-light, most people would have taken them for a sleeping beggar and her dog. 'Damn it all,' he hissed, 'what are you doing here?'

'Guarding y—'

'Shhh, later.' Jamie had heard the sound of rapid footsteps and moved away from them so that anyone coming out of the cemetery would focus on him. A man exited, looking right and left, then stopped as he caught sight of Jamie. Pretending he'd never realised he was being followed, Jamie stood up and raised his hand, holding his fob watch. 'Aha,' he exclaimed, 'found it!'

The man looked startled and Jamie tried to explain by miming that he'd dropped his watch and only just retrieved it. With a curt nod, the man walked off and Jamie smiled to himself. He hoped he had fooled him into thinking he was oblivious. At least now he knew what this new spy looked like, even if he didn't know who he was working for.

Roshani provided the answer to that question. 'He bad man,' she whispered, erupting from her position by the wall the moment the spy was out of sight. 'Work with Uncle.'

'Really?' Jamie wondered how her uncle had become involved in this affair. 'Is your uncle in the gem trade?'

'What?'

'Does your uncle like diamonds? Shiny stones, like this.' Jamie unscrewed the top of his cane and took one out of the secret compartment to show her. 'Diamond,' he said, pronouncing it clearly so that Roshani could copy him.

She shrugged. 'He like, yes. But he and bad man no look for dai-ah-munds. Work for other bad man. Rich.'

'Ah.' Jamie thought he understood. 'Is his name Mansukh, by any chance?'

'Yes, yes, Mansukh very bad man. More bad than Uncle.'

'I thought so. We must make sure we stay out of his way then.' He fixed Roshani with a glare. 'That means you do *not* follow me when I go out at night, is that clear?

It's dangerous! Stay away from that man, from your uncle, and most of all from this Mansukh person, understand?'

Roshani pouted, but nodded reluctantly.

'Good, now let's go home and have supper. I'm starving.'

'Me too. Kutaro too.'

Jamie laughed. 'You two are always starving. In fact, I'm convinced you're bottomless pits.'

'What that?'

'A hole with no end.'

Roshani smiled at him. 'Is bad?'

He took her small hand in his and gave it a reassuring squeeze. 'No, it's not. I'm glad you're eating well. It means you will grow and be healthy.'

And her well-being, he realised, was becoming important to him.

Hell, he really was going soft.

'I shall be going away for a while within the next few weeks, but you'll have the servants to protect you, so you should be all right.'

William was speaking casually, but Zar could tell he was tense as his hand shook slightly when he lifted his cup. They were having supper together for once, as they were going to the English Factory afterwards for another social evening.

'I see. Where are you going?'

'None of your concern. A short journey, that's all. Well, depending on favourable winds, of course.'

'You're going somewhere by sea?' Zar was surprised since he'd never done so before, at least not while she'd known him.

'Yes. Now stop plaguing me with questions and finish your meal so we can go to this infernal gathering.'

'I thought you enjoyed going to the English Factory. You always say you find good customers there.' Zar couldn't help teasing him a little. 'And friends,' she added, her mood darkening at the sort of friends William kept, Richardson among them. She'd caught the man staring at her on several occasions, but so far he'd heeded Jamie's warning and not come close. Still, she'd make sure she didn't go anywhere on her own, especially not to the roof terrace.

'I suppose, but I'm not in the mood. Things to think about. Lots to do.'

Zar didn't press him further, but resolved to tell Ali to be particularly watchful. She felt bad about having to spy on her stepson in this way, but she simply didn't trust him. She'd tried her best to get along with him and work with him since Francis died, but he refused to meet her halfway. In a way, she could understand his continuing resentment. As an only child, and a son at that, he had expected to inherit everything. To suddenly have his father turn all his attention on his new wife and then give her half his business must have seemed extremely unfair. She'd tried to tell her late husband, but he'd shrugged it off and now she had to live with the consequences.

Poor William – neglected while his father was alive and slighted afterwards. Still, Zar had had her own crosses to bear and she knew one had to make the best of what fate handed out. It was time William grew up.

At the English Factory, she found herself once again staring at Jamie across the room, but her feelings had undergone a transformation since that first time. She no longer felt like glaring at him, quite the opposite. And she didn't dread speaking to him, the way she had only a couple of weeks before. Was it really less than two weeks ago that they'd met? It felt like longer.

He waited a while, then made his way through the other guests and arrived at her side, where he stood patiently as she finished speaking to an elderly man who'd been friends with Francis. She breathed a sigh of relief when the man took himself off and stopped looking at her as if she were a prize ewe.

'Another suitor?' Jamie asked, amusement lurking in his eyes as always.

'I hope not. At least he's never asked outright, although there's still time I suppose.' She knew she sounded bitter, but she couldn't help it. Why should someone like that feel she ought to marry them just so they could live in comfort for the rest of their life? What about *her* comfort?

'Come, let us take a turn on the roof terrace,' Jamie suggested and put a hand on her elbow to steer her towards the stairs.

She frowned. 'Not you as well?'

He chuckled. 'Stop bristling. I merely wish to speak to you. There's something we need to discuss, remember?'

'Oh, yes, of course.' She felt foolish now.

Once up on the roof, he took her hand and towed her to an empty corner. She tried to extricate her fingers, afraid that someone would see them, but the roof garden was empty for once and they were alone. His hand was warm, but dry, and having her own smaller one engulfed by his felt wonderfully safe, just like it had when he rescued her from Richardson. When he let go of her fingers, she had to stop herself from trying to grab his back.

Jamie dug a hand into his pocket and then held it out to her, palm up, showing a small item. 'Here, I brought something for you.' The something sparked with red fire in the faint light from the nearby lanterns and Zar picked up his offering with reverence, knowing immediately what it was.

'A Burma ruby?' she breathed. 'Goodness, it's breathtakingly beautiful!'

About the size of her thumbnail, the stone wasn't huge, but she saw at once that it was very special. Not just of the so called pigeon's blood colour; even in such poor lighting there was clearly a star shimmer on its surface – the coveted asterism effect. Despite being used to handling lovely gemstones, Zar was mesmerised by this one.

'So you like it?' Zar heard amusement in Jamie's voice, as if he was teasing her again.

'What woman wouldn't?' she retorted, somewhat waspishly. She knew she should give it back to him immediately, but she couldn't stop looking at it, turning it over to admire the lustre and deep red flashes of brilliance.

'I should think you appreciate it even more than the average woman, being a connoisseuse of such things.'

Zar looked up to see if he was mocking, but his expression was serious. She nodded. 'Indeed I do, although I have to say I feel its beauty purely as a woman too,' she admitted. With some reluctance, she held it out to him. 'Thank you for showing me.'

He shook his head. 'Keep it, I have several more and I acquired them for a pittance.'

'But I couldn't possibly ...' As always, fear rose within her at the thought that he might require something from her in return, but he put her mind at rest with his next words.

'Look on it as a gift from me in gratitude for your promise to take on Roshani when I leave. I really am indebted to you for that. Please, I insist.'

He put both hands over hers, as he had done once before when he gave her the two diamonds, and closed her fist around the exquisite ruby. She tried not to notice how his touch sent a shiver of awareness up her arms.

'If you're sure?'

He smiled. 'I am.'

'Very well, thank you very much. I shall treasure it.'

'Good.' Then he sighed. 'And now we'd better speak of other matters. We don't have much time. I had a meeting with your stepson yesterday. He let slip who the talisman belongs to – the Rajah of Nadhur.'

'Oh, no! I've heard of him and that particular jewel is said to be powerful. It gives good luck, but only to its rightful owner. To anyone else, it's dangerous.'

'I thought there might be some superstition attached to it. There always is with that type of object. Anyway, I think William's going to try and sell the talisman himself. And I believe he's hired one of Mansukh's ships to take him wherever it is he's going. Although it seems to me the merchant might know exactly what is happening because he sent someone to spy on us.'

'That tallies with what William told me at dinner tonight. He said he's going on a journey by sea. You think he involved Mansukh? Honestly, what a lackwit he is!'

'Indeed. Or the original thieves arranged it all with Mansukh and for some reason he hired William to be the carrier.'

'I don't quite understand it though.'

'What? William's involvement or the merchant's?'

'Mansukh. Why would a man like that allow William to be the go-between when he could so easily have taken the talisman himself? He'll have to give William a part of the profit. Unless he means to murder him ... oh no!' Much as she disagreed with her stepson, she wouldn't wish such a fate on him.

Jamie looked thoughtful. 'You're right and actually, I think you already provided the answer – didn't you say that the talisman was cursed?' Zar nodded. 'Well, then, Mansukh must be using William to physically carry it to its new owner so that if there is any retribution, it won't fall on him. None of the other local jewellers would take on something like that, I should think. Most Indian people would shy away from handling an item that was thought to bring bad luck to anyone but its rightful owner. Whereas a foreigner like William would consider it superstitious nonsense.'

'Yes, that must be it. So where will they go, do you think? Persia?' she asked.

'Probably. I know there is a rich market for gemstones and jewellery there and some of the buyers don't care about provenance, or so I've heard.'

Zar bit her lip. 'What are we going to do? We must stop him.'

'Don't do that, it's very distracting.'

'Huh?' Zar looked up at him and frowned, her lower lip still caught between her teeth.

'Oh, hell,' he muttered. She saw him glance round swiftly as if checking that they were still alone, then he put an arm around her and pulled her close, covering her mouth with his. She felt his tongue trace the part she'd been biting, and Zar opened up in surprise, giving him a chance to delve deeper.

There was a bench right next to them and he sat down, tugging at her so that she ended up sideways on his lap. He didn't stop kissing her, however, just continued as if nothing had interfered, and Zar soon forgot where she was. At least until his hands started roaming.

'No, please!' His fingers had skimmed the underside of her breast and she flinched, the old fears rising to the surface so fast she felt as if she'd been doused with ice. Her response was instantaneous, unthinking. Pure reflex.

He blinked, looking slightly dazed, and stared at his hand which she was attempting to dislodge. 'Sorry,' he mumbled. 'Got carried away ...' Then he scowled. 'I didn't hurt you, did I?'

'I ... no, but ... argh!' She stood up, shoving at his chest to get to her feet faster, then turned her back on him, wrapping her arms around herself. She took deep breaths to try and stop the panic which was still threatening to swamp her while her heart refused to settle back to its normal rhythm. She felt it beating against her arms.

Jamie got to his feet behind her. 'I apologise,' he said. 'I only meant to kiss you. The sight of you nibbling your lip just ... You're safe now, I won't touch you, I swear.'

She managed to control herself and turned round to face him again. 'It's all right. I over-reacted.'

He regarded her for a moment, searching her gaze in the moonlight, then he nodded as if he accepted her words. 'Very well, where were we? We need to stop your stepson, right? Sooner rather than later, otherwise I'll be forced to give him the fake talisman and I don't think that's a good idea.'

'Yes. I've set Ali to watching him more closely and I'll try to listen in to any conversation he might have with people at the house.'

'Good. Let me know if you hear anything more. We had best find a way of returning the talisman to the Rajah as soon as possible once I know my friend's family are safe.'

There wasn't much else to be said after that, so they made their way below, although separately, Zar going first leaving Jamie to follow a while later. She was grateful for once that everyone was used to her coming down from the roof garden looking either flustered or annoyed. No one batted so much as an eyelid at this sight tonight either.

Thank the Lord for small mercies.

What the hell was that all about? Jamie took a turn around the roof garden by himself before descending the stairs. Zarmina had been pliant in his arms while he kissed her, hardly reacting when he pulled her down to sit on his lap. But the moment he tried to touch her in any other way, it was as if she'd sat on a wasp's nest.

She was terrified. He recognised the signs of panic. He'd seen it before on the face of a man in his father's employ who'd been afraid of the sea, but who had tried to come on a sailing trip with them once. Pure, abject terror had made him react the same way Zarmina just did. But why was she scared?

Someone must have hurt her. The elderly husband, most likely. Had he taken his young wife by force? Had no one warned her about the marriage bed? It was a common occurrence, but most women seemed to become used to it after a while. This didn't seem to be the case here. *A pox on the man!*

Jamie was fairly sure Zarmina had never been kissed properly before, so that obviously didn't trigger the panic. Anything else, however, and she recoiled. How was he to help her overcome this? Because he knew now that he wanted her and she wasn't immune to him either, whether she realised it or not.

He'd have to think about it, but now was not the time. There were more important things to do. Like saving William's worthless neck.

Jamie sighed. Why was his life never simple?

Chapter Fifteen

'Forgive the intrusion, Highness, but my servant Tufan
has brought me something I thought you might want to
see.'

Bijal had carefully chosen his moment and approached
the Rajah when he was alone in his chambers. Ostensibly
the prince was resting, but from what the vizier could see,
he was more like an animal prowling round a cage. His
master stopped and turned towards him, his face looking
drawn and grey with fatigue.

'What is it, Bijal? More bad news?'

'Possibly. I'm not sure but … this was brought back
among your half-brother's belongings. Tufan recognised it
as it wasn't long since you presented it to Dev as a special
gift.' He held out a small wooden box, with an intricately
carved lid inlaid with precious stones, gold and silver. The
Rajah had given it to his half-brother and filled it with
jewels, hoping, as Bijal well knew, that this would re-
establish the peace between them. But the jewels had soon
been squandered and only the box remained.

Now it contained something else entirely and Bijal
couldn't wait to see how his master would react to the
sight of it.

The Rajah opened the box and frowned. 'What is this?
Surely it's not …?'

'I'm afraid it might be, Highness.' Bijal tried to sound
as apologetic and pained as possible, since the implication
was clearly not lost on his master.

Inside the box was what looked like the uppermost
part of a turban ornament, the gold mount with feathers

usually placed at the top. And not just any ornament, but the sacred talisman, which was still missing. Bijal had had this copy of the top feathers made to look as though it had been broken off from the two jewels. He knew it was first-rate. No one could possibly tell the difference, he was sure.

The Rajah recognised it immediately. His face went pale and he picked up the feathers and held them between forefinger and thumb as if they were repugnant to him. Which they probably were as they ostensibly proved that his brother had sold the rest of the talisman and just kept this.

Bijal sighed and shook his head. 'I'm so sorry, Highness, but I felt it was your right to see it.'

His master dropped the offending object back into the box and slammed the lid shut. 'Thank you, Bijal, you may leave me now. I have much thinking to do.'

'Of course, Highness.'

Bijal backed out the door, bowing. Outside he had to force himself to walk slowly rather than run and skip the way his heart was soaring inside him. He was making great progress and very soon the Rajah would realise the talisman was lost for good. With a bit of luck, it should be well on its way to Persia by now and soon Bijal would be able to buy a new symbol of power with the money from the sale of the old one. He'd have something made, or perhaps pretend to rediscover a truly ancient talisman with powerful magic attached to it.

A new talisman for a new dynasty. How fitting was that?

Zarmina felt like a thief herself as she crept down the stairs from her bedroom to skulk in the darkened courtyard near the *divan*. The door was closed, but since there was a window covered in nothing but latticework, Zar hoped she would be able to overhear any conversation taking place inside. This proved to be the case and as usual William wasn't being particularly careful, which was to her advantage but made her despair of him. Honestly, he was so loud anyone could hear him. Would he ever learn caution? She settled down on a bench just below the balustrade of the raised walkway that surrounded the courtyard, and tried to blend into the shadows.

William was entertaining a guest and he'd asked her to dine by herself in her room. 'We'll be discussing men's business,' he'd informed her airily, but that only served to pique her interest.

By the sound of things, they were very merry. She hoped the guest wasn't a Moor since they weren't supposed to drink anything intoxicating. It was against their religious beliefs but Zar knew that behind closed doors this rule didn't always apply. Perhaps this was the case tonight? It certainly sounded like it, although perhaps they were drinking arrack? For some reason coconut arrack wasn't banned, even though it was intoxicating, as it was considered to be made from a fruit they permitted.

For a while she heard nothing of particular interest. There was only the usual male banter, with a few ribald jokes that made her cheeks burn. Then the conversation finally took a more interesting turn as William banged his cup onto the table, like a judge passing an important sentence, and changed the subject. 'So, let us move on to more serious business. Are we agreed then? You'll take me wherever I want to go on board your ship?' William's words sounded a bit slurred, but not nearly as bad as he sometimes was.

What on earth was he up to now? Surely he wasn't trying to go behind Mansukh's back and go to Persia without him to sell the talisman himself? But it certainly seemed that way. He'd be a dead man.

A slight pause. 'You swear on the Quran you will pay me half the profit of whatever it is you're selling? Enough for me to build more ships and rival Mansukh, the sly cur?' Zar didn't recognise the voice, so she didn't know who the guest was, but she could guess. She'd heard rumours that one Feroz was trying to set himself up as a rival to the other merchant. William confirmed it with his next words.

'Yes, I swear, on my honour, or whatever holy book you want. Mansukh's little empire will be over, gone. You, Feroz, are the man who can break his stranglehold of the trade here. I know it. The only one with the courage and cunning to do so. '

He was going a bit too far with the flattery, in Zar's opinion. She shook her head. Surely the other merchant wouldn't fall for such outright obsequiousness? But he did.

'Yes, you are right, my friend. All I need is more money. And Mansukh thwarts me at every turn.'

Zar could only assume the man had drunk far more than was advisable. He may come to regret this in the morning – both the drinking and his bargain. But that was his problem, not hers.

From the reference to the holy book, the Quran, she gathered Feroz was a Mohammedan, which would add to the rivalry since Mansukh was a *bania*, or Hindu merchant. The various ethnic groups ostensibly lived in harmony in Surat, but there were tensions below the surface and competition was fierce. Each kept to their own parts of the city and their own kind.

The two men went on to discuss their plans and Zar

heard William mention that the item in question would be his in just under a week's time. Jamie hadn't said anything about handing it over so soon and she doubted he would. He'd stall William somehow.

Now she knew who her stepson's new accomplice was, she could ask Ali to find out the name of his ship and when it was due to sail, just in case. And then she'd tell Jamie.

The thought of seeing him again, even if it was just to discuss this deplorable business, made her tingle all over. Which was not a good thing.

She must stop thinking about him. He wasn't staying here, he'd said so.

And anyway, she wasn't interested. *Definitely not.*

A slight movement to her right stopped her thoughts in their tracks and she turned swiftly to scan the courtyard. There was nothing but shadows, but she couldn't help feeling as though someone was watching her. Or was it another spy, listening in on William's conversation? That wouldn't be difficult, as noisy as he was. She shivered and with a last glance behind her, hurried back to her room.

This was getting too serious. She needed to speak to Jamie.

Jamie was woken in the middle of the night by a crash, followed by frenzied barking. He cast aside the thin sheet under which he slept and leaped out of bed, taking the stairs three at a time down to the ground floor. In the *divan,* at the front of the house, he found Roshani and Kutaro. The latter was trying to spit out a piece of material which appeared to be stuck between his teeth. His small mistress was muttering 'Good boy' over and over again, while attempting to help him.

'What the hell is going on here?' Jamie glanced around

the room which looked, in the moonlight spilling in from the windows, as though a storm had swept through it. He lit a lantern and held it up to better gauge the damage. 'What did he do? Has he run mad?' Jamie stared accusingly at the dog, who gazed back with eyes that indicated he was innocent of all and any wrongdoing.

'Kutaro brave. Bite man who come steal.' She mimed a dog biting someone's hand with a pretend growl. 'Blood, hurt, good!'

'There was someone here? A thief?'

'Yes.'

'The one in the cemetery? Or the one with the strange nose?'

Roshani shook her head. 'Yes and no.'

'What?'

'Yes, man in cemetery. No, not nose man.'

'Oh, I see.'

So, Mansukh's spy. Why on earth was he ransacking Jamie's house? Had the merchant decided to take matters back into his own hands and not risk Jamie handing the talisman to William after all? That would be understandable. He went to the doorway and glanced out into the courtyard. In the light of the moon all was serene, the little pond in the middle still. Not a single ripple creased the water's surface and that told Jamie all he needed to know. The fake talisman was safe.

He'd hidden it in the water under a loose tile at the bottom, inside a mud-coloured pouch. The feathers would get very soggy, but he thought that was a small price to pay to keep it safe. They would dry out or could easily be replaced. And secrets were always best concealed in plain sight, where no one would think to look. This seemed to be the case tonight.

So what was going on? He tried to sort it all out in his mind. Someone had stolen the talisman from the Rajah, then passed it on to Akash for transport to Surat. That someone had also hired Mansukh to sell it for him abroad, but the merchant must have insisted William was to carry it so he didn't have to touch it and be cursed with bad luck. But now William was proving useless, and Mansukh had lost patience and sent his spy to take it back.

Only, he hadn't succeeded. So what happened next?

All Jamie knew was that he couldn't let any of these people have the fake talisman until he had more information. Where was Sanjiv? Why hadn't he arrived yet? And was Akash's family safe? He sighed and rubbed his face, feeling very weary. He'd have to be extra careful from now on, and on his guard.

'Did the man see you?' he asked Roshani.

She shrugged. 'Don't know. Maybe.'

'I thought I told you to stay away from these people. They can hurt you, much worse than Kutaro did to them. Next time, if there is a next time, find someone to help you before rushing in. And where's the nightwatchman?'

'Don't know.'

'Perhaps he's been hurt? I'd best go and see. You and Kutaro go back to bed.'

'Dog hear something, just come to see,' she defended herself. 'Good dog.'

Jamie bent to fondle the dog's ears. 'Yes, he is a good dog. Here, give me that.' He pulled the last of the material out of the dog's mouth and held it up. 'Just plain cotton, so we can't use it to prove the man's guilt.' He swore under his breath. Who would believe him anyway? He was a foreigner here and couldn't really prove anyone was in his house.

The main thing was that the thief had left empty-handed. For now.

'The man might come back,' he said to Roshani. 'Can I borrow Kutaro for the rest of the night, please? The next place for someone to look would be my bedroom.'

'Yes. Kutaro stay with you.' Roshani gave the dog an order in her own language which Jamie took to mean for him to be on guard.

'Thank you. Please go back to bed now and don't tell anyone about this. Stay close to Soraya. I'll sort out the mess here after I check on the watchman. And remember, if you hear anything else, you come and wake me first, understood?'

'Yes, Jamie *sahib*.'

Jamie stared around the room. It was going to be a long night.

'Mr Kinross, to what do we owe this honour?'

Zarmina had been keeping watch from the *divan* and rushed down the stairs to intercept Jamie in the courtyard. She sent him a speaking look to indicate that he must follow her lead and play-act and thankfully he seemed to understand her silent message.

'I, er ... came to enquire about your health. I do hope you suffered no ill effects from our little outing the other day?' he improvised. 'It was rather hot and I was afraid you might have found it fatiguing.'

'No, not at all. It was most pleasant, thank you.'

'Good, good. Is your stepson about?' His gaze held another question, but he didn't ask it outright. He must have guessed that she wanted to speak to him alone and probably knew as well as Zar did that they might be under surveillance. At least he'd come quickly. She'd only sent a note round to his house an hour ago.

'No, he's gone out for a while, but he may be back soon. Would you care for some refreshment?'

'Thank you, that would be most welcome. Perhaps we could partake of it here in the courtyard? Sitting outside is lovely in the mornings.'

'Of course.' Zar realised they were less likely to be overheard outdoors if they kept their voices down, which was all to the good. She needed to tell him about last night, even though she didn't yet have the information from Ali about the ship.

Cold *sharbat* was sent for, a sweet drink made of fruits and sugar. It was very welcome as the heat was still intense even though the sun had not yet reached its zenith. They were coming very close to the monsoon season now and the temperatures had soared in the last couple of days. Zar would have preferred to sit in the shade, but was prepared to put up with the discomfort in order to have a little privacy. She glanced around, making sure there was no one about. The small courtyard was empty and quiet, apart from the buzzing of insects who were busy in the various flower pots. A brief feeling of satisfaction flowed through her at the sight of the pretty blooms, which she often tended personally. She had orchids of various kinds, marigolds, lilies and jasmine, as well as water lilies in the little pond and lots of small shrubs and bushes. It was truly a peaceful place, the splashes of colour vivid in the sunlight.

The chance for a hushed conversation came once the refreshments had been brought and the servant departed. Zar told Jamie her news first, then he related what had happened at his house during the night and the conclusions he'd drawn.

'You're sure the man didn't find it?' Zar shaded her eyes with one hand to look up at him and was once again startled by the clear crystal of his irises in the bright light. They were far more beautiful than any diamond. But why was she thinking about that now? Impatient with herself, she broke eye contact and fiddled with the ruffles of her sleeves. She was dressed in the English fashion today, as she always was whenever she received foreign guests or visited other foreign residents.

'Yes, I checked this morning. It's still safely hidden away.'

'So what are we going to do then? Ali hasn't reported back yet, but when he does we'll know for sure what day William is leaving. I can't believe he's thinking of double-crossing Mansukh. He must be mad.'

Jamie nodded. 'From what you've told me, it doesn't sound very wise. But we don't know anything for sure yet. Let us meet again tomorrow and confer. We may have more information then.'

'Good idea. What excuse can we give though? I'm sure William will find out that you've been here today. He'll think it strange if you return so soon, won't he?'

'How about if I bring Roshani for a visit? She's been chattering about you ever since the picnic.'

'Oh, yes, do! I'd love to see her again and hopefully I'll have heard from Ali. In fact, he should have been here by now. It can't be that hard to find out such a simple thing.' Zar frowned, wondering what was taking her spy so long. 'I—'

She was interrupted by the sound of voices coming from the main entrance to the house and a moment later,

William strode into the courtyard, his face screwed up in an expression of fury. Zar stood up, realising just how close to Jamie she'd been sitting, and called out to her stepson. 'William, what's the matter? Has something happened?'

He jumped, as if he hadn't noticed them there, and turned his steps towards them. 'Kinross.' He nodded curtly to the visitor. 'Didn't expect to find you here.'

'Mr Kinross just came to enquire about my health,' Zar hurriedly explained.

'Your health? Why, are you ill?'

'No, I …' Zar's brain seemed frozen and she couldn't think what to say, but fortunately Jamie came to her rescue.

'I took Mrs Miller and her *ayah* on an outing the other day and I was afraid the heat may have been too much for them,' he interjected smoothly. 'Happily, that was not the case.'

William's scowl told them he found this suspicious, but whatever was preoccupying him obviously took precedence. 'It's the damnedest thing,' he burst out, starting to pace in front of them. 'A merchant friend of mine has just been found murdered. His throat slit from ear to ear.' He must have heard Zar's gasp as he added, 'Beg pardon, but really, it's the outside of enough.'

'Wh-what merchant?' Zar asked, although she was afraid she knew all too well who it would be.

'Name of Feroz,' William confirmed. 'He was here only last night, discussing a, er … business proposal. I can't believe it!' He raked his fingers through his fair hair, making it stand on end at the front where perspiration had made it limp and wet.

Jamie had remained silent throughout this exchange, but he and Zar shared a glance. He shook his head at her, the gesture so slight she doubted William noticed. 'That is indeed unfortunate for the poor man,' Jamie said. 'And for you, of course. I do hope this won't cause you any problems.'

'What do you mean?' William scowled at him. 'Why should the death of Feroz cause *me* problems?'

Jamie held up his hands in a placating gesture. 'I only meant it might be an inconvenience to you to have to change your plans. You did say you were negotiating a business deal with the man, didn't you?'

'Oh, that.' William looked relieved. 'Yes, yes a bloody nuisance.'

'Well, I shall take my leave,' Jamie said. 'This is obviously not the time for a visit. I shall see you tomorrow, Mrs Miller, when I will bring my ward as agreed. She is looking forward to seeing you.'

'Ward? I didn't know you had one.' William sent him a look of disbelief.

'Yes, but it's a long story and I won't bore you with it now. Good day to you both.'

As Jamie bowed and left, Zar watched William who seemed restless and nervous. What would happen now, she wondered? Who had murdered Feroz? It could only be someone connected with Mansukh, unless the other merchant had enemies she knew nothing about. If she'd been right, and there really was another spy in the courtyard the previous evening, he'd reported to his master. Feroz's death was the result.

She shivered. This whole business was becoming much too serious.

William slumped down at his desk and with an angry curse, swiped his hand across the surface, dislodging various papers and quills. These fluttered to the floor, spreading out around him, but he didn't care. He'd have liked to throw something heavy at the wall, just to take his frustration out somehow, but there wasn't anything to hand other than the ink stand. He wasn't stupid enough to throw that, as the contents would completely ruin the walls and floor.

'Devil take it!' He slapped his palms down onto the now empty desk. How could Feroz be dead?

He'd seen the man only last night and he'd seemed like someone who could take care of himself. From the rumours William had heard, Feroz had been setting himself up in opposition to Mansukh for quite some time, so he'd thought he was more than capable of looking after himself. That obviously wasn't the case.

More worrying though was that if his death was a result of his deal with William, then William himself was in danger. How had Mansukh got wind of his plans? He'd not mentioned it to a soul, other than Feroz and his broker. And he'd been so careful, not even selling any of his assets yet. Instead he'd agreed with the broker that everything would be sold after his departure and the funds brought to Persia by the man personally. William would await him there and he trusted him implicitly. He'd been in his father's employ for years.

Mansukh had spied on him. Spies were everywhere and he shouldn't have assumed he was safe from them in his own home.

He shivered. He'd thought it would be easy to escape with the talisman and the rest of his fortune without Mansukh being any the wiser. But the man must have eyes and ears everywhere. How was he to extricate himself from this mess?

Perhaps he could blame Kinross? Say that it was his idea and he'd forced William into an agreement?

It was the only plan he could come up with for now. In the meantime, he'd try and find another way of leaving, and quickly.

Chapter Sixteen

'How kind of you to bring Roshani to visit me this afternoon, Mr Kinross.' Once again Zar met her guests in the courtyard, hoping to keep them there so she could discuss the previous day's happenings with Jamie. First she had to greet her younger guest though. 'How are you, my dear?' Zar smiled at the little girl, who grinned back, mischief lurking in her eyes. She reminded Zar very much of Jamie himself, who'd taken the tiny thief under his wing. Perhaps he saw a kindred spirit in Roshani and that was why he'd agreed to let her stay?

'We were very pleased to be invited,' Jamie said, replying for them both she noticed.

'Shall we stay outdoors?' Zar gestured to the courtyard. 'Roshani may wish to run around for a while.'

'Yes, she certainly has a lot of energy.' Jamie smiled and for a moment Zar almost forgot the serious purpose of his visit.

She pulled herself together and ordered refreshments, just like the day before. Roshani chatted to her hostess for a while. Then, having gulped her *sharbat*, she began to explore and set off along the paths. Zar turned to Jamie and whispered, 'Ali never came yesterday so I am none the wiser. Have you any news?'

He shook his head. 'Not much, no. I sent Kamal out to try and glean what information he could, but there was nothing but the bare facts. Feroz the merchant was found with his throat cut and no one had seen or heard a thing.'

'It must have been Mansukh, right? I mean, no one else had a motive.'

'We don't know that. Feroz could have been a cheat and a liar, disliked by others.'

'No, his death fits in too well with the rest of what we know.' Zar unconsciously grabbed his forearm and almost shook it. 'What are we to do? If Mansukh is angry, he might murder William next, and then you ...' She trailed off, unable to bear the thought of Jamie hurt or worse.

His mouth quirked and he put a hand over hers where it still rested on his arm. 'Are you worried about me, Zarmina? I'm touched.'

She pulled her fingers away and made an impatient noise. 'I'm worried about all of us. This is too dangerous. We have no idea what we're up against.'

'True. So what do you suggest?'

Zar tried to order her thoughts. She watched Roshani, who was now skipping around the perimeter of the courtyard on one leg in some game of her own. How she wished she was as young and carefree as the little girl. Life had seemed so simple at that age. She sighed. 'I don't know, but I suppose our only option is to do as the thief or thieves wish.' She looked up at Jamie. 'You'll have to give William the talisman.'

'I can't. Not yet. You know that.' Jamie's mouth tightened. 'Not until Sanjiv arrives with news of Akash and his family.'

'But—'

A scream rent the air, interrupting Zar in mid-sentence, and Priya came rushing into the sunlight, her face a mask of terror. Right behind her swarmed a group of men armed with daggers and curved swords. They spread out to cover all the exits from the courtyard, searching each room in turn. Two of the men came out of a side room dragging a swearing William between them just as one more person came in through the entrance – Mansukh.

'Oh, no,' Zar whispered, her heart practically jumping into her throat. Their discussion had been too late.

'Shield me for a moment,' Jamie hissed and ducked behind Zar.

'What?' She frowned, but did as he asked, while William started shouting for his *sepoys*. Anyone of standing had hired soldiers to guard them whenever they ventured out. They came cheap and it was a sign of status, as well as protection. The household employed four such men, but none of them answered the summons. Zar tried not to think what might have happened to them, but feared they could have shared Feroz's fate.

She took a deep breath and tried not to give in to the panic rising inside her.

Jamie turned and took his place beside her again. Zar looked up at him, wondering what he'd been doing, but his expression gave nothing away.

The portly *bania* made his way towards them, his black eyes glittering with barely suppressed anger. Priya continued to wail and he flapped a hand at one of his henchmen. 'Get her out of here. And her child. This is nothing to do with them.' Zar realised Mansukh thought Roshani was Priya's daughter, as the girl happened to be standing near her. She watched as the merchant's men ushered the two into the house and shut the door on them. *Good, at least they'll be safe.* She knew Priya would look after the little girl.

William now stood silent, as if petrified, staring at Mansukh with the wide-eyed gaze of someone trapped by a tiger or other wild animal. Jamie seemed made of stouter stuff. 'What is the meaning of this?' he asked, glaring at the merchant. 'You dare threaten a lady in her own house?'

Mansukh came to a halt in front of their little group and pursed his lips. 'I'm sure you know exactly why I am here, foreigner. I do not like being cheated.' His English was good, if heavily accented, and Zar remembered he had been doing business with the English factors for some time.

'No one has cheated you,' Jamie said, and added under his breath, 'Yet.' Zar hoped she was the only one who heard him.

But Mansukh fixed his gaze on William, who squirmed visibly and turned a nasty shade of pale. 'Yes, they have. Or planned to. So you thought you could go behind my back, eh? That is not how I do business. Now where is it?'

'I don't have it.' William's tone was both sulky and defiant, yet with a quaver of terror in it, like a small but frightened boy.

'You lie.' Mansukh gestured to his men. 'Take them away for questioning. I'm tired of this game now.'

He repeated his order in Gujarati and his men rushed to do his bidding. Mansukh himself turned and walked away without a backward glance. He ignored the sounds of the scuffle when Jamie tried to resist, laying about him with his fists like a prize fighter, to Zar's surprise. But although he fought well, he was but one man against a dozen and with no help from William, who still stood like a statue, he had no chance. Zar herself could do very little, as her arms were quickly pinioned behind her and tied with a rope around the wrists.

For the sake of modesty, middle-class Mohammedan women of the town always covered themselves with a white enveloping garment called a *burqa* when they went out. It had a small white net over the eyes so they could see. Such coverings were now thrown over their heads before they were led out of the house and into three palanquins. As the conveyances started to move, each borne swiftly by six servants, Zar swallowed hard and tried not to give way to tears.

Jamie's plans had all gone spectacularly wrong.

Rich merchants lived in fine brick houses and Jamie already knew Mansukh's was situated next to the city wall facing the river. He'd been to reconnoitre after Zar mentioned the man and recognised the four storey building as they approached it. Most of the ones around it were lower, with two or three floors at the most, but Jamie reckoned Mansukh wanted to show off his wealth by having the extra space.

All such houses had thick, sturdy walls and this particular one had upper floors that overhung the lower levels and were supported by carved wooden pillars. The three prisoners were quickly hustled in through the main entrance and frog-marched towards a staircase that led down into arched cellars. These appeared to be as extensive as the floor above and Jamie tried to memorise the layout. Zar and Jamie ended up in a large room which had to be very close to the river, judging by the amount of moisture that covered the walls.

The *burqas* were pulled off and they were shoved to the floor. Jamie rolled in order to avoid being hurt, since his hands were tied behind him, but he heard Zar give a muffled cry and guessed she hadn't known to do the same. 'Bastards,' he snarled, but the men who'd brought them took no notice. Instead they dragged their captives over towards the wall and clamped iron cuffs round their wrists. These were attached to a chain each which had only enough slack for them to sit with their backs against the wall.

'Wasn't the rope enough?' Jamie taunted, but again, he was ignored.

The guards went off with William, who was obviously to be taken somewhere on his own, and his shouted protests echoed round vaulted ceilings.

'Sounds like he's found his voice again,' Jamie muttered. 'Shame.'

'Wh-what are they going to do to him?' Zar whispered, sounding breathless as if she was battling to keep her emotions under control. Jamie was pleased she hadn't started weeping at least. He couldn't bear women who cried for the slightest thing. He'd had enough of that with Elisabet …

He turned to look at Zar. There was a small amount of light coming in from a grille set high in the wall, enough for him to be able to make out the fact that she was keeping fairly calm. He leaned back and studied her face. The lovely peridot eyes were huge, but he couldn't allay her fears. 'I think we can guess,' he said, bluntly. There was no point shielding her from the obvious. She wasn't stupid. 'We'll be next, once they realise William really doesn't know anything.'

'So will you give them the talisman?'

'I don't see that I have a choice.' He sighed. 'If only Sanjiv had arrived, but he must have been delayed. You know I couldn't really do anything until he got here.'

'What were you doing in our courtyard when you asked me to shield you?'

He smiled and opened his mouth to show her what he'd hidden under his tongue – three diamonds, each about the size of his smallest fingernail. 'Emergency supplies,' he said, once he'd put them back. It wasn't too difficult to talk with them there. It was something he'd practised.

She blinked. 'What? Where did those come from?'

'I usually keep some in the hilt of my dagger, which is hollow, but I thought they'd probably take that away from me, which they did, so I removed them. You never know when you might need something to bribe people with.'

'You're going to try and bribe the guards?' She perked up at that idea, but he shook his head.

'No point. I'm sure Mansukh has them well-trained and he'll pay them more. No, I'll hang onto these for a while. Although perhaps it's better if you have them, in case I'm taken away for questioning.'

Her nostrils flared, as if the mere thought of that scared her. He wasn't so keen on the idea himself. Still, at least he had something to bargain with, unlike William.

'If I give them to you, can you keep them hidden the same way?' he asked.

She looked doubtful. 'Probably not three of them. I won't be able to speak normally. I think I could manage one under my tongue maybe?'

'Then I'll have to put two of them elsewhere. It's probably a good idea not to have them all in the same place anyway. Come closer, please. I think these chains might just be long enough.'

'Why? Where are you going to ... *Jamie!*'

Jamie had shuffled over and bent to put his face in her décolletage. He dropped two of the diamonds down the cleft between her breasts, making her gasp, although he wasn't sure if it was with outrage or because what he was doing tickled.

'Jamie, really!' she protested.

'Let's hope they don't look there,' he said with a grin, as he reluctantly removed his lips from the vicinity of her breasts after placing a kiss on each swell. Zar opened her mouth, presumably to remonstrate with him some more, but he forestalled her by leaning over to kiss her instead. He kept it light and playful, using his tongue only to trace the outline of her bottom lip, and heard her sigh as if she'd given up the fight to stop him. He noticed she didn't back off and soon entered into the game wholeheartedly, meeting him halfway each time. That was just as well as he couldn't have reached otherwise.

'Jamie, this isn't really the time,' she murmured between kisses.

'Yes, it is. It's the perfect time.' It took their minds off the surroundings, which to Jamie's thinking couldn't be a bad thing. And he hoped to distract her so she wouldn't think about their predicament. It was certainly helping him. 'This doesn't … scare you?' he added, tugging a little on her lip with his teeth which made her shiver.

'No.'

'Is that because I can't touch you?' he whispered, trying to keep his tone light and flirtatious, even though he desperately wanted to know the answer.

She stopped for a moment and looked into his eyes, then nodded. 'I … think so.'

'I would never hurt you. I swear.' He feathered kisses along her cheek and leaned his forehead against hers. 'Do you believe me?'

'I-I don't know. You might not mean to, but—'

'If you'll let me, I can show you that lovemaking doesn't have to be painful. One of these days, I'll teach you to enjoy it, I promise.' He knew he was treading on eggshells here, but nothing ventured, nothing gained. 'You liked my mouth on your skin just now, didn't you?' He glanced towards her bosom. 'Just imagine what it would feel like lower down, if your, um … assets were free from constraints.' He bent down to kiss his way from her collarbone towards her cleavage, nuzzling the velvety skin before grazing it ever so slightly with his stubbly chin.

She trembled, but drew back a bit and swallowed hard enough for him to hear it. 'I can't. I just … no, it's not possible.'

'Yes, it is.' He allowed his mouth to dip lower down, rubbing against the material that strained across her bust. He felt her nipples harden and smiled up at her. 'See?'

She drew in a sharp breath and shook her head. 'Please, don't.'

He sat up straight again. 'It's entirely your choice,' he emphasised. If he was ever to make love to her, it had to be on her terms so there was no point pushing her. 'Just think about it, all right? You'll need to trust me.'

Not that there seemed much chance of anything happening between them at the moment. Who knew if they'd even get out of here alive? But at least if he could keep her mind focused on thoughts of lovemaking, she wouldn't think about their incarceration.

She nodded, looking torn, and he decided not to press her further for the moment. There was just one thing left to do.

'Now, I need one more kiss, that's all,' Jamie said. When she leaned forward, he pushed the remaining diamond into her mouth. 'Don't swallow it. That might be dangerous. Go on, place it under your tongue.'

'Mmm-hmm.' It took her a moment to move the stone, but once she had, she was able to speak again. 'That feels awkward.'

'You'll get used to it. And if you find it impossible, I can always take it back. Now then, let's see how tight these bonds are.'

'So you really thought you could outwit me, Miller? I knew you were stupid, but not quite *that* idiotic.'

Mansukh was standing in front of William, glowering at him, while two of his burliest men held onto their prisoner. A third, at a nod from the merchant, punched William in the solar plexus, making him retch painfully.

'I didn't! It was Kinross. He was threatening me. I swear it.'

Another couple of punches, to the jaw and side of the head. William's vision swam and he began to see that he'd been extremely foolish indeed.

'The other foreigner was just a courier. He knew nothing of what he carried, so how could he threaten you? Do you take me for a moron?' Mansukh's cheeks were mottled with anger and his eyes shot sparks of fury.

'No, I was going to tell you, but ...'

'Ah, that must be why you bought passage on board one of that cur Feroz's ships, eh?' Mansukh nodded. 'Oh yes, I know all about that. He talked before we stopped his vocal chords for good.'

William felt physically sick and his knees trembled with fear at the thought of what had happened to Feroz. If his hands had been free, he would have raised them to protect his neck. A neck he'd prefer uncut.

'Now, I want you to tell me exactly where you've hidden the talisman in preparation for your journey. And believe me, you *will* tell me!'

William only wished he could.

* * *

Zar was still shaken by the sensations Jamie had caused without even using his hands. No one had ever touched her breasts other than Francis, and certainly not in a way she enjoyed. *But I liked it!* She had to be honest with herself, even though the thought terrified her. Dear Lord, but what could he do to her if she allowed his hands free rein?

No, that was a step too far.

There was no point thinking about it now, though, as they were trapped here and not likely to be let out. Fear of what Mansukh would do to them gained the upper hand in her mind and she forgot all about lovemaking. 'Is he going to kill us, do you think?' she blurted out. 'Can he get away with that? We're English. Surely, as foreign nationals, he has no right to detain us?'

'Huh?'

She became aware that Jamie was wriggling and jangling the chain behind him. 'What are you doing?'

'Trying to free myself, of course.' He grunted and suddenly she heard the sound of metal clanking down onto the floor. 'There we go, that's one of them.' He grinned, his teeth flashing white in the near-darkness.

'How did you do that?'

He shrugged. 'These irons must have been made for a large man, because they were quite loose on me, and the bones in my hand are very flexible. Remember when I put on your bangles? Not enough to get out of these damned ropes though. They've tied them too tight. But perhaps you can undo the knots if I sit with my back towards you? Let me just free my other hand from the cuff first.'

Zar wondered if she too could free herself, but the heavy shackles around her wrists were very small, perhaps made for a child. What a horrible thought. The only thing she could do would be to help Jamie.

It took her a while, but eventually she managed to undo the knots on Jamie's bonds. He bent to investigate hers. 'Can you get out of these?' he asked.

'No, I don't think so.'

Feeling with his fingers, he checked, but Zar knew it was the truth.

'*Fan också!*' he swore.

'What does that mean? And what language is it?' Zar was curious and realised she still didn't know very much about the man she'd kissed three times now. She really ought to rectify that if she was going to continue to allow him such liberties. Although she wasn't. She shouldn't.

'It's Swedish and you don't want to know the meaning, trust me.' He chuckled. 'Not something a well-brought up young lady should ever say.'

'So why Swedish? That's a country to the far north, isn't it?' Zar had only been to England once and her knowledge of the geography of Europe was very limited.

'Yes, very far. There is snow all winter, deep and numbingly cold. I long for it sometimes when the weather here is at its hottest, like now.' He hesitated, then added, 'It's where my parents live. My father is Scottish, but he moved to Sweden as a young man and then he met and married my mother.'

He seemed reluctant to talk about it, but Zar pressed on. She sensed a mystery and her interest was well and truly piqued. And she'd rather pursue this subject than sit quietly and contemplate their possible fate. 'Tell me about them. Do you have other family? A wife?' The thought had only just occurred to her and sent a sliver of ice into her stomach. Why hadn't she asked before? What a fool.

'No, I'm a widower. I have … a daughter though.'

The admission sounded as if it had been pulled out of

him against his will and Zar didn't understand why. 'Well, that's lovely. Isn't it? How old?'

'Um-hmm. Four and a half.'

He didn't appear to be convinced that having a daughter was a good thing and Zar was about to take him to task, since a man ought to care for his own child, especially one as young as that. Then a thought occurred to her. What if his wife had died giving birth to the baby? Sometimes when that happened, a husband could find it difficult to take to the child, she'd heard.

'I'll tell you about that some other time, but not just now,' Jamie muttered. 'It's complicated.'

That seemed to confirm her assumption, so Zar decided to drop the subject. 'Well, tell me about Sweden at least. How do you survive such cold? I found it hard enough in England. My father took me there once and we arrived in March. The weather was awful and I was chilled to the bone for months! Luckily we left before autumn began.'

Jamie laughed at that. 'You found that unbearable? You'd never survive in Sweden then. Imagine snow drifts up to waist height, icicles hanging from the roofs and every tree branch covered with frost. It's beautiful, but harsh.'

'I can't even begin to picture that.'

'Of course, you wrap up warm. There are garments made of fur, which helps. Hats, gloves, layer upon layer of clothing and hot bricks to put in your sleigh when you travel.'

'Sleigh?'

'A carriage without wheels that glides along the snow. Wheels would only get stuck.'

'I'd like to see that.'

'Would you?'

'Maybe just once. Briefly, before I froze to death.'

That made him chuckle. 'Then perhaps I'll take you one day.' He sighed. 'As for now, I'm afraid we're stuck here.'

He'd been trying to find a way of freeing her while they talked, tugging at her chain, presumably to see if there were any weak links, but it was no use. '*You* don't have to be,' she said. 'Why don't you try and go for help? Surely the English factors would come and rescue me and William if you could but reach them?'

'I would, but there's no way out. The door is locked, so until someone comes, I'll have to wait. Are you sure you wouldn't rather I stayed? If I promise to give up the talisman, I'm sure they'll at least let you go free.'

'No, why would they? I doubt they'll risk anyone knowing about it.' She swallowed hard. 'I think they mean to silence us for good, once they have it.'

Chapter Seventeen

They waited for what must have been hours. Complete darkness fell. All was silent apart from the distant shushing noise of the tide coming in or out on the river, and the *muezzin* calling faithful Mohammedans to prayer. Mohammedan churches, or mosques as they were called, were everywhere in Surat. The larger ones had arched cupolas, while smaller ones only had little turrets. Three or four of them also had minarets, the tall round towers with a walkway at the top from whence these reminders to prayer were issued to believers. Jamie was so used to hearing them now, it was merely a background noise.

At first, Jamie stood by the door, trying to listen for sounds of movement and hoping someone would come so he could overpower them. But as time passed, he went back to sit next to Zar, making her lean her head on his shoulder.

'Try and sleep,' he said. 'I promise I'll wake you if I hear anything.'

'Very well, but you'd better take the diamond back first.'

He did, with a quick kiss, but he didn't linger over it this time as he wanted her to get some rest. To his surprise, she dozed off, and something inside him stirred at the thought that she trusted him, at least when it came to her safety. No one had relied on him for such a long time, it was a strange feeling. But he shouldn't have involved her in this business at all. It was his fault she was down here in this dank cellar in the first place. The thought made him clench his fists. Although really, it was Miller's fault for being so greedy.

He wasn't sure what to do next. Overpowering one or maybe two men as they entered the room would be possible, but how would he escape through the house? And could he really leave Zar behind, not knowing what Mansukh and his men would do to her? He could guess and after what he suspected she'd already been through with her husband, such treatment might rob her of her sanity.

No, I can't leave her. He must find a way out for both of them.

In the end, the decision was taken out of his hands. Some time after midnight, Jamie heard footsteps approaching and implemented the first part of his plan. He shook Zar's shoulder and put a hand over her mouth.

'Someone's coming. Keep quiet,' he breathed and felt her nod. 'And take the diamond, quickly, in case they intend to question me.'

He passed it to her with a light kiss, then got up and positioned himself behind the door. When the first man entered, he knocked him senseless with a punch that landed just above the left ear. A second man, having seen what happened, fought back, but there was someone else behind him carrying a lantern. Mansukh himself.

'Stop or I shoot!' he ordered.

Jamie gave his second adversary a thump in the gut which had him doubling over, then stood tall, facing the *bania*. The man was indeed pointing a pistol at him and although Jamie couldn't be sure it was loaded, he didn't want to take any chances. A dagger he could have handled, but not this.

'Good. I see you are a man of sense.' Mansukh stepped into the room and glanced at Zar. 'Unlike the relative of the lady.'

Zar gasped. 'What have you done to William?' she whispered. Jamie saw her blanch as the light from the lantern illuminated her features.

Mansukh's mouth tightened. 'It's not what I have done, *sahiba*, but what he has done to *me*. He is a fool, thinking he can outwit me.' He scowled at them. 'After some ... persuasion, he told me he would fetch the item he was supposed to pass to me. I sent him on his way with several of my men and he went to your house. He said he knew exactly where you kept it.' He nodded at Jamie. 'But after spending an age in there, he tried to escape by jumping out of a window at the back. Naturally, I had taken precautions and he was caught. He will soon be on his way down river to my ship.'

'He didn't give you the, er ... item?' Jamie knew this couldn't be the case, but had to make sure.

'No, of course not. How could he, when you have it? I did not think he was telling the truth, but I had to make sure.'

Jamie nodded. No point pretending any longer.

'I am tired of playing games,' the merchant barked. 'You will go and fetch it quickly or the lady dies. And if you try to get help from your fellow English, I will make sure there is proof that you killed her, which means the authorities here will execute you instantly. Do you understand?'

'Yes. You swear to me she will be unharmed?'

'You are not in a position to make demands of me, but this I will promise anyway because Mrs Miller has always stayed out of my business and dealt fairly with everyone else. She is a woman of sense.'

The words rang true so Jamie nodded. 'Thank you. After you then.' He indicated that they should leave and threw Zar a reassuring glance. 'I'll be back soon,' he promised her.

The two men Mansukh had brought were on their feet by now and jostled him out the door, one giving Jamie a surreptitious kick, but he ignored them and strode off after the merchant once he was satisfied that Zar had been locked in again. At least they didn't stay with her. He hoped Mansukh would keep his word.

He would be as quick as he could.

'Jamie, Jamie! You good?'

Roshani came hurtling towards him as soon as Jamie entered his house. Kutaro, as usual, followed on her heels, barking with excitement. Luckily Mansukh's men had stayed outside in the street, after telling him to hurry. Jamie bent to pick the little girl up and she wrapped her arms around his neck and hugged him hard.

'I'm fine. Are you? Those men didn't hurt you, did they?'

'No. Priya take me back. She here. But ... *Sahiba* Miller?'

'Zar is all right, but I need to give the bad men something before they will let her go. Come, I need to talk to you first. Quickly.'

He led the way up to his bedroom, bringing a lantern which had been left by the stairs. It was probably best if the men outside thought he was up here fetching the talisman. 'Now sit down, I need you to listen to me.'

He put Roshani on a chair and knelt in front of her. 'The bad men have Zarmina because I have something they want, a jewel. I'm going to give it to them and I hope that will make them release Zarmina. I want you to promise me you will stay with her if I don't come back. I might have to, er ... go on a journey with the bad men. And if Zarmina doesn't come back either, you stay with Priya, understood?'

Roshani nodded, but her lower lip jutted out. 'Want to stay with you.'

'I know, but that may not be possible. We'll see. I just want you to be safe and I will give Priya some money so she can look after you.' He went to get his cane, which he'd left at home earlier, and unscrewed the top, tilting it to make a small pile of gemstones fall into his hand. In his pocket he had a handkerchief and he quickly tied the stones into it with a secure knot. 'See? These are for you and I trust Priya to keep them safe for you.'

The little girl's eyes were huge at the sight of so much wealth, but she didn't contradict him. 'Thank you,' she whispered.

He smiled at her. 'All will be well, but it might take a while.' He wasn't convinced of this himself, but he needed her to believe it for now. 'Now, I need to tell you what to do when a man called Sanjiv comes looking for me. I'm relying on you, understand? Good, then listen ...'

Soon after, he found Priya weeping in the courtyard and reassured her as best he could, before retrieving the talisman from the fountain. 'I must go now. I'll help your mistress, don't fret. Just look after Roshani, please. And tell Kamal what has happened.'

'I promise.' Priya dried her tears.

Jamie walked back into the street and waited for Mansukh's men to surround him. As they walked off into the night, he glanced back at the house and a shiver hissed down his spine.

It might be the last time he saw it.

* * *

Zar sat alone in the darkness, trying in vain to suppress the tremors that coursed through her body at regular intervals. I'm just exhausted and the shock of being abducted is causing me to shiver, she tried to tell herself. But she knew it was terror, pure and simple, that had her in its grip.

She didn't trust Mansukh, no matter what he said. It was reassuring that he thought highly of her and had noticed her policy of not becoming involved in anything he did. But once he had the talisman, how could he possibly stop any of them from telling everyone that he dealt in stolen goods? The answer was that he couldn't and therefore he had to kill them.

After what felt like ages, but was probably no longer than an hour, she heard footsteps and the bar to the door being lifted. She took a deep breath, hoping she could at least show courage as she went to meet her fate, but she couldn't stop her heart from beating so hard she was sure it must be visible through the material of her gown.

One of Mansukh's servants came in and crossed the room. He hunkered down next to her and unlocked the horrible iron cuffs. Although Zar's arms were still behind her, it felt marginally better to be free of at least one of type of bond.

'Is the foreigner back?' she asked the man in Gujarati.

The man only grunted in reply and said, 'Come.' He pulled her to her feet and tugged her along towards the door. Zar knew it was pointless to struggle, so she went with him without demur.

Up in the courtyard, in the pearly light of pre-dawn, she found Mansukh waiting with a group of his men. William stood to one side looking scared and nervous, his face covered in bruises. There was blood trickling out from his nose, and he kept sniffling as if to get rid of it. Like hers, his hands were still bound behind him. Zar sent him an enquiring glance, but he just scowled at her.

She felt anger surge through her. It wasn't as if it was her fault. He'd got himself embroiled in this all by himself. But at the same time she did feel sorry for him. He'd never been very bright and his father should have helped him to learn how to go on, instead of pushing him away in favour of his new wife.

To her relief, Jamie came down the steps from the entrance, escorted by more of the merchant's men. He appeared unruffled and assured, which helped to calm Zar's heartbeat somewhat. His eyes found hers and she thought she saw relief in them at finding her unhurt. *Does he really care?* She told herself it didn't matter. The only person here who should have been concerned for her welfare was William, but it was obvious he was merely looking out for himself.

'You have it?' Mansukh asked as Jamie came to a halt in front of him.

'Yes. Now will you let Mrs Miller go, please?'

Zar noticed he didn't plead, just asked as if he expected a positive reply. For a moment, the merchant seemed to waver, then he shook his head almost regretfully.

'Not yet, I'm sorry. I cannot risk it. You are all coming on a journey with us.'

Jamie's mouth tightened and Zar saw his eyes flash, but he made no comment. Instead he extracted a pouch from inside his waistcoat which he handed over. 'It's a bit wet, but I don't believe it has come to any lasting harm.'

Mansukh opened it, turning away from his men as he did so. Zar caught a glimpse of something that blazed with red fire, then blue. Everyone waited while the *bania* examined the item more closely. The atmosphere was tense and several of the men shuffled nervously. Zar guessed they feared their master's temper and were hoping he'd have no cause to display it.

The merchant nodded his satisfaction and stowed the talisman in his girdle before giving a command to go. Zar guessed that greed or impatience must have made him overcome his superstitions at last or else he would have made someone else carry the jewel. 'To the boats, and be quick about it.' He pointed at Jamie. 'Someone bind him again, now.'

Jamie submitted to this without showing any emotion, then came to walk by her side as they were prodded into motion. 'Are you well?' he whispered.

'Yes, thank you. He kept his word.'

'I had hoped he would leave you out of this now, but I can see his point – it would be too dangerous. We must look for a way to escape later. Perhaps they'll let down their guard when we are out at sea.'

Zar felt her insides tighten at the thought of a sea journey with this band of ruffians, but with Jamie at her side, at least she wasn't entirely alone. Her thoughts were interrupted as William reached them and barged a shoulder into Jamie so that he stumbled slightly and bumped into Zar. 'Stupid bastard,' William snarled. 'If only you'd given it to me as you were supposed to have done, we wouldn't be in this pickle now.'

Jamie rammed him back, sending him into one of the guards, who grabbed William's arm and shook him, while swearing loudly.

'And you shouldn't have tried to play your own little games when you don't have the brains for it,' Jamie retorted.

'Enough!' Mansukh had stopped and turned around. 'We don't have time for this. Men, separate them.'

William was dragged away to walk at the back of the group, while Jamie resisted attempts to part him from Zar. She was grateful for his tenacity, as the guards eventually left him to walk next to her.

Dear Lord, please don't let them take him away when we reach the ship. I don't think I can bear it …

The tide was flowing out towards the sea with its usual noisy, strong current, and the barges they boarded were soon far from a city that was barely awake. Yet another call to prayer could be heard in the distance, the sound echoing across the water, but other than that, all was peaceful.

Zar sat impassive as they floated past densely wooded areas interspersed with cultivated fields and the occasional village. Jamie had made sure he was seated next to her and as there wasn't much space, he'd been squashed up against her by the men flanking them. From time to time he felt her shiver and wished he could do something to make her less afraid, but since he had no idea what fate awaited them, there was nothing he could say.

At the mouth of the river, they followed the coast round to deeper waters and eventually boarded a larger ship. A native craft, it was smaller than the English and Swedish vessels he'd sailed on previously, but it looked fast. Jamie guessed time was indeed of the essence since the monsoons were due to arrive soon and no one wanted to be out at sea once the hurricanes of the season began. Perhaps that was partly why Mansukh had become impatient. In fact, all the European ships had already left – the one Jamie had arrived on being the last to go.

Jamie and Zar were taken to a small cabin below deck, while William was led in the opposite direction. Jamie was glad they didn't have to share with him. The way he felt at the moment, he'd be likely to beat the man senseless the first chance he got.

'You can have your hands free if you give me your word you won't attack any more of my men,' Mansukh said just before they were escorted below. 'If you so much as hurt a hair on their heads, I will take it out on the lady,' he added.

Jamie nodded. 'You have my word.'

It was a relief to be rid of the bonds and Zar sighed with pleasure as she stretched her arms and shoulders. 'Thank the Lord for that,' she murmured. 'I never realised how horrible it is to have your limbs stuck in the same position for any length of time.'

'Here, let me massage them for you,' Jamie offered and put his hands on her shoulders.

She jumped. 'No, I don't think—'

'Zarmina, relax! I swear, I'm only trying to help you.'

She threw him a doubtful look over her shoulder, but subsided, and soon she was leaning into his fingers as he worked the tension out of her cramped muscles. 'Ah, that does feel good.'

'Told you.' He couldn't resist placing a light kiss on one of her cheeks, but refrained from doing more than that. He didn't want to give Mansukh's men any ideas in case they came into the cabin unexpectedly or they'd think Zar was anyone's for the taking. The thought made his stomach tighten. *They're not laying a finger on her, if I can help it.*

After a while they sat down on the bare floor planks, which at least didn't feel as cold and damp as the cellar they'd come from. The cabin was clean though and smelled only vaguely of oriental spices. Zar again leaned her head against Jamie's shoulder and he made her more comfortable by putting an arm round her back.

'Shall we take turns to sleep for a while? I think it's best if one of us stays awake,' he said. 'You go first.'

'But you haven't had any sleep yet, have you?'

He smiled down at her. 'No, but you don't look as though you can keep your eyes open for much longer. I'll be all right.'

'Very well, if you're sure? Thank you.' She added, 'Let me just give you back the diamond,' and took it out of her mouth. 'Here.'

'Thanks.' Jamie put it in his pocket for now.

She was asleep in seconds. Jamie sat still, adjusting to the sensation of holding her again. It felt frighteningly tender, an emotion he'd steered well clear of for the last five years. But somehow with Zar it wasn't quite as bad as he'd thought it would be. She hadn't forced him to protect her, hadn't flirted with him or tried to coerce him into anything. She was the exact opposite of Elisabet.

The thought brought him up short.

He'd believed that Elisabet had soured his opinion of women for the rest of his life. She'd made him unable to trust any female, viewing them all cynically as if they were only out to entrap him for their own gain. Zar had tried to push him away from the very beginning. She was the hunted one, the prey, the one everyone was trying to catch. Just like him. And that changed things.

The anger he'd felt towards Elisabet would never quite go away, he realised that, but perhaps it was possible to put the past behind him and move forward? Dare he put his faith in a woman again? Could he possibly fall in love?

He didn't know and didn't really want to think about it.

Zar had a luscious body and a beautiful face. He wanted her, there was nothing more to it. Who wouldn't? So what if she was courageous and honourable? Those were traits he could admire, but they didn't mean he loved her.

Zar mumbled in her sleep and snuggled closer to him, wrapping one arm around his waist. Jamie felt a surge of something fizzing through his veins, but again put it down to lust. The bodice of her low cut gown gave him a wonderful view from above and he felt a definite pang of desire. But at the same time he just wanted to pull her tight to his side and keep her safe.

He shook his head. Why complicate things? If she let him, perhaps he'd teach her about lovemaking, then she could marry someone else. Someone who could give her what he couldn't – complete trust and love. A man who'd stay in one place for more than a month at a time.

Besides, who knew if they would even live for another day, so there was no sense in contemplating the future. There was only the here and now.

Chapter Eighteen

'I have decided to leave tomorrow. Arrange it, please, Bijal.'

'I beg your pardon, Highness? Tomorrow? Why, the wedding is two months hence!'

Bijal stared at his master and closed his mouth which had fallen open in surprise. He felt a stirring of unease deep inside. He had counted on the Rajah staying put for at least another month before setting off. That way the talisman would be well out of the way before the Rajah and his entourage came anywhere near Surat. Not that they would be heading for that city in any case, as the intended bride lived near Ahmedabad to the north, but it was still too close for comfort. And although it was quite some distance for a cavalcade to travel, it wouldn't take two months, of that he was sure. Damnation.

'I've made up my mind to visit a kinsman at Baroda for a few weeks beforehand. He sent me an invitation as soon as he heard about the nuptials. It might serve to distract me from the constant worries and the grief. You are pursuing your enquiries, I trust?'

'Why, yes, of course.'

'Good. I must have the talisman back, and quickly.'

'I am aware of that, Highness. But to leave so soon? Your entourage ... it will take days – weeks – to organise everyone for travelling and—'

The Rajah held up a hand to stop the Grand Vizier in mid-sentence. 'Bijal, I know you well enough to be perfectly certain that you will have everything arranged in a trice. I am resolved, we leave at dawn. Anyone who is not ready can follow on later.'

Bijal had no choice but to bow his acquiescence, but inside he was seething. *I don't want him anywhere near Surat until the talisman has been sent on its way.* He had a bad feeling about this. A very bad feeling.

But he had to play his role for a while longer.

They were fed some kedgeree – a dish made of boiled rice, some kind of peas or lentils, pieces of cooked fish, butter and cream – towards evening, by which time Jamie had taken a turn at sleeping. Zar felt on edge, but managed to eat. She knew she needed to keep her strength up, just in case they had an opportunity to flee. Although how that was to happen in the middle of the ocean, she had no idea.

'Perhaps we can steal the ship's boat,' Jamie mused. 'There must be one either on board or floating behind us. We don't seem to be moving very fast at the moment, so I'm guessing the winds are contrary, which is good. That means we haven't gone too far from the coast yet.'

'We'd need to get out of this cabin first. How are we going to do that when you promised not to hit anyone?' Although Zar was grateful to have her hands free again, she couldn't help but feel Jamie's oath had been a bit hasty.

He grinned at her now. 'You seriously believe I'll keep my word to a group of abductors?'

'Oh, I see.' She felt her cheeks heat up, but wasn't sure if it was because she felt foolish about believing his words to Mansukh, or because his smile did strange things to her pulse rate. Maybe it was both.

'Don't worry, I'll only use my fists if it proves necessary, and never if there's any chance they could carry out their threat and harm you in return.'

This only vaguely reassured her. After all, how could he be certain?

He changed the subject abruptly. 'So how tight is your bodice?'

'I beg your pardon?' She turned to frown at him. Was he trying to seduce her? Here of all places?

'The diamonds,' he whispered, 'are they still safe?'

'Oh, oh that.' She patted her bodice and felt the small lumps. 'Yes, they're there.'

'And the third one? Want to give it back to me again?' He'd given it to her before he took his turn at sleeping.

She turned away to hide the fact that her cheeks were firing up again. Why did the mere thought of kissing him affect her this way? It was madness! Especially as they no longer needed to pass it from mouth to mouth. 'No, I put it with the rest while you were sleeping.' She glanced at him from under her lashes. 'I didn't want to swallow it and it was becoming uncomfortable. Besides, shouldn't you have asked that *before* we ate? It could have become part of my supper.'

'You're right, I'm sorry.' But his eyes danced with mischief, as if he had read her thoughts just now. 'Or perhaps you just didn't want me to kiss you again.' His grin widened and she found herself thumping him on the arm.

'You wouldn't have had to, now we're not tied up any longer.'

'Ah, but maybe I wanted to?'

'You're impossible. Don't you ever think of anything else?'

He pretended to consider, then shook his head. 'No, not really.'

She thumped him again and he chuckled. It probably hurt her more than him since his arms seemed to be made of corded rock.

'Very well, of course I do,' he said. 'It's just that I'd rather think about kissing you than the fact that we're still imprisoned.'

She'd felt the warmth of his skin through his shirtsleeve and was tempted to touch him some more. Instead she made herself consider his appearance, which was disreputable to say the least. He wasn't wearing a coat, only the shirt and long waistcoat, both of which were dusty and stained with dirt. His neckcloth and breeches were no better and his stockings were more brown than the white they should have been.

'What happened to your coat?' she asked, without thinking.

'Left it at my house. There didn't seem any point in ruining it further and it's so hot I don't know why I was wearing it in the first place. Why, are you cold?'

'No, of course not.' In fact, it was stifling in the little cabin and she wished she'd been wearing Indian clothing instead of the tight English gown. It might be good for concealing diamonds, but it was also restricting her breathing. 'I hate English clothes,' she muttered. 'Why do they have to be so constricting?'

His mouth quirked. 'It's just the fashion. There are more comfortable garments than what you're wearing, you know. And if you want me to help you take anything off, just say the word.'

She threw him a look of exasperation, which was answered by another bone-melting grin. Zar had to look away. *Any moment now, I'm going to make a complete fool of myself.* Damn him. Why did he have to be so attractive? It wasn't fair.

William walked back and forth across the small cabin he'd been shoved into. It had a couple of hard bunks without bedding, but he didn't feel like lying down. He'd tried it at first, but quickly realised it made him feel the motion of the ship much more keenly and his stomach had nearly rebelled. He'd never been a good sailor, which was why he normally left travelling to other people. Standing up helped a little, but it was probably only a question of time before the *mal de mer* struck. He swallowed down bile.

'Bloody hell!' he shouted to no one in particular.

He knew they wouldn't hear him anyway, as the noise from the wind and waves would drown out any sounds from him.

'Damn Mansukh. Damn Kinross. And damn that bitch Zarmina!'

This was all their fault, not his. If his father hadn't taught Zar about business, William would have been able to sell it all without problems. If Kinross had done what he'd been paid to do and handed over the talisman, William could have been on his way to England via Persia with it now. And if that devil Mansukh hadn't had spies everywhere, he'd be none the wiser ...

If, if, if ... But it had all gone wrong. So completely wrong.

What was going to happen to him now? Would he become shark food?

'Then what the hell are they waiting for?' he growled. He'd rather they got it over and done with. The waiting was killing him.

At least it would be over quickly as he couldn't swim. With any luck, he'd drown first, before any of those blasted predators turned up.

But he didn't want to die at all ...

There was one porthole in the little cabin and Jamie

watched as the sun began to disappear beneath the horizon. The sky flamed orange, then turned red, pink and lilac in quick succession. It was a beautiful sight, but also a reminder that time was passing.

Were they going to be thrown overboard soon? What the hell was Mansukh waiting for, deeper water?

Jamie guessed that was the intention, but hoped the *bania* would wait a bit longer. That would give them a chance to try and escape. If not ... No, he wouldn't think about that.

Despite the gusts of wind coming in through the porthole, it was sweltering in the enclosed space and Jamie felt perspiration meandering down his back. He wiped his forehead with his sleeve and tried to think cold thoughts. Oh, for some snow right now. Frost, ice, soft white flakes that melted on your tongue ... But he was as far away from that kind of weather as he could possibly be and now wasn't the time for regrets.

During the night, he tried to open the door, using an old nail that had been sticking out of the woodwork on one side, which he'd managed to prise loose. It didn't work, however, and he had to give up.

'I think there is a stout bar on the other side and I can't lift it with the nail,' he told Zar. 'I could probably break the door down, but that would alert Mansukh's men to what I'm doing so it's pointless.'

No one came to give them any more food and they tried to ration the water they'd been left. Again, they took turns to sleep.

Another morning passed with only one visit from their gaolers. They were given some bread and more water, but nothing else.

'I suppose we have to be grateful they feed us at all,'

Zar grumbled. 'But my stomach is used to several proper meals a day, not just one.'

So was Jamie's, but taking sips of water every so often helped and he thought the fact that they were given any food might be a good sign. If Mansukh was planning on killing them, there wouldn't be any point in feeding his prisoners, so perhaps there was something else in store for them?

Towards midday, Zar was sitting in a corner, leaning against the wall and dozing in the heat, while Jamie paced the floor. He was too restless to relax; he hated inaction and the feeling of being caged in. As he turned for the umpteenth time, a loud explosion suddenly disturbed the peace and the ship shuddered, making Jamie stumble. Zar cried out and got to her feet.

'What was that?' They both rushed to the porthole and looked out.

'Pirates, I think,' Jamie said. 'Let's hope they're ours.'

'What do you mean?' Zar grabbed his arm and her fingers dug into his skin. He put his hand over hers and gave it a reassuring squeeze.

'Just that I hope they're not Maratta – south Indians – but English, or at least European. If so, they might kill Mansukh and his crew. There aren't many of them left in this area now though, but let's pray they're not natives.'

'And will they k-kill us?'

'We'll see.'

They listened for a short while as a cacophony of sounds erupted up on deck and outside their cabin. More shots were fired, the ship taking a few hits, and through the porthole Jamie saw the pirate ship come close enough for its crew to board the merchantman, but he didn't catch a glimpse of the name. From what he could see of its shape, it could be a European vessel, but that didn't necessarily mean its crew was. The Maratta captured and used whatever ships they could.

They listened to the shouting and at last Jamie heard what he'd been hoping for. He smiled at Zar. 'That was English swearing, for certain. Right, time to go, I think.' He went over to the door and gave it a couple of mighty kicks, aiming for the middle where the bar would lie across on the outside. He made quite a ruckus, but he didn't think anyone would notice with everything else going on. The wood began to splinter and after another kick, it gave way. He turned to Zar. 'Go and try to find William and let him out. I'm going to join in the fighting on the pirates' side. Hopefully that will make them favourably disposed towards us. Tell him to do the same.'

He gave her the long nail, which he'd kept in his pocket. 'Take this and if anyone attacks you, jab them in the face with it, preferably the eyes. Hold it between your fingers, like this, so the tip sticks out.' He showed her and Zar nodded, her face white, but determined. 'And come and find me as soon as you can.'

He watched her for a moment as she ran towards the other end of the gun deck, which was empty. It seemed Mansukh and his men had been taken unawares and now it was too late to retaliate with cannon shots. He climbed up the steps to join in the fray.

Emerging up behind one of Mansukh's men, Jamie surprised him and was able to knock him down with a blow to the head. He grabbed the man's weapons – not a moment too soon – as another crew member came hurtling towards him. While fighting this one off, Jamie scanned the deck and noted that he'd been right – the pirates were mostly Europeans, or at least not Asians of any kind. A motley crew, some very ragged, led by a man dressed in a crimson silk coat, they all had the look of desperate men who thought nothing of killing to gain what they were after. Jamie didn't know if Mansukh had a cargo other than his captives and the jewel, but hoped so. He didn't want to imagine what would happen should the pirates have to leave empty-handed.

Zar found to her relief that the lower decks were empty and no one was on guard outside the cabins at the other end.

'William? Are you there?' she called out and he answered immediately from the left hand one.

'In here. What's going on?'

She lifted the bar and pushed the door open as fast as she could. 'Pirate attack. You need to come and fight.'

'Fight? Have you gone mad? Untie me, please.'

He looked rough, his face still bruised and dirty, and his eyes were bloodshot as if he hadn't slept much. His hands were still bound, albeit in front of him and not behind. Zar made quick work of the knots and he breathed a sigh of relief when the bonds fell off.

'Jamie's gone up on deck to assist the pirates,' Zar told him. 'He says they might be English so perhaps they'll help us if we help them. It's our only chance and—'

'Not me!' Pushing past her, William headed for the steps leading to the back of the main deck. 'I'm leaving while they're all busy battling each other. No one will notice me taking the ship's boat.'

'But Jamie said—'

'I don't give a fig what bloody Jamie said! And since when are you on first name terms? Had a good night, did you?' William sneered.

'It's not like that, he—'

'Spare me the details. I need to leave. Now.'

'We can't leave without Jamie.' Zar stood her ground and tried to block his way.

'We? Why would I take you with me? I'll be glad to be rid of you. Besides, from what I've seen of him, Kinross can take care of himself. You should be more concerned about your own skin, being the only woman on a ship full of men!' He shoved her roughly to one side, making her stumble.

Zar righted herself and watched in disbelief as he rushed off towards the hatch. 'William, for heaven's sake …' He couldn't mean to leave her here, surely? And Jamie as well?

'I hope you end up as a pirate's doxy.' He laughed and climbed the steps without looking back.

She clenched her fists, fury surging through her. 'Just you wait, William, just you wait!' she shouted after him, but he'd disappeared and she didn't think there was any point in following him. She could only hope he got caught trying to steal the boat, then maybe he'd be thrown over board. *Serve him right, the little whoreson.*

It didn't help her own predicament though. As he'd said, she was the only woman on a ship full of dangerous men. There was only one person who could help her now, but he was one against many. Jamie may be strong and good at fighting, but could he keep her safe? She had to hope his plan of helping the pirates would pay off. It was their only chance.

Zar ran to the steps at the other end and climbed up to peek out at the chaos. She flinched at the gory sights before her and had to swallow hard to keep the contents of her stomach down. There were mutilated bodies, blood everywhere and even severed body parts, but she concentrated on finding Jamie in the melee. Where was he? Finally she spotted him, but he was over on the other side of the deck, fighting off a fierce little man in a yellow turban.

'Aha!' One of Mansukh's men appeared next to Zar and charged at her with a dagger. She sidestepped at the last second and turned to slash out at his arm with the nail in her hand, the way Jamie had shown her. The man dropped his weapon, bellowing with rage and – she hoped – pain. With a furious expression, he careered towards her again and managed to grab her arms so she couldn't hurt him again. Zar tried to free herself from his grip, twisting her arms and kicking at his shins, but he was much stronger than her.

No! He's going to kill me … Fighting down the rising panic, she tried to think of something to do and suddenly remembered Jamie's lesson after Richardson's attack. Without hesitation, she bent her head at an angle and quickly bashed her forehead into the man's nose. It hurt, but hopefully his pain was greater as she thought she heard bone crunching, but couldn't be sure. It had the desired effect though. Her assailant let go of her and stumbled backwards, only to fall foul of a pirate who stuck a dagger into his back.

Zar took a couple of deep breaths to quell her revulsion as the man's blood spilled out beneath him on the planks. The pirate flashed her a grin, which showed the blackened stumps of his teeth, but thankfully another of Mansukh's men soon distracted him and she was forgotten for the moment. Feeling very vulnerable, she picked up the dead man's *tulwar* and scanned the deck to see where Jamie was now. When she caught sight of him, he seemed to have beaten off his opponents, at least temporarily, and was headed towards her. Along the way, he bumped shoulder first into Mansukh, who was busy with a wicked-looking curved sword. It seemed almost as if Jamie had gone out of his way to trip over the merchant, which puzzled Zar, but there was no time to think about it.

'Are you all right? Did anyone hurt you?' He checked her from top to toe with a frown.

'No, not really.'

'Then please, go back below deck and stay down for now,' Jamie said. 'I'll try to make sure no one goes down there from here at least. Keep an eye out and let me know if anyone comes down the other steps.'

'No, I'm not going anywhere without you. Stay next to me, please!'

'Zarmina …' he began, a warning in his voice, but there was no time for more as they were soon attacked again.

Zar had never fought with a sword of any kind before, but she soon found that the *tulwar* was extremely sharp and she was able to inflict quite a lot of damage whenever she managed to slash at someone. She had to hold it with both hands, as it was heavy, but sheer determination and terror gave her added strength. From time to time she glanced at Jamie, fighting alongside her, and tried to copy his moves. Mansukh's men hesitated when confronted with her, as if they'd never battled against a female before, and this gave her a much-needed advantage.

It wasn't long before she felt she couldn't hold out much longer, however, and she began to wonder if it wouldn't be better to do as Jamie had asked and retreat below deck. Then she heard Mansukh's voice bellowing, '*Stop! Wait!*' Strangely enough, everyone halted in their tracks, like some macabre tableau, and all eyes turned towards the merchant.

'I have something of infinite value,' he shouted. 'I will give it to you if you leave our ship alone.' Seeing that no one moved, he put a hand inside his sash. Zar assumed he was going to hand over the talisman and thanked the gods that at least it wasn't the real one. But something was wrong. Mansukh's hand fumbled around in the makeshift pouch while his expression turned into a massive scowl. Frustration, anger, then near panic showed in his eyes, and eventually he looked up and fixed his gaze on Jamie. 'You!' He pointed his sword at him and let out a cry of rage. 'Where is it?'

Everyone turned to look at Jamie instead, but he just shrugged. 'I've no idea what he's talking about.'

The pirate captain had had enough. 'So you've lost this valuable something?' He glanced at his men. 'Then what are we waiting for? *Charge!*'

The fighting started up again, as if it had never stopped. Zar badly needed a break and ducked below for a while. As she peered out of the hatch though, she saw Mansukh heading straight for Jamie, his face a mask of fury. She hoped Jamie could fend the man off.

What had happened to the talisman? Mansukh must have dropped it during the fighting.

The merchant never reached Jamie, as he was intercepted by someone else. Zar lost sight of him after a while and concentrated on Jamie instead. She watched and waited, while time dragged on. If her fingers had been cleaner, she would have chewed her nails, her nerves ragged with worrying about the uncertainty of their fate. Once she'd regained her breath and felt ready to join the fray again, she went back on deck, but just then it seemed it was all over. A great cheer went up and as it sounded like 'huzzah!' she assumed that meant the pirates had been victorious.

'Zar! Over here.'

Jamie's voice was exactly what she needed to hear and when he reached out a hand to her, she rushed over to him. There was still chaos on deck, with the pirates now swarming down towards the hold and cabins, so Jamie moved over to the railing and guided her to stand slightly behind him. She noticed he kept hold of her hand, while with the other he gripped a bloodied sword. Taking more deep breaths, she steeled herself to face whatever was to come next.

The stench of unwashed bodies hung over the ship and she could almost taste the blood that had been spilled as the smell of it floated through the air. She'd never witnessed such violence before and had to swallow hard many times in order not to be sick. She couldn't believe she'd actually taken part in a fight, wounding and perhaps even maiming people. At least she hadn't killed anyone, which was a relief.

She gripped Jamie's hand as hard as she could. He was her only rock in a very stormy sea.

Chapter Nineteen

Jamie stood still and waited. He knew the crimson-coated pirate captain had noticed him during the fight, but the man hadn't said anything, only thrown him a curious look. Now he came to look them over.

'You English?' he asked, his eyes gliding over Zar, who shrank back further behind Jamie.

'Scottish. My wife and I were taken captive by these natives – no idea why – but when I heard you, I kicked the door down and came to help you best them.'

The pirate nodded. 'I noticed.' He regarded them for a moment with narrowed eyes. 'We don't usually attack our own kind and as you've done us a favour, I s'pose I owe you. Want to join us? Plenty of booty to go round in these here waters. And we've a comfortable hideaway in Madagascar.'

Jamie bowed to show he was grateful for the offer. 'Thank you. If it was just me, that would be very tempting, but ...' He nodded towards Zar. 'I'm sure you'll understand if I'd rather not share my wife with all and sundry. Haven't tired of her yet.' He grinned and winked at the man. 'Newlyweds, you know. A rather memorable honeymoon, you could say.'

The pirate guffawed, his face splitting into a somewhat toothless grin. 'Yeah, I see what you mean. Nice little filly.' He eyed Zar again and Jamie surreptitiously tightened his hold on his sword. He didn't trust this man an inch, for all that he was behaving civilly at the moment.

The captain screwed up his face, as if deep in thought, then shrugged. 'I can let you go since you helped us out, but my men'll expect the lady to stay. Unless you have something to offer as ransom for her?'

Jamie gritted his teeth. He'd expected as much. Zar was too beautiful and could probably be sold at great profit as a slave girl or some such. The thought made his blood boil, but he tried to stay outwardly calm and shook his head.

'Not with me, no. You'll appreciate these brigands robbed us already. However, what about a fair fight? Me against any one of your men, fists only – winner takes the lady.'

Jamie heard Zar gasp behind him, but pretended he hadn't noticed. He couldn't be sure the captain would honour such a deal, but it tallied with the sort of code these men lived by so it just might work. If the worst came to the worst, however, he had an ace up his sleeve.

The captain nodded, an even bigger grin spreading over his features. 'I like that, but we do things by vote so let me put it to my men.'

The pirate did so and after some deliberation, a unanimous decision of 'aye, cap'n!' seemed to be reached.

'If you can best Jonah, the lady is free to leave with you.'

Jamie nodded and handed Zar the sword he was still holding. She took it reluctantly and stared up at him, her eyes huge green pools of worry. Quickly, he bent to kiss her hard on the mouth and whispered, 'Have faith.'

Zar felt faint and the sword was extraordinarily heavy in her hand, even heavier than the one she'd used earlier which she'd put down now. *What in the name of all the gods is he thinking?* This would never work.

'Have faith,' he'd said. Did that mean he knew

something she didn't? Or was he just confident in his own abilities?

She leaned against the railing as she needed something to support her shaking legs. Things didn't improve when she saw who Jamie was to fight – an enormous man with a neck like a bullock and arms as thick as small tree trunks. *Jonah!* As in Jonah and the whale? But this *was* the whale. It was going to be a disaster and Zar had seen the way the pirate captain had eyed her up. He'd had no intention of losing the deal, she was sure …

Jamie looked calm, but Zar could hardly bear to even peek as he and the big man began to circle each other. Everyone else had formed a ring around them and she was happy to stay on the outside, hopefully forgotten, at least for the moment. It meant she couldn't see very well what was happening, but she wasn't sure she wanted to in any case. Jamie beaten to a bloody pulp, screaming in agony, lying on the deck in a lifeless heap … Her mind supplied more than enough images, all of which she tried to suppress.

And then there was her own fate. She had no trouble imagining that either. Hordes of men – dirty, disgusting men – all touching her, using her, until … She shook her head. No, she wouldn't let them lay so much as a finger on her. She'd rather jump overboard.

As for this fight, she simply had to watch.

She caught hold of some ropes and climbed up to stand on the railing, carefully not peeking at the water, which seemed very far below. Just then, Jonah charged forward and swung a meaty fist towards Jamie's head. Jamie moved out of the way and seemed to somehow use Jonah's momentum to unbalance him, sending him sprawling onto the deck with a tackle to one shoulder.

A huge roar went up from the onlookers and suddenly there were shouts of encouragement for both sides as they realised perhaps the fight wouldn't be as one-sided as they'd thought.

They were all mad. Zar guessed these men lived by fighting and the only way to gain their respect was to act like them. Jamie must have known this, but could he keep Jonah at bay for any length of time?

The big man got to his feet and to his credit, Jamie waited and didn't kick him while he was down. He went in close and threw a couple of punches at Jonah's middle, which seemingly had no effect whatsoever. Then the big man landed a blow to Jamie's chin, which sent him staggering backwards. Zar closed her mouth tightly to stifle the scream that rose in her throat. *No!* Please, no …

Jamie shook himself like a dog and began to dance around Jonah, punching wherever and whenever he could and taking a few more hits, although none as bad as that first one. The crowd was raucous in the extreme, egging on the two fighting men, and Zar saw coins change hands as they were obviously betting on the outcome. She clung to the ropes with a trembling hand, the sword still held in a death-grip with the other.

Sweat was pouring down Jonah's face and when Jamie managed to punch him on the temple he blinked as if confused. His movements became slower and more erratic, while Jamie kept up a shower of smaller blows, mixed in with the occasional hard one to the head.

He'd done this before. Zar realised Jamie must have been trained in fisticuffs, although why she had no idea. He hadn't seemed like the brawling kind, but then did she really know him that well?

She almost laughed when Jamie practised what he'd

preached and head-butted Jonah on the nose, catching the big man off guard. With blood flowing freely down over his mouth and chin, Jonah blinked. Jamie took advantage of his momentary lapse in concentration and landed two swift blows – one to the temple again and one under Jonah's chin. The last punch felled the huge man like an ox at slaughter and he lay still on the deck.

A massive cheer went up from the onlookers and Zar wanted to join in, but couldn't find her voice. She was frozen into immobility, unable to move so much as a muscle, and hung onto the ropes for dear life. Was this it? Would they really let them go? Or had they just been toying with them, wanting some sport to liven up the day?

She very much feared the latter.

Jamie felt sore all over and one eye was half shut where it was swelling up, but he tried his best not to show any weakness as he slowly made his way through the circle of pirates to join Zar. She looked stunned and was standing up on the ship's railing, holding onto some ropes. He guessed she was extremely shaken by everything that had happened this day, and the one before, and probably unable to move of her own accord. He reached up and gently disentangled her hand, then lifted her down to stand beside him. Just in case she felt faint, he put an arm round her waist to prop her up, and felt her trembling.

There was no time to reassure her though. The pirate captain had followed him and Jamie looked at the man, wondering what would happen now.

'Excellent bout,' was his comment on the fight. 'Poor Jonah won't live that down for a while.' He chuckled, then his expression turned serious. 'Well, fair is fair and I did promise you and the wife your freedom. Best I can do is set you afloat in the ship's boat, but you'd better hurry before everyone's good mood disappears and they change their minds. There's no saying what they'll do when they're in a celebratory mood.'

Relief flooded Jamie, but he knew the captain was right and they shouldn't hang about. He felt Zar tug on his hand and bent down so she could whisper in his ear, 'William's taken the boat and left already.'

He swore under his breath. 'Thank you, captain, but there appears to be a problem. The ship's boat belonging to this vessel has already been appropriated by a coward who slipped away earlier, or so my wife tells me.'

'Ah, I see.' The captain used the tip of his sword to scratch at his scalp. 'Well, there's our boat, but we need it ourselves.'

'I can pay you a little something towards the cost of a new one,' Jamie said. 'And seeing as how you'll probably find one for free,' he said with a grin to show he meant the word 'find' to be a euphemism, 'that will be pure profit for you. One moment, please.' He turned to Zar. 'Have you still got that item I asked you to hide earlier, my love?'

He saw that she caught his meaning and after turning around for a moment, handed him one of the diamonds from inside her bodice.

Jamie held it out to the pirate. 'Will this do? I'm not sure of its value, but it looks fairly big to me. I got it off an Indian trader a while back and was going to have it set for the wife, but ...' He tried to keep his expression neutral so the captain didn't guess that he knew exactly how much it was worth. He needn't have worried – the man's eyes lit up at the sight of the little treasure and he held it up to the light when Jamie handed it over.

'Yes, I reckon that'll do nicely. Thought you said

as how you didn't have anything to barter with? You could've saved yourself the fight with Jonah if you'd told me about this earlier. Anythin' else you're not telling me?'

Jamie shook his head. 'No, I was hoping to save that for my wife, that's all. You know what women are like with baubles. It'll fair break her heart to lose this.' He tried to look downcast and saw that Zar followed suit. Good girl.

The captain threw him a considering look, then nodded as if satisfied that Jamie was telling the truth. 'Yeah, but needs must, eh?' He shouted to one of his men. 'Oy, Jonesy, go get the *Reckless*'s boat for this gentleman here. And be quick about it.'

'What?'

Jonesy got a clip round the ear while the captain repeated his order. 'Now, man!'

Not long afterwards Jamie and Zar climbed down a rope ladder while Jonesy held the smaller craft steady. Zar went first and Jamie clenched his jaw when he noticed the pirate looking up her skirts as she descended. But after the clout he'd received earlier, the man didn't do more than get an eyeful, and soon clambered back up to the main deck. Jamie wasted no time. After thanking the pirate captain, he made his way down and took the oars of the smaller boat. It was fairly heavy for just one man, but he could manage. He breathed a sigh of relief as soon as he'd put some distance between them and Mansukh's former ship. It was his guess it would soon either be torched or sailed to Madagascar.

Good riddance.

As for Mansukh and his crew, they were either dead or taken captive and right now Jamie didn't have the energy to care.

* * *

Zar sat at the back of the boat and stared out across the sea, which thankfully wasn't too agitated at the moment. She bit her lip to stop tears from spilling down her cheeks. For some reason, now the danger appeared to be over, she felt like crying and her legs wouldn't stop shaking.

'Are you all right?'

Jamie's voice, soft with kindness, made her want to cry even more, but she swallowed hard and took a deep breath before looking at him. She tried to smile, but it was probably a rather wobbly effort. 'Yes. Or I will be soon. I just … Do you want help with the rowing?'

He gave her a lopsided smile. 'Thank you, but no. We'd probably end up going in a circle if I let you have one oar.'

That made her giggle, as he'd probably intended, and she blinked away the last of the moisture in her eyes. 'I'm sure you're right. What about you – are you hurting? You must be!'

He looked like he'd been trampled by an elephant, or in this case perhaps more aptly, rammed by a whale. His poor face was bruised and battered, one eye almost swollen shut. 'Would you like me to bathe your face in salt water?'

'Perhaps later. I'd rather put some distance between us and the pirates first. I don't trust them an inch.'

Zar didn't either and she was having a hard time believing they'd got away from them. 'Why did they let us go? That man could easily have taken the diamond and still kept us prisoner or killed us.'

'I think they live by their own code of honour, which as far as I've heard, includes not harming fellow Europeans unless they fight back. The natives they consider as scum and I've been told some hair-raising tales of what's been done even to women passengers, but with our ships they just take the cargo.'

'I see. Lucky for us then.' She frowned as she remembered something else. 'What happened with Mansukh by the way? I can't believe he lost the talisman, or rather, the fake one.'

Jamie grinned. 'He didn't exactly *lose* it.' He stopped rowing for a moment and reached inside his shirt, bringing out the bundle she'd last seen in Mansukh's courtyard. Zar gaped at him.

'How did you ...?'

His eyes twinkled. 'I have a friend whose father used to be a pickpocket. He taught me a thing or two. It's not a profession I normally follow, but the knowledge has its uses. The trick is to bump into your victim so that they're not paying attention to anything else you're doing, and at the same time slip your hand into their pocket, quick as a flash. It takes practice, but if you're young and bored with nothing better to do ...'

'You're friends with a pickpocket?' Now why didn't that surprise her?

'No, his son. The former thief is more like an honorary uncle.'

Zar was confused, but decided it was probably better not to know. 'So we have it back, that's wonderful!'

'Indeed.' He threw the little parcel to her. 'Perhaps you'd like to stow it somewhere safe? I think your bodice is tighter than my shirt.'

'Jamie!' The look that accompanied his words made her cheeks catch fire, but she knew what he said was true, so she pushed the package down to join the remaining two diamonds, which still nestled somewhere inside her clothing. It wasn't massively comfortable, but if they should happen to be thrown into the water, she reckoned it might still be safe. As long as they didn't drown or get eaten ...

She returned her gaze to the endless ocean. 'And do ... do you think we can reach the coast in this little boat?' She felt her insides churn with anxiety at the thought of just how tiny it was compared to the hundreds of fathoms of sea that lay beneath and around them.

'Yes,' he replied firmly. 'I'm keeping an eye on the sun so that we're heading east. We hadn't been sailing for that long, so it can't be too far. A couple of days at most. You might want to tear off a piece of your chemise to cover your head though. The sun will burn out here. Or pull up the back of your gown to act as a sun shield?' He stopped rowing for a moment and tugged his shirt out of his breeches. 'Come to think of it, I'd better cover up too.' He ripped a large piece off the bottom of his shirt and tied it round his head as a makeshift turban. He looked so funny, Zar had to laugh.

'Go on, your turn. You'll probably look like a fishwife,' he teased, sending her a pretend glare while he picked up the oars again.

She copied him, pulling a large chunk of material from the edge of her chemise with her teeth, then tied the cotton material at the nape of her neck. 'There, happy now?'

He smiled and nodded, but there was a glint of something in his eyes and his voice sounded quite husky as he told her, 'I was wrong. You look lovely.'

Zar felt her cheeks become suffused with heat and looked down. 'I doubt it very much,' she murmured. 'I feel disgustingly dirty.'

'We can have a swim once we reach shore. It looks inviting, doesn't it?'

'Not here it doesn't, but perhaps closer to land.' She shuddered at the thought of the many sea creatures that must be swimming beneath them, including the dreaded sharks.

They fell silent and Zar realised it was probably a good idea not to talk too much. They didn't have any water and using your voice made you more thirsty.

She prayed to all the gods she could think of to help them get to the coast safely. But how long would it take?

Chapter Twenty

Jamie rowed on and off for a day and a night. His arm muscles were screaming in protest and his palms were raw with blisters, but he pulled off his neckcloth and tore it in half to bandage his hands. Then he just gritted his teeth and got on with the task. *It's either this or die and what's a couple of sore hands compared to certain death?*

The sea remained relatively calm at first, apart from a couple of minor squalls accompanied by rain showers. These came and went quickly. Too quickly, as they only managed to collect a tiny amount of rainwater in a scoop they found in the boat. This helped quench their thirst for an instant, but no more.

'The monsoon is on its way,' Zar said, peering anxiously at the sky where dirty clouds were gathering. 'We always get these little bursts of rain before the main downpour begins.'

'Let's hope they stay light until we reach land,' Jamie replied. If the waves became too high, he wouldn't be able to make much progress.

Unfortunately, his wish wasn't granted. On the second day, the wind picked up considerably and the waves around them became more like hills that had to be climbed and then descended. Jamie tried his best to keep rowing, but soon he became confused about the direction since the waves tossed them this way and that. Every time he thought he'd corrected their course, they were thrown off it again and he couldn't see the sun in any case, so had nothing to aim for except what he thought seemed like a marginally brighter part of the sky. It was maddening.

'Jamie? Can you see where you're going?' He heard the anxiety in Zar's voice and tried to soothe her, despite his own worry over their situation.

'Not just now, but as soon as this calms down, I will. Can you swim?'

'Yes, but I've never tried any long distances.'

'No matter. If we capsize, we can always hold onto the boat.'

Jamie knew that even if she'd been a great swimmer, it probably wouldn't do any good in the middle of the ocean. And holding onto a boat in weather like this could be difficult, to say the least. No point telling her that though.

He continued to try and guide the little craft over the crest of the waves, but it was an uphill struggle, literally. They were soon soaked with spray from the white tips and a particularly large wave jolted them sharply. Zar gasped.

'Hang onto something,' Jamie shouted. 'Or even better, come and sit here with me.'

He made room for her next to him and held out his hand towards her. She stretched out her own hand and as she started to stand up he called out a warning. 'No, don't st—'

But she'd already risen and just as he was about to grab her fingers, another massive wave hit the side of the boat, making her lose her footing. Zar stumbled, then fell overboard with another scream before he could stop her. Jamie stared at the water as she disappeared beneath the surface, frozen in horror at first, but then his limbs were galvanized into action. He had to save her.

'*Zarmina*!'

He hung over the side, frantically looking for her, but

when she appeared, she was too far away for him to reach her. Then she was sucked under again. 'Noooo!' Grabbing the oars, he rowed hard to try and keep the boat near the spot where he'd last seen her and to his relief, he saw her head come up once more, her arms splashing. 'Zar, over here! Keep afloat, I'm coming!' he bellowed. He wasn't sure if she heard his words, but she turned her head towards the sound of his voice at least, and seemed to be fighting to stay above water.

The next few minutes were the longest of Jamie's life as he battled to push the boat close to her. Several times he lost sight of her and was afraid she'd slipped under the surface, dragged down by her heavy skirts, but to his relief, she came up repeatedly. Finally, when he thought for sure he was going to lose her because he simply didn't have the strength left to fight the waves any more, her head suddenly appeared right next to where he was sitting and her arms flailed above the edge. He let go of the oars and threw himself sideways, grabbing hold of one of her hands.

'I've got you!'

Relief swept through him, but her fingers were wet and slippery and he almost lost his grip. Fighting down the rising panic, he quickly caught hold of her wrist with his other hand and hung on for dear life, then tried to haul her upwards. 'Can you grab the side of the boat? Come on, help me out, Zar,' he urged.

He could see that she was in shock and near exhaustion, but she nodded and tried to do as he asked. Once he was sure she had a firm grip on the side, he leaned over and put his hands under her armpits, heaving her back into the boat where she landed in a sodden heap on the bottom, coughing and spluttering. The boat rocked dangerously, but a rogue wave helped them for once by pushing in the other direction and saved them from overturning.

'Zar! Zarmina? Talk to me. Did you swallow much water?'

She shook her head. 'Yes. No. Maybe, just … a little.'

'Good. Come here. Shhh, it's all right now. You're safe. You're fine.' Jamie sank down onto the bottom of the boat and sat next to her, pulling her close. They were both trembling with exertion and fear, but they were alive, at least for now.

He made sure the oars were inside the boat so they couldn't fall out, then bent his head to lean it against Zar's. He closed his eyes and let the waves take them where they wanted to. There was no way of steering at the moment. Where they went from here was in God's hands, but at least Zarmina was alive.

He thanked the Lord for that.

William whimpered, almost out of his mind with fear, as he watched one huge wave after another rising above and around him.

He was going to die, he was sure of it.

Was this his punishment for leaving Zar behind? Was God angry with him? But she'd deserved it, the stupid conniving woman, and she wasn't his responsibility. Not really. She'd brought it all on herself by acting so wilfully.

She should have married Richardson, then she wouldn't be in a fix now.

Still, the thought of her alone with the pirates or Mansukh's men, whichever group triumphed, sent a frisson of guilt through him.

'Badly done, son, badly done,' he almost heard his father's voice admonishing him.

Nothing he could do about it now though. And she had Kinross to fight her corner. That left a sour taste in his mouth as well, the way she'd spoken of the man as if he was their saviour, a knight in shining armour. *Hah!* William had saved himself, he didn't need the infuriating Scotsman.

Or so he'd thought.

He huddled low inside the boat, desperately seeking shelter underneath the seat at the stern, but the foamy water still reached him. He could taste it on his tongue, smell it, feel it oozing over his skin. His eyes stung, partly from tears of terror, but mostly from sea water. The storm had been raging for hours and he'd lost his oars. Trying to hide from the sight of all the water, he lay down and closed his eyes tightly, wrapping his arms around his head. That way he didn't have to look at the horror all about him. But in his mind's eye, he continued to see the waves coming towards the boat, rolling over him, drowning him …

Eventually, he fell asleep from sheer exhaustion, and when he woke up, he thought he really had died and gone to heaven. All was calm, blessed peace. Tiny waves lapped against the sides of the boat, but none rose up above him. Best of all, the sun was shining in a mostly blue sky.

And then he heard a shout.

Confused, he sat up and looked across the water where he spied a ship. It looked like a fishing vessel, but although it was small and somewhat bedraggled, he thought it was the most beautiful sight he'd seen in his life. He waved his arms and saw answering gestures from the crew, then the ship slowly turned towards him.

They were coming to pick him up. He was safe.

* * *

Sometime towards dawn, the waves and the wind died down at last and Jamie breathed a sigh of relief. He'd been sitting on the bottom of the boat with his back leaning on the seat and Zarmina in front of him, slumped within his arms. They were both wet through, but luckily it wasn't too cold and by huddling down in this way they were spared the worst of the wind. It was still extremely uncomfortable though and a couple of times he'd had to bail out the water that kept filling up the inside of the boat as well. It was one thing being squelching wet, they didn't need to sit in a puddle too.

'Zar? Are you awake?' He whispered the words, just in case she'd managed to doze off.

'Yes. I think so.'

He smiled at that. 'If you're talking to me, I'd say you are. Listen, I think the sun will be rising soon and then we'll be able to steer a course towards land again.'

He didn't add that it might be a hopeless endeavour, as he had no idea how far out into the ocean the storm had pushed them. They had to try, at least, and hope for the best. The alternative didn't bear thinking of.

'Good. Maybe we'll dry out a bit.' She shivered. 'I'm so wet. I must look like a drowned rat. I certainly feel like one.' Her skirts were spread out around their legs, heavy with brine.

'The most beautiful rat I've ever seen,' Jamie murmured, for although her hair hung in sodden tangles, her face was as lovely as ever, if a bit paler than normal.

She sent him a look of disbelief over her shoulder. 'You've got sea water in your brain, or possibly your eyes.'

'I wouldn't be surprised,' Jamie agreed. 'Once the sun is up, we'll have to remove our clothes one by one and wring them out, then try to dry them. I have no idea how you managed to stay afloat with all that material weighing you down. You must be a stronger swimmer than you thought.'

He felt her shudder once more, the memory of her terror obviously still fresh in her mind. 'Yes. It was as though they were alive, trying to pull me under,' she murmured. 'I'd almost given up ...'

'Don't think about it now. You're safe.' He tightened his grip round her torso and hugged her close. He didn't want to think about it either. He'd come so near to losing her and he knew now he didn't want that. He ... cared about her. His mind stuttered over the unfamiliar feeling and he quickly turned his thoughts to more practical matters.

'Did you lose the fake talisman or is it still there?'

Zar patted her bodice. 'It's there, as are the diamonds I think. Amazing that they didn't fall out!'

'Yes. I guess it was a good thing for once that you're laced up so tightly. Never mind, we'll get you out of that soon.'

'I'm sure the clothes will dry even without us taking them off,' she said, a slightly prim note creeping in.

'You're not seriously going coy on me now, after all we've been through?'

'Well, I'm not going to sit naked in front of you, if that's what you think.' She sounded cross now and he shook his head behind her back. Honestly, she was such a contradiction – shy one minute and courageous the next.

'I swear, I'll keep my eyes closed. Or you can blindfold me if you want, but you're not sitting around in wet clothes all day.'

'We'll see.'

In the end, they compromised. He took off his shirt and waistcoat first, while she removed her gown. Once these garments were dry, Zar made him turn around while she took off her chemise and petticoat, then put his shirt on instead, together with her now very stiff gown. Once her chemise had dried in turn, they swapped back again so he could take off his breeches. He tucked the shirt securely underneath him, but it made him smile to see her attempting not to look at his legs.

A bubble of laughter rose up within him, despite the predicament they were in. Perhaps it was time for some teasing, to take their mind off things …

'Sorry they're a bit hairy.'

'What?' Zar's eyes flew to Jamie's, then down to his legs, before she turned away again. She'd not wanted to look at his naked limbs, but it was difficult to resist. Hair or no hair, he was beautifully made. And as for his upper body, which had been on display for hours earlier while he lent her his shirt … well, words failed her.

He was a veritable god. No, that was probably blasphemy, but he was definitely shaped like one. Tanned an even, golden colour, his skin had gleamed in the sunlight which played across the muscles working underneath. Rowing made his biceps and shoulders bunch up, then relax in the most amazing way, and his taut stomach had flashed in and out of her vision as he bent to his task. It was incredibly distracting.

She'd had no idea a man's body could be so fascinating.

'My legs,' he said, bringing her thoughts back to the present. 'Not a pretty sight, are they.' He made a face.

'I wouldn't say that.' She felt herself blush. 'I mean, I

understood all men to have hairy limbs. That is to say … really, why are we discussing this?'

Jamie chuckled. 'Just passing the time. We could discuss yours instead, if you prefer? They're much daintier than mine. Very shapely, in fact.'

She sent him a glare. 'You promised you wouldn't look. I should have blindfolded you after all.'

'Then you would have had to navigate. It's a bit difficult to see the sun with your eyes closed.'

'I took my turn at rowing.'

'So you did. With your lovely legs.' He smiled and she wanted to get up and box his ears, but knew she'd never again stand up in a boat. It was too risky.

'Can we change the subject please?' she almost growled at him. 'I don't want to discuss body parts.'

'Ah, perhaps you'd rather touch them? I don't mind. Feel free. I could do with a back massage actually. I'm cramping up.'

'No!' She tried to suppress her outrage. 'No, thank you. I have no wish to do any such thing.' Then guilt flooded her. He was, after all, doing all the work. Or most of it anyway. 'Do you really need your back rubbed?' she asked. She wasn't sure if he was still teasing or genuinely hurting.

He grinned. 'Maybe later. I'll let you off for now.'

Zar was annoyed to feel disappointment well up inside her. Damn him, he was right – she'd wanted to touch him.

For a while she sat in silence, just staring at the water flowing past as Jamie rowed. Each time he dipped an oar into the water and pushed, a small whirlpool was created which made its way past her. She watched these in fascination, sometimes turning her head to follow their progress behind them. It became mesmerising, almost soporific, and she was in a near trance when something jolted her out of it and she sat up straight, swallowing a gasp.

'Jamie? *Jamie!* Is that what I think it is?' she hissed.

'What?' He looked up and craned his neck to see what she was pointing at. 'Ah. Yes. Hell and damnation!'

A triangular fin had appeared not far behind them and seemed to be heading their way. Zar felt as if all the blood had drained out of her head and pooled in her stomach. She clenched her fists to stop from screaming out loud.

'What are we going to do?' she whispered, as if the large fish could hear her. Perhaps he could? She had no idea if sharks had good hearing or not. It must have found them somehow. Had it been their voices that lured the beast towards them?

'You're not bleeding anywhere, are you?' Jamie asked, squinting at her in the sunlight, before checking himself over.

'No, why?'

'I've heard they're attracted to the scent of blood.'

'I can't see any and I don't hurt anywhere. Do you? Your face?'

'No, I'm fine. That's all dried long ago. It's probably just out for a leisurely swim then.' Jamie was clearly trying to sound calm, but Zar wasn't fooled. She saw him scan the water behind them and turned back to look as well, afraid of what she'd find.

The fin came closer and she could see part of the body now. It was huge, several yards long at least, but moving through the water with sinuous grace. She shuddered. 'Jamie?'

'Shhh, just stay really still and hopefully it will tire of following us.'

Zar tried to keep the panic at bay as she watched

the massive shark begin to circle their little boat. Was it curious? Investigating? Or just plain hungry? She could see it clearly as it was so near the surface – grey back, white underside, enormous mouth and large bulging eyes on either side of its head. A monster. The fin cut through the water, occasionally joined by a flip of the tail, but there was no urgency about it as if the fish knew it had all day. Jamie and Zar had nowhere to hide from it. Slowly, Zar inched her way down to sit in the bottom of the boat so that only her head would be visible to the shark, although how that would help she wasn't sure.

Jamie continued to row, keeping his movements smooth and deliberate Zar noticed, and the big fish stayed away from the oars. After a little while, however, she nearly jumped out of her skin as the shark appeared behind them and nudged the back of the boat, as if testing what it was made of. They heard the thump as the shark's nose connected with the hull and felt a juddering movement. Zar put a hand over her mouth to stifle a scream of pure terror, while Jamie stopped rowing.

'Wh-what should we do?' she whispered.

'Let's just wait a moment. If it doesn't desist, I'm going to have to try and bash it over the head with one of the oars.' Jamie still sounded calm, but she could see that he was on full alert. 'Or maybe poke it in the eye.'

It sounded like a good plan to Zar, but she had no idea if it would work. Presumably the shark could overturn their craft if it wanted to before Jamie had time to hurt it much. It didn't bear thinking about. What else could they do though? They were trapped.

They sat quietly, waiting for what seemed like hours, until finally the monster seemed to tire of the game and the fin disappeared into the distance.

'It's gone,' Jamie said and started rowing again. 'Let's hope it doesn't come back.'

Zar let out a shaky sigh of relief. 'Amen to that.'

Thankfully, the shark didn't return. Towards late afternoon on the third day Jamie was so thirsty he thought his tongue would soon shrivel up, and his stomach was tied in knots with hunger. Zar must be in the same state, he thought, but she sat stoically in the stern apart from the few times she insisted on having a go at rowing. Whenever she did, he could see the effort it cost her to propel the boat even short distances, but she had a tenacity he couldn't but admire and he'd left her to it while he slept for a while.

'Just keep the sun behind us and you should be all right,' he'd told her.

Now the sea was beginning to turn rough again, the water churning around them as the sky darkened. Jamie frowned at the thought of another possible storm or even the main monsoon and pushed his tired muscles ever harder. They must reach shore before this storm hit or they'd never make it. But he said nothing to Zar. He didn't want to worry her more than she probably was already.

'Look, seagulls,' she exclaimed and pointed behind him.

Jamie turned to see and a wave of relief washed over him. Despite the increasing wind there was indeed a large flock of birds circling not far away. That could only mean one thing – land. 'Thank the Lord,' he muttered. Now if only he could row fast enough.

The currents began to help them and they sighted the coast faster than Jamie could have hoped for. A long strip of empty beach appeared, backed by palm trees and other vegetation and Jamie redoubled his efforts. Finally he was able to just steer with the oars as the waves carried them towards the sandy shore. Jamie had long ago pulled off his shoes and stockings, as had Zar. He jumped into the shallow water, pulling the boat behind him onto the sand at the water's edge, where the waves were lapping furiously.

'Throw our shoes up onto the beach, please,' he ordered Zar, and when she'd done as he asked, he reached out his arms to help her onto dry land. So as not to get her skirts wet again, he simply put his hands on her waist and lifted her out of the boat, carrying her as far as was necessary.

'Thank you,' she said, sounding a little breathless.

'You're welcome. Now we need to drag the boat as far up as we can. I think there's a storm coming.'

She put a hand up to shield her eyes and scanned the horizon. Heavy black and pewter coloured clouds were rolling in towards them, moving as if a giant was blowing his horrible breath landwards in a rush. They looked angry and threatening and Zar shivered. 'You're right. We must find shelter, but where?'

There were no dwellings in sight in either direction. In fact, it might be a deserted island or even just a sandbar for all they knew and not the Indian coast at all. Jamie decided not to think about that now. He was just happy he didn't have to do any more rowing for the moment.

'We'll just have to use the boat. Come on, help me pull this please.'

Together they dragged the boat as far as the line of coconut trees and then they heaved it upside down behind a row of thick trunks, leaning the side that faced inland on top of a fallen tree. To make sure the boat stayed put, even in high winds, they scooped sand around it to shore it up.

'There,' Jamie said, 'we'll have to crawl in, but we have shelter. Now let's go in search of coconuts, but quickly. The wind is picking up and I think I felt a raindrop just now.' As if to confirm his words, a flash of lightning split the sky just then and thunder reverberated above them.

There was an abundance of coconuts, with more falling as gusts of wind shook the tree tops, and they helped themselves to as many as they could carry and brought them back to the boat. 'Would you mind if we used your petticoat to sit on?' Jamie asked. 'I know it's immodest, but it's better than lying directly onto the sand.' He shrugged. The situation wasn't exactly normal. 'Besides, I've already seen your legs. We can use my waistcoat too.'

He saw Zar flush, but she nodded and fumbled with the ties at her waist before pulling it off. That left her with only her gown, which was open from the waist down where the petticoat had been displayed, and the chemise that reached her knees as she'd torn a strip off it on the first day. Jamie tried not to look as the latter was rather see-through. He'd done more than enough staring in the boat and her shape was already seared into his memory.

They crawled in underneath the boat and settled on the clothing. If he sat crosslegged, Jamie could almost remain upright. As long as he bent over a little, his head didn't touch what was now the ceiling – the bottom of the boat. Not perfect, but better than nothing and they were drier than they'd been for days.

'How are we going to open the coconuts? We need a rock or something.' Zar shook hers and just the sound of the liquid inside made Jamie swallow in anticipation.

'I've got one. Here, this should do the trick.'

He banged the stone along the middle part of the coconut, rotating it until a crack appeared. The milky water inside began to trickle out and they took turns drinking. For a while they were occupied with slaking their thirst and chewing contentedly on bits of coconut, which Jamie pried loose with the help of the rock.

'Ah, that's heavenly,' Zar murmured. 'I don't think I've ever tasted anything so good.'

Jamie chuckled. 'I agree. But we'd better eat slowly or we'll get a belly ache after so long without sustenance. Let's save some for later.' He put the other coconuts to one side. 'Listen, the rain is coming down in earnest now. Let's build up a wall of sand on this side too so there's only a small opening. Maybe that way we won't get drenched or flooded.'

The boat wasn't huge, but it was solid and although the rain and wind were soon lashing against it, the hull was watertight. They could see the lightning and felt as though the thunder shook the very ground they were sitting on. Fat raindrops fell, increasing in number and velocity until it sounded like someone was throwing nails or pebbles onto the ground and at the outside of the boat. Their little shelter stayed put though and they remained dry and warm underneath. Darkness fell and soon they could see nothing but vague outlines of each other. Jamie felt his eyelids droop as exhaustion finally claimed him.

'I need to sleep. Let's rest for a while. Do you mind lying next to me? There's not much space on this clothing.'

'No, you're right.'

As Jamie lay down and closed his eyes he heard Zar yawn and then felt her stretch out beside him. She managed to keep a small distance between them, which made him want to smile, but he was too tired to even think about it.

Within moments, he was asleep.

Chapter Twenty-One

Bijal looked back along the long line of elephants, wagons and men on horseback and on foot that constituted the Rajah's cavalcade. It was a small miracle that he'd managed to gather them all together so quickly, but as the Rajah had said, he was good at his job. It helped that he'd been able to delay his master by two days, calming him down and assuring him they would travel faster if they packed properly.

'After all, Highness, you wouldn't want to stop at a common inn, now would you? We need all the tents, cooks and provisions to see to your comfort.'

Not that he gave a fig whether the man was comfortable or not, but he still had to keep up the pretence. For now.

He leaned back inside his *hathi howdah*, a precarious construction that looked like a small carriage without wheels, set on top of an elephant's back. His was almost as luxurious as the Rajah's, which was covered in gold leaf and precious stones. Bijal's was silver with semi-precious jewels, but personally he thought this combination was more aesthetically pleasing as it went well with the elephant's colouring.

The domed silk canopy above his head kept the sun off him and matched the large embroidered covering that hung down the elephant's sides beneath the *howdah*. Both were a brilliant scarlet hue that gleamed in the light. The soft cushions inside were a similar, but lighter, red. Bijal chewed slowly on a handful of dried fruit and contemplated the next step of his plan, while the animal's lumbering gait lulled him into a drowsy state. The *mahout*, the man who rode just behind the elephant's ears, was guiding him along at a steady pace. They weren't moving quickly, but that suited Bijal just fine. The longer it took, the better. Although naturally he'd prefer to arrive before the monsoon began. It was as well not to spend time in a tent in pouring rain.

The talisman must be almost in Persia by now, he mused. It should fetch a staggering sum, money that would be put to good use.

Oh yes, very good use indeed.

In the meantime, his thoughts turned to the lovely Indira, who must be waiting for her bridegroom by now. She may be in for a surprise, but hopefully she wouldn't mind marrying a slightly more mature man instead of the Rajah. Bijal had had his eye on her for some time. A connoisseur of women, he'd spotted her potential years ago and fostered the connection with Indira's father. Now, the long planning stage of his campaign was coming to an end at last and soon she would be his.

He would enjoy her charms all the more, knowing she should have been the Rajah's.

When Jamie woke, he had no idea how long he'd been asleep. It was still dark outside so either they'd slept a night and a day, or morning hadn't arrived yet. He felt Zar shiver next to him and guessed she was awake. 'Are you cold?' Jamie whispered, keeping his voice down just in case he was wrong.

'No. Yes. Maybe a little.' She sat up. 'How are your hands?'

'I'll live. I rinsed them off in the sea and the salt water will help them heal. I'll do that again later.' He laughed. 'I might not be able to move my arms for a few days though, so you'll have to feed me then.'

'Your muscles are sore? Would you like me to, er ... massage them for a while?'

Jamie sat up straight with surprise and banged his head on the boat. 'Ow!' She was asking to touch him of her own free will? That was a step in the right direction. 'Yes, please, if you're sure you don't mind?'

'No, it's the least I can do after you've done all the work these past days. Turn around.'

'Well, you did some rowing too, but if you insist ...'

Jamie did as she'd asked and when her hands began to knead his aching shoulders and biceps he had to clamp his mouth shut so he wouldn't groan out loud. *God, that feels good!* But he didn't want to scare her off. He decided the best thing would be to make a joke of it for now, so he said, 'Please, don't ever stop, woman! Can I employ you to do this for the rest of my life?'

He waited to see what her response would be.

Zar knew Jamie wasn't serious about that, but in truth, she didn't *want* to stop. Ever. It was sheer bliss touching him like this at last, feeling the knotted muscles under warm skin relaxing slightly because of her ministrations. He was so altogether perfect – wide shoulders tapering down to a narrow waist, arms beautifully defined and hard from all the rowing, his long hair, as soft as goose down, loose across his neck and upper back. Even though she couldn't really see him, the shape of him became imprinted on her brain, bit by delicious bit. It was as though her fingertips were making a mental map of him.

'No, thanks. You can find someone else to be your slave,' she replied, but she had come very close to saying she'd love to fulfil such a position. The sun must have

243

addled her brain. Or maybe it was the shock of nearly drowning and then being scared witless by the shark.

'You're good at this. You must have done it before,' Jamie said, his voice sounding drowsy and content.

'No, never.'

'Not even with your husband?' He half turned and Zar was grateful he couldn't see the blush she felt staining her cheeks.

'Especially not with him,' she muttered.

'Can you tell me about it?' He sounded gentle now, non-threatening, and the darkness invited confidences as if it would swallow them up as soon as they were out in the open. It was tempting. Very tempting.

Zar hesitated. 'It's difficult,' she managed at last. 'It's something I'd rather forget, but my brain won't let me.' She moved her fingers further down and massaged the base of his back, hoping to distract him. A small groan made her think she'd succeeded, but then he spoke again.

'Perhaps if you tell me about it just this once, you will? I've heard people say that it helps to share thoughts, although I've never tried it myself.'

She sighed, capitulating. 'There's not much to tell really. I was seventeen and he was … well, old and repugnant to me. But he had rights. I was made to be a dutiful wife, stand still and let him …' She tailed off, swallowing past the obstruction that appeared in her throat as the horrible images came crowding into her mind, as always.

'Stand?' Jamie sounded puzzled. 'What the hell? I mean, beg your pardon but I thought we were talking about bedroom duties here?'

'We are. It's just that … he kept wanting to look at me. All of me. Without a stitch of clothing on. He would stare and stare, with that horrible gloating look in his eyes, as if he owned me. I mean he did, obviously, but you know, like an animal or a chattel, his to do with as he pleased. It was so humiliating. And *then* he'd touch.' Zar felt her whole body flaming with embarrassment. Why was she telling him this? She must be mad.

She'd stopped massaging his back and he turned and found her hands in the dark, enveloping them in his big, warm, damaged ones. 'He hurt you? And then he bedded you?'

'Mm-hmm.'

'He didn't use … whips or anything, did he?'

'What? No! No, just his hands, but they were like the claws of an animal, his fingers rough and hard, his nails long and disgusting. Grasping, squeezing, pawing.' She shuddered at the memory, her stomach curdling. 'I can't bear to be touched now.'

Jamie lifted her up and pulled her onto his lap as if she were a child, putting his arms around her. One hand guided her head to rest against his shoulder, while the other stroked her back. 'I can hold you like this though. You don't mind?'

'No.' And she didn't. This was different.

'It's all right,' he whispered. 'It will never happen again. Not that way. I won't let it. From now on, you'll always be safe.'

Zar closed her eyes and let the feeling of safety he promised envelop her. She wanted to believe him. Wished with all her heart that it could be true. But eventually she stirred and sighed. It was just an illusion. 'How? I'll never be able to marry again. Never ha-have children …' Her voice broke on that final word, because she'd craved one so much. *A baby of my own.* Someone to love.

'Shh, of course you will. Listen, I think I know a way to

245

help you. But you're going to have to put your whole trust in me. Can you do that? I'll never hurt you. I promised you that already once.'

Zar thought about the last few days and how he'd been with her every step of the way. Protecting her, buoying up her mood, fighting for her, pulling her out of the terrifying ocean, rowing her to safety. *If I can't trust Jamie, then who can I trust?* 'Yes,' she said. 'I believe so.'

'Then please tell me truthfully – do you find me attractive? You are not repulsed by my looks or behaviour?'

'No. Yes. I mean, I'm sure you're fully aware that most ladies think you very handsome.'

'I'm not concerned with "most" ladies, only you.'

Zar took a deep breath. 'And if I do? Consider you handsome, that is?'

'It would be a good start. In fact, it's essential for the purposes of this exercise.'

'Hmm, well all right then. I do.'

'Thank you. And I think you are exceedingly lovely.' He stroked her cheek and cupped it with his blistered palm. 'Now have you ever thought of my kisses, my body, when I wasn't with you? Do you desire me?'

'Jamie! A lady isn't supposed to think that way.'

'To hell with that! Forget everything you've ever been told. All that nonsense about what's correct, about duty. What happens between a man and a woman when both are willing is pure, wicked and delicious, and it isn't wrong. It's very right, trust me on that. Now confess.' He kissed a particularly sensitive spot beneath her ear. 'What does that make you think of?'

She squirmed and once again blessed the darkness for hiding her expression at least. 'Very well, it makes me think of how I felt when you kissed me.'

'Good. Anything else?' He continued to feather kisses along her neck.

'Um, skin?' She decided to go a little further. 'Warm, unclothed skin?'

'You mean nakedness. Use bold words. The words your brain is thinking, not the ones you think you ought to say.' He kissed the underside of her chin.

'Naked skin,' she repeated obediently, and hearing herself say that out loud made a frisson of awareness sizzle through her that was exciting.

'Even better. Remember what my stubble did to your breasts?' His voice was very husky now and that word made her shiver and sent another spark shooting downwards. 'Did you like it?' he prompted.

'Yes.' No point denying it when he could easily confirm for himself that her body remembered the episode very well indeed.

'Then I promise you will feel that way again, but a hundredfold – no a thousandfold – more intensely. I want you to make love to me, Zarmina.'

'N-now?' Zar sat up and stared at his shadowy form. 'But you just said—'

'That I wouldn't hurt you, yes. And I won't. I will not lay so much as a finger on you unless you tell me to. *You*'re going to make love to *me*.'

'I don't understand.'

'I'm going to lie down and I want you to touch me anywhere you please and do whatever you feel like to my body. All of it. Explore. Kiss. Tickle. Tease. Use your fingers, palms, mouth, tongue. Absolutely anything you want. Just do it. It's time to teach your body a new lesson.' He made her get off his lap and she felt, rather than saw, him lie down on top of her petticoat. 'Would you like me to take my shirt off?'

Zar was too stunned to reply at first, but she thought about his invitation to do exactly what she had to admit she'd been wanting to do and forced herself to be honest. What if he was right? She did want to touch him, but how far could she go? And if she stopped, would he make her continue? She'd never find out if she didn't try.

I have to be bold, he said.

'I'll remove it,' she said, trying hard not to sound as scared as she felt.

'Good, be my guest.'

He'd already pulled it out of the waistband of his breeches, so Zar was able to just grasp the bottom of the shirt and tug it up and over his head. She threw it to one side and ran her fingertips over his chest. More warm skin. More hard muscles. And nipples? She circled these and he made a noise like a contented cat which made her smile.

She explored lower and found a line of hair bisecting his ridged stomach. It stopped by the edge of his breeches and her fingers became timid, turning away. *It's too soon. I can't go that far yet.* It astonished her that she could even think of venturing that way later, but the thought was tantalising.

Could she go through with this? It was wrong in so many ways. And there could be consequences. A child. Ostracism.

To hell with it, as William would say. She would deal with that if it happened and surely doing this just once wouldn't matter? She'd almost died out there on the vast sea, come close to ending her life without ever knowing what lovemaking was really like. Lovemaking with Jamie. She wouldn't want to miss out on this chance to find out. She couldn't.

'You might like to straddle me,' he suggested. 'Then you can kiss me if you're so inclined.' She heard a smile in his voice. He was enjoying this, the scoundrel. But then, so was she ...

She hesitated, then did as he'd said and sat down on his stomach. Though she made sure her chemise covered her nether regions, it was such thin cotton she still felt the hardness in his breeches branding her behind. She tried to move away from it, but couldn't.

'Er, best if you sit still for now. I'm not a saint,' Jamie murmured.

'Me just sitting on you affects you?' she asked, worry creeping in. 'Then how do I know you'll be able to keep your word? I mean, can you really control yourself?'

'I'll manage. But I'm hoping I won't have to. Remember, you can give me permission to move at any time.'

'Hmm.' Zar was acutely aware she was playing with fire here, but she liked it too much to stop yet. She decided to kiss him. That worked before, making her forget all about the past for a while.

It did so again. She placed her palms on his smooth chest and touched her lips to his. He didn't move and let her rain little kisses on his mouth, nibble his lower lip with her teeth and lick the contours of it. He tasted of coconut and salt, a strange but delicious combination. 'Kiss me back,' she demanded softly.

He did and she felt him smiling at first, before she lost herself in a much deeper kiss. One that sent flames shooting all the way down to her toes, even though he was only using his tongue.

'Damn, you're a master at this, aren't you,' she muttered.

'Language!' He chuckled. 'Of course I am. I told you,

I'm not a saint. Saints are boring. Trust me, you wouldn't like one kissing you.'

Shaking slightly, she scraped his chin ever so lightly with her nails, then moved on to kiss his throat, his chest and, backing up a bit, his stomach. His skin smelled of sea and wind, with a faint tang of sandalwood soap, and she loved it. Again, she stopped at the waistband of his breeches.

'You're allowed to take them off too, you know.' Again, the amused voice which goaded her. No, dared her. She accepted the challenge.

'Very well.' There were buttons either side of a flap which her trembling fingers had some difficulty with, but she managed to undo them at last. She moved off him to pull the breeches down and he helped by kicking them off. Swallowing hard, she sat back down on his thighs, a bit lower this time and then she reached out and followed them up to …

'Holy Shiva! That's … that's not what Francis was like.'

A strangled laugh escaped him. 'I should hope not. I'm half his age, I think.'

Her fingertips explored, curiosity overcoming her nerves. 'It's so soft, so warm, and yet … not soft at all.'

He drew in a sharp breath. 'Mm-hmm.'

Throwing caution to the wind, she grasped the whole length of him in one hand and stroked it. He jumped and gave a muffled cry. 'Oh, am I hurting you?' She let go.

'No, quite the opposite.' His voice sounded strained, as if he was talking through clenched teeth. 'Is it my turn yet?'

'Your turn?'

'I want to touch you too. Explore, the way you are doing.'

His words made alarm bells clang inside her mind, but she silenced them with an effort of will. 'I … I suppose that's only fair.'

He reached up and began to undo the laces of her bodice, one by one, with what seemed like deliberate slowness.

'Wait, the diamonds and the talisman!'

'I'll find them.' Jamie sounded as though he'd relish that task and she felt his fingers brushing the skin of her torso while he searched. When he had located the items and put them to one side, he pulled out the final lace and sat up to push her gown off her shoulders and down her arms. She helped him by shrugging out of it completely. Then he put his hands on her waist and moved his thumbs in lazy half-circles, while leaning forward to kiss her.

It started off as a gentle kiss, but she found that wasn't enough. She became greedy, her tongue playing with his, teasing, tasting. Zar loved the way this made her feel, the little spears of flame that shot down into her stomach and lower. The way her breasts tingled and the tips hardened. She made a noise in her throat which turned to a gasp as his hands slowly moved upwards to cup her breasts through the chemise. The old fears crept into her mind, but she tried to keep them at bay. *This is Jamie. Jamie.*

'Shh, relax, I'm only exploring, remember?' he whispered. He kept his hands still until she became used to the sensation, then his thumbs began to work some kind of magic on her nipples.

Zar marvelled at the difference to her previous experiences. There was no pain, no squeezing, just butterfly caresses that were driving her wild. When Jamie stopped she murmured in protest and he chuckled.

'I just want to dispense with this,' he said, and tugged at her chemise. 'I too want naked skin.'

Another spark fizzled through her at his words and she allowed him to pull the garment off. He started, as before, at her waist, his hands stroking upwards in a leisurely fashion as if he had all the time in the world. Just as Zar was becoming impatient, he bent to replace his thumbs with his tongue instead, and she arched back in surprise. 'Jamie!'

'I told you, anything goes. Don't you like it?'

'Yes. Yes, I do.'

She didn't protest when his hands traced the contours of her stomach and dipped lower, finding her innermost place. It was all she could do not to cry out at the exquisite sensations his tongue and fingers were creating. 'Take me inside you,' he murmured, lifting her up and lowering her onto himself, slowly, gently, giving her time to pull back if she'd wanted to. But by now her brain wasn't registering anything other than the need for something more. Something she didn't know she wanted until she felt the tip of him entering her.

'Ah, yes, that's it. Ow!' He'd pushed all the way inside and she'd felt a small ripple of pain, but it wasn't too bad.

Jamie froze. 'You've never …? He didn't …?'

'No, he couldn't.' Zar moved cautiously up then down and found that it didn't hurt any more. Instead, a delicious warmth was spreading through her and somehow her body knew what to do now. 'Go on,' she urged him. 'Please!'

'No, you do it, you're in charge,' he murmured, guiding her, showing her what to do, and she did, moving faster and faster until her entire body exploded and it felt as though she was bursting into a thousand tiny pieces.

'Jamie!'

He cried out too and she felt him shuddering. Eventually they both stilled and he put his arms around her, pulling her down to lie on top of his chest. It was as if they were one, with them still joined together so intimately, and she revelled in the sensation, clinging to him as their breathing slowed down to a more normal tempo and their heart rates became steady once more.

She closed her eyes and smiled.

Chapter Twenty-Two

'Are you all right?'

Jamie stroked the silky skin of Zarmina's back, feeling gloriously sated but niggled by guilt. She'd been a virgin. *Bloody hell!* It wasn't something he'd even contemplated. He just assumed the old man had bedded her, but she said he couldn't. He was impotent. No wonder the bastard had enjoyed touching her so much – it must have been the only thing he could do and he'd taken out his frustration on her.

'I'm very well, thank you.' She sounded sleepy and not at all distressed, which he took as a good sign.

'You didn't tell me you'd never … I suppose I should have asked. I'm sorry.'

She lifted her head and traced the line of his jaw with her finger, making him shiver as she rasped through four days worth of stubble. He couldn't see her expression, but the small caress was tender. 'It wasn't important. And that bit was over with very quickly. It was the rest that was difficult, to begin with anyway.'

She wasn't upset. That was a relief.

'And then?' he dared to tease.

'And then, you worked miracles, as I'm sure you know. If I could only see you properly right now, I'd wager you are smirking at me, am I right?'

He did then, but denied it. 'Absolutely not. Why would I?'

'Because you were right, damn you.'

'And that's a bad thing?' He reached down to cup her luscious behind, softly raking his fingernails across them.

'Yes! No. What are you doing?'

'You didn't think we were finished, did you?' He pushed her up so he could kiss her. 'That was just the beginning. We have all the time in the world and now it's definitely my turn to be on top.'

'You mean, you can do it more than once?'

Jamie laughed. 'Oh, yes. As many times as you want, depending on whether you'd like to be able to sit tomorrow or not, of course. Kiss me back, and I'll show you.'

'But we shouldn't. What if …?'

Jamie didn't wait to listen to her protests. If he let her talk herself into panicking again, she'd never get used to his lovemaking, and that wasn't something he wanted. Far from it. He knew now he wanted to continue with this for the rest of their lives. He wanted her in his bed, and his heart, forever.

'Eurgh, I don't think I ever want to eat another coconut as long as I live.' Zar swallowed a mouthful, knowing she had no choice unless she wanted to go hungry.

'Well, there's gratitude for you. Your man goes out to gather food for you and all you do is complain. You're a hard woman to please.'

Zar narrowed her eyes at him. She doubted very much he was 'her man'. He probably had a woman in every port, the way they said sailors did. The thought was depressing, but she couldn't blame him. She hadn't asked for his undying love and to be fair, he'd done her a huge favour in curing her of her fears.

They'd spent two nights under the boat now – or at least that was how long they thought it was, although they couldn't tell for sure – and she no longer minded him touching her anywhere. In fact, she positively welcomed his caresses. Just the thought of his hands on any part of her anatomy sent darts of anticipation shooting through her. She shook her head. She must stop thinking about Jamie and his lovemaking. It was shameless of her and it had to end. Just because they were cut off from the rest of the world here, didn't mean they wouldn't have to rejoin it again soon. And then, she'd have to come to terms with what she'd done. Allowed Jamie to do.

She must have been mad. Reckless, wanton, irresponsible ... Her cheeks heated up and she turned away so he wouldn't notice.

'As you're becoming bored with the fare, perhaps it's time we did some more reconnoitring. Shall we go for a walk to see how far this sandbar stretches?' Jamie suggested. 'It's still raining, but it's not a torrential downpour at the moment.'

He'd been out during the previous day, heading inland, and reported back that they seemed to be on nothing more than a sandbar. There was a strip of water separating them from what might either be the coast or an island, but it had looked too deep to negotiate.

'We'll still get wet,' Zar protested, although in truth, she wasn't really afraid of a bit of rain. It was more that she didn't want their time here to come to an end. But of course it had to soon in any case.

'It's monsoon season, it's going to rain on and off for months! We can't stay here for that long. At least, I hope we don't have to. If there's no way to cross to the next piece of land by foot, we'll have to drag the boat across to the inner shore and row again. Or try to row around the sandbar, but it could go on for miles so I'd rather not.'

Zar nodded. 'Very well. Let's go now then, while it's daylight.'

She was dressed again, albeit in a very creased, stiff and uncomfortable gown and petticoat. They'd taken turns to go down to the shore to wash as best they could in the saltwater, but this had left her skin itchy and rough, so it wasn't ideal. They didn't dare go swimming because the current seemed very strong, sucking at their legs and feet as they stood in the shallows.

They set off, going left first. 'Let's see how long this strip of sand really is,' Jamie said, striding out so that Zar had to walk very fast to keep up. To her relief, he took hold of her hand and pulled her along, which helped.

After some time, the beach began to curve slightly and as they rounded it, they caught sight of smoke rising into the air. 'Ah, we're not as alone as we thought we were,' Jamie muttered. 'Can you give me one of the little diamonds, please? We might need something to barter with.'

Zar had returned them to their hiding place before leaving the boat, just in case they weren't coming back, and she took one gemstone out and handed it to him.

The smoke turned out to be coming from a group of fishermen's huts clustered together at the southern end of what they said was indeed a sandbar. One of the men spoke some Gujarati, so Zar was able to communicate with him.

'Where exactly are we?' she asked. 'Is the Indian coast far?'

The man smiled and shook his head, pointing to his left. 'This is Juhu and the islands of Salsette and Bombay are over there. You can walk to the first one at low tide.'

Zar quickly translated for Jamie, who seemed to have understood the gist anyway. 'Can you show us the best place to cross, please? We can pay you.'

Once Jamie held up the diamond, the man and his friends became extremely helpful indeed. They even went so far as to lead Zar and Jamie along the inner side of the sandbar to a precise point where they said it would be safe to cross very soon. It appeared to be some sort of tidal creek, negotiable during low ebb.

'Just watch the water. We'll leave you now,' the fisherman said.

'Thank you. *Namaste*.'

The men waved goodbye and hurried back to their dry huts. While the water ebbed, Zar and Jamie settled down to wait beneath a tree. The water did seem to be receding, so Zar hoped they'd been told the truth.

'So if that is an island called Salsette over there, how far is it to Bombay, do you know? And can we get help there?' she asked. 'There are English people, right?'

'Yes, but we won't need them.' Jamie was smiling, obviously pleased with the news. 'I have a house there.'

'In Bombay? Why?'

Once again, Zar had the feeling she didn't know this man at all, even though she'd 'known' him in the most intimate sense. He was an enigma.

'It seemed like a good idea to buy one. It was the only place in India where an Englishman – or in my case a Scotsman – was allowed to buy a property, and I was tired of living like a complete nomad. I wanted somewhere to keep a few things permanently. I don't spend a lot of time there, but it's been handy.'

'I see.'

'Bombay isn't as nice as Madras – it rains a lot more and the temperature and humidity are unbearable a lot of the time, but it's become an important port for trade with the Red Sea countries and the Persian Gulf. It made sense to have a foothold there, even though I don't like it much. Madras is a much better place in my opinion. But Bombay is good for my trading ventures.' He slung an arm round her shoulder and pulled her to his side, giving her a brief hug. 'Don't worry. Once we get there, I'll be able to provide you with food, clothes and shelter from this infernal weather. Then we can make plans.'

'Plans?' Her stomach did a somersault. Was he already plotting how to get rid of her now he'd had what he wanted? Well, why should she care? She had a perfectly good life in Surat. As long as she wasn't with child ...

As if he'd heard part of her thoughts, he said, 'We need to go back to Surat and see what's been happening there. I do hope Sanjiv has finally arrived. And don't you want to know if William made it home?'

'Not particularly.' She called her stepson something very nasty in Gujarati and Jamie chuckled.

'I've no idea what that means, but I can guess,' he said when she raised her eyebrows at him. 'But if I was William, I'd be afraid of meeting you again, after he abandoned you like that.'

'Yes, I still can't believe he did that, but even so, I'm sure he's not afraid of me in the slightest.'

'I would be. I'm sure you have quite a temper when you're riled and I wouldn't want to be on the receiving end of it.' Jamie grinned and then laughed out loud when she punched him on the arm. 'Enough, woman. We have some walking to do. Look, I think it's safe now. The water looks shallow. Shall we try?'

'Very well.'

Zar hiked up her skirts and followed him, holding on to his hand so as not to lose her footing. She didn't tell him that leaving the little sandbar felt like leaving Paradise. She didn't think he'd agree.

'To think it was so easy to reach civilisation! We could have been here two days ago if we'd known.'

After crossing over to Salsette, an island that seemed to be mostly made up of mangrove forest and marshland, they had found another fisherman to row them across to Bombay. From the shore, they'd been able to walk to Jamie's house as it wasn't far.

'Indeed. We could probably have rowed down too if we'd realised how close it was, but we would have risked getting caught in strong currents. This way was better.'

And if they hadn't stayed on the sandbar, he may not have had the chance to make love to this beautiful woman. Jamie took a deep breath and tried not to look at the lady in question. He had some decisions to make and seeing her clean and dressed in native clothing, with that glorious hair hanging down her back while it dried out after recently being washed, wasn't helping his thought processes one whit.

'But we had no way of knowing and I, for one, was too tired to go exploring when we reached the shore.' His muscles had recovered and the swelling around his eye had gone down, but his hands were still a bit sore, despite him washing them frequently with sea water.

'Well, it's wonderful to be properly clean again. I didn't think I'd ever get rid of the feeling of salt water.' Zar finger-combed her long tresses and shook her head so the mane of dark brown hair rippled. Jamie had an urge to bury his own fingers in it this instant.

Jamie's two servants, a Hindu man and his widowed sister who looked after the property when he wasn't in

Bombay, had been very efficient in providing them with baths, clean clothes and food with a minimum of fuss. They hadn't batted an eyelid when Jamie asked them to procure Indian clothing for himself and Zar. Jamie paid them very well for their services, but he was pleased to know it was money well spent.

Zar was standing by a window in his salon now, looking out over the small garden that belonged to the property. He came up behind her and put his arms round her waist, bending down to bury his nose in her hair. 'Mmm, I must say you smell better too,' he teased.

'Jamie!' She turned her face to glare up at him, then obviously noticed his amusement. 'I'm sure you do as well,' she murmured, turning a delicate shade of pink when his hands began to roam higher. To his frustration, she pushed them away and stepped out of his reach, putting some distance between them. 'Please, don't do that.'

'Why not? There's no one to see us. And besides, even if there were, they'll have to get used to it.'

'What do you mean?' She wrapped her arms round her middle, the way he'd noticed her do before whenever she felt vulnerable. Jamie wondered why she was doing it now. He thought he'd managed to put her thoroughly at ease in his company.

He took a deep breath. Time to get serious. Just touching her and breathing in her scent had made up his mind for him and he knew what he had to do, even though a part of him still panicked at the thought. But did he really have a choice? Not if he was an honourable man and he realised now that was what he wanted to be.

'I'd be very honoured if you'd be my wife, Zarmina.'

Her eyes opened wide in alarm. 'What? No!'

She took another step away from him, but he reached out and captured her hands.

'You want me to get down on bended knee?' He tried out his most charming smile on her, but it didn't work.

'No, please don't.'

'As you wish.' Her expression was not encouraging in the least, but he ploughed on regardless. 'Zar,' he said, trying his best to stay calm and reasonable. 'After what we did on the beach, do you really want to stay unmarried? I thought I'd convinced you there was nothing to be afraid of. You don't think I'm going to turn into an ogre overnight, the moment I put a ring on your finger, do you?' He smiled again to show he was joking, but there was no let-up in her scowl.

'I don't need a husband. I'm fine on my own,' she insisted. 'I thought you were different. You were the only one who *didn't* ask me to marry you.'

'That was before we made love.'

'Well, what we did, it doesn't mean … doesn't have to lead to marriage.'

'Making love usually does.' *And call a spade a spade. I thought I'd taught you that by now.* 'Zarmina, there are other things to take into account here. If William has managed to get back to Surat, he'll probably think you dead, or at the very least a slave to the pirates, never to return. He'll be busy taking your half of the business and if he has any sense – which I grant you, he may not have – he'll sell what he can and go back to England. He will never be safe in India again after his treachery. Whoever stole the talisman will be after him, for one thing.'

'Then I need to hurry back to Surat to stop him. If he even made it through that storm, which is unlikely.'

'How will you do that? You are a woman and I doubt

262

there will be much you can do about it. William is a desperate man now, if he's survived. I don't think he liked you much before all this happened and now you'll be in his way. He probably won't hesitate to kill you. Equally, if he hasn't survived, do you seriously think you can carry on running a business like that? A woman on your own?'

'Yes, I'd hire someone to help me. Someone trustworthy. In fact, I have a good broker already.' Her chin went up and he saw determination in her eyes. Normally, he admired her for it, but just now he wished she'd be more biddable. Damn it all, he was offering her his life here, his very soul, something he hadn't thought he'd ever give a woman after his marriage to Elizabet.

'But why go to all that trouble? If I was your husband, I could take care of matters for you.'

'Yes, because all I own would be yours.' She pulled her hands out of his and thumped him on the shoulder with one fist, then flung away, only to pace back and forth instead. 'And I would be owned by you too,' she said bitterly. 'I'd have no freedom. No money of my own. While you'd be rich at my expense. That doesn't seem like a very good deal to me.'

He shook his head. 'I think you are forgetting something – I'm already rich in my own right. I don't need your assets. In fact, I'm willing to sign a document to say I will give your share all into your keeping to do with as you please, as soon as we've dealt with William. It will just need to be mine temporarily so that I have a right to act in the matter.'

Zar stopped and regarded him from under lowered brows. Her arms were wrapped around her again in a defensive gesture and Jamie longed to undo them and put them around his waist instead. But he knew this wasn't the time to persuade her that way. He had to allow her to agree to this with her brain, not her body.

'How would I know you're rich? You've never told me anything about yourself.'

'Well, I can show you all the gemstones I have hidden away in various places. Or you can ask the people at the English Factory to vouch for me if you like. My parents own a merchant company in Sweden and their ships often come to Surat, so they are well known there. And although I'm a younger son, they have promised that I'll inherit half their possessions one day, once my sisters have had a dowry or the equivalent in silver. But I don't really need their wealth; I've done quite well for myself here in the gem trade.'

Zar seemed to digest this for a moment, but it was clear she wasn't convinced. 'And how do I know you won't renege on your promise as soon as we're married? Most men can never have enough riches.' Her eyes were filled with suspicion and Jamie stifled a sigh. He thought he'd banished her demons, but they were obviously deeply rooted.

'Because I can also sign a document to that effect if you don't feel you can take my word for it. I had hoped you trusted me by now, but if not …'

They stared at each other in silence for a while. Jamie stood still, waiting for Zar's mind to accept what he was saying. He knew it made sense. The fact that he also wanted her as his wife for other reasons was probably something better left for another time. She wouldn't believe him now anyway, even though it was the truth.

The thought of losing her made him almost breathless and it wasn't something he wanted to contemplate. How had this happened? How had she come to mean so much to him in such a short space of time? He hadn't believed in love. He'd thought his brother a sap for being so enthralled by Elisabet, but he could see that he just hadn't met the right woman until now.

'I'm sorry, Jamie, but the answer is no,' she said firmly.

She looked so sad and confused, he again had the urge to pull her close and persuade her the only way he knew how. That would be wrong though, he sensed it instinctively. If he did that, she'd regret her decision.

Somehow, he had to make her listen to the voice of reason instead. He knew she desired him, he'd already proved that. Now all he had to do was persuade her marriage wasn't as bad as she feared. But he could see he needed to go slowly. First things first though, they had to find out how matters stood in Surat.

'Very well,' he said, pretending to capitulate. 'But can we at least pretend we're married so that I can help you deal with William? He'll never know whether it's the truth or not and if he believes I'm your husband, it will rattle him no end, I guarantee it.'

She bit her lip in that distracting way that had Jamie's insides clenching with lust, but he hung onto his composure. 'All right,' she agreed. 'But only if it's necessary.'

Zar felt as if she was being pulled in half. One part of her wanted desperately to marry this man because now that she'd tasted the heady pleasures of being in his arms, the thought of living without him made her go all cold inside. But the rational part of her brain told her he wouldn't stay anyway. He wasn't born and raised in India. He'd want to go home eventually to that cold country he talked about so longingly, where his family lived. And his little daughter.

And then he'd leave her behind. Just like her father did.

He couldn't possibly take her back to Europe because then he'd have to be just as ashamed of her as her father had been when he'd taken her to England. Jamie's family and neighbours would no doubt be horrified if he arrived home with a half-foreigner. She was well aware that despite her magnolia-coloured skin, her looks were exotic and different to any of the women there. The tiniest bit of sun and she acquired a darker hue. There was no masking the fact that she wasn't all white. She well remembered her aunt's reaction, which had been as far from favourable as it could possibly be.

'What on earth were you thinking, Thomas? No, actually, don't answer that. I don't suppose you were using your brain at all,' had been her aunt's verdict when first catching sight of Zar. She had felt humiliated beyond belief.

And when Jamie sailed home, she'd be left here, presumably with enough money to keep her and any children they may have in comfort for the rest of their lives. She doubted Jamie would return. *No, I couldn't bear it!*

She'd seen it happen before, to Indian women who had been concubines or wives of the foreigners. They were provided for and the children sometimes remembered in their father's will, but they weren't taken to England or Europe. Girls were married off if possible, boys sent to become officers in the armies of native princes. Zar closed her eyes. She didn't want that for her children. But would there be a choice? She might already be carrying a child.

She had to pray that wasn't the case.

Now she had to be strong. *I can cope.* And Jamie would soon forget her. He had his own demons, she'd gathered that much, and she was sure marriage had been the last thing on his mind when he arrived in Surat. He was gentleman enough to offer her the protection of his name and his assistance with William, but love had nothing to do with it. Only business.

And lust perhaps.

She couldn't live with that.

Chapter Twenty-Three

'At last we have come this far! I've never known a journey to take so long. It was exceedingly boring.'

Bijal was standing behind a thick banyan tree in the grounds of the Rajah's cousin's property outside Baroda, which wasn't too far from Surat. The slow progress of the wedding entourage had made him want to scream in the end as he became impatient for news about the talisman. Now, finally, he had managed to get a message to Tufan, who'd come to report on progress.

'I'm glad you have arrived safely, Excellency.' The servant bowed.

'What news? You've sent me no messages these last few weeks and I'd expected to hear from you.'

'I'm sorry, but I'm afraid there has been a complication.'

'What complication? Tell me this instant.' Bijal felt an icy finger of foreboding scratch along his spine.

'Well, first of all the foreigner who brought it from Madras refused to give it to the go-between as arranged. I think he was pressing for a larger payment.'

'Outrageous! Did he not remember his friend's family was at stake? I thought you made sure he knew the consequences of failure.'

'I did, Excellency, but it's difficult to understand these foreigners.' Tufan spread his hands and shrugged. 'The other one, the go-between, then became greedy as well and started to negotiate for passage to Persia with another shipowner. I was just about to intervene when the merchant Mansukh took matters into his own hands.'

'How so? I paid *him* well, at least.'

'He grew impatient, I believe, and had the second shipowner killed, then abducted both the foreigners concerned, plus a lady. I'm assuming he forced them to give up the, um, object as they then set sail as planned. He took the foreigners with him, presumably in order to dispose of them at sea.'

'Sensible man.' Bijal nodded, the feelings of unease receding. 'Then the problem was solved so there is no need for panic.'

'Ah, yes, but you see, there are rumours that the ship was attacked by pirates. I've not been able to verify this, but someone from another ship they'd also attacked reported hearing the pirates talk about a prize they'd recently captured. I don't know what to do or how to find out more. I was just about to set out in search of you to see what you suggest.'

Bijal ground his teeth together. *Of all the bad luck ... pirates!* 'The only way we will know for certain is to wait and see whether Mansukh returns. It may be some time since the monsoons have now begun, but until then, there's nothing we can do. You must go back to Surat and lie in wait. Keep your eyes and ears open for any other developments.'

'Yes, Excellency.' The servant bowed once more.

'And report to me immediately you have news, understood? I will be here for a while.'

'Of course.'

The Grand Vizier stayed under the banyan tree and paced back and forth for some considerable time after Tufan had left. He had come this far, he must not fail now. *I can't!*

But what if the talisman really was cursed and the gods were against him?

No, it can't be because it's rightfully mine.

'We had better set out for Surat first thing tomorrow morning,' Jamie said the following day. 'I know we need to rest, but I'm afraid time might be of the essence. Do you mind riding? We'll get wet, but it will be a lot faster.'

'That's all right. Any other mode of transport would be just as unbearable at the moment.'

It was true. They couldn't go by ship, as the monsoon kept the sea in constant ferment. And carriages or bullock carts would invariably get stuck in mud this time of year as the roads turned into quagmires during the constant rainfall. Any progress would be agonisingly slow. Riding would be risky too, but they'd have to hope the horses didn't slip and hurt themselves.

'Then that is what we'll do. Would you think me unbearably rude if I leave you for a while to go and make arrangements for our journey? I promise I'll be as quick as I can.'

'No, not at all. I think I'll have a rest.'

Jamie nodded. Zar seemed to be trying to avoid his company – not easy in the small house – and would probably be glad of a chance to be alone in order to gather her thoughts. And so would he. He needed to find a way to persuade her to marry him for real, but he wasn't sure what the best course of action would be.

He needed time to think.

That evening, they dined in the salon, sitting on cushions on the floor, on opposite sides of a low table. Jamie's servants had brought in a selection of delicious smelling dishes – curried stews, saffron rice, bread and fruit – and left them to help themselves. It seemed very intimate, and

Zar mostly kept her eyes on her plate, concentrating on her food.

'I don't bite, you know. At least not so it hurts.'

She looked up to see Jamie across the table, giving her one of his special smiles, although it didn't quite reach his eyes the way they normally did. It was as if sadness lurked behind it, but she thought she was probably imagining that. After all, she must have just hurt his pride by refusing his offer of marriage. His heart didn't come into it. Only desire, which was what he was alluding to now, judging by the teasing note in his voice.

'That's reassuring,' she replied somewhat drily. 'I'm not afraid of you.'

'Good. Then perhaps we can have a conversation with our meal? I find the silence somewhat oppressive.'

'Sorry.' She hadn't realised how quiet she was. They'd both been deep in thought. But what could they talk about? They'd already planned how to deal with William and the talisman so what else was there to discuss? Zar stifled a sigh, then wondered if perhaps she should turn the tables on Jamie for a change. 'Jamie?' she asked tentatively. 'You remember how I told you about my marriage while we were on the beach?'

'Mm-hm.'

'Well, would you tell me about yours? I ... you never mention anything about your wife.'

She saw him stiffen, then he hesitated, as if he wasn't sure he wanted to talk about this. Eventually he replied though. 'There's a reason for that. I hated her and try to think of her as little as possible.'

'Oh.' Zar didn't know how to react to such a statement, but she was puzzled and ventured to ask, 'So why did you marry her then?'

He gave a short laugh, completely devoid of mirth. 'I had no choice. She tricked me.'

Zar was taken aback. She had heard of women employing their wiles to catch husbands, but this sounded much worse somehow.

Jamie sighed and shook his head. 'I'm sorry, it's a sore subject with me, but you're right, it's only fair that I tell you since you confided in me. It's not a pretty tale though. Are you sure you want to hear it?'

'Yes. Please.' She was curious now. 'If you don't mind?'

'No, actually I'd like you to know and I swear I won't lie to you.'

'I believe you.'

She leaned back as he began his story, slowly peeling some fruit, but she soon forgot to eat it. He told her of his older brother Brice's love for a beautiful girl, which appeared to be reciprocated. He recounted how Brice had gone on trading ventures to China in order to be able to provide for his young bride-to-be. 'Because he knew she was spoiled and he was determined she'd want for nothing,' Jamie said.

Then he went on to recount how he'd encountered Elisabet in the forest, thought her violated, and acted as a knight in shining armour. And how she and her maidservant tricked him into falling asleep in her bed.

'They must have undressed me and heaved me under the covers, knowing full well Elisabet's father would find me there the following morning.' Jamie's voice was hoarse with bitterness and Zar felt for him. 'And she'd not been raped at all. It was all an act, a sham. She had lain with her lover out of her own free will, many times as she told me later, but she knew her father wouldn't consider him good enough to marry her. So when she became with child, she needed another solution. She set her sights on me.'

'So what happened then? Surely you explained to the man about being drugged?'

Jamie snorted. 'I tried at first, believe me, but he wasn't listening. Elisabet was his only child, his pampered daughter. There was no way he'd believe me over her and you have no idea how convincing an actress she could be. I'd already learned that the night before. And I'm afraid I had a bit of a reputation, which didn't exactly help matters.'

'That's terrible! Tell me exactly what happened, please.'

Zar found it hard to understand why Elisabet had acted that way and felt she needed all the facts. Only then could she try to make sense of it.

'Very well,' Jamie said, 'but as I said, it's not a pretty tale ...'

When Jamie had woken up that morning, his head was pounding like the very devil and this wasn't helped by a voice that shouted out imprecations. Someone shook his shoulder and he opened one eye, blinking against the sharp morning light.

'Wake up, you lout! You have much to answer for.'

Jamie opened the other eye and squinted at the angry face before him. Farmer Grahn, Elisabet's father, was glaring at him, his cheeks a mottled red. 'What's the matter?' Jamie mumbled. Then it all came back to him. Finding Elisabet, the rape, the Walloons. Had her father found out? But why was he shouting at Jamie?

'I'm sure you know exactly what the matter is. We'll be discussing this with your father present,' Grahn told him grimly.

Jamie winced at the loudness of the man's voice, but as he became aware of his surroundings, he realised a hangover was the least of his problems. He turned his head, which had been resting on a snowy pillow bordered with lace, and his eyes met the guarded gaze of Elisabet. Jamie shot upright, then noticed he was stark naked. He clutched the sheet to his chest, while bringing the other hand up to cradle his aching head. 'What the hell ...?'

He stared at Elisabet, who shrugged, giving him an apologetic little smile, which managed to be coquettish at the same time. 'I'm sorry, Jamie,' she murmured. 'Father came home earlier than I thought.'

'And a good thing I did,' Grahn shouted. 'How long has this been going on? That's what I'd like to know. I've sent for your father, boy, he should be here any moment.'

Jamie ignored the man, who continued his tirade, and focused on the girl next to him. There was no sign of the tears from the night before. Instead she was calm and collected, as if she was caught in bed with men every day of the week and it was nothing out of the ordinary. The scratches on her face were very faint, and it was almost as if everything that had happened in the forest had been a dream. No, not a dream – a charade for his benefit. Jamie felt anger explode inside him, his stomach muscles clenching. 'Why you little ...' he started saying, but she put up a hand to cover his mouth.

'Think, Jamie,' she said quietly. 'I told you, this is all for the best. There was no other way.'

For whom? Elisabet, obviously. He opened his mouth to argue with her, but realised he didn't have a leg to stand on. It was her word against his and he'd been caught naked in her bed. No one would believe him, even if he swore blind he'd found her the night before, the victim of rape. He had a reputation as a ladies' man, something he'd been rather proud of until now. God, what a fool, he berated himself. He narrowed his eyes at Elisabet and stifled the impulse to throttle her. Had she even been raped at all, he wondered? No, it was all a ruse. No woman could look that pleased with herself the night after a brutal attack.

'You planned this,' he hissed, while Grahn ranted on in the background, oblivious to their whispered exchange. 'Why? I thought you loved Brice.'

'Of course I still love Brice, but he's not here to save me, so it has to be you,' Elisabet replied.

Jamie shook his head. 'I'm not buying it. He'll be back soon and you know he'd do anything for you. He wouldn't have blamed you if you'd truly been hurt, which I no longer believe to be the case. No, this was all part of a scheme, wasn't it? You couldn't bear the fact that I've never paid you any attention, so you've trapped me. Well, you may have won, but believe me, you'll regret this.'

Elisabet's façade crumbled slightly. 'You were just being stubborn and unnecessarily noble,' she whispered. 'Every man for miles around wants me, you included. You just wouldn't admit it because you're scared of your big brother. Well, now I've solved the problem for you. You should be glad.'

Jamie had never wanted to kill another person before in his life, but he did now. The only thing that stopped him was the thought that somehow he'd get his revenge.

'You're wrong,' he said, staring her straight in the eyes. 'I've never wanted you and I'll never willingly touch you again. Ever. You can rot in hell.'

'And ... and did you?' Zar could barely make herself ask

the question, but she wanted to know. She could see the pulse at the base of his throat fluttering wildly in agitation and felt bad about making him relive these memories, but hoped it might help him to talk about them, the way he'd helped her by encouraging her to open up.

'No. I married her, because my father said I had no other option, but I insisted on separate bedchambers. It drove her mad.'

'But didn't you tell me that you have a daughter?' Zar frowned.

'Yes, but she's my daughter in name only. I never slept with Elisabet. As I said, she was already pregnant and the Walloon boy was the father of her child. The baby arrived six months after our wedding day, but fully formed and healthy. I'm sure everyone took that as proof I had seduced her. If only they knew!'

'What happened?'

Zar saw him tense and take a deep breath. 'Elisabet died.'

The screaming had gone on all night and Jamie was close to breaking point. He hadn't wanted to be in the house for the birth, but his father had told him it would have looked bad if he stayed away. After all, everyone thought the brat was his.

'Much they know,' he muttered, clenching his fists.

Still, no matter whose child it was and how much he hated Elisabet, Jamie would never have wished this much pain on anyone. It sounded as if the baby was being extracted from her body with red-hot pliers or some other barbaric device, judging by her screams and moans. If he hadn't been reassured by the midwife that this was normal, he'd have kicked the door down and demanded to know why his wife was being tortured unnecessarily.

His wife. As always, his mood turned black whenever he so much as thought the words. She'd had her way – as always – and they had been married within weeks of being discovered in bed together. And unfortunately, Brice returned just in time to witness the wedding. He hadn't stayed long. He told Jamie to go to hell, then left as soon as possible. In all conscience, Jamie couldn't blame his brother. He would have thought the worst too if the roles were reversed. But although Jamie hadn't seen him since, they'd made their peace by letter. Brice had found a better woman, far away in Scotland, while Jamie was left with Elisabet, his life in ruins.

Another shriek penetrated the thick oak ceiling and Jamie covered his ears. How much longer? 'For the love of God,' he whispered. 'Enough is enough, surely …'

Soon after, Karin knocked on the door and entered at his curt command. 'The baby has been born at last, but I think you'd better come,' she said, without looking at him.

Jamie had refused to address the woman after her collusion with Elisabet. It was clear to him she'd helped her young mistress to ensnare him and it wasn't something he was willing to forgive in a hurry, if ever. But he'd let her stay because he knew she'd only acted the way she had out of love for her young mistress.

'So it's over?' he asked, pushing past her out of the room.

'Yes, but …' He heard Karin sob behind him and turned to stare at her. 'She … she'll not pull through, my dear mistress.' Tears were flowing freely down the woman's face and a momentary dart of pity shot through Jamie, but he hardened his heart. Besides, he wasn't sure he believed her. She'd lied to him before.

He took the stairs two at a time and flung open the door to Elisabet's room. She was lying there now, propped up by a mountain of pillows, looking whiter than the sheets around her. The midwife was over by the fire, bathing a small mewling creature, but Jamie wasn't interested in that. It wasn't his child, so he didn't care what happened to it right now.

'Elisabet?' He sat down on the coverlet next to her, remembering that other night when he'd done the same, thinking she'd been hurt. He knew now it was all lies. The child had gone full term, the midwife had assured him, which meant Elisabet was already three months pregnant when she enacted her tragic rape scene. Jamie tamped down the fury coursing through him yet again.

'Jamie.' Her eyelids fluttered open and she stared at him, a strange expression in the blue depths. 'Damn you,' she whispered.

'I think that's my line, isn't it?' he answered, but softly since he could see she wasn't in any state to argue properly. They'd done their fair share of that already over the past months. 'Anyway, I wasn't the cause of your discomfort. You brought that on yourself.'

'Had to. Only way to catch you. Always so stubborn, so sure of yourself.'

'So you're saying that you seducing a Walloon boy or two was all because of me? I don't think so. But we can argue the point when you're recovered. You should get some rest now, for the sake of your …' He realised he hadn't even asked if the child was a boy or a girl, so finished with '… child.'

'It's too late. I heard them. I'll not live long enough to even feed her.' Elisabet stretched out a hand and grabbed Jamie's, squeezing hard despite her weakened state.

'Swear to me you'll take care of her. She's innocent, it's not her fault.'

So it was a girl. Well, the baby's sex was irrelevant. Jamie took a deep breath and looked at Elisabet. She was right. A child was never to blame for a parent's wrongdoing. But damn it all, how was he to raise another man's child as his own? And without the child's mother? He looked away and murmured, 'Very well, I'll provide for her,' but he didn't actually say the word 'swear'. He'd find a way to have the child cared for, without him being involved.

Elisabet must have noticed because her grip tightened even further. 'I hate you,' she hissed.

'Yes, that must be why you wanted to marry me so badly. Shame you picked the only man around these parts who wasn't interested.'

'You were! You just wanted to punish me for trapping you. I should have found another way.'

'No, you should have left me alone. If I'd really wanted you, I would have squared it with Brice somehow.'

'Very well, you're right. I don't hate you. I was so sure I could make you love me. Everyone else did ... But you've got what you wanted now – your freedom back and the farm to run as you please.'

Her father had died unexpectedly just a few months after the wedding and Jamie found himself the owner of one of the biggest farms in the area. Elisabet refused to believe he'd never wanted that either.

He shook his head. 'You're deluded. I never wanted you or your inheritance and nothing you could have done would change that. Can't you see? All you did was make me despise you. You should have stuck with Brice, he's the noble one.'

'He gave in too easily. I wanted someone who stood up to me.'

Jamie sighed. 'Well, you got that. Perhaps more than you bargained for? Now shouldn't you rest? Save the arguing for later.'

'I told you, there won't be a later.' She gave him a wan smile. 'Perhaps we'll meet up in hell?'

'I sincerely hope not!' Jamie stood up, freeing himself from her grip. 'Strangely enough, I find I wish you a better fate than that.'

Elisabet started to cry but Jamie didn't know what to do about it. What did you say to someone who was dying and who knew it? Words seemed pointless. Jamie could tell her strength was fading and he really didn't want her life to end this way. Perhaps if he left her to rest, she'd recover. And knowing Elisabet, she might just be trying to fool him into feeling sorry for her.

He patted her shoulder awkwardly, then went over to look at the infant, who was now clean and trussed up in blankets and clothing that was too big for her. He stared at the small face and felt nothing. How different it would have been if it had been his daughter lying there. Moving the blanket aside slightly, he saw the pitch black hair which matched tiny eyebrows and long dark lashes. The baby's skin wasn't milky white like her mother's and Jamie knew without a doubt this child would tan in the sun the way her father had done. *A pox on that Walloon!* But knowing Elisabet, that boy had probably been as much a victim of her machinations as Jamie himself.

'What are you calling her?' he called out over his shoulder, but Elisabet's eyes were closed and she didn't reply.

'She said it was up to you, master Kinross,' the midwife said.

'Really? I'd have thought she'd want to choose. She decided everything else.'

'No, she refused. Didn't even want to see her.' The midwife shook her head and picked the baby up. 'Poor little mite,' she murmured. 'But it takes some of them a while. All that pain can do funny things to you.'

Jamie felt a twinge of pity for this child, whose mother couldn't even be bothered to name her. 'She's to be called Margot,' he said. He just picked a name at random. What did he care? But it was a good name, he felt, and suited the dark little girl. 'Yes, Margot,' he repeated with a nod.

He left the room after a last glance at Elisabet, and went downstairs in search of *snaps*. He didn't normally resort to drink in times of trouble, but he needed it tonight. And he couldn't bear to stay here and watch her die. Although he'd wished her ill, he couldn't quite bring himself to be that vindictive.

'And she died that night?' Zar felt her own heart beating too fast, appalled by Jamie's sad tale.

'Yes. I didn't speak to her again.'

'But the child lived?' Zar found her emotions focusing on the little dark-haired scrap named Margot by a man who didn't want her. All her latent maternal instincts surfaced in a rush. *I want her! I'll care for her.* But that wasn't possible because it would mean she'd have to marry Jamie first. And even if she did, he wouldn't take her to Sweden, she was sure. Little Margot would never even know she had a stepmother.

'Yes, she's doing well. I left her with my mother when I went to India so she's being cared for.'

'That's good.' She didn't dare voice the true extent of her feelings when hearing about the little girl.

Somehow she sensed Jamie wasn't ready to talk about his responsibilities with regard to the child. 'What about your brother? Did he forgive you?'

'Yes, eventually. I haven't seen him since it happened, but I sent him a letter and he replied. He said he understood and that actually I'd done him a favour because I made him see Elisabet's true colours.' Jamie smiled. 'He found love with some other woman in Scotland apparently, one who was everything Elisabet wasn't – honest, brave and loyal.' He shrugged. 'So it worked out well for him.'

'But not for you.' Zar felt for him but was pleased at least the quarrel with his brother had been cleared up.

'Do you think badly of me?' Jamie's voice sounded strained and, for once, unsure.

Zar struggled to keep her tone even. 'No. You were wronged and I think you did the best you could in the circumstances. I hope you will one day be able to forget about it, the way I'm learning to put my memories of Francis out of my mind. Such thoughts are destructive, if we allow them to be, I can see that now. But it takes time. I don't believe it happens over night.'

Jamie sent her a sad smile across the table and nodded. 'You are a very wise woman, Zarmina. I wish I'd met you first.'

So did she.

Chapter Twenty-Four

'Cover yourself with this blanket and let us go. It should protect you from the worst of the rain showers.' Jamie handed Zar a blanket, which his servant had procured. There was one for him as well, and a pair of Arabian horses he'd paid through the nose for.

They set off early in the morning and rode steadily throughout the day, stopping only a few times to give the horses and themselves a break. Zar had agreed it was best they posed as Hindus, so they were both dressed in native clothing. Jamie's skin had tanned even more while out in the boat for so long, and with his hair covered in a turban and the beginnings of a moustache, as well as a lot of stubble, he was able to pass muster.

'Although my Hindi is fairly fluent, it's better if you do the talking in Gujarati,' Jamie told Zar. 'Pretend I have a sore throat or something. I think that's safer.' She'd agreed.

The rain came and went in massive rain showers where the wind blew the raindrops into misty clouds that came at them sideways, spooking the horses. Jamie was sure he'd never been this wet before, except for that night in the boat, and began to wonder if he'd ever be dry again. The roads turned into muddy rivers, the horses' and riders' legs splattered with mire. The heavy showers were interspersed with blazing sunshine, which made for uncomfortable levels of humidity. But neither of them complained as it was just something that had to be endured.

Jamie was on guard the entire journey, scanning the countryside around them for possible danger. All travellers had to keep an eye out for bandits, who could appear at any time, and he'd brought pistols and a sword and dagger, just in case. If a group of brigands ambushed them, however, Jamie doubted they'd have a chance. He prayed the weather would keep such men away.

In a little village they found a *sarai*, a type of small hostelry, to spend the night in. It was none too clean, but at least it was dry and the horses were able to rest under a roof of sorts as well.

'Stay next to me at all times,' Jamie warned Zar sotto voce. 'It's safest if they think you're my wife.'

'I suppose so.'

The grudging response made Jamie realise it was time to put his plan into action. He'd decided to try and woo Zar in any way he could in order to make her change her mind about marrying him. Now was as good a time as any to begin.

'You didn't mind sleeping in my arms on Juhu,' he reminded her, putting a proprietary arm round her waist, ostensibly for the benefit of any onlookers, but really to test her response to his proximity.

She stiffened slightly, but stayed put. 'That was … different.'

'In what way?'

'We'd just been through a shocking experience. We weren't thinking clearly. Or I wasn't anyway.'

'You seemed fairly lucid to me.' He gave her a lazy smile and nuzzled her ear.

'Please don't remind me. And could you stop that?'

'I'm only acting the lovesick husband. We have an audience.' They were sitting in a shabby room with other travellers and although no one was looking directly at them, they were bound to be watching surreptitiously.

There was nothing else to do, after all, except eat the unappetising meal. 'Don't you want someone to adore you?' he teased.

'No. I could never be sure it was my person they adored, rather than my fortune.'

'You could with me. I told you, I'm already rich and money isn't important to me.' Jamie wasn't sure how to persuade her on this point. Her previous experiences had obviously tainted her views on prospective husbands and this was a massive hindrance. 'Shall I tell you what matters more?'

'If you wish.' He'd kept his arm around her waist, and she was still stiff, but he sensed a slight unbending as though he'd piqued her curiosity.

'Family. Happiness. Loyalty. Friendship. Those are the things I value. And honesty.'

She glanced at him from under those lovely long lashes and gave him a measuring look. 'That's all?'

'All? Sounds like quite a lot to me. It's not often you find someone who can give you all those things.'

'I don't think such a paragon exists.'

'I'm holding one.' He kissed her cheek and pulled her closer, but while she didn't resist, she didn't quite unbend either.

'Now you're just teasing me.'

He sighed. What would it take for her to believe him?

Zar hoped that Jamie couldn't feel the rapid beating of her heart. Sitting so close to him, one of his strong arms around her, it was extremely tempting to just give in. Live for the moment. Make love to him again in the tiny room they were allotted for the night.

That was obviously what he was hoping for.

285

But she had the future to think of and she didn't believe he'd want her for any length of time. He'd soon tire of bedding her and then what? Misery. Loneliness.

As she lay down next to him, however, she had to use all her determination not to turn around and roll into his arms. It was extremely tempting. *He* was so tempting and she wanted him so badly. If only she could be sure he'd stay with her forever.

'Let us hope it doesn't take too long to reach Surat,' Jamie muttered the following morning. 'I don't think my back can take sleeping on such rough surfaces for too many nights!'

He was feeling grumpy because his charm offensive wasn't having any effect whatsoever. Zar had slept next to him, but with a careful space between them. Did she really regret their lovemaking that much?

But perhaps she was just worried about the immediate future and who knew what awaited them at their destination?

They arrived in Surat a few days later, just before the city gates were closed for the night, and were able to make their way to Jamie's rented house without meeting anyone they knew. A suspicious Kamal opened the door and took a moment to realise who was outside. When he did, his eyebrows rose almost to his hairline, then his face broke into a huge smile.

'Kinross *sahib*! Come in, come in. We thought you gone! Maybe even …' He shook his head. 'We have been so worried.'

He didn't have a chance to say more as a bundle of fur came hurtling round a corner and jumped around Jamie, barking and yapping excitedly. Jamie bent to pick Kutaro up and hugged him close, unexpectedly touched at such a rapturous welcome. He allowed the dog to lick his chin while he scratched him behind the ears.

'Hello, you little rascal. I'm pleased to see you too.'

'Jamie! And *Sahiba* Miller!'

Roshani wasn't far behind her pet and flung herself at the pair of them at once, her skinny arms holding the three of them together. Jamie and Zar both bent to hug the little girl back and their eyes met over her head. They smiled at each other, while Roshani bombarded them with questions.

'Where you be? Why so long? Where bad man? You go on ship?' Her curiosity knew no bounds and Jamie let Zar calm her down and answer in Gujarati, while he gave Kamal a shortened version of their adventures. Then Soraya arrived from the kitchen, wondering what all the commotion was about and had to be told as well. It was quite a while before all explanations had been given and everyone settled down.

'We've been travelling for days. Please can you organise some water to wash with for me and my wife, Kamal?'

'You wife?' Roshani, ever quick to pick up on things, looked from one to the other. When Jamie nodded, she grinned from ear to ear and jumped up and down. 'I knowed it! I see you look at *Sahiba* Miller—'

'Mrs Kinross now, actually.'

'Yes, yes, Mrs Kinross, and she look back. I knowed!'

'You knew, did you? I don't know about that, since I didn't,' Jamie muttered, but he shot Zar an amused glance. Zar looked slightly awkward as she'd only agreed reluctantly to tell this lie at first, but if William was to believe them married, they had to pretend to everyone else too for a while. She managed a smile for the little girl.

'I'm glad you're pleased, Roshani,' she said. 'It's, er ... all a bit new to us as yet.'

Kamal and Soraya both bowed and beamed at Zarmina. '*Sahiba*.' Kamal spoke for both of them. 'We wish you very happy.'

'Thank you,' she replied, returning their smiles, but Jamie thought her answer sounded slightly muted. He hoped she could keep up the pretence for as long as it was necessary, but she obviously wasn't comfortable with that notion.

Before heading to his bedroom, Kamal took him aside to whisper, 'You have a visitor. The man you said would come is here.'

'Sanjiv?' Kamal nodded. 'Oh, excellent. Where is he?'

'I have put him in the corner room at the back. He has stayed there for two days.' Kamal shrugged. 'Didn't know what to do.'

Jamie clapped him on the back. 'You did well. Please go and tell him I'll see him as soon as I'm clean. Ask him to join us for a meal in an hour.'

'It will be as you wish, *sahib*.'

Roshani wouldn't leave Zar's side, so Jamie shrugged and directed Soraya to take her to the room next to his. 'I will see you both downstairs as soon as you're ready,' he added before disappearing through his door.

Zar felt a bit awkward having to ask Soraya to lend her some clothing, but the woman was all smiles and seemed to think nothing of it. Soon she'd brought new garments, hot water to wash with and some lovely scented soap. Zar hurried to wash herself piecemeal with a wet cloth, while Roshani chattered away in Gujarati about how she'd been fretting ever since Jamie left.

'I was so scared!' she told Zar, her brown eyes wide to show how distressed she'd been. 'But I knew Jamie would come back. He promised.'

Zar wondered how he could have promised any such thing when he hadn't known what would happen, but guessed at the time he didn't want to worry Roshani. It was fortunate that he'd been able to keep his word and not disillusion the girl.

'Now you are here, all is well, yes?'

'I'm not sure. We still have a few problems, sweetheart, but hopefully all will be well. Now come, I believe Jamie is waiting for us. And I, for one, am starving.'

That was obviously a sentiment the little girl understood perfectly. 'Me too,' she declared, even though Zar was sure she'd have eaten her evening meal already. She had to smile. Oh, to be so young and innocent again.

'Sanjiv, it's good to see you! Any problems?'

Jamie had arrived downstairs first and greeted Akash's brother with a big smile, which was reciprocated. They spoke in Hindi as they'd done in Madras.

'That depends on what you mean by problems. Everything went well in Madras. I waited until Meera and the children were returned safely, then I left.'

'So the thieves kept their word then? Thank God for that!'

'Indeed. Akash was ecstatic and I'm sure he's taken precautions so that they can never be taken hostage again.'

'That's very good news. And your journey?'

'Well, no one seemed to be following me, but it took longer than I thought as I decided to go by ship the last part. Unfortunately the weather turned bad, so I ended up almost shipwrecked and then I had to continue on foot, just to make sure I could get here.'

'What about the snake? Did everyone believe you to be a snake-charmer?'

'Of course! I told you, my friend showed me what to do and I liked the serpent. In fact,' Sanjiv looked vaguely embarrassed, 'I … er, let him go. You know, into the wild. He had done his job and I had no more need of him.'

Jamie laughed. 'Excellent. I would have done the same.'

'Really?' Sanjiv seemed relieved to hear that.

'Absolutely. But to be serious, we should have taken the monsoon into account more, I think. Still, you're here now and we need to make plans. I take it you have the talisman?'

'Yes, here it is. I'd rather you keep it from now on.' Sanjiv handed Jamie the bundle containing the jewel and he stowed it in his sash next to the fake one.

He turned as Zarmina and her young companions entered the *divan*. 'And here is my wife. Sanjiv, may I introduce Zarmina? And Roshani, my, uhm … ward and her furry friend Kutaro.' Jamie translated for Zar and Roshani, as neither spoke Hindi and Sanjiv's English was rudimentary at best.

'I didn't know you had a wife.' Sanjiv looked confused, but greeted Zar politely.

'That's because we were only married a few days ago. It's a long story, but let us eat first, then I'll fill you in.'

After the meal, Jamie did so, and related their adventures once more, apart from the more private ones. 'So now we need to find out what has become of Zar's stepson and then figure out what to do with the talisman, while unmasking the thief. At least we know who its rightful owner is now – the Rajah of Nadhur.'

'We suspected as much, didn't we.' Sanjiv nodded. 'He is the ruler over the region where Akash and I come from, so the thief could have found out about my brother being a lapidary and living in Madras.'

'That makes sense.'

'I passed him along the way, you know. He's in a nearby town on some sort of state visit, or so I was told. He's about to be married.'

'He is?' Jamie frowned. 'Doesn't that seem like too much of a coincidence? You don't think he's set up the whole theft himself because he's in need of money, do you? Zarmina and I wondered about that.'

Sanjiv looked horrified. 'No, never! A talisman like that is too sacred. He would be terrified of the bad luck which would be sure to befall him, should he do such a thing.'

'But maybe that's why he's pretending it's a theft?' Zar put in and Jamie nodded. He'd been thinking the same thing.

'No, absolutely not. The talisman is sure to be blessed by the gods and they would know of his deceit. Such a ruse would never work and the Rajah knows that.'

'Hmm, I'm not convinced, but let us say for argument's sake that you are right. In that case, it would have to be someone else, someone who had access to the ruler's private quarters. Any ideas?'

'I'm sure a *rajah* has many attendants, even in private.'

'Then we must find a way of visiting him to see if there is anyone we recognise.'

'Bad man from Mansukh? Or nose man?' Roshani said, proving that she'd been following the discussion with avid interest. Jamie narrowed his eyes at her. He'd almost forgotten her presence and wondered if she could be trusted to keep quiet. But he knew she'd never do anything to harm him, as her next words confirmed. 'Want to help,' she said. 'Kutaro too. Can bite.'

'Thank you, but I'd rather you kept out of this, both of you. Tell Kutaro to guard *you*, that's his most important job. And no, it couldn't be Mansukh's spy because I saw him on the ship and ... er, he was killed by the pirates. Now we need to—'

He was interrupted by wailing coming from the courtyard and stood up, reaching for the dagger he'd strapped to his waist. What now? Were they never to have any peace?

Kamal knocked on the door and was shoved out of the way by a wild-eyed Priya. The maid searched the room with her eyes and gave a little shriek when she beheld Zar, who stood up and met her former *ayah* half-way. 'Priya, what are you doing here?'

The two women clasped hands, and Priya opened and shut her mouth several times before she was able to speak coherently.

'It is that misbegotten cur, your stepson,' she began, shaking with what seemed to be fury rather than fear. 'He is ransacking your room, stealing things! I tried to stop him, but he threatened me with a pistol. And ... and ... *Sahib* Evans is helping him! I didn't know what to do, so I thought to ask Kamal for assistance.' She glanced at the servant, who was still standing by the door. 'He and his wife were so supportive after you were taken away, it ... I ...' She shook her head, as if unable to speak further.

'Mr Evans? You mean, my father?' Zar looked thunderstruck.

As well she might, Jamie thought. What on earth was he doing back in Surat? He was supposed to have retired to England.

But there was no time to ponder these things now. This called for action.

'Priya, you did the right thing and we're back now. We'll deal with this.' Jamie gritted his teeth and reflected that it appeared they hadn't arrived a moment too soon. 'Sanjiv, Kamal, can you come with me, please? We need to stop them.'

'I'm coming too,' Zar said. Her voice was quiet, but determined, and as Jamie looked into her eyes he knew she had a right to be present at the confrontation.

'Very well, but you stay back at first, please. I don't want you harmed in any way.'

She nodded.

'Good, then let's find some weapons.'

It didn't take them long to reach Zar's home and Jamie made her enter the house last.

'We don't know if William has any henchmen around,' he whispered. 'It's easy enough to employ a few *sepoys* as they come cheap. And we've no idea what your father is doing here either.'

Zar knew he was right to be cautious. William wasn't the brightest man in the world, but when people were cornered and desperate, they sometimes acquired a cunning that was normally alien to their nature. There was no saying what he'd be capable of. And as for her father … She doubted he had any tender emotions or he wouldn't have sold her to Francis.

They all used the back door, which Priya had left unbarred in her haste to leave, and made their way on silent feet into the courtyard. Jamie stopped to listen and the others followed suit. Zar heard noises coming from upstairs, but nowhere else. She scanned the upper walkway and saw light spilling from the door to her quarters.

Jamie must have seen it too, as he gestured for continued silence and for them all to move towards the stairs. Sanjiv and Kamal went to one set of steps, while Zar followed Jamie to the other. They kept their eyes open for any threats, but the house seemed empty apart from whoever was in Zar's rooms.

Near the doorway, Jamie stopped and waited until the others were ranged on either side. 'Me first, alone,' he mouthed and received nods in reply. Then he took a quick look into the room and entered with a pistol in one hand and his dagger in the other.

'Exactly what do you think you're doing, Miller?' he asked, his tone low and deadly.

Zar peeked round the door frame and caught sight of her father and William, both standing stock still with their hands full of her jewellery and a couple of bags of coins she'd kept under her mattress. They looked like two children caught with their hands in a jar full of sugary treats – guilty and defensive. As well they should, since they'd made quite a mess. Her father turned a dull red.

'Who the hell are you?' he asked, but his question was answered by William, whose ludicrous expression of surprise quickly turned to black fury.

'Kinross!' he snarled. 'I should have known the pirates wouldn't finish you off. I suppose you've joined them, have you? Deceitful bastard.'

'I'm glad you think so highly of me,' Jamie replied, his voice dripping with sarcasm. 'But no, I declined their kind offer. I am here to reclaim what is mine.' He nodded at the items in William's hands.

'What are you talking about? I'm taking what should have been *mine* all along. If my father hadn't had his head twisted by that little strumpet … Beg pardon, Evans, but honestly, everyone else could see she was playing him for a fool, but not him, oh no.'

Her father kept silent, which made Zar furious. So he couldn't even defend her against such slurs on her character? *By all the gods, he's the outside of enough!*

'Is that so?' Jamie asked. 'Yet he deemed her wise enough to run half the business after his death. He obviously didn't trust *you* to look after it properly.'

'He was bewitched, I tell you! She had him eating out of her disgusting, grasping little hands!' William was so angry, his eyes were bulging, but Zar noticed that Jamie stayed calm.

'I think you'll find you are wrong. I talked to quite a few of the other Englishmen here and they all told me you wouldn't have survived six months as a trader without Zarmina and your broker. But it's a moot point now, isn't it? I take it you're leaving India? And you, sir, what's your part in this?'

Zar's father shrugged. 'I came to support my daughter in her trading ventures,' he said. 'I heard from friends that she'd been widowed and thought she would appreciate her father's guidance. Unfortunately, young Miller here informed me of her demise. Naturally, as her father, I claim a share of her estate.'

'A very small share,' William muttered, pulling a coin bag out of Evans' hands.

Zar felt the fury inside her almost boil over, but she clamped her teeth together and stayed quiet as Jamie had asked. She trusted him and would wait for his signal.

'Damn right I'm leaving this stinking place!' William

spat. 'Not staying a moment longer than I have to. So get out of my way, Kinross!'

'Not so fast.' Jamie raised his pistol a fraction. 'Before you leave, you will put those trinkets down. And the money. They belong to Zarmina, not you.' He turned a fraction towards Evans. 'She's very much alive, so I regret to inform you there is no inheritance to share out.'

'The pirates let her go? I don't bloody well believe it!' William was almost jumping up and down with rage.

'Well, it's true. So you can't sell her share of the business before you go either.'

'Says who?' William sneered. 'I've torn up that infernal will – oh, yes, I found it hidden in here,' he gloated. 'So she can't prove ownership and she can't fight me, she's too weak.' He snorted. 'I doubt she'll call me out.'

'No, but I will. I always fight for what's mine. Or I can just shoot you on the spot, I suppose. My servant will testify that it was in self-defence.'

But William had only listened to the first half of what Jamie had said. 'What do you mean "yours"?' he challenged.

'As Zarmina's new husband, all she owned belongs to me now.'

Chapter Twenty-Five

'What? No! You're making that up.' William's face was a mottled red, his eyes wild. 'She's sworn never to marry again. In fact, she was being a right nuisance about it when my friend Richardson wanted her.'

'I think you'll find she's changed her mind and I'm not making it up. Zar, tell him, will you please?' Jamie didn't turn his head and Zar was glad. She knew he couldn't afford to let William out of his sight for even an instant. The man was obviously seriously unstable, if not totally deranged. Perhaps the terrifying journey back across the sea all by himself had unhinged his mind? She wondered how he'd managed it at all.

She stepped slowly into the room, but stayed behind Jamie. She didn't acknowledge her father with so much as a nod, even though he exclaimed 'Zara!', his old pet-name for her. She addressed William. 'Yes, Jamie and I are married,' she confirmed. 'We have proof in the form of marriage lines from the English minister in Bombay. So you need not deal with me any longer, William. You should be pleased.'

'Pleased? Why you … aaargh!' William exploded into a torrent of curses and abuse that made Zar want to put her hands over her ears.

'*Enough!*' she shouted at the top of her voice and William stopped in mid-rant, staring at her. 'Have you heard of the *Qazi*?' When he didn't reply, she continued, 'Yes, I know you have. He's the man who dispenses justice here in Surat and together with a *Mufti*, a man who is learned in matters of law, he registers all types of deeds.

The fact that you tore up your father's will is irrelevant – the *Qazi* has a copy. Several probably. I have lodged a will of my own with them, giving all my worldly goods to Priya should anything happen to me. And to be extra secure, I gave the English Chief Factor a copy too.' She finally gazed at her father and added, 'So you wouldn't have been entitled to anything whatever happened.'

Her father shrugged as if he didn't know what to say, which was just as well, since Zar didn't want to hear from him anyway. She turned back towards William, whose mouth worked as if he couldn't get the words out, then he sneered, 'Why you dirty little whore, you have it all planned, don't you? I'll just have to—'

But Jamie had apparently had enough. He marched over to William and punched him on the chin. 'Shut up, Miller. Don't ever call my wife names again, do you hear?'

William staggered backwards, dropping most of Zar's trinkets. Blinking at Jamie, he put up a hand to cradle his face. He glared daggers and was just about to say something, when another voice interrupted them. It came from the direction of the balcony, where a shadowy figure appeared.

'Which one of you is William Miller?'

William spun round and Jamie looked over towards the now open shutters. The figure stepped slowly into the room, followed soon after by several others. He heard Kamal hiss that there were people in the courtyard and realised they were surrounded. But by whom?

He didn't like this. Not one little bit.

'I am. Who the hell is asking?' William snarled.

'Then kindly hand over that which doesn't belong to you.'

'The talisman? You'll never see that again, it's been lost at sea.' He pointed at Jamie. 'He knows all about it. I'm going now.'

He bent to pick up a few of Zar's necklaces and rings, whatever was closest to hand, then set off for the door.

Jamie's hand shot out and caught William by the arm. 'Aren't you forgetting something?' he hissed. He didn't want to shoot the man in front of witnesses, but he wasn't letting Miller go with Zar's possessions. 'Our discussion wasn't finished, but it looks like we'll have to continue it later.'

'Oh, devil take it, I just want to leave this godforsaken country. I hate it here!' William threw the bits of jewellery at Jamie and bolted through the door, but Kamal and Sanjiv stopped him. Together they restrained the kicking and screaming man and one of them must have put a hand over his mouth as the noise became muffled and then stopped altogether.

Jamie considered his options and decided on the truth. Or part of it at least. 'The talisman was not lost at sea,' he told the man by the balcony. 'Do you truly represent its rightful owner or just the thief who stole it from him?'

'We serve Bijal, the Grand Vizier of the Rajah of Nadhur.'

That didn't really answer the question as such. Still, Jamie doubted he had a choice here. He pulled the fake talisman out of his belt and held it out. 'I think this is what you're after?' He nodded towards William. 'Please feel free to take him with you. He was lying.'

The man moved forward and took the packet, unwrapping it to check the contents. When the fake talisman was revealed, he nodded as if satisfied, then turned to a group of men who had followed him into the room. 'Bring them,' he ordered. 'All of them.'

'Now hold on a moment,' Jamie protested. 'Miller is the man you want. We were just trying to make him return the stolen item. This is nothing to do with us.'

'That's for the Rajah to decide. Now either you come of your own accord, or we can make you. Your choice.'

'But you came for Miller. He was the one who was hired by the thief to sell the jewel abroad.' Jamie reckoned that as they'd been asking for William by name, they must know he was the go-between.

The leader of the group shrugged. 'The Rajah wants the truth. You had his sacred object so you are as much a thief as the others. I'm sure he will wish to hear your explanation.'

Jamie gave up. It would seem they had no choice but to try to appeal to the Rajah himself. 'Very well.'

Evans tried to protest in his turn, but received a cuff on the back of the head for his trouble. After that, he kept quiet, although he obviously had no idea what was going on.

Jamie tried to send Zar a reassuring glance, but could see that she was terrified. He took her hand and squeezed it, trying to imbue her with courage, and she nodded as if she understood. To the Rajah's man he nodded at Kamal and added, 'This man is but my servant. He knows nothing of the other matter. May he stay here to safeguard my wife's possessions until our return?'

They both knew there may not be a return, but it wasn't something Jamie wanted to say out loud.

'Yes, yes.' The man nodded impatiently. 'Now hurry. The Rajah is waiting.'

Jamie seemed taken aback to find elephants waiting outside the house, but Zar was relieved they wouldn't have to walk at least. It was still raining and the roads a muddy mess.

'Climb up,' they were ordered, as the elephants obediently bowed their front legs to allow them access to the seating platform mounted on their backs. Unfortunately it wasn't a proper *howdah* with a canopy, but just two seats.

Jamie held out his hand to help Zar and then scrambled up himself to sit beside her. She had been wearing a large shawl and pulled it up over her head now, as well as around herself. Then she clung to the sides of the seat for dear life when the elephant followed the instructions of its *mahout* and got to its feet. She'd been on one before, but didn't like the swaying sensation and the fact that she was so far off the ground. But she trusted the handler, who sat just behind the large beast's ears, to get them to their destination safely.

Sanjiv and William were on the animal in front of them, with her father next to one of the Rajah's men behind them. The strange procession made its way through the dark streets and out of one of the city's gates, which appeared to be opened especially for them. Zar guessed someone had been bribed for this purpose.

It felt strange to ride through the silent night. There was no moon as the rain was falling steadily and the wind was up, but Zar could still make out the fields and tree groves by the sides of the road. Jamie took her hand and held it tight. Even though they were both soon wet through, his palm felt warm and solid as always. Safe. But they were anything but safe at the moment.

'Will the Rajah believe us?' she whispered.

'I hope so, but not if he arranged the theft himself. In that case, he'll be looking for scapegoats.' Zar shivered and Jamie continued, 'But I have a feeling he's not the one who sent for us. I doubt the Rajah knows anything about the Surat connection, so someone else must be the criminal.'

'I don't understand.' Zar tried to look at Jamie, but could only make out his profile.

'Think about it – unless the Rajah has found out who stole the talisman in the first place, he won't know it's been sent to Surat. The only one who does is the original thief. Now everything has gone wrong and he may have given up on the idea of selling the jewel. Instead, he'll try to curry favour by being the one to find it and return it. That's what I would do, if I were in his shoes.'

'Of course, that makes sense. But who is he?'

'The man behind us said he was acting on the orders of the Grand Vizier. That sounds like a person who might have access to the Rajah's private quarters. I'd wager it could be him.'

'But we can't prove that. We can't prove it's anyone other than ourselves.' Zar felt despair engulf her. How could they possibly come out of this alive? 'And now they have the talisman too.'

She heard Jamie chuckle softly. 'No they don't. I do.'

'Oh, you mean …?'

'I gave them the fake. Now all we have to do is try and guess who the real thief is and then unmask him.' Jamie squeezed her hand. 'I'll need your help. Listen carefully now, this is what I want you to do …'

Some considerable time later, they arrived at a high wall that proved to enclose a large, sprawling building in the Indian style surrounded by trees and ornamental gardens. It was just after dawn and grey light seeped in through the many windows and doorways and highlighted the high cupolas of the roofs. A walkway surrounded by ornate pillars ran along the front of the building, with a large entrance in the middle. Massive double doors opened to reveal a courtyard, where everyone dismounted. Once inside the palace itself, the 'guests' found themselves led through a series of corridors. Finally, they arrived outside another formidable set of doors, which their lead captor knocked on.

'Enter,' came from inside, and they were ushered in, followed by their guards.

Zar made sure she was walking next to Jamie. He still held her hand and it was comforting, but inside she was quaking. What if his ruse didn't work? Were they all going to die this day?

At the end of the room was a dais and here a man sat waiting. Zar almost gasped when she caught sight of him, as she'd never seen such magnificence. He was dressed almost exclusively in white, but the material was embroidered with gold and silver thread that sparkled in the light of several candelabras as he moved. A sash of purple silk was tied round his waist, with the hilt of a bejewelled dagger sticking out at the top. This too flashed and glittered, as did a large ornament of precious stones fastened to the front of his turban. Not as big as the talisman, but a costly object nonetheless. Underneath was the handsome face of a man in his prime, perhaps mid to late twenties. His expression was haughty, but to Zar it looked as though he had an intelligent gaze that missed nothing.

The Rajah, for it couldn't be anyone else, was surrounded by guards and courtiers. One stood further forward and Zar guessed he might be the vizier as he had an air of authority about him. His demeanour was calm, but a watchful look in his eyes told her he didn't miss anything either. If anyone threatened his master, this man would know about it instantly, she was sure. The Rajah regarded them from under hooded eyes as they all bowed and put their hands together in the traditional greeting. He didn't reciprocate, but then they hadn't expected him to.

The possible vizier bowed to his master and said, 'Highness, once again, I apologise for waking you so early, but I believe this is a pressing matter. I present to you the thieves who have stolen the sacred talisman. My spies found them at last.'

'Thank you, Bijal. So finally I meet the people responsible for stealing my most treasured object,' the Rajah said. 'Is there no end to your greed, foreigners?'

One of the men near the dais translated the Rajah's words into accented English, but soon found there was no need.

'I'm afraid we are being wrongly accused, Highness,' Jamie replied in near-perfect Hindi. The Rajah's eyebrows rose slightly in surprise at such fluency, but he waited while Jamie continued. 'Only one of us was acting as an accomplice.' He pointed at William. 'The rest of us were forced to help through blackmail.'

'And why should I believe you? Accused men will say anything to save their skins.'

'Of course,' Jamie acknowledged. 'But in this case it may be in your best interest to believe us because if we speak the truth, there is a traitor in your midst. Someone who will no doubt try to harm you again in future if he or she isn't caught now.'

All the people clustered round the Rajah began to look

at each other as if they worried they'd be accused next. Everyone except the man called Bijal, who kept his gaze on them while his mouth curved into a small smile.

'Well said, foreigner, but still a futile attempt. No one here will believe you as it is well known your people want only riches,' said Bijal.

'And you don't?' Jamie challenged.

The vizier scowled at him, his eyes flashing with dark fire. 'I have all the riches I need in the service of His Highness.'

'Ah, so you're only a servant.' Jamie nodded, as if he understood the position now, which seemed to anger the man further.

'I am the Grand Vizier, I'll have you know.'

Jamie shrugged. 'A servant nonetheless.' He turned towards Zar and nodded in the vizier's direction, winking at her surreptitiously. She understood and spoke up.

'Well, we're going to end up as servants too, husband, thanks to you and your little intrigues,' she said loudly and angrily, pushing at Jamie with both hands on his chest.

'Watch your tongue, wife.' Jamie pretended to scold her. 'I'll not have a shrew in my household, I've told you.'

'I will not! Not this time. I'm used to having my own servants, not serving others, and now see what you've done. It's unbearable, I tell you. What were you thinking?'

On the final word, she shoved him again, as hard as she could, in the direction of the vizier. Jamie stumbled backwards and into the man, treading on his toes. So off-balance did he seem to be that he had to grab hold of the vizier's belt to right himself, and the man snarled furiously and tried to free himself from Jamie's grip.

'How dare you? Get your filthy hands off me!'

'Sorry, sorry,' Jamie smiled apologetically. 'Women, eh? Such temper, some of them.' He turned back to Zar and spread his palms. 'None of this is my fault, surely you can see that? It's all William's. He's the one you should be berating.'

William, who'd been standing just behind them, seemed to have his own agenda. Without warning, he sprang into action and tried to attack the man holding his wrist in a firm grip. He swung his fists in all directions, catching the man a blow and making him let go. Then he tried to fight off another guard, who'd come to his comrade's assistance. 'I'm not taking the blame for this, I was but the go-between!' he shouted. 'Mansukh told me who was really responsible. He told me—'

'Silence, prisoner!' the Grand Vizier had moved to stand before William. 'One more word out of you and you will die immediately.'

Zar tried to signal to William to calm down, but all that had happened during the night seemed to have tipped him over the edge into near insanity. William managed to free himself yet again, and lashed out at the vizier, striking the man's nose. A gasp went up from the assembled company and in the next moment Zar saw a flash of metal, then William sank to the floor with a strangled noise.

'No!' she cried out, and would have gone to her stepson, but Jamie held her back.

The vizier straightened up and she could see that in his hand he held a *katar*, a strange type of push dagger, which had an H-shaped handle above a short, almost triangular blade. The tip was dripping with blood. William's blood. Zar felt faint and leaned against Jamie for a moment.

'No one strikes a vizier,' Bijal announced in grand

tones, and glided back to his original position as if nothing out of the ordinary had happened.

Zar glanced at her father, who hadn't said a word so far, and whose expression was as shocked as she herself felt. He must be regretting coming back to Surat. But then it served him right. He should have stayed in England. Why would he think she'd welcome his help with trading? No, it had to be a ruse for getting his hands on some of her fortune. Well, he wasn't having so much as a rupee. Zar had earned it and she felt sure Francis had paid him enough for her already.

Returning her thoughts to the here and now, she stared as William's lifeless body was removed by the efficient guards and someone cleaned up the mess on the floor. Within a very short time, it was as if William had never been there.

Was that going to be their fate too?

She stared at the only thing in her life that seemed to be stable at the moment – her pretend husband.

Chapter Twenty-Six

Jamie took a deep breath and tried to concentrate on the matter at hand. He could think about William later. Right now, he had to extricate the rest of them from this mess.

Bijal, the vizier, had signalled for the man who'd captured them to go to his side. 'Tufan, you have the object, I take it?' The man nodded and handed over the pouch containing the fake talisman. Bijal extracted the exquisite jewel and placed it across the palms of his hands before bowing and holding it out to his master.

'Highness, your talisman.'

The Rajah took it from him, seemingly pleased at first, but then he frowned. 'But how is this? It still has its feathers. That means the ones in Dev's box were fake, doesn't it? So he had nothing to do with the theft.'

Jamie didn't know what this comment referred to, but saw the vizier's smile falter for an instant before he replied smoothly, 'No doubt the thieves saw fit to add new ones. If they were planning to sell it, they could hardly do so with bits missing.'

That's my cue. Jamie cleared his throat. 'Excuse me, Highness, but there may be another explanation.'

'Silence!' the vizier hissed. 'You will speak only when spoken to.'

Jamie shut his mouth, but stared hard at the Rajah. The man narrowed his eyes and put his head to one side. 'No, let him speak, Bijal. I should be interested to hear his theory, even if it proves to be wrong.'

The vizier's expression turned stormy and his lips

tightened, but his master had spoken. Jamie almost smiled. Now it was time to see if his theory was correct.

'Well, my belief, Highness, is that the real thief was none other than your vizier himself.'

'How dare you?' Bijal roared and took a step towards Jamie, the *katar* once again making an appearance.

'Bijal! Let him finish.' The Rajah at his most imperious waved his vizier back. 'Continue, foreigner. What proof have you of such an accusation?'

'For one thing, the talisman in your hand is a fake.'

Another gasp went through the crowd and everyone's eyes turned to the object in their master's hands. He frowned and held it up to the light in order to study it more closely. Jamie saw him scrutinising the ruby and wondered if the Rajah could tell the difference between that and a red diamond. Possibly not. But surely he must be familiar enough with this jewel to see that part of the inscription was missing from the sapphire? He held his breath, waiting for the verdict.

The Rajah nodded at last. 'He is right. This is not mine.' He fixed his gaze on Bijal. 'What is the meaning of this?'

'I ... I ... what? I don't understand. There must be some mistake. My spies assured me ...'

'I'm sure it's not my place to dictate to you, Highness, but if I might suggest a search of the vizier's person?' Jamie cut in.

'Yes, immediately.'

The guards hurried to do their master's bidding, surrounding Bijal at once. He tried to shove them off, but two of them grabbed his arms while the others patted his clothing and checked the contents of his sash. It wasn't long before one man held up a package that was very similar to the one in the Rajah's lap. He rushed to hand it over.

'No! But what …?'

The expression on Bijal's face was almost ludicrous, but Jamie didn't allow himself so much as a smile. They weren't out of the woods yet.

Again, the Rajah held up a talisman to the light and checked the inscription in detail. When he had finished, he had a face like an avenging god.

'So, you thought to make a fool of me. Why, Bijal?' The vizier said nothing. He had stopped struggling and stood with his head bowed, seemingly a broken man. 'And my brother?' the Rajah continued. 'You tried to make me think he had stolen from me, but it was untrue, wasn't it? Did you have him killed also?'

Jamie didn't understand any of this, but assumed it made sense to the Rajah. The more crimes the vizier had committed, the better, in his opinion, as that might be in his and Zar's favour.

'Answer me!' the Rajah roared, as formidable as a tiger in his wrath. 'Why have you done this to me? I have always treated you fairly.'

Bijal lifted his face at last and sent his master a look of venom. '*You* may have, but your father did not. He was my father too and I was the eldest, yet he chose not to marry my mother and therefore you inherited the throne. But it was my birthright. *Mine!*' he hissed.

'Your mother was a *nautch* girl. My father couldn't marry her. How could you even think such a thing? Preposterous.'

'She was not always a dancing girl. She was highborn, but her father's kingdom was taken away.' Bijal had a haughty expression now, defiant and almost regal. Jamie supposed the man had nothing left to lose.

'If she told you that, it was a lie,' the Rajah insisted. 'My father told me exactly where she came from. Trust me, she was no princess.'

'How dare you speak thus of my mother? She was royal, I tell you, she was! More royal than you!' The vizier's face darkened and he wrenched himself free from the men who were holding onto him. Before Jamie had time to move, the man threw himself forward and grabbed hold of Zar's wrist, yanking her hard up against him, her back to his front. The gleaming *katar* made another appearance, this time held against Zar's neck. She stared at Jamie with eyes that were huge with terror. Jamie froze.

'Take one step closer to me and the woman dies,' Bijal hissed, backing slowly towards a side door. 'I may have lost this throne, but I'll find another.' Zar had no choice but to follow.

Jamie looked around, his brain working furiously to find a solution. He saw both Zar's father and Sanjiv trying to edge towards the exit, presumably to attempt to intercept Bijal, but the vizier saw them and nicked Zar's chin so that a few droplets of blood oozed over her magnolia skin. She didn't make a sound, but her face was now drained of all colour.

'Stop right there,' Bijal ordered. They did.

Jamie felt numb. He glanced at the Rajah, who was scowling, obviously at a loss as to what to do.

'You gain nothing by killing her,' Jamie shouted. 'The Rajah's men will capture you outside. There's no escape.' He hoped to stall the man by talking to him until he could come up with a solution.

'We'll see about that,' the vizier muttered, but he didn't stop moving.

He was almost by the side exit now and Jamie tried to

gauge how quickly he could reach them. If he could make Zar kick the man or something, there might be enough time for him to tackle Bijal to the ground. He stared into Zar's eyes, willing her to understand that he wanted her to create some kind of diversion and saw her blink, slowly and deliberately. She got the message. *Good!*

Before either of them could do anything, however, a small brown streak came tearing along the wall and jumped up with a growl, attaching itself to Bijal's backside. *Kutaro?* What the hell was he doing here, Jamie wondered fleetingly, but there was no time to think about it. Bijal let out a shriek of pain, losing his concentration for a moment, which was long enough for Zar to kick the man's shin and duck out of his grip. From behind the crowd, another small shape hurtled into the vizier's legs, toppling him off-balance at the same time as Jamie sprinted across the room and grabbed the hand that was holding the deadly *katar*.

'Nooo!' The vizier flailed as he fell to the floor, but Jamie didn't give him a chance to get up. He threw himself on top of the man, fighting for possession of the *katar*. Desperation made Bijal strong, but Jamie was stronger and forced the man's fingers to open until the weapon clattered to the floor. Quickly, Jamie picked it up and pointed it at Bijal's throat.

'Don't move so much as a muscle or you're dead,' he breathed.

'Help the foreigner,' he heard the Rajah order, and very soon Bijal was once again being gripped by two sturdy guards. This time they didn't take any chances, however, and tied his hands behind his back.

Jamie got off the floor and he and Zar both turned to Roshani and her dog, who were standing panting next to them. 'What on earth are you doing here?' Jamie asked. 'I thought I left you safe at home.' Although part of him was angry with the little girl for disobeying him, there was no doubt she and her furry friend had saved the day. Without them ... no, he didn't even want to think about what could have happened. It had been too close a call.

'We follow. Walk. See bad men take you away. No like. Elephants very slow.' Roshani explained in a whisper.

Zar shook her head, but said with a smile, 'You're impossible, but thank you, you saved my life.' She opened her arms to the little girl and hugged her close, while Jamie grabbed Kutaro's collar and made a fuss of him, murmuring 'Good boy, yes, you're a very good boy.'

'Who are these newcomers?' The Rajah's imperious voice interrupted their reunion.

Jamie stood up and lifted Kutaro, cradling him in his arms so he wouldn't escape and cause any mayhem. He bowed as best he could. 'Apologies, Your Highness, this is my, er, ward and her faithful dog. They must have followed us here, although I'm not quite sure how they were able to enter the building ...'

The Rajah waved a hand. 'No matter. I'm pleased that all has ended well.'

'For you maybe!' Bijal had seemingly found his voice again, and began to shout imprecations at the Rajah. 'You're occupying someone else's throne. You're a sham, an impostor, a bastard and—' One of the guards hit him, cutting off the sound.

'And you're deluded,' the Rajah said, quietly but firmly, then nodded to the guards. 'Take him away. I will deal with him later. And his henchman too.'

Bijal's black gaze swept over Jamie, Zar, Sanjiv and Evans, as well as the little girl and the dog, but they all stared back. The vizier couldn't harm them now and after his callous dispatching of William, he'd not receive any sympathy from them.

When Bijal and his servant had been led out of the room, the Rajah turned back to Jamie. 'What is your name, foreigner?'

'James Kinross, Highness.' He indicated his companions. 'And this is my wife, Zarmina, my ward Roshani, my friend Sanjiv and my wife's father, Thomas Evans.'

His Highness stood up and bowed formally to all of them. 'You have my eternal gratitude and my apologies for any inconvenience caused. You shall all be rewarded and you are, of course, free to go.'

Jamie and the others bowed back, even Evans although Jamie wasn't sure the man understood what had happened.

'Thank you, Highness. No reward is necessary, we were pleased to be of assistance.'

'I insist. I always reward those who help me.'

'Then I thank you again and may we wish you good fortune for your forthcoming nuptials.'

The Rajah smiled and held up the talisman. 'Now that I have this, that is assured. And having a duplicate might help fool any future thieves. Thank you again, my friend. I wish you a long and happy married life also. Ravi, bring one of the diamond caskets.'

The man returned very quickly with a beautiful little chest, inlaid with mother-of-pearl and ivory, but Jamie soon found that the outside was the least valuable part. The servant lifted the lid to show them that it was filled to the brim with uncut diamonds.

'I hope you can have something done with these. I am

told they will yield stones of good quality,' the Rajah said. 'I'm sorry, but as I am not at home, I regret I don't have any finished ones to give you.'

'This is more than generous, Highness, thank you!'

Jamie knew that he could cut these stones himself and with eyes trained by Akash, he saw at once that the Rajah spoke the truth – these would be uncommonly fine diamonds.

As they stumbled out into the early morning, Jamie took Zar's hand and guided her towards the waiting elephants, making sure that Roshani and Kutaro were close behind.

'Come on, you two, you'll have to sit on our laps.'

'We ride on elephant? Yes! I never before.' Roshani's face was wreathed in smiles and she hurried over to the *mahout* who helped her up into the *howdah*, lifting Kutaro up as well. Jamie pulled Zar towards the waiting animal.

'He's truly letting us go? I can't believe it.' Zar had a dazed look on her face, but sounded almost breathless with relief. 'Your plan worked.'

Jamie twined his fingers with hers and gave them a squeeze. 'Well, it would have done if it hadn't been for Bijal, but thankfully Roshani and Kutaro came to our aid. You helped as well though, thank you. I couldn't have planted the real talisman in Bijal's sash without you.'

And as they set off back towards Surat he realised that he'd spoken nothing but the truth. He couldn't have managed it without Zar. They made a good partnership.

In fact, they were made for each other.

Now all he had to do was convince her of that, because he wasn't at all sure she felt the same.

Chapter Twenty-Seven

'There you are! How are you feeling now?'

It was late afternoon of the day after their ordeal at the hands of Bijal, and everyone had slept late. Zar had eventually woken up, had a leisurely meal in bed and then ventured outside as the rain had stopped for a while. She was now sitting in Jamie's courtyard, on the rim of the little pond, trailing her hand in the water. The courtyard wasn't as nice as her own as it lacked flower pots, but was still beautiful in a less cluttered way. She looked up to find Jamie standing next to her.

'I'm fine, thank you,' she told him. 'Relieved it's all over and, truth to tell, a little sad about William.' She saw Jamie raise his eyebrows in surprise. 'I know, he didn't treat me well, but to be honest, he did have some cause. And whatever he did, his life ended too soon.'

'Well, I'm glad you can find it in you to forgive him. I think it might take me a little longer,' Jamie said drily. 'May I?' He indicated the space next to her.

'Of course.' She laughed. 'It's your pond after all. I should really go back to my own house, but somehow I can't face it yet. In fact, I was thinking perhaps I ought to sell it and buy another property. There are too many bad memories.'

Jamie nodded. 'Good plan. I need to sell some property myself now.' He looked away. 'I don't suppose you've changed your mind about marrying me? Now we have a whole chest full of diamonds to share, you needn't worry I'm after your fortune.' He glanced at her, his mouth quirking into a teasing half-smile.

Zar took a deep breath before answering. She couldn't let on that his smile affected her and didn't return it with one of her own. 'No, I … don't think it's a good idea.' She managed to keep her voice even, but it was amazingly difficult to remain outwardly calm. Part of her wanted to throw herself into his arms and say 'yes, of course I'll marry you, I love you', because she'd had to admit it to herself now. She'd fallen in love with this man, even though it was no use, for by the sound of things he was preparing to leave India soon if he was selling his assets and she'd be left behind. Why put herself through such humiliation? He didn't love her and she was sure he was only asking her because of some chivalrous notion that he ought to.

'Right.' He stared at the ground. 'Well, feel free to stay in this house for as long as you like. I need to travel to Madras with Sanjiv and then on to Bombay. I shall be gone for at least a month, possibly more. Are you still happy to take care of Roshani for me? You'll have Kamal and the new *sepoys* I hired to guard you and if she's a nuisance, I can always take on more staff.'

'No, that will be perfect. She'll miss you, of course, but I will continue her English lessons and perhaps try and teach her some other ladylike accomplishments. It will help pass the time.'

'Good, thank you. I appreciate it.'

'No thanks necessary, she is a delight.'

He grinned. 'And a handful, but I'm sure you can manage.' Then he grew serious. 'Will you meet with your father? Or do you want to wait until I'm back so I can offer you my support? He deserves to kick his heels for a while.'

Zar's spirits sank even lower. She'd refused to even speak to her father the night before, claiming exhaustion, and she wasn't sure she wanted to talk to him ever again. Thomas Evans was currently staying at the English Factory, he'd said, and had threatened to remain there until she'd agree to a meeting. She could ignore him, but she supposed it would be better to get it over with. Let him have his say, then he could leave too.

'I might,' she said. 'We'll see. I can deal with him myself though. With Kamal here, he wouldn't dare hurt me and I'd make sure the *sepoys* were within calling distance.'

'You do that. I wouldn't want any harm to come to you while I'm gone.'

But what about when he left for Europe? Would he care then? She didn't say the words out loud. What was the point?

The conversation was becoming awkward and stilted. Zar wished he would just go so she could get on with starting her new life, on her own, and come to terms with a lonely future. As if he'd read her mind, he stood up, but then he hesitated.

'Zar? If there should be … consequences, of our actions on Juhu, you will tell me, won't you?'

Zar nodded. 'Yes, of course.'

But she had her fingers crossed behind her back in a childish gesture because she had no intention of doing so. The last thing she wanted was to keep him here because he felt it was his duty. If there was a child, it would be much better if he never knew.

'Please be seated.'

Zar indicated a rug on the floor, even though she guessed her father would have trouble sitting crosslegged at his age. She refused to pander to him. He'd asked for this meeting so it was on her terms.

'Thank you,' her father replied and managed to sink down, his knees creaking slightly. He winced, but Zar pretended not to see.

'What was it you wanted to discuss with me?' she asked instead, keeping her voice neutral and icily polite.

'I know I deserve your scorn,' he began. 'Perhaps even hatred, but I just wanted to explain. I truly thought I was doing what was best for you.'

Zar felt her eyes open wide. 'In selling me to an old goat like Francis? You must be joking.'

He shook his head. 'No. Of course I know he was old, but don't you see? I was sure he wouldn't last long. Not many Englishmen do out here. And then he'd leave you well provided for, able to choose a husband more to your liking. There's never a shortage here, you must admit.'

Zar just snorted. She didn't believe a word of this. But he sounded sincere, she had to give him that.

'You know I didn't have the money for a dowry,' he continued. 'What little I had was needed for living expenses in England. Everything costs so much more there and … but the point is, I could never have found you a decent husband in London, not without a dowry. And because of your …' He hesitated.

'My foreign looks,' she put in, scathingly.

'Those, yes. Because of that, no man would have taken you without a large payment. You would have ended up an old maid. I didn't wish that for you.'

'That is your defence?'

He shrugged.

'And now, I suppose you've come to tell me you made the long, hard journey here just to help guide me in my life as a wealthy widow. Because obviously I'm too stupid

319

to look after my own affairs, having been abandoned at the age of seventeen to fend for myself.'

'No. I mean, yes. I mean … I genuinely thought you might appreciate my assistance.'

Zar stared at him. He was unbelievable. 'May I remind you that in the twenty years you spent here you barely made a profit once, from what I've heard? How on earth did you think you could possibly help me?'

He sighed and his shoulders slumped. 'I admit I wasn't very successful, but I believed that because you're a woman, people would try to take advantage of you. Simply through being by your side, I thought I might convince them to act differently. But it's a moot point now, since you have acquired such a … decisive husband. I'm sure he'll see to everything.'

'Actually, no he won't. The business is still my own. He's not having any part of it.' She didn't tell her father that this was because they weren't married for real. Everyone still believed this lie and Jamie didn't appear to have divulged the truth before he left. Why, she had no idea, but she'd decided to play along with it for now. It made it less awkward for her to be living in his house.

'Really? How extraordinary!'

'Yes, well, apparently he has a mother who helps run the family business, so he is used to managing females. Besides, I made it a condition of our marriage,' she lied.

'I see.' He stared out into the courtyard, where Roshani was playing some game that seemed to involve jumping up and down a lot. 'Then there isn't much more for me to say. I apologise wholeheartedly for any hurt I caused you, whether you accept that I acted in your best interests or not. When you have children of your own, you will come to realise that it's not always easy to do the right thing.'

He looked sad and Zar noticed all the new lines that creased his face. Years of living in India had made his skin sallow and old age had crept up on him rather quickly. *When I have children of my own …* His grandchild. If there was one, could she really be callous enough to deprive him of the joy he or she might bring to him in his final years? Was she that cruel?

She wasn't.

All the hurt she'd carried around for years had been washed away by her love for Jamie. And if he was leaving her behind, she *would* need a man to help. Who better than her own father? She could run the business by herself, but he was right in thinking his mere presence would lend respectability to her enterprises and make people take her seriously.

'Look,' she said, 'perhaps you're right and it's time to let bygones be bygones. I accept your apology, but I don't need your help. At least not right now. Who knows what the future may bring?'

He blinked and stared at her, hope dawning in his eyes. 'You truly mean that? You can forgive me?'

'I think so, but … it may take some time.'

'I understand and that's fine. Take as long as you need, only don't cut me out of your life entirely, I beg of you. I … I don't have anyone else.'

'No, I won't do that.' She hesitated, then made another decision. 'Would you like to lodge here for the remainder of your stay? There is plenty of space.'

'Thank you, yes, if it's not too much trouble? I wouldn't want to be in the way.'

'You won't be, it's a big house and I'm sure Jamie won't mind. I'll send the servants to fetch your luggage from the Factory.'

He nodded and thanked her again, and as Zar watched Kamal show her father to a guest room, something hard inside her began to thaw.

It took Jamie two months to complete everything and he was burning up with impatience to get back to Surat. He missed Zar and Roshani so much, it was almost like a physical pain.

I love them! He'd reached that conclusion long ago and it made him both terrified and elated at the same time. But how could he take them to Europe with him? They'd hate it. On the other hand, there was no way he could leave them behind. He simply had to persuade Zar to marry him somehow. If she wouldn't listen to reason, he'd woo her with lovemaking. She'd responded to that before, why not again?

It was with some trepidation he entered his house, but it was late and everyone seemed to have retired for the night. Only Kutaro came to greet him and even he looked sleepy. 'Go, little one, back to your mistress,' Jamie urged, after making a fuss of him for a while, and the dog seemed to understand and trotted off.

Looking up, Jamie saw a light spilling out from Zar's room and decided to take her by surprise. He ran up the stairs two at a time, then entered her room after a quick knock and without waiting for a reply.

'Zar? I'm back.' He closed the door behind him and turned as he heard her gasp. She'd been seated in front of a looking glass, brushing her long, glorious hair, but the brush was discarded in an instant. He thought he saw pure, unadulterated joy in her eyes, but then she schooled her features into a calmer expression.

'Jamie! You shouldn't be in here.'

'I'm sorry, but I couldn't wait until morning to see you again. Have you missed me?'

'Well, yes, I mean, of course … welcome home,' she said, looking flustered.

Home. He realised that's what this was. Any house which had Zar in it would always be home, no matter where in the world it was situated. And Roshani. But Zar was still keeping him at arm's length and it was time for action. He had nothing to lose.

He crossed the floor in a couple of long strides and gathered her into his embrace, almost crushing her. Then he kissed her, slowly and thoroughly, and there was nothing wrong with her response to that. In fact, it was nothing short of explosive and he was all set to ravish her there and then, but she suddenly pulled back and put a hand on his chest.

'Jamie, please, don't. I can't bear it.' Her chest was still rising and falling, showing that she was as agitated as he was, but she was clearly trying to keep her emotions under control.

Jamie frowned. 'Why? You don't exactly seem to abhor my touch.'

'No, that's the problem,' he thought he heard her mutter. She walked away from him and stood by the balcony doors, staring out into the night. 'So how did it go? Was your journey successful?'

Jamie raked a hand through his hair and decided to play along with her for the moment. Perhaps she needed some time to get used to his presence again. He had rather startled her. Where was his finesse? His charm? Had he really thought he could just pounce on her like that? He was losing his touch obviously. 'Yes, I've sold the property in Bombay,' he told her. 'And I said goodbye to Akash and his family. They are truly safe and well.'

Zar closed her eyes, but he'd seen a shadow passing over them before she masked it. 'That's good,' she managed to say in a somewhat wobbly voice.

'You don't sound convinced. Zar, what's wrong? Has something happened? Your father, did he upset you?'

'No, no, we've cleared the air and he's staying here as a guest at the moment. I hope you don't mind? I … it's nothing, just … I suppose you'll be going soon then. Roshani will miss you.' She still wouldn't look at him, but appeared to be making a thorough study of the night sky. In a voice that was nothing more than a whisper, she added, 'And so will I.'

Jamie felt as if a vice was gripping his lungs, preventing him from breathing properly. 'Will you really? But there's no need.'

'How do you mean?' She sounded confused and turned to frown at him.

'It's simple – come with me, both of you. I have given it a lot of thought, Zar, and I know it will be difficult for you at first, but I managed to become used to the heat here so I honestly believe you can both acclimatise yourselves to the cold in due course. If you'll just give it time.'

Her eyes flew to his and he almost drowned in them. Huge and of that strange peridot and aquamarine mixture, they were so beautiful he wanted to gaze at them forever. But now they were brimming with tears that threatened to spill over the edge and he reached up to catch one as it fell. 'You want me to go with you to Sweden?' she asked. 'Roshani too?'

'But of course! Look, I know you're dead set against marriage, but please, give me a chance to prove to you that it's not as bad as all that. I promise to give you as much freedom as you want. You can keep your business, run it any way you wish. I won't interfere. And we could adopt Roshani as our daughter. I just can't bear to leave either of you behind.'

She closed her eyes and he saw her take a deep breath. 'But it would be so difficult for *you*.'

'For me? Why? I'm sure I'll soon get used to it again. It's you I'm worried about. You said you almost froze to death in England, in June for heaven's sake!'

'Not the weather, Jamie. Forget the damned weather!' She thumped him with a small fist and he grabbed it and brought it to his lips to place a kiss on her knuckles.

'What then, my love?'

'Don't call me that when you don't mean it. And I'm talking about the reaction you would get when you arrive with us in tow. The shame ... Everyone will be whispering behind your back.'

Jamie shook his head. 'I have absolutely no idea what you're talking about. Why should anyone whisper about me?'

'Because you'll have a strange-looking wife and child. If you meant what you said and you think we should adopt Roshani as our own.'

'Yes, of course. I already feel as though she belongs to us.' He put his hands up to cup her face. 'But Zarmina, you do *not* look strange! Slightly different perhaps, but beautiful. Stunningly lovely, in fact. If anyone is going to stare at you – and me – it will be out of envy. The women will wish they had your looks and the men will be jealous that I have such a lovely wife. And daughter.'

Zar shook her head. 'I saw them, in England. Heard them too. My aunt—'

'Was probably an ugly old spinster who'd never had any man interested in her at all. You must trust me on this, my love.' When she closed her eyes at his use of the endearment again, he kissed her and ordered, 'Open your eyes, Zar, and look at me.' She did, although reluctantly. 'I call you my love because that is what you are and always will be. I love you. Completely and utterly. Every inch of you. Truly.'

Her eyes changed from wary to a kind of wonder, making them seem even more luminous than before. 'You do?' she whispered.

'Yes, I swear it on everything I hold sacred.'

'But you said Elisabet ...'

'Forget her. She can't hurt me any more. It's in the past. You are my future, Zar, you and Roshani and if she'll have us, little Margot too. We'll be a family, if you agree to come with me, that is? Can you bear it?'

She threw her arms round his neck and buried her face against him. 'Yes, oh yes! I'll put up with anything in order to be with you. Just don't leave me, please.'

Jamie smiled. 'Never. If I need to come back to India to trade, you'll be going with me. We'll keep a house here. I'm sure Kamal and the other servants will look after it for us, then we can come and go as we please. How does that sound?'

'Wonderful! Just wonderful.' Zar looked up at him, her eyes shining. 'I love you too, Jamie, so very much.'

'Then that is all that matters. I don't give a tinker's cuss what anyone else thinks! Now please, may I ravish you, my lovely wife-to-be? I've been gone for what feels like years and I really don't want to wait any longer.'

'Mmm, please do.'

The smile she gave him told Jamie everything he needed to know. All was well and the future was suddenly very bright indeed.

Epilogue

'Rosh, sweetheart, please sit still. You're letting all the cold air in underneath the furs.'

Jamie tried to sound stern – putting on what he'd privately dubbed his 'fatherly' voice – but he couldn't help a smile from tugging at his mouth. He, Zar and Roshani were travelling by sled towards Askeberga, his parents' manor house deep in the Swedish forests, and it was as cold as it could possibly be. He'd tried to warn Zar and Roshani of what awaited them, but he wasn't sure they'd believed him – until now. Kutaro, dressed in a little padded coat that Zar had made for him, was snuggled up somewhere by Jamie's feet. Although at first he'd seemed as enchanted by snow as his young mistress, he had the sense to burrow deep inside the furs that lined the sled now.

Another sled followed with some of their belongings – they'd left a lot more in Gothenburg – but Jamie was glad to be huddled with his little family. A family which had increased a few months previously, which was why it had taken them over a year to finally arrive in Sweden. He put a gloved hand on the bundle of furs Zar held which contained young Thomas, named after his incredibly proud grandfather Evans, whom they'd left in London on their way north. In reply, he received a kick and a whinge which told him it was very close to feeding time. It was a good thing they were nearly there. Master Thomas did not like to be kept waiting.

'Don't wake him up,' Zar murmured. 'It was so peaceful while he was keeping still.'

'He'll soon have to emerge to meet his Scots-Swedish grandparents. Although my guess is he'll be more interested in his next meal. I've never known such a glutton in my life.'

Zar smiled. 'Just as well if he wants to grow up big and strong like his father.' She leaned her head against Jamie while grabbing the back of Roshani's cloak with one hand to make her sit down. 'Rosh, for heaven's sake. We're nearly there, your father said. Please, don't make me any colder than I am already.'

The little girl was beside herself with excitement. 'But I can't sit still. I can't wait to meet my sister.'

Jamie felt anxiety swirl inside him. 'Remember what I said, Rosh. She might not take to us straight away. She doesn't even know we're coming.'

With all the snow, it hadn't seemed worth it to try and send a messenger when they could travel as quickly themselves. Jamie hoped his parents wouldn't mind them descending on the place en masse.

'I know, Papa, I know. I will take it slowly, like you told me. But I just know I'm going to love her and she me.'

Jamie wished he was as certain, but at least he was willing to try his best. If only Margot could forgive him for abandoning her for so long …

Before he knew it, they were making their way up that long avenue of ash trees, the one he'd last travelled all those years ago with a different baby in his sled. The yellow manor house looked warm and inviting, smoke coming out of several chimneys and the windows all lit up. It was nearly Yuletide, so perhaps his parents had other guests? Jamie suddenly wondered if they'd be welcome.

He swallowed down his doubts. His mother, at least, would be thrilled to see them. He'd had yet another letter from her before leaving India and her last words had been 'Come back soon, please!'

Well, here he was.

They got out of the sled on cold feet and Jamie lifted both Zar and Roshani in order to speed up the process. Kutaro shook himself and jumped out after them, yawning hugely. Jamie knocked on the door and waited, his heart thumping painfully, but the last thing he'd expected was for it to be opened by his brother. They stared at each other in shock, before Brice's face split into a huge grin.

'Jamie, by all that's holy! Welcome home, you rogue.'

To Jamie's surprise, his big brother enveloped him in a bear hug which almost cracked several of his ribs, but he returned it with feeling. Somehow it seemed his brother really had forgiven him completely and it was as if Elisabet had never existed, never come between them. This was how it had always been with the two of them before she came along and spoiled things.

'Brice, I didn't expect you to be here. Did you bring your family?'

'But of course! I don't go anywhere without them.' Brice looked past Jamie. 'Looks like you don't either?'

Jamie remembered he had a very cold wife and daughter waiting to come in and hastily brought them forward and into the large hall. 'No, me neither,' he confirmed. 'This is my wife, Zarmina – Zar – and our daughter Roshani.' He smiled at the others and added, 'This is my brother, Brice.'

Zar gave him a shy smile. 'Pleased to meet you.' She looked as though she wasn't sure how to greet him, but he solved her dilemma by giving her a hug too, although

Jamie could see Brice had taken in the fact that she was holding a baby as he treated her like a glass ornament.

'And who is this?'

'Thomas, our son,' Jamie replied. 'I wouldn't talk to him right now though, he's about to scream the place down. Supper time.'

'Oh, I know all about hungry babies, trust me. We've just had a new arrival – named after you, actually. Then I'll talk to this little lady instead.' Brice gave Roshani a much more robust hug and lifted her high in the air. 'My brother's daughter, eh? Well, this is a nice surprise. I'm your uncle Brice. You'll have to come and play with your cousin Ailsa, my little girl. She'll love that.'

He stood up again and smiled at Jamie, who shook his head. 'Brice, I … there's so much I want to say to you, and you have no idea how sorry I am that—'

Brice cut him off and held up a hand. 'Don't. There's no need. Mama has explained it all, many times over, and really, it's fine. I never realised Elisabet's true character – I must have been completely blinded by love – but I know now. And I understand that you were the victim, not me. She manipulated us both and you paid the price. As for me, I escaped to find something far better. Believe me, I couldn't be happier.'

'You're sure?' Jamie had thought about this meeting for so long. Had believed it would be awkward in the extreme, but here was Brice, acting like nothing had happened. Smiling, relaxed, the older brother Jamie had always known and loved. 'You're really willing to forget everything?'

'Absolutely. You were right in that letter you sent me. No matter what, we're brothers and best friends first and foremost, and no one can take that away from us.

We won't let them. Trust me, it's all in the past. And now—'

He was cut off by a bark and Jamie belatedly remembered Kutaro, who had followed them inside. He was staring up at a much bigger dog, grey and shaggy, who'd come into the hall on silent paws. 'Kutaro, behave!'

'Don't worry, Liath won't hurt him.' Brice bent to stroke both dogs. 'He's my wife's dog and he's the gentlest creature on earth unless you threaten his mistress. There now, be friends you two. Good boy, Liath.' He chuckled. 'But what the hell is he wearing, poor thing? I've never seen anything like it, ha ha …'

'He feels the cold, like the rest of us. You would too if you'd spent your life in India,' Jamie defended Kutaro, who admittedly did look rather silly. He joined in the laughter. 'Come here, boy, let me take that off. We can't have the local dogs making fun of you.'

To Jamie's relief the canines began to wag their tails and circle each other, before starting some strange doggy game of chase. 'Oh, hell, I hope they don't break anything,' he muttered. 'Brice, maybe we should—'

He wasn't allowed to finish his sentence as the hall was suddenly crowded with people and echoing with cries of welcome. Jamie's parents, Killian and Jessamijn, Brice's wife Marsaili, daughter Ailsa and her two younger brothers all had to be introduced and hugged in turn. Then Jamie noticed that behind his mother's skirts hid a dark-haired little girl, peeking out with enormous brown eyes. 'Mother?' he prompted, and Jessamijn nodded and pulled the girl forward.

'Margot, love, aren't you going to greet your Papa? You've been wanting him to come back for ages and here he is at last.'

Margot bit her lip and looked at Jamie, who decided to do what felt most natural. He got down on his knees on the floor and opened his arms. 'Hello, Margot. I'm really sorry I've been away for so long. Have you a hug for me?'

It was as though a fence was torn down and Margot ran forward, straight into Jamie's embrace, throwing her little arms around his neck. 'Papa, you came!' she whispered, as if she couldn't quite believe it. Jamie blinked hard, emotion clogging his throat. He knew now how wrong he'd been to leave her and he didn't deserve her forgiveness. That she was willing to give it to him was a minor miracle and he was incredibly grateful.

'Yes, I promised I would and here I am.' Jamie closed his eyes. It felt so right to hold her and she *was* his, no matter the circumstances of her birth. This was his daughter, just as much as Roshani was. 'I'll never leave you again.'

'What took you so long?' Margot raised her eyes to his and he could see her question wasn't accusing, just curious. 'And did you bring me a present? *Farmor* said you would.'

He smiled at her. 'Of course I brought you something, I'll show you in a minute. And the reason I couldn't come back earlier was that I had to find you a Mama first and here she is.' He indicated Zar, who bent down to embrace the little girl too, although more cautiously. 'Hello, Margot, I'm so pleased to meet you at last.'

Margot nodded as if acquiring new mothers was something that happened every day. Jamie marvelled at the way children took everything in their stride.

'I'm glad your grandmother has taught you English. *Du talar väl svenska också?*' Jamie asked.

'Yes, *så klart!*' Margot looked at him as if he'd asked a stupid question.

Yes, of course she did. Jamie laughed at the way she'd mixed her words – he'd done the same as a child. He had wondered if the little girl would be bilingual, but he'd assumed his mother would teach her both Swedish and English. It was just as well since he'd thought it best for Roshani to stick to learning English properly first before tackling another language. 'I have another surprise for you,' he told Margot. 'Along the way, I found you a big sister too. What do you think of that?'

Margot turned shining eyes to him and her smile widened. 'A sister? Oh, yes please!'

Roshani came forward and threw her arms around the younger girl. 'It's me. I'm your sister, Rosh. See, I told you, Papa! I knew Margot would want me. We're going to be the best of friends, aren't we, Margot?'

Her new sister nodded, but added with an impish look. 'But sometimes we might fight because Ailsa and I do even though we're friends, isn't that right?'

Their cousin, who'd been watching everything, agreed. 'But not today because now we're going to play. Come on, you two, let's leave the babies to Mama and Auntie.'

Taking charge, Ailsa disappeared with Roshani and Margot in tow. Jamie looked at Brice and the others and they all burst out laughing. 'Well, that didn't go too badly,' Jamie said, pushing his fingers through his hair. Truth to tell, he felt rather shaken, but knew that would pass. He put an arm round his wife's shoulders. 'I don't know about anyone else, but I could use a strong drink!'

'Whisky!' Brice and Killian shouted in unison.

'Eeeuww,' Jamie heard Zar mutter. 'I don't suppose you have tea?'

'Of course, and trust me, that tastes a lot better,' Marsaili told her, linking her arm with hers. 'Come, let me take you and baby Thomas to the kitchen to thaw out while someone prepares a room for you all. Mama, are you coming with us? Let's leave the men to their foul beverage.'

Jamie sent Zar a questioning look, asking with his eyes if she'd be all right if he left her with his mother and Marsaili. She smiled and came over to give him a quick kiss. 'Go!' she ordered. 'Thomas is getting impatient.'

Jessamijn gently pushed Jamie in his father's direction and took Zar's other arm. 'Yes, do.'

Killian hugged his son again as if he couldn't quite believe he was real. Jamie knew how he felt. 'They'll join us when it's time for supper,' Killian said. 'Come into the parlour.'

Sitting by the warm tile stove, with a whisky glass in his hand, Jamie felt as though it was all a bit surreal, but he couldn't stop smiling. It was so wonderful to be here.

'So you two have made your peace, have you?' Killian looked at his sons and Jamie saw the love and pride in his eyes. He had to swallow down a lump in his throat. Why had he stayed away for so long? He should have known his family would help him face anything. He took a sip of the delicious whisky, which burned a warming path all the way down to his stomach and steadied him.

'So Brice says,' Jamie replied.

Brice grinned. 'What, you don't believe me? You think I'm about to pounce on you and beat you black and blue?'

'No, because you couldn't. I'm the same size as you now. Well, almost.' Brice had always been bigger and brawnier, but Jamie was quick, with lightning reflexes. They were evenly matched.

'Hah! No way. I'd trounce you in a flash, but we won't

be putting it to the test. I think we'll soon have our work cut out separating our children, rather than acting like them. Ailsa may be a girl, but she's as feisty as they come.'

'Hmm, yes, you may be right there. Roshani isn't exactly ladylike either.'

'They take after their grandmother then,' Killian said drily, and they all laughed. It was a family joke that Jessamijn had been a right hoyden when she was younger, but as it was a trait Killian loved, the teasing was good-natured.

'I was beginning to think I'd have to come and fetch you home, you've been gone so long,' Brice said.

It was Jamie's turn to grin. 'From what I've seen already, you couldn't bear to leave your family for that long.'

'True, but needs must ...'

'Your mother and I wouldn't have let him,' Killian put in. 'We'd have gone ourselves, but she insisted you would see sense in the end. You just needed time.'

Jamie nodded. 'She was right. She knows me so well. I'm guessing she didn't think I'd require quite this much time though. Her letters were getting rather sharp.'

'Ah, so you read between the lines then? She was rather hoping you would.' Killian laughed. 'But tell us about the jewellery business. Are you going to set up a branch here? It sounded intriguing and you've obviously made good contacts ...'

The conversation turned to business, until they were interrupted by a small dark-haired whirlwind who came dashing into the room and threw herself at Jamie, wrapping her small arms round his legs. 'So are you really my papa? The other children said I'd made you up. I didn't, did I?'

335

Jamie pulled her up onto his lap and hugged her close. She smelled of some kind of flowery soap and biscuits and he breathed in her fragrance, storing it in his memory. He didn't know why he'd been so scared of acknowledging this daughter. It was so simple and he already loved her. 'Yes, I really am your papa, you can tell them that from me. And if anyone says anything different, you let me know, all right?'

She nodded. 'Or I'll punch them on the nose. That's what I did with Ola. He was being 'noxious.'

Brice, Killian and Jamie all burst out laughing. 'Another fighter,' Brice murmured. 'Ye gods, is the world ready for the next generation of the Kinross family?'

'I hope you don't go round hitting people without reason, Margot.' Jamie tried to sound stern, but had a hard time hiding his smile.

'No, only when they're stupid. Rosh says I won't have to now though, she's going to do it for me.'

'Oh, wonderful.' Jamie sighed, but a warm feeling spread through him. He'd gone from being totally alone to having a wife and three children in the space of little more than a year. It was going to take some getting used to.

Just then, Zar came into the room carrying Thomas, with Brice's wife in tow, holding her own baby and with a three-year-old boy, Brice's oldest son, Kenelm, hanging onto her skirts. Jessamijn brought up the rear, directing two maids who were bringing in a tray.

'Time for some celebratory cake, I think,' she announced. 'We can make another one for Yule, this one is needed now.'

'Hurrah, cake!' A stampede of little girls materialised next to their grandmother, with Margot jumping off

Jamie's lap so quickly he hardly had time to register that she was gone. Even Kenelm forgot to be shy and elbowed his way to the front of the queue.

Jamie watched for a moment as everyone crowded round his mother, his new family already instantly absorbed into the clan. Everything inside him fell into place.

They were truly home.

About the Author

Christina Courtenay lives in Herefordshire and is married with two children. Although born in England she has a Swedish mother and was brought up in Sweden. In her teens, the family moved to Japan where she had the opportunity to travel extensively in the Far East.

Christina is chairman of the Romantic Novelists' Association. She won the Elizabeth Goudge Trophy for a historical short story in 2001 and the Katie Fforde Bursary for a promising new writer in 2006.

Monsoon Mists is Christina's eighth novel with Choc Lit. She also has a number of novellas published under the Choc Lit Lite imprint, which are available online.

In 2011, Christina's third novel, *The Scarlet Kimono,* won the Big Red Reads Best Historical Fiction Award. Both *Highland Storms* (in 2012) and *The Gilded Fan* (in 2014) have won RoNA Best Historical Romance Novel awards, and *The Silent Touch of Shadows* won the 2012 Best Historical Read Award from the Festival of Romance. Christina's debut novel, *Trade Winds*, was also shortlisted for the 2011 Pure Passion Award for Best Historical Fiction.

www.christinacourtenay.com
www.twitter.com/PiaCCourtenay

More Choc Lit

From Christina Courtenay

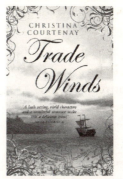

Trade Winds

Marriage of convenience or a love for life?
It's 1732 in Gothenburg, Sweden, and strong-willed Jess van Sandt knows only too well that it's a man's world. She believes she's being swindled out of her inheritance by her stepfather – and she's determined to stop it.

Short-listed for the Romantic Novelists' Association's Pure Passion Award for Best Historical Fiction 2011

Highland Storms

Who can you trust?
Betrayed by his brother and his childhood love, Brice Kinross needs a fresh start. So he welcomes the opportunity to leave Sweden for the Scottish Highlands to take over the family estate.

But there's trouble afoot at Rosyth in 1754 and Brice finds himself unwelcome. The estate's in ruin and money is disappearing. He discovers an ally in Marsaili Buchanan, the beautiful redheaded housekeeper, but can he trust her?

Winner of the 2012 Best Historical Romantic Novel of the year

Sequel to Trade Winds and prequel to Monsoon Mists

The Scarlet Kimono

Abducted by a Samurai warlord in 17th-century Japan – what happens when fear turns to love?

England, 1611, and young Hannah Marston envies her brother's adventurous life. But when she stows away on his merchant ship, her powers of endurance are stretched to their limit. Then they reach Japan and all her suffering seems worthwhile – until she is abducted by Taro Kumashiro's warriors.

Winner of the 2011 Big Red Read's Best Historical Fiction Award

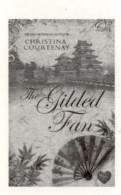

The Gilded Fan

How do you start a new life, leaving behind all you love?

It's 1641, and when Midori Kumashiro, the orphaned daughter of a warlord, is told she has to leave Japan or die, she has no choice but to flee to England. Midori is trained in the arts of war, but is that enough to help her survive a journey, with a lecherous crew and an attractive captain she doesn't trust?

Sequel to The Scarlet Kimono

Winner of the 2014 Romantic Historical Novel Award

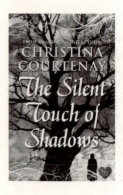

The Silent Touch of Shadows

What will it take to put the past to rest?

Professional genealogist Melissa Grantham receives an invitation to visit her family's ancestral home, Ashleigh Manor. From the moment she arrives, life-like dreams and visions haunt her. The spiritual connection to a medieval young woman and her forbidden lover have her questioning her sanity, but Melissa is determined to solve the mystery.

A haunting love story set partly in the present and partly in fifteenth century Kent.

Winner of the 2012 Best Historical Read from the Festival of Romance

New England Rocks

First impressions, how wrong can you get?
When Rain Mackenzie is expelled from her British boarding school, she can't believe her bad luck. Not only is she forced to move to New England, USA, she's also sent to the local high school, as a punishment. Rain makes it her mission to dislike everything about Northbrooke High, but what she doesn't bank on is meeting Jesse Devlin …

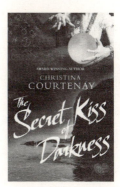

The Secret Kiss of Darkness

Must forbidden love end in heartbreak?
Kayla Sinclair knows she's in big trouble when she almost bankrupts herself to buy a life-size portrait of a mysterious eighteenth century man at an auction. Jago Kerswell, inn-keeper and smuggler, knows there is danger in those stolen moments with Lady Eliza Marcombe, but he'll take any risk to be with her.

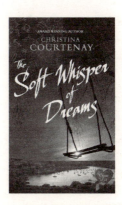

The Soft Whisper of Dreams

Some dreams shouldn't come true …
Maddie Browne thought she'd grown out of the recurring nightmare that plagued her as a child, but after a shocking family secret is revealed, it comes back to haunt her – the same swing in the same garden, the kind red-haired giant and the swarthy arms which grab her from behind and try to take her away …

Sequel to The Secret Kiss of Darkness.

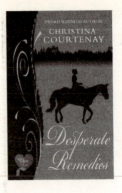

Desperate Remedies

'She would never forget the day her heart broke ...'

Lexie Holloway falls desperately in love with the devastatingly handsome Earl of Synley after a brief encounter at a ball. But Synley is already engaged to be married and scandal surrounds his unlikely match with the ageing, but incredibly wealthy, Lady Catherine Downes. Heartbroken, Lexie resolves to remain a spinster and allows circumstance to carry her far away from England to a new life in Italy. However, the dashing Earl is never far from her thoughts.

Once Bitten, Twice Shy

'Once was more than enough!'

Jason Warwycke, Marquess of Wyckeham, has vowed never to wed again after his disastrous first marriage, which left him with nothing but a tarnished reputation and a rather unfortunate nickname – 'Lord Wicked'.

That is, until he sets eyes on Ianthe Templeton ...

Marry in Haste

'I need to marry, and I need to marry at once'

When James, Viscount Demarr confides in an acquaintance at a ball one evening, he has no idea that the potential solution to his problems stands so close at hand ...

Amelia Ravenscroft is the granddaughter of a earl and is desperate to escape her aunt's home where she has endured a life of drudgery, whilst fighting off the increasingly bold advances of her lecherous cousin. She boldly proposes a marriage of convenience.

Visit www.choc-lit.com for more details
including the first two chapters and reviews

CLAIM YOUR FREE EBOOK

of

Monsoon Mists

You may wish to have a choice of how you read *Monsoon Mists*. Perhaps you'd like a digital version for when you're out and about, so that you can read it on your ereader, iPad or even a Smartphone. For a limited period, we're including a **FREE** ebook version along with this paperback.

To claim, simply visit ebooks.choc-lit.com or scan the QR Code.

You'll need to enter the following code:

Q231405

Introducing Choc Lit

We're an independent publisher creating
a delicious selection of fiction.
Where heroes are like chocolate – irresistible!
Quality stories with a romance at the heart.

Choc Lit novels are selected by genuine readers like yourself.
We only publish stories our Choc Lit Tasting Panel want to
see in print. Our reviews and awards speak for themselves.

We'd love to hear how you enjoyed *Monsoon Mists*.
Just visit www.choc-lit.com and give your feedback.
Describe Jamie in terms of chocolate and you could win a
Choc Lit novel in our Flavour of the Month competition.

Available in paperback and as ebooks from most stores.

Visit: www.choc-lit.com for more details.

Keep in touch:
Sign up for our monthly newsletter Choc Lit Spread for
all the latest news and offers: www.spread.choc-lit.com.
Follow us on Twitter: @ChocLituk and Facebook: Choc Lit.

Or simply scan barcode using your mobile phone QR reader:

Choc Lit
Spread

Twitter

Facebook